Faewalk

Book 4 of the Living Myth Saga

Gabriella Creighton

GABRIELLACREIGHTON.COM

ISBN Information

Print: 979-8-9939808-3-6

eBook: 979-8-9939808-2-9

You can find more books by this author at:
GabriellaCreighton.com

About the Author

Gabriella Creighton is a life long lover of the Fantasy and Science Fiction Genres. She has been fascinated by Dragons and other mythical creatures from a young age and grew up dreaming of being a writer. Inspired by great authors like Jane Yolen, Anne McCaffrey, JRR Tolkien and Phillip Pullman, she loves to take an alternative view of myth and weave her own versions.

Growing up in Rural New York and around many of the real life versions of the locations in this book, as well as having been thrown all over the United States, Gabriella has learned she has only three desires. To write until the nail her coffin shut, to never answer the phone and for a cool glass of Salted Caramel Crowne Royal mixed with Cream Soda and Dr Pepper, which she calls a magic elixir. It helps get the writing done.

You can find more of her works at:
GabriellaCreighton.com

To Colin,
You've always been into my weird.
You probably have realized you're Marcus and Eric combined.
If not, then there you go.

Contents

Prologue

Lilith

Lilith stood at the heart of the canyon and watched the world try to pull away from her.

Black glass rose on every side, jagged and polished, catching her reflection in warped fragments. In one shard she wore a crown of horn, in another a veil of shadow, in a third her eyes were nothing but ember ash. Infernal sigils glowed beneath her bare feet, sunk deep into stone that had once been a mountain. Now it was a hollow, carved out by centuries of ritual, a place where Hell leaned close to other worlds.

Heat pressed against her like a weight. The air tasted of iron and roses that had died in their vase. High above, at the crack of sky, colors shifted slowly from bruise purple to coal red. The lesser hosts lined the cliffs in patient rows. Winged things clung to the walls. Tall armored figures waited in the hollows, weapons resting point down, visor slits burning.

Lilith did not look up. She could feel their expectation, bright and eager, humming along her skin. The circle at her feet was their answer, the promise she had called them here to witness.

She lifted her hand and sigils flared, molten script bursting along the grooves in the stone. The circle reached almost to the canyon walls, edged with spires and obelisks. Old tongues wound through the pattern, fragments of bargains and broken names. This was no summoner's toy, no doorway for a single demon to crawl through. This was a war gate, a wound she meant to cut into reality wide enough for legions.

"Earth," she said, letting the word fall like a stone.

Sound sank into the circle. Light rushed up to meet it. The canyon floor shuddered. The walls groaned as if something inside them remembered being whole. She began the invocation.

Infernal consonants cracked the air. Vowels stretched into notes that twisted into a kind of song. Every time her voice dropped, the circle answered, rising in a low echo that shook dust from the cliffs. The sigils drank power from the hosts that watched, drawing it out without touch. Winged creatures hunched lower. The tall armored figures gripped their weapons as strength flowed from them into the pattern.

Beyond the circle, the air thickened. Colors layered like veils. A ghost of a city formed inside them, no more than an outline at first. Towers and rooftops. A jagged skyline. The faint suggestion of moving lights. Earth lay on the other side of that blur. She felt the wards that wrapped it, old protections that had turned aside a thousand petty intrusions.

They would not stop this.

Crowley's failure with the mortal girl had annoyed her, not humbled her. He had been useful once, a clever tongue that slid easily between faith and doubt. Losing him had been the true insult, and losing him in the Dreamer's shadow had been a reminder that she had allowed too much to unfold without her hand on the scales. That ended now.

Her fingers curled. More sigils lit, bright as spilled suns. The ghost city grew sharper. Clouds. Spires. Cars crawling along streets like insects. A storm rolled along the higher sky. Bells and sirens ghosted through from the other side, stretched thin as if pulled through water. The circle fought her.

Wards on the far side tensed, a web of holy light and ancient agreement. For a moment the city vanished, replaced by a white glare that pricked her eyes. Lilith leaned harder into the spell. Her voice cut the glare. The circle deepened its pull. The hosts above hissed as strength bled out of them.

Obelisks trembled. One toppled and shattered, scattering molten shards across the ground. The war gate swelled, its edge pushing outward as if it meant to swallow the entire hollow. Then everything stopped.

Silence fell so completely that it felt like impact. Echoes died mid syllable. The war gate froze, its surface a sheet of imperfect glass that showed a half formed city and half remembered light. The glow beneath her feet held steady, caught between pulses.

Someone had touched her spell.

The air smelled different, less of iron and more of old incense. A figure stood in the circle where there had been only empty space. He wore a robe that might have been black or deep gold, depending on where the light found it. A simple circlet rested on dark hair. His face could have passed for human, but it was too still, arranged with deliberate care.

"Lilith," Bel said, voice mild, as if greeting her in a quiet hall.

She did not turn toward him at once. That would have been concession. She kept her gaze on the frozen gate, feeling how threads of power had twisted around his presence, drawn aside by a gravity that was not hers.

"You are in my way," she said.

"It seemed a good place to be," Pride replied. "You are very close to making a very loud mistake."

Heat rose around her, stronger than any furnace. Cracks raced outward from where she stood, spiderweb fissures scoring the floor. She pushed the invocation forward, layering new commands over the held ones. The sigils strained against his interference.

Bel sighed. It was not a mortal breath. It moved through the spellwork, a small act of refusal. The gate clouded. The city blurred. The white glare did not return. Instead the surface turned a neutral gray, the color of ash and stone.

"You would burn yourself against the old wards," Bel said. "Again. For what. Another clash where both sides lose blood and nothing important changes."

Lilith turned then, slowly, as if drawing a weapon. Her eyes glowed molten copper. "Earth is where the prophecy began," she said. "Earth is where the Dreamer lives. The mortal realm is the board that matters. You would have me ignore that."

"I would have you use it properly," he said.

He walked toward the edge of the circle, hands clasped behind his back. The spell parted around him, unwilling but obedient, like water forced aside by stone. The hosts above did not move. Only the glass walls recorded him, copying his shape until the canyon was full of slender robed silhouettes.

"Earth is locked," Bel said, studying the gray surface. "Warded by Heaven. Shielded by terms even you cannot break without bleeding for them. Yes, you can force this gate through. You always can. You will simply spend power we do not need to spend, fighting in a place where every inch is contested."

He lifted his hand. The gray quivered and folded inward. The half born gate shrank, drawing tight until all that was left at the center of the circle was a single dull point.

"There are other doors," he said. "Ones that are already open."

Lilith watched the point flicker. Fury sheared into a thinner, sharper interest. "Speak," she said. "Quickly."

Bel smiled, a precise expression that never reached his eyes. "I am not here for caution," he said. "I am here for opportunity."

He closed his hand over the point of light.

The canyon vanished. The place he made instead was a plane of smooth dark stone, stretching in all directions until it dissolved into haze. Above and below it hung windows, turning slowly in the empty sky, each one holding a world behind its thin skin. There was no scent here, no heat. It was not nothingness, merely a space that belonged to his pride and no one else's.

"You have been amusing yourself," Lilith said.

"Someone had to," he replied. "Watch."

He moved his hand and one of the nearer panes swelled, sliding close until it hung before them like a tall door. The surface cleared. On the other side lay a forest.

Trees rose in pale silver columns, their bark catching stray light and sending it back as a soft glow. Leaves layered overhead in an emerald canopy threaded with gold. A river slipped between the roots with a sound like quiet laughter. The air shimmered with fine motes of magic in shafts of sunlight that never seemed to shift.

"Summer," Bel said. "One of the Courts. The bright face they show the rest of creation. Warmth. Hospitality. Happy endings."

The forest changed. The view did not move, but defects slid into focus. In the distance, a patch of trees sagged as if something heavy leaned on them. Flowers near the river's bend had lost their color, edges browning and curling. Thin fractures webbed the air above a moss covered stone.

"This," Bel said, "is what is happening while you argue with locks."

Lilith stepped closer to the pane. She set her palm against it. Cold met her skin, a chill that did not belong in Summer. Beneath it, something faint and familiar stirred.

"Hell," she said.

"Not yet in any way they will admit," Bel answered. "Whispers. Spores. Little knots of doubt and hunger. The Fae are fond of bargains and stories. It was simple to let a few of ours slip into their games."

The image narrowed on the sagging trees. Between the trunks, a dark knot pulsed in the soil, veined with dull red. It beat slowly, like a heart not fully awake. Branches above it shivered. Hoofbeats rang once, very faint, and a shape moved in the distance, horn catching the dimmed light like a spear.

Bel let the vision widen again before it could sharpen further.

"Their anchors are proud," he said. "They think their stories protect them. They do not imagine that someone would rewrite those stories from beneath."

Lilith lowered her hand. "You would have me abandon Earth to tear their gardens apart," she said.

"I would have you notice that the board has changed," he said.

Another pane slid closer, overlapping the first. This one did not show a single world. It showed two layered together. On one side, a landscape that never settled, melting from cities to deserts to oceans in the span of breaths. On the other, the echo of Summer's forest, blurred, as if someone had dragged wet paint across it.

"Dream," Bel said quietly. "And Fae. Once they nodded to each other at a distance. Now the seam between them bleeds. Do you know why."

The space itself seemed to provide the answer. The Dreamer.

For a heartbeat a girl's outline crossed the overlapping realms, framed by shifting images. Crown. Mask. Book. Blade. Eyes bright with a color that did not belong to anything simple. The vision passed before Lilith could reach for it, but its taste lingered.

"Since she woke," Bel said, "the old locks have been under strain. She walks in Dream and the fabric between places remembers being thinner. Fae loves stories. The Dreamer is a story given teeth. They pull at each other."

He pressed his fingertip to the place where the two realms met. Colors there trembled. Fine cracks spread along the seam.

"Every time she takes more of the Dream's power, the boundary weakens," he said. "When it passes fully into her hands, there will be a moment when nothing is firm. That is when you strike. Not into Earth. Not into Heaven's teeth. Into Fae. Into Summer. Into the place where the stories are already half corrupted and no one knows which enemy they should fear."

Lilith considered that. Her anger thinned into a sharper edge. "If Summer falls," she said, "the other Courts tilt."

"They scramble," Bel said. "The mortal realm loses one of its oldest shields. We can always go to Earth later, if we still need to."

The overlapping pane drifted aside. A new window approached, showing a narrower stretch of wild land between courts. Darker trees. A deeper river. No palaces, only old magic.

"That is where our corruption will grow," he said. "The Emerald Forest. A pleasant place to walk if one believes they are safe."

"You are certain the Dreamer will go," Lilith said.

"I am certain anyone who tries to stand between that rot and those she loves will go," Bel said. "If Summer asks for help, she will not ignore it."

"And while she tends the fracture," Lilith said, "we tear it wider from the other side."

Bel inclined his head. "Very well," she said. "Call this what you like. Hear me, Pride. If this fails. If the Dreamer slips free and the Courts hold. I will open every gate I can and drown Earth in war, no matter what it costs me."

"Of course," Bel said. "I would only prefer to win first."

The windows folded inward. The stone plane lingered for a breath, then vanished.

They stood in a tunnel of rock.

The air here was cold. The walls were close and rough, veined with lines of dull red that pulsed to a slow, heavy rhythm. The passage sloped downward, deeper into a darkness that did not come from lack of light.

Lilith's smile had teeth now. "You mentioned other doors," she said. "I assume you also brought a key."

"Several," Bel said. "One in particular."

He walked ahead. Shadows leaned toward him in the way of things that had once learned to bow and never stopped. Lilith followed. The floor trembled faintly under each of her steps.

The tunnel opened into a vault.

Sigils cut into the rock spiraled down the walls and across the ceiling, converging at the center of the chamber. Chains hung from those spirals, hundreds of them, each inscribed with its own warding script. They met around a dark cocoon of fused bone and iron, suspended above the floor.

The slow rhythm she had felt in the passage beat stronger here.

"Sleeping so close to the surface," Lilith said. "Bold."

"Efficient," Bel answered. "There is no point hiding a blade that must be drawn quickly."

He stepped toward the cocoon. The chains groaned. Wards stirred, testing their own strength. The thing inside the shell turned its attention toward them with an instinct so old that it made even the elder demons feel recent.

"What do you call it," she asked.

"Names are for those who will try to pray to it," he said. "For now, think of it as an answer."

He touched one chain. Sigils flared along its length. For a heartbeat every binding in the chamber lit, turning the room into a cage of fire. Then the light died back. One chain fell slack. The others held.

The cocoon cracked. A line split its surface. Dark radiance seeped from within, heavy enough to seem almost solid. The shell opened. Something unfolded out of it, dragging chains, armor ringing as it straightened.

It did not settle into a single shape. For a moment it was a hulking beast on too many legs, head low, horns scraping rock. Then it rose and narrowed, becoming roughly humanoid, though its proportions were wrong. Plates of bone and metal layered along its limbs and shoulders, forming a shell of living armor. Where flesh showed between plates it was the color of old scars.

Its face shifted like smoke. Features formed and slid away, as if it searched through stolen visages and discarded each one. Only the eyes stayed the same. They were rings of eclipsed sun, black at the center with circles of searing script instead of light.

Frost crept along the chains.

The General looked at Lilith and Bel in turn. When it spoke, its voice carried every sound a mountain made when it broke. Grinding. Cracking. The slow fall of stone.

"Where," it asked, "will you loose me."

Bel studied it as a craftsman might study a finished weapon. "A realm of bright masks," he said. "Endless summer and careful kindness. A place that thinks it understands danger because it writes rules about it."

"Faerie," Lilith said. "The Summer Court."

The General turned the word over, weight testing it. "What is required," it said.

"Break their balance," Bel said. "Strike when Dream screams and the boundary with Fae thins. Shatter their anchors. Turn their bright forests into ground that answers to Hell."

Lilith's smile sharpened. "Kill anyone who stands beside the Dreamer," she said. "Anyone who thinks to die for her. Make their sacrifices worthless."

The chains trembled as the General straightened. It bowed, a slow motion with a predator's poise. Sigils along several bindings flared and dimmed, adjusting around the agreement.

Bel traced a line of fire in the air, beginning at the vault and running upward through stone and shadow. For a moment it vanished. Then points along it lit, one after another, like sparks on a rising wind.

"At the height of the transfer," he said, "this path will ignite. It will carry you through the cracks between Dream and Fae and deliver you into Summer's heart. Until then, you wait."

"I will wait," the General said. "Not forever."

"You will not need to," Bel said.

The burning path faded. The chains settled into a restless stillness. Lilith could feel the General already testing the leash, learning its limits, measuring the space where obedience and defiance might one day meet. She liked it.

"Far above," Bel said, "there is a land of green light and laughter that has never had to imagine you. They will not be ready."

"Good," Lilith said.

She looked upward, though there was only rock. In her mind's eye she saw again the forest beyond the pane. Sunlight through leaves. River bending in careful curves. A girl walking beneath the trees with dreams in her hands and strange allies at her side.

"Then let Summer burn," Lilith said.

The vault held the words. Chains shivered. The slow beat in the stone quickened, taking on a rhythm that matched a heart somewhere very far away.

In the realms above, where the sky was still clean and the forests still sang, the season turned by a fraction of a degree. No one noticed that tiny shift, not yet.

CHAPTER 1

Crossing the Green

SIA

THE GREEN DOOR DID not exist yesterday. Today it sat where a plain wall used to be, wood the color of wet leaves and a vine tucked neatly into the keyhole like a bookmark. The Museum felt extra quiet around it, the kind of quiet that means behave yourself or the building will remember.

Kaelan stood with her palm flat on the frame, listening like the door might talk back. "Three times for a true introduction," she said. "Say your name and mean it. The old ways keep score."

Sia let out a breath and set two fingers on the vine. "I am Sia." The leaf cooled under her touch. "I am Sia Mason." The chill moved deeper, like clean water under skin. "I am Sia of the Dream." The keyhole softened into green light and the faint smell of rain came through.

"It heard you." Kaelan's voice relaxed a notch. "Ask for guest-right."

Sia lifted her chin and kept her tone steady. "We ask to cross as guests. We offer a small favor in return, one dawn of service if Summer calls within a year and a day." She did not add anything flowery. The door did not feel like it wanted extra.

"I stand surety," Kaelan said. "Kaelan Kuzunoha, Miko of Tsukiyomi, ally of the Summer Court. I will keep our conduct in order on Summer soil."

Somewhere down the corridor, a bell gave one clear note and faded. That was usually the Museum's way of agreeing without getting in the way.

Sia looked to Marcus. He had been quiet for the naming, hands loose, weight on one leg like he could wait all day. In this light the silver thread at his temple looked like a river drawn in metal. He met her eyes and gave the small nod that meant ready.

"Anchor first," Sia said.

They had rolled up a rug to make space. No chalk circle, no heavy gear, just a clear rectangle of wood floor. The Museum liked simple when the plan was to be a guest and not a warder. Sia breathed in and found the point behind her ribs where dream and breath usually met. A thin thread of light rose out of that point, soft and steady, the kind of glow that makes shadows more honest instead of erasing them. She guided it toward Marcus and set it around his wrist like a weightless cord.

Fuzanglong's lessons lived in the space between breaths. Doors are conversations. Speak first of what you bring. Second of what you will not take. Third of what you will repay. Walk like you are not alone, because you will not be.

Sia spoke to the cord and to Marcus at the same time. "I will hold you steady while you walk beside me. You will keep my count. We walk as one." The thread brightened, a clean little pulse.

"I accept," Marcus said. No performance. Just the words. Kaelan tapped two fingers to her lips, then to the cord, a witness touch that tied a tiny knot of light. Sia felt it settle, neat and sure.

"Projection," Sia said, and matched her breathing to his.

One shared breath. Then a second, deeper. On the third, the light at Marcus's wrist slid up his arm and pressed the air into shape. A second body stepped forward, faintly blue and speckled like a night sky, the height of a tall man. For a heartbeat the echo moved a half-beat late. Marcus adjusted to Sia's count and the lag closed. When Kaelan asked permission to test it, Marcus nodded once. Her fingers met the echo like the surface of a pool and left a scatter of points that sank back into the lines.

"It holds," she said.

The vine at the keyhole lifted. The green beyond the door was not Museum light. It carried warmth without heat and the scent of clover and clean water. It felt like an open hand waiting to see what they would place in it.

"Right foot," Kaelan reminded gently. "Say what you bring."

Sia set her right foot to the threshold. "We bring our names in order." She placed her left. "We will not take what is not given." On the third step she said, "We will repay what we owe." The leaf brushed her knuckles like approval. Kaelan followed. Marcus came behind, careful with the cord. His echo paced Sia's shoulder in time. The door closed after them without a sound and turned into a normal stretch of wall on the other side.

They stood in a tight stand of alder and birch. Moss laid slick green scales over the ground. Light showed through in thin seams between the trunks, not bright spots, more like fabric pulled just short of transparent. The air tasted like rain that had not fallen yet and the sweetness that lives in the white of a broken stem.

"Safe path," Kaelan said, checking the lean of ferns and the way the moss ran over stone.

"Safe path," Sia answered. The cord warmed on her wrist, a small yes.

Marcus tapped his claw to the inside of his foreleg, a habit from training. "Three bells on the projection," he said. "Then I need a break."

"Three," Sia repeated, and the number felt right here. She turned, taking in the tiny signs Fuzanglong had taught her to read. Do not hunt for a trail. Read one. The leaves will point with their faces. The water will tell you how to move. Choose the way that matches who you are, not the way that makes you feel clever.

She put her palm to a birch. The bark was cool and dry under her hand. "We will walk clean," she said for the record of the place. The tree did not answer. It did not need to. The forest's attention shifted a fraction, like a room turning its head. They were noticed. Not judged. Simply logged.

Kaelan took the lead without making a big deal of it. She walked like someone reading a language in the ground. Sia fell in behind her with the cord loose between her and Marcus. Marcus's body watched their backs from the doorway, and his echo paced Sia's shoulder with an easy stride that made her wonder if anyone else would ever get used to how normal that looked when you were around it long enough.

They moved. The Museum's hush drained away and the sound of this place took over, a long, low breath that matched the rise and fall in Sia's chest. Somewhere, bees worked like they always did. Somewhere, water thought about speaking. The path did not appear. It read itself into their bodies instead, in the angle of Sia's foot, in the run of moss, in the way the ferns leaned toward a bend she could not see yet.

"Markers say keep the water to our left until we can hear it," Kaelan said over her shoulder. "A dozen slow breaths."

"Got it," Sia said. She listened and felt the air cooler on her left by the width of a hand. The moss shone a little more in that direction, like fish scales under a cloud. She adjusted a step at a time until the cool stayed steady.

The Green Door's rules stayed with her, quiet at the base of her thoughts: ask, do not take; repay, do not forget. She mentally counted their entry favor and set it at one. The Museum would not enforce anything here. Summer would. And Summer kept ledgers.

They came to a natural lintel where branches had grown into a low arch across the way. It was not a wall, exactly, but the shape asked for respect. Kaelan stopped and tilted her head, listening. "We should ask," she said. "Properly."

Sia squared her shoulders, stepped to the arch, and kept it simple. "We request passage. We offer a small task in thanks before sundown. We thank you for the road." The branches lifted just enough to let them through. The Rule of Three did its job the way it always did here. Ask, offer, thank. Simple beats, old power.

They passed under and did not touch the leaves. On the far side, the air smelled faintly of apples and clover again. The cord tugged once at Sia's wrist, not a warning, more a check-in. She glanced at Marcus. He nodded. The echo's breath matched hers.

"How long can you hold it if we have to move fast?" she asked.

"Fast costs more," he said. "But I can sprint if we need it. Better if we don't."

"Better if we don't," she agreed.

They walked on. The forest's attention never turned sharp. It stayed like a librarian who sees you put a book back where it belongs and decides to trust you with the rare shelf next time. Sia found herself relaxing into the rhythm without letting her guard drop. It felt good to be moving for a reason that did not end in a fight. It felt better to feel the Dream inside her line up with something outside her that wasn't trying to use her.

They reached a spot where the ferns thinned and the ground dipped into a shallow swale. Sia paused. She did not see the river yet, but she could hear it now, a low thread off to the left, exactly where the markers said it would be. The cord pulsed once. Marcus breathed in. Kaelan lifted her hand and pointed without pointing, a little line of two fingers that said there and keep to the right edge.

"Fuzanglong said to follow the water until we see a split birch with a stone at its base," Kaelan said. "That will mark the first real turn."

"Then that's what we do," Sia said.

She checked the door behind them out of habit. The forest had already let it go. Wood, vine, and keyhole belonged to the Museum again. Out here, there was only green and the rules they had agreed to. Ask. Don't steal. Repay your debts. Keep your oath. Speak it three times when it matters.

Sia let the list settle and moved. The water's sound grew clearer with every slow step. The cord stayed easy. The echo kept pace. The path stayed a conversation instead of a struggle. It felt like starting on the right foot. It felt like the first clean page of a new notebook, and for once she did not think about drawing on it. She thought about not messing it up.

"Left keeps singing," she said quietly.

"Then left is right," Kaelan said, and smiled. "Keep it on your ear. A dozen breaths."

They counted together, slow and even, and the forest kept its own count with them. On the twelfth, the wind shifted and carried the river's voice into the open. Sia looked up and saw a split birch with a smooth stone at its base exactly where Fuzanglong said it would be.

"Marker found," she said.

"Turn made," Kaelan answered.

They climbed toward it, and the Green Door felt further away in a good way, like the start line had finally dropped behind them. Ahead, Summer waited with its ledgers and its paths and whatever had gone wrong in the Emerald Forest. They were on the road now.

SUMMER SPREAD OUT AS they walked. No road, just space that let them through. The air stayed clean and green. Light slipped between trunks. Every so often Sia caught a wrong note, quick and easy to doubt, like a metallic breath, a patch of ferns leaning the wrong way, birdsong that stuttered and then fixed itself.

"Left is cooler," Kaelan said, eyes on the moss. "Keep the water on your ear."

Sia felt the cord warm against her wrist. Marcus's echo paced beside her, quiet and steady now. His real body watched their backs.

They found the stream by sound first. Then the line of water showed up, sliding around smooth stones. Their bank dropped to damp sand. A few steps later, they saw him.

A satyr knelt by the water with one leg stretched out wrong. Human torso, goat's leg, short dark horns that curved back from his temples. Fur matted from dragging himself. Clover stuck to him, bruised the same way as the patch they had seen earlier. A thorn vine had cinched around his calf. The thorns were too dark. A gray film clung to them like cooled ash.

He heard them and went still. His hand shifted toward a belt knife but did not draw it. His face stayed careful.

Sia stopped where the sand started and kept her hands in view. "We are guests," she said. "We will not take your name. We ask to help."

Kaelan angled herself to keep both the river and the satyr in sight. Her voice dropped for Sia. "Oak behind us. Good witness if he agrees."

The satyr glanced at Sia's cord, then at Marcus's echo, then back to Sia. "You walk doubled," he said. His voice rasped with fatigue. "Strange, not unwelcome."

"Temporary," Marcus said. "I keep my own leash."

The satyr almost smiled. He looked down at the knot and then up again. "If you can cut what clings without cutting what it clings to, I will not refuse."

"Permission to approach?" Sia asked.

"Granted, guest," he said.

Sia crossed the sand. Up close the wrongness was worse. The thorn's shadow did not match its shape. The film smelled like wet iron. She looked to Kaelan.

"River water," Kaelan said, opening a clay vial. "Light touch. No names."

Sia crouched and set two fingers near the knot without touching. "I am going to ask the ground to remember your leg before this," she said. "I will slide that under the thorns so they lose their grip."

"Memory is fair," the satyr said. "Do it."

Sia matched her breath to the stream. In. Out. The Dream stirred like a picture coming into focus. She did not force it. She brought up the exact scene that should be here, a leg with fur and stride, not briar and pain. When the memory settled, she slid it under the knot, thin and flat. The thorns scraped once, resisted once, then started to let go. Kaelan poured a thin line of river water over the rest. The gray film bled into the water and ran off in a dark sheet that broke apart before it reached the stream.

The satyr hissed through his teeth, more relief than pain.

"Almost done," Sia said. She lifted one thorn free with two fingers and dropped it on a flat stone. It stopped looking real as soon as it left him. The last of the ash skin washed away. Angry punctures showed beneath, already less angry without pressure. Sia set her hand a breath above the skin and gave the memory back one more time, then released it. The punctures sealed to clean pinpricks. She did not push for more. Bodies finished better when you gave them a start.

Kaelan pressed a blank ofuda to the stone and spoke a short, firm line. The thorn husks lost their shape and turned to dust.

"Done," Sia said, sitting back.

The satyr flexed his leg, slow and careful. It held. He ran his fingers through the fur once, checking. Then he bowed his head to Sia, to Kaelan, and to Marcus. Three short bows.

"I owe," he said. "I do not like to owe. Listen and take this as payment. The Emerald Forest has gone strange."

Sia kept quiet. Let people choose how to pay.

"Paths double back," he said. "Light looks right and then goes flat. The trees at the center do not hold witness. Something presses under the ground like a hand on thin ice. Sick patches like this show up where they should not. Do not follow the first bright turn. If you taste iron, you are near it."

"How far?" Kaelan asked.

"Half a day if you read true," he said, tipping his chin upstream. "Less if the Forest wants you to find it. More if it does not."

"Anyone else go in?" Marcus asked.

"Two hunters," the satyr said. "Both came out wrong in the eyes. One speaks names when he sleeps. Not his own. Names he should not know."

The cord warmed against Sia's wrist like it wanted her eyes. She kept her tone even. "Thank you for the warning," she said. She said it again, and then a third time, each slightly different. The Rule of Three mattered here.

"You work clean," the satyr said, surprised and pleased. He pulled a reed, tied a quick knot with three flat turns, and set it on the sand. He did not hand it over. He slid it toward them with the back of his fingers. "For your pocket. River folk will know you did right by one of ours today."

Sia looked to Kaelan.

"Take it," Kaelan said. "He offered it on his own."

Sia picked up the reed. It felt like any reed, smooth and cool, but the knot held a little warmth. She tucked it inside her jacket with her pencils.

"If you are going to the Emerald Forest, go with your deals tidy," the satyr said. "Do not leave small debts open. Do not take shortcuts. If something asks your name three times, do not give it unless you mean to bind to it."

"We will keep our deals straight," Sia said. "We will not give what we should not."

He pushed to his feet and tested his leg. It worked. He looked at the bruised clover on the bank and frowned. "This does not belong here either. I will speak to a warden. That is my part."

"Then we are even," Sia said.

"For now," he agreed. He gave one more short bow and moved upstream, quiet on wet stone, until the trees took him.

They watched the water for a moment. The wrong taste faded back to green.

"Emerald Forest," Marcus said.

Kaelan nodded. "We were headed that way. Now we know why."

Sia checked the cord and the echo at her shoulder. "How long on the projection?"

"Two bells strong," Marcus said. "A third if I do not need to sprint."

"Let's not make you sprint," Sia said.

"Fuzanglong's line meets this stream near a split birch," Kaelan said, pointing along the water. "We stay with it until then. No shortcuts."

"No shortcuts," Sia repeated. She let the warning sit so she would not forget. Bright paths can lie. Light can trick. Names asked three times have weight.

They moved on with the stream to their left. The signs stacked up. More bruised clover. Birdsong that slipped. Shadow where it should have been open. The canopy darkened a shade at a time. "Emerald" started to feel less like a jewel and more like deep water. Sia felt the same thing she had at the door, a quiet yes about the road they were on. It did not make her relax. It made her want to get there soon enough to fix what still could be fixed.

THEY STOPPED BEFORE THE trees turned emerald and the light went heavy. No one pushed to keep going. The line of forest looked like deep water you do not step into at night.

Kaelan picked a flat spot near the stream and checked the ground the way she always did. "Edge territory," she said. "Safe to camp without waking a warden."

Sia dropped her pack and shook out the tarp. Kaelan helped stake the corners. Marcus's projection hovered beside Sia, steady and bright, matching her breathing through the anchor thread.

"Projection check," Sia said.

"One bell left at full size," Marcus said through the echo. "Two if I ease off."

"Ease off," Kaelan said. "We need you sharp tomorrow."

The echo pulled its light inward, folding down until it was a hand-sized dragon with bright pinprick eyes and a neat tail. It settled on Sia's shoulder like it owned the spot.

Sia grinned. "There he is. Baby Marcus."

The tiny dragon tilted its head, offended. Marcus's voice came out of it, dry. "That is not the name."

Kaelan tried to keep a straight face and failed. "Pocket Marcus?"

"Please stop helping," Marcus said.

They ate simple trail food. Sia and Kaelan handled the real work. Kaelan warmed water on the camp stove and poured it into a shallow brass bowl. The surface stilled, then turned bright like a sky catching light.

"Fuzanglong may speak on the water," Kaelan said.

The brightness shifted. A ripple moved across the bowl as if something breathed through it. Sia leaned in. The outline of a long whiskered face suggested itself in the shine.

"Student," Fuzanglong's voice said, calm and clear. "Do not enter the Emerald Wood in darkness."

"We are camped at the edge," Sia said. "We met a satyr. He warned us about strange paths. The signs are off."

"You are listening," he said. "Good." A pause, like he weighed what to add. "First rule once you cross. Emotions amplify in Faerie. Yours, the land's, your enemies'. If you feel fear, the wood can hand you more of it. If you feel joy, it can pull you off the path. Keep steady."

"Steady," Sia said.

"Second," he said. "The Law of Three. You already used it at the Green Door and with your thanks. Inside the Emerald Wood, it sharpens. Ask three times, and a gate may open. Speak your name three times, and you bind it to the moment. Hear your name three times, and consider whether to answer at all. The third asking costs someone something."

"Then we do not give names lightly," Sia said.

"Correct," Fuzanglong said. "Third, the Law of Debt. The Courts keep ledgers. Do not go to sleep with an unbalanced ledger on borrowed ground." The water dimmed, then smoothed flat. His presence faded.

Kaelan set a reed across the bowl to mark the lesson. "Law of Debt in simple terms," she said. "If you take comfort, leave a token. If a path holds for you, seal it with a small task. If you accept a gift, say how you will repay it and then do it."

Sia took the satyr's reed knot from her jacket. "This is a gift?"

"Offered freely," Kaelan said. "He paid you for the healing with the warning. The knot is like a receipt. River folk will read it and know what you did. It can nudge expectations. Not a trap, a reputation."

"Do we owe for camping here?" Sia asked.

"A little," Kaelan said. "Three hands of clearing, three thanks spoken, and three sips left in the bowl for whatever drinks at night. That balances the rest."

Sia and Kaelan did the work. They gathered fallen twigs and cleared the threshold path to the stream. The tiny projection pointed things out like a tiny foreman but did not touch much. Kaelan poured the last of the warm water back into the bowl and set it on a flat stone by the bank.

When they were done, Sia faced the trees. "Thank you for the ground," she said. "Thank you for the water. Thank you for the quiet." She said it clean and simple. The Rule of Three mattered more than fancy words.

The wood seemed to settle. Not magic fireworks. Just a small shift, like a place that had decided they were fine to be here.

They sat again. Night pressed in. The stream kept talking. Every now and then the wrong metallic taste flickered at the back of Sia's tongue and went away.

Kaelan tipped the bowl and skimmed a line with the reed. "One more thing. Do not joke with names inside. If something asks three times, it is fishing for a bind."

Sia glanced at the tiny dragon on her shoulder. It met her look with serious little eyes. "You do not count," she told it. "You are Baby Marcus."

The small dragon puffed a bright speck and turned its head like a cat. Marcus's voice was unimpressed. "Still not the name."

"Marcus, regular," Sia said, pointing at the empty air where his real body would be. Then she tapped the mini. "Marcus, travel size."

"I am filing a complaint," he said. He did not sound upset.

They set the watch. Kaelan would take first, Sia second. Marcus's projection would spot quietly between them to save anchor power, but he would not hold a full watch so Sia could rest. The stream kept its small sound. The edge of the Emerald Wood sat dark and patient across the way.

"Emotions amplify," Sia said. "Say it out loud if something hits hard. We do not let the forest steer us."

"Copy," Marcus said from her shoulder. "I will not surge the projection unless you call it."

"No shortcuts," Kaelan said. "No following odd lights. If something wants to talk, we either make a clean deal or we keep walking."

"Deal," Sia said.

They cleaned the last three sips from the bowl onto the stone, left the empty vessel as a sign, and settled in. Sia watched the dark line of trees until her eyes blurred. She woke before dawn to damp air and the cold edge of morning.

They packed. Sia slipped the reed knot back into her jacket. The tiny projection stretched, then unfolded to full size with a bright shiver and held steady on the anchor. Kaelan checked the way forward. First light washed the trunks gray, then green.

They faced the Emerald Forest together. The breeze carried a faint iron taste, like a warning on her tongue.

"Emotions steady," Sia said.

"Ledger clean," Kaelan said.

"Dragon not Tiny," Marcus said, keeping a straight face on Sia's shoulder, both girls eyed him slowly.

Sia stepped to the front with the stream on her left. "Let's go meet what is wrong," she said, and they moved toward the emerald dark.

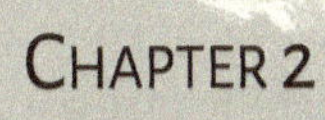

Sickness in Emerald

Sia

THEY STEPPED INTO THE Emerald Forest at first light. The green was different here. Bark looked wet where it should have been dry. Leaves showed a bruise tint around the edges. A rabbit froze under a fern and stared too long with cloudy eyes, then hopped away with a back leg that didn't bend right.

"Eyes up," Kaelan said. "Emotions steady."

Sia kept the stream on her left, just like Fuzanglong taught. The anchor cord lay warm around her wrist. Marcus's projection rode her shoulder in the small dragon form, claws catching on her jacket fabric with a careful grip. Its tiny chest rose and fell in time with her breathing.

A sound rolled through the trees. Low at first, like wind in a pipe. It swelled, widened, then broke into a messy cry that didn't belong to any animal Sia knew. Marcus flinched and slipped. Sia caught him with two fingers before he tumbled.

"Got you," she said.

"I felt that in my bones," Marcus answered through the tiny echo. He dug in and steadied. "Not my best look."

The sound faded, came again from a new angle, then melted back into the leaves. Under the roar was a smaller noise she didn't like. Wet and tight, like someone trying not to sob.

"Do you hear it?" Sia asked.

Kaelan tilted her head and listened. "I hear the shape of it. Don't answer it."

Air shifted in front of them, as if heat rose off the ground. It slid together into a pale ribbon of light, and Fuzanglong flowed out of it. He looked like himself, long-bodied and antlered, but thin as fog against sun. His scales carried no weight. The light came through him.

"Projection reduced," his voice said, calm and clipped. "The air in this wood interferes."

"How bad?" Sia asked.

"I can travel with you," he said. "Do not expect power. Expect warning and sight."

"Good enough," Kaelan said. "We keep moving."

They did. The path was never a real path. It was the way the ferns leaned and the way the moss climbed the stones. Every twenty steps Sia saw another wrong thing. A cluster of mushrooms grew in a perfect ring on bare mud where there should have been leaves. A crow perched with its wings half open and didn't blink. A young maple had a glossy patch at its base that reflected like a puddle, only it was part of the trunk.

The sound came again. Closer. Marcus jolted, then locked his claws and stayed put. Sia set her hand near him to give him something to brace against. The anchor cord warmed, a small check-in that told her the projection was still in step.

"We are not answering a cry," Kaelan said. "Keep your mouths shut unless you are speaking to each other."

Sia swallowed and kept her breathing even. The forest felt like a place that watched and waited to see what you would do wrong. She didn't plan to give it anything to work with.

"Move on the dips," Fuzanglong said. "Listen for the low tide in the sound."

The cry rose, dipped, and rose again. They walked during the quiet slice, then paused behind a thick birch when it swelled. Through the birch leaves, Sia watched a pair of deer step across a patch of bruise clover. Their ribs showed. Their heads turned too slow, like the neck joints were stiff. One stamped and left a print in soil that looked a shade darker than it should.

"That clover again," Sia said. "Same as the patch by the satyr."

Kaelan nodded. "We're close to whatever is spreading it."

The noise shifted. It tried to sound like wind. It didn't. It tried to sound like a person moving branches. It didn't. The tight crying sound sat under everything, the way static sits under a bad radio station.

Sia stopped listening to the shapes and listened to the rhythm. It wasn't random. It came in sets. Four heavy exhale sounds, then that thin weeping noise, then three more heavy breaths, then quiet. She counted it twice. It matched.

"Patterned," she said. "We can move on the threes."

"Do that," Kaelan said. "Two more dips to the next marker."

They slid through narrow space between mossed stones. Fuzanglong's spectral body passed a handspan from the trunk of a beech and left a thin frost line on the bark that faded right away. He saw Sia watching and shook his head.

"Not power," he said. "Only interference showing itself."

The cry rolled again. Marcus gripped her collar, then eased when the dip came. He shifted on her shoulder like a cat trying to pretend it hadn't been startled.

"You okay?" Sia asked quietly.

"For now," he said. "The interference makes the echo want to lean." He paused. "Thank you for catching me."

"You're welcome."

They reached a shallow rise where ferns thinned. Kaelan lifted two fingers, the signal for stop. She crouched, touched the soil, and nodded toward the left.

"Marker should be a split birch with a stone at its roots," she said. "Do you see it?"

Sia scanned the trunks. Lines of light slipped between them and caught on smooth bark. She found the split, a V-shape that opened toward the stream. A river stone sat at the base like someone had placed it there, round and gray, damp along one side.

"There," she said.

Kaelan stood. "Then we stay with the water and we don't answer any voices."

The sound surged again. This time the weeping cut through clear, like someone took a breath to scream and couldn't. Sia felt it hit behind her ribs the way a big drum hits in your chest.

"It is real," she said. "Not a trick of wind."

"No one said it wasn't real," Kaelan said. "We said we don't answer it."

Sia nodded and kept moving. The ground underfoot felt normal enough. The trees didn't. Several had glossy bands around them like glue had dried on their trunks. A cluster of bluebells grew upside down out of a crack in a rock and rang a thin bell sound when the low cry passed through.

Fuzanglong's spectral head turned in a slow sweep. "The wood remembers something wrong and keeps playing it," he said. "Stay out of the center of clearings. Edge travel is safer."

They hugged the edge of a shallow bowl where the ground dipped and the air felt colder for no reason. Sia kept her hand near Marcus in case he jolted again. He didn't. He watched, eyes bright and steady in the tiny head.

"Count holds," he said after a minute. "I can keep this for a while."

"Good," Sia said. "Tell me if it doesn't."

The sound dipped. They crossed the bowl's narrow mouth and climbed a short rise where the moss grew in scales. At the top, the stream they had been tracking slid into view again, tighter and darker here. A thin skin rode its surface, not full film, just a hint of gray.

Sia noted it, filed it next to the bruise clover and the glossy bark bands. The stack of small wrong things built into a picture she didn't like. The forest wasn't just sick. It was trying to make them feel the sickness, and then make them act on it.

Kaelan looked back at her. "You good?"

"Yeah," Sia said. "I want to fix it. That's all."

"Keep that want steady," Kaelan said. "The wood will try to turn it into rush."

"Noted."

They moved again, same rhythm. The cry rose. The cry dipped. They went on the dip. When it came back, they waited with their backs to trees that still felt normal. Fuzanglong kept his coils low to the ground and his head high, like a banner that didn't need wind to fly.

The next dip opened a longer window. They used it to cross a section where the understory thinned and the canopy pulled tight overhead, turning the light cool and green. A fox slunk across the space ahead of them, ribs sharp, tail thin, eyes flat. It didn't look at them. It looked at the ground and walked like every step hurt.

Sia swallowed. Her chest felt tight for a second. She said it out loud so the feeling wouldn't get bigger. "I'm angry."

"Good," Kaelan said. "Anger is honest. Keep it small and useful."

Sia breathed in, breathed out. The anchor cord kept its warm pulse. The tiny dragon on her shoulder matched her count without fuss.

The sound rose and fell like the ocean, only it wasn't water. It was something alive that had learned how to be loud.

"Two more dips to the next turn," Fuzanglong said. "Then the stream forks. We take the left fork."

They nodded and kept moving, careful and quiet, until the cry fell away again and gave them room to walk.

THE STREAM NARROWED UNTIL it was the width of a hallway and turned dark for no good reason. Not depth dark. Surface dark. A gray skin rode the water and wrinkled when it moved. The smell shifted too, clean river undercut by something like cold iron.

"Offshoot," Kaelan said. "It should be clear."

Shapes flitted over the film. At first Sia thought dragonflies. Then one turned and grinned. Too many teeth for something that small. Another dipped through the skin, popped up, and jittered in the air like someone was yanking it on a wire.

"Pixies," Kaelan said, frowning. "And they are wrong."

The little things giggled in bursts. One tried to say hello and made a scraping noise like glass on glass. Another dragged a gray smear down its wing and kept going as if it did not feel it.

Sia raised both hands so they could see them. "We are guests," she said. "We will not take your names."

Three of the pixies turned their heads in the same jerky way and stared at the tiny dragon on Sia's shoulder. Marcus's voice stayed level. "Eyes on the water, Sia."

Kaelan was already moving. She pulled a brush, a small pot of ink, and three paper slips. She drew tight lines in one smooth pass on each, whispered short words, then flicked her fingers. The ofuda snapped into the air and spread like flat birds. The pixies froze mid-flight. Not slammed. Paused, wings stuck a half-beat from the next flap.

"Go," Kaelan said. "While I can hold it."

Sia crouched at the bank. The gray skin eddied against the charm stillness and stacked up near her knees. The stuck pixies wobbled in place, eyes too wide.

"I am going to clean the water," Sia told them. "If any of you want to keep the slime, say so now."

A leader, if there was one, squeaked, "Dirty hurts."

That was enough. Sia set her palm a breath above the surface and called up the picture of this stream without the film. It was simple and clear in her head. Quick water. Stones with shine. Insects that were not pixies, just insects doing their job. She laid that picture over the present and pressed. The gray sheet peeled off in one long piece as if it had been painted on and the paint finally gave up. It slid into her other hand and held there as something that was not water anymore.

The smell of iron doubled. Kaelan tapped a fresh slip against the sheet. It cracked like thin candy and turned to ash. The ash did not fall into the stream. It fell backward onto the bank and stayed there.

The ofuda holding the pixies released. Wings fluttered hard, then leveled. The faces shrank back into the right size. One by one, they dipped to the water and sipped. The first one let out a tiny laugh that sounded like a real laugh, not the broken giggle from before.

"Clean," she said. "Thank you."

"Thank you," a second said.

A third repeated it, because that was how Faerie liked to lock a thing. "Thank you."

Sia nodded once. "You are welcome."

"We will repay," the first said quickly. She put both hands on her chest like she was saying a pledge. "We will stand watch. We will scream warning. We will not lie." The words came in a practiced rhythm, like rules learned at home.

"We are looking for the forest guardian," Sia said. "Do you know where to find them?"

The little group spun in place, then pointed upstream. All arms. All feet. One of them added, "Twist twice. Avoid the sick circles. Go when the bellows get quiet. The Guardian sleeps wrong."

"Wrong," another echoed, softer.

Kaelan looked to Sia. "We accept wards?"

Sia thought of the ledger. They had taken safety, water, time. They had given a fix. Balance was good, but the offer was clean and useful. "We accept," she said. "You can ride with us until nightfall. If a warden asks, we will speak for your good conduct."

The lead pixie cheered and zipped to hover just above Marcus's tiny head, which immediately annoyed him. Two more took positions on the edge of Sia's hood, eyes forward.

"Stay out of my face," Marcus said, deadpan. "And no hair pulling."

"We will not lie," the pixie said solemnly, which did not actually answer the hair question. She glanced at Fuzanglong's thin, spectral shape and visibly decided not to engage.

Fuzanglong studied the water, then the bank. "Move when the sound dips," he said. The layered cry rose, wobbled, then dropped. "Now."

They followed the stream. The wards paid for themselves immediately. One hissed and pointed at a ring of mushrooms sitting too clean on mud. They detoured without stepping inside the circle. Another slapped Sia's ear with both hands and jabbed a finger at a place where the air moved the wrong direction, up from the ground. They bent low and let it pass over their heads before crossing.

"Twist," said the leader when the stream took a sharp bend to the right. They did. "Twist again," she said after a short run, and they did that too, back around a stand of oaks with glossy bands at their bases. Sia kept her breathing even and her pace steady. The cord stayed warm. The small dragon matched her count without complaint.

The cry rolled louder, then quieted again. It had a chest to it now, as if a huge thing was breathing somewhere hidden, not far.

"It is closer," Sia said.

"Keep the dips," Kaelan answered. "No hero moves."

They crossed two more sick patches without touching anything that looked like a border. A fox watched them go from behind a fern. Its eyes looked right again. It blinked. That felt like a win.

At a narrow cut between low ridges, the leader flicked her fingers in a tiny circle. "Twist-twice ends here," she said. "Guardian sleeps ahead."

Sia nodded. "You did good," she said. She split the sentence into three parts without making a big deal of it. "You watched. You warned. You told the truth."

The three wards beamed like kids who had just been told they did their chores right. The leader tapped the knot in Sia's jacket pocket, the one the satyr had given them, and nodded. "Reputation carries," she said, proud of herself for using a big word.

"Stay on the edges," Kaelan told them. "If something heavy moves, do not try to help. Just scream."

"We are loud," one promised.

"Yeah," Marcus said from Sia's shoulder. "We noticed."

The next swell of sound climbed, fell, and left a wide quiet in its wake. They used it. The wards zipped to the perimeter, eyes sharp. Sia stepped into the cut, kept the stream within sight, and pushed forward toward whatever counted as a guardian in a forest that felt this wrong.

THE WARDS LED FAST once the stream bent left. "Twist," the leader said, and they cut around a stump glazed with glossy bark. "Twist again," and they slipped between two oaks rooted in bruise clover. The crying sound ran on a steady cycle now, four heavy breaths, a thin weeping note, three more, then quiet.

"Move on the quiet," Kaelan said. "Edges only."

They stayed to the edges. A perfect mushroom ring sat on bare mud. The wards hissed, and Sia guided them wide. Farther on, the air shoved upward in a flat sheet. The wards slapped Sia's hood and pointed down. Everyone crouched and let it pass. Marcus's tiny claws bit into Sia's jacket and held.

The next quiet opened wider. They crossed a shallow dip where the light turned sick green. The cry came back close enough to buzz in Sia's ribs. Meaning slid underneath the sound whether she wanted it or not.

"What is it saying?" Kaelan asked, eyes on the ground.

"Some of it asks to be killed," Sia said. "Mercy, again and again."

"We do not answer that," Marcus said from her shoulder.

"We won't," Sia said.

The wards slowed at a narrow cleft between low ridges. "Guardian," the leader whispered, drawing a small circle in the air and pointing ahead.

They stepped through and entered a hollow where the light thickened. In the center stood a tree that had grown around a person. Not strapped. Grown. The trunk bulged to fit plate armor and kept going. Bark crusted across the shoulders and helmet. Vines threaded the joints like cables. The man's hands hung half free, palms up, fingers locked in green cuffs.

The armor was not plain. Green enamel clung in flakes. Verdigris bled from scrollwork shaped like oak leaves and holly. A short, heavy axe haft, stained deep green, was trapped in roots at his hip. A buckler half-swallowed by bark showed a quartered field in green and gold with three oak leaves in one corner. Along the gorget, just under the helmet rim, a thick seam ran across the neck plate, as if the metal had once been cleanly split and forced back together. Bark had scarred over it like a healed cut.

"Human make," Kaelan said, taking the right edge. "Old crest. Summer colors."

Sia moved up the left, careful of ribbed roots. Under the helmet's shadow she saw a jawline and slack skin. Sleep that had gone past sleep. The chest plate carried a burned sigil that matched the oak-leaf motif. Even under the rot the armor smelled faintly of crushed holly.

"I can ask the tree to remember before it took him," Sia said. "Give it space to let go."

"Do it quick," Kaelan said. "Listen."

The bellows rose again. Sia tuned them out and focused on the trunk. She pulled up the picture of this tree before it met metal. Younger bark. Clean grain. No plate. The memory came thin, then steadier. She slid it between wood and steel like a wedge. Bark flexed under her palm. A hairline crack popped around one pauldron. The green axe haft twitched a finger's width, like it wanted out.

The wards all snapped their heads to the ridge and screamed together.

Sia turned. Hoof on stone. A ragged snort. A shape stood on the rim, backlit and heavy. Horse body, too tall at the shoulder, neck built like a lever. A single horn, long and spiraled, wrapped in fungus sheets. Vines gripped the mane in tight knots that pulled skin. Each breath whistled and cut, grief forced through a broken pipe.

Sia reached for her umbrella without thinking and flipped the catch. The canopy stayed closed. The carved ferrule caught the light. Runes along the shaft came up faint, ready. She set the tip to the ground and felt the anchor cord warm on her wrist. The umbrella steadied like a staff in her hand.

Fuzanglong's spectral head lifted. "Hold the edge," he said. "Do not run."

Kaelan slid in front of Sia, ofuda between her fingers. The tiny dragon on Sia's shoulder tensed, claws biting fabric.

The unicorn screamed. Up close the weeping inside the sound shredded into jagged pieces. It dropped its head and drove the horn at them, straight down the slope.

"Left," Kaelan snapped. "Sia, on me. Hands safe. Marcus, eyes front. Wards, scream if it shifts."

Sia braced the umbrella like a staff and kept one hand near the cracked pauldron in case she got a second to pull. The ground shook under the first hammer of hooves on the lower stones. The charge did not slow. The horn lined up on the hollow like a thrown spear. The green enamel on the trapped armor flashed in the corner of her eye, and the oak-leaf crest caught a shard of light.

The monster came straight at them.

CHAPTER 3

The Unicorn

SIA

THE UNICORN HIT THE slope like a battering ram. Fungus tore on its horn. Knotted vines snapped off its mane and whipped the air.

"Big form," Marcus said from Sia's shoulder.

Light stacked around her in a rush. The tiny dragon stretched into a man-sized projection and planted himself between them and the charge. He took the hit square. The horn drove through his chest-light and lifted him like a doll. The projection blew sideways, crashed through a sapling, and slammed a larger trunk hard enough to shake leaves loose. Sia felt the anchor yank hot against her wrist, then settle into a painful throb.

"Marcus!" Sia ran left with Kaelan, using the quiet edge of the hollow. The unicorn skidded on stone and re-aimed, breath whistling through a wrecked throat.

Sia snapped the catch on her umbrella. The canopy stayed closed. Runes along the shaft woke in a clean line. She set the ferrule to the ground and let the heat climb into her hands. When the beast lunged

37

again, she swept the umbrella like a staff. Fire tore out in a straight bar and hit the shoulder. Fungus flashed. Vines curled black. The unicorn reeled and screamed, grief breaking into the sound like glass.

Kaelan was already moving. A katana slid into her hand from nowhere, clean as a card trick. She cut across the front leg when it staggered. The blade bit and forced weight off the strike. The horn gouged rock instead of ribs.

"Eyes," Kaelan said.

Fuzanglong rose in a white loop, big as the air would let him. His spectral head crossed the unicorn's vision once, twice, three times, drawing the next lunge wide each time. He left no wound, only confusion and badly placed hooves.

Sia sprinted to Marcus. His projection crouched against the tree, outlines fuzzy, fighting to hold shape. She grabbed his forearm. The cord hummed, then steadied as their breathing matched.

"Still with me?" she asked.

"Barely," he said. He pulled himself upright and glanced at the fight. "You need more fire than you have."

"I have what I have," she said.

"Take mine," he said. "I will feed it. You shape it."

"Do it."

Sia planted the umbrella and held the shaft vertical like a flagpole. The runes brightened. Marcus set his palm over her hand. Heat surged up the cord and into the steel. It rolled through her like a furnace door opening and wanted to become a single blast.

"Not a beam," she said. "Hold and count."

He listened. The heat steadied into a pulse. Fuzanglong swept past the unicorn again and bought them a heartbeat.

Kaelan moved to the right flank, blade low, waiting for the next bad step. "Now, Sia," she called. "Give me something to work with."

Sia lifted the umbrella, pointed the ferrule above the unicorn's withers, and pulled the heat into a shape she trusted. Not a wall. Not a river. A summer storm. She broke the fire into drops the size of fists and threw them high. The first wave fell in a tight circle on the beast's back and shoulders. Each strike burned fungus away and left skin beneath that did not know what to do with air.

The unicorn bucked and slammed a forehoof where Kaelan had cut. It misjudged and stumbled. Kaelan stepped in and scored the same leg again to keep the weight off. She did not try to cripple it. She tried to keep it from spearing anyone by accident.

"More," Marcus said, voice tighter now.

Sia widened the pattern. Fire fell in a ring that tracked the horn and shoulders whenever the beast turned. The smell of wet iron rose and mixed with something sweet and rotten. The wards spun at the edge of the hollow, squeaking warnings at anything that moved in the brush.

The unicorn threw its head and screamed. Under the scream Sia heard a word push through like a hand through a curtain. Not a language, but a meaning. She locked it away for later and kept her hands steady on the staff.

Fuzanglong flashed across its eyes again. The horn stabbed empty space. Sia dropped a double volley on the neck where the vines had knotted tight. The knots smoked and then snapped. The unicorn stumbled and caught itself on the far rim with both forehooves.

"Keep the rain," Kaelan warned. "If it gets free it will run straight through us."

"I have it," Sia said.

She bled Marcus's heat into the pattern without dumping him dry. Every second she felt him adjust to her pace, and every second the anchor cord cooled a fraction. The projection brightened again around his edges. He was not safe. He was stable enough to fight.

The unicorn gathered for another charge. Sia cut the rain to a narrow strip and dropped it like a line across the path. The beast hit the line with its chest and flinched. Kaelan used the recoil to rake the weakened foreleg again. The knee slid and the beast went down on it, scrabbling for a purchase that was not there.

"Left side," Marcus said. "Shoulder joint."

Sia shifted the point of aim and brought the next wave down where he called it. Fire ate fungus. Fire ate vine. Real skin showed through. The scream changed. It sounded less like a broken instrument and more like something living that hated every second of this and needed them to keep going anyway.

"Hold it," Fuzanglong said, voice level. "Hold until the rot lets go."

Sia held. Her forearms burned from the grip. Her shoulders shook. She kept her feet set the way Eric had taught her. No fancy stance. Just a stance that did not roll an ankle when a monster tried to plow straight through her.

The unicorn bunched to spring again and then faltered. The rain found a seam along the neck, ran under the plates of fungus, and ripped a sheet of rot off like old tape. The horn flashed clean along one side. For a blink Sia saw a true spiral under the mess.

"There," Kaelan said, breathing hard. "Now we can reach it."

Marcus pushed more heat. Sia broke it into smaller drops and threw them faster so the fire would eat and not drown. The wards screamed at the trees. The cry from the forest answered in deeper notes and rolled back at them like a threat.

Sia kept her eyes on the fight and did not look away. The umbrella shook in her hands. She reset her grip and counted out loud to keep the pattern even.

"One. Two. Three."

Fire fell in sheets that Sia kept tight and angled. She planted the umbrella like a staff and let the runes climb to her hands. Marcus fed heat through the anchor, steady this time, not the flood from the first volley. The umbrella turned it into arcs that smashed fungus plates and burned through vine knots. Every hit threw off sparks and the smell of wet rot cooking.

"Keep me lanes," Kaelan called. She circled the unicorn's shoulder, blade low, ready to chop if it tried to break through.

"I've got them," Sia said. She split the next wave into three narrow bands and dragged them down the spine, then across the ribs. The beast staggered, hooves gouging the dirt. It reared and screamed. The scream cracked in the middle and turned into words pushed through a broken throat.

"Do not stop," it forced out. "Burn it down."

Sia felt herself pull the fire back on instinct. She hated the idea of cooking a living thing. The plea punched through that hesitation. "You asked," she said under her breath. She pulled the feed tighter and hotter and aimed at the thickest plates along the withers.

Kaelan stopped moving for a heartbeat, eyes narrowed like she was listening to something under the noise. "There is a will beneath this," she said. "It is not only a body under rot. Let me add mine."

"Do it," Sia said without looking away. Heat licked along her sleeves. Sweat ran and stung the corner of her eye.

Kaelan touched two fingers to her lips and blew. Blue-white fire streamed out, not a gout, more like a ribbon. It braided into Sia's pattern and changed the feel of the burn. The heat stopped feeling like a bonfire and started feeling like a forge. Where foxfire touched fungus, it did not char. It came apart. The sheets of growth unstitched and fell as clean ash that skittered back from the stream like it had been told to behave.

"Hold that," Sia said. She shifted her grip, passed the umbrella to her left hand, and drew the next arc higher to catch the horn. Fungus there flared and cracked. Knots in the creature's mane snapped with popping sounds that reminded Sia of breaking heavy thread.

"I can hold," Kaelan said. "Not forever."

"Long enough," Marcus said through the projection, voice clipped but even. "I am holding the feed in the middle. Pull when you want it."

The wards did their part along the rim. They zipped from perch to perch, shrieked when a sick patch crept, and slapped Sia's hood twice to warn her away from an updraft of wrong air. Fuzanglong floated along the far side of the hollow and lifted his head when the unicorn lined a charge. He cut the eyes again, bright and simple, and the point of the horn dipped an inch away from Kaelan's shoulder instead of through it.

Sia set the triangle for real. Marcus sent her clean flame. She grabbed it with the umbrella and made it behave. Kaelan fed foxfire into the center so the heat purified instead of cooked. They kept their lanes. They did not cross each other. The pattern fell in a rhythm the unicorn could not outrun. Fungus burned and slid away. Vine knots snapped. The raw skin under it hissed and showed white hair in patches. It was the wrong kind of beautiful, but it was progress.

The unicorn slammed its horn into the soil and threw a wave of dirt in a circle. Sia adjusted and took the fire rain wider for two beats so Kaelan could lean back out. She narrowed it again when the head came up and drove the next set straight down the spine. The smell shifted off rot and into something cleaner. Ash. Steam. Hot metal.

"Almost there," Sia said. She did not say it twice. She needed the breath.

The creature tried to run in a line through the rain and stumbled instead. It knelt on its forelegs and dragged itself three steps. The horn cut a groove like a plow, then lifted. The cry tore out of it again. The words inside were weaker now but still there.

"Do not stop," it said. "Please."

Sia held the edge of the purge like she had been taught to hold a cutting spell. Enough to break the foul thing. Not enough to take the host with it. She kept the umbrella firm and let Marcus pour. She tugged Kaelan's foxfire across three trouble spots where the rot tried to cling. The ash fell away in heavy sheets. It never went near the stream. It hit the bank and stayed where Fuzanglong's earlier wave had flattened the ground.

Heat rolled back at them. Sia widened her stance, set the ferrule deeper, and held the pattern from going wild. She felt her arms shake and made them stop. The anchor cord kept its clean pulse on her wrist, Marcus in step with her count. Kaelan's breath came in measured pushes that matched the bursts of blue-white fire.

"Enough," Fuzanglong said. His voice cut straight through the crackle. "Stand clear."

Sia broke the channel. The umbrella's runes dimmed a shade at a time. Marcus closed the feed. Kaelan pinched the foxfire closed like a candlewick. Fuzanglong reared, spectral and huge as the air would let him, and scratched both front claws down into nothing. A wall of river water burst into the space and hammered down. It was not a rolling flood. It was a single, heavy sheet that smacked fire flat and shoved ash back from the center. Steam blew up and out. The wards tumbled in the gust and came up swearing in voices the size of thimbles.

Silence hit fast. It sounded wrong after all that noise. The only thing left was the low run of the stream and a soft crackle where hot stones cooled.

Sia blinked into the steam and wiped the side of her face with her sleeve. Her hands shook, then steadied when the umbrella settled to a normal weight again. Kaelan took one slow breath and let it out. Marcus's projection kneeled, head bowed, holding shape like a boxer on one knee waiting for the count.

They stepped forward together. The hollow looked different without the heat bending the air. Ash coated the ground in a shallow bowl. It had pulled away from the stream in a clear line. Fuzanglong held the water with invisible edges until the last wisps of smoke were gone, then let it fall flat into damp soil.

In the center lay the truth of it. A unicorn, lean and long, hide patchy and raw where the growths had been, but alive. The horn was clean and bright, not a weapon at the moment so much as a sign. The mane lay free where vines had been. Every breath made the ribs show and then hide again.

Sia kept her hands visible. "We can help," she said, even and plain. "If you want it."

The unicorn's ear flicked. It turned its head without trying to rise. The eye that finally met hers looked like a storm letting go. It did not speak with a human voice. It did not need to. The feeling that came off it was the same as a nod.

Kaelan slid her sword away and worked a charm tin open with her thumb. "Salve with cooling and knit," she said, mostly to Sia so they would be on the same page. "No binding."

"Good," Sia said. She knelt on the clean side and set the umbrella down within reach. Her hands hovered a breath above the worst of the raw patches. She did not try to make new skin. She asked the body to remember the exact step just before this damage, the one where the flesh had been stressed but still whole. She nudged it to that point and held it there so it would not tear further. Kaelan spread thin lines of salve in a pattern that looked like frost and smelled like peppermint and pine.

Marcus watched from a few feet away, shoulders loose for the first time since the hit. He kept the anchor quiet and let Sia work. The wards perched on roots and fence-watched with serious faces, ready to scream if any of the ash shifted.

Fuzanglong lowered his head until his nose was almost level with the horn. "Name yourself, Lord," he said, respectful and soft.

The unicorn closed its eyes for a second like it had been waiting to be asked that the right way. Then it opened them and gave them the kind of look you give people you are willing to trust for a little while. Whatever he said was not for Sia's ears in words. It sat around her chest anyway. Relief. Pain. Thanks. A promise that the asking to burn had meant what it sounded like.

Sia touched her fingers to the clean base of the mane and let a last whisper of heat settle out of her hands. It ran along skin and faded where it met Kaelan's salve. The horn caught a line of light and threw it into the ash at their feet. It looked like a clean line drawn across a page full of mistakes.

"Welcome back," Sia said. "We will keep watch while you catch your breath."

STEAM THINNED OVER THE hollow. Ash lay in a wide ring where the fire had pushed it. The stream ran clear again, snapping quietly around stones.

The corruption didn't retreat. It struck.

Air shoved up from the ground in a hard sheet, the same wrong draft the pixies had warned about, only bigger. Soot twisted off the ash bowl and reached like fingers. Thorny vines shot from the shadows at the rim, green at first, then slick and gray as they crossed the line of light.

"Shield," Kaelan said.

Sia planted the umbrella. The ferrule bit dirt. Runes flared up the shaft. She pulled a dome into place with a quick, practiced motion—one ring, then a second, then a third. The first took the hit. The second angled it. The third bled it off into the ground. The push of air broke and slid. The vine tips hit the field and smoked instead of sticking.

"Hold for three," Sia said. "I'll make us a lane."

She swept the umbrella left to right, etching a narrow corridor in the shield where the field thickened rather than thinned. "Path open," she called. "Go."

Kaelan moved through first, light on her feet, katana down and ready. Sia kept the dome flexed and followed. Marcus's projection stayed tight at Sia's shoulder, small again to save anchor power, eyes bright and tracking. The pixie wards fanned out to either side, tiny faces set, ready to scream if anything shifted.

The unicorn pushed up to his knees, legs shaking. He planted a forehoof, then the other, breath loud in the quiet. The horn caught daylight and threw a clean line across the ash.

More corruption hit. Tendrils whipped the shield. A gust tried to pull the ash back onto the unicorn like a blanket. Sia shoved the umbrella down and threw a flat front into the gust. It broke around them and went wide.

"Enough," the unicorn said.

It wasn't human speech. It pressed into the space like a command. The horn brightened from base to point. The air tightened around Sia's ears the way it does right before thunder.

"Out of my forest," the unicorn said. "Out."

The order rolled. It wasn't loud so much as complete. The vines went slack and shriveled where they hung on the dome. Ash peeled back from the center in a dry tide and stuck fast to the bank. Glossy bands on nearby trunks cracked and flaked. The bruise clover at the hollow edge greened right in front of them, as if someone turned a dial. The iron taste blew off the air and left wet leaves and cold stone behind.

Sia eased the shield down in steps, ready to throw it back up if anything bucked. Nothing did. The dome collapsed into a single ring at their feet, then into a thin shimmer around the umbrella ferrule, then into nothing. She let out a breath she hadn't noticed she was holding.

The unicorn stood on all fours for exactly three heartbeats, head high, horn bright. He checked the trees like a captain scanning a line after the volley. Satisfied, he exhaled hard and folded, first to his knees, then onto his side. Hooves twitched once and went still.

"Down," Kaelan said, already sheathing the blade. "We've got you."

They moved in. Sia set the umbrella within reach and put both hands above the worst of the raw patches along the shoulder. "No deep work," she said, reminding herself as much as Kaelan. "Stabilize. Close edges. Stop bleeding that hasn't decided to stop." She asked the body for the moment right before tearing, found it, and held the tissue there so it could choose to knit instead of split.

Kaelan opened her tin and traced thin lines of salve in frost-patterns that guided heat away. Peppermint and pine cut the last of the smoke smell. "Three lines," she said. "Three circles. Three breaths." She matched the old rule without making a ceremony of it.

The wards perched on root-knobs and watched like little sentries, wings quivering. One pointed at a last curl of gray that hadn't decided if it wanted to behave. Sia flicked a spark from the umbrella ferrule and turned it to proper ash. The pixie nodded, very serious.

Marcus's projection shook out his tiny wings and settled on a rock a safe distance from the horn. He glanced at Fuzanglong's spectral coil, then at the unicorn, then back at Sia. "I am very grateful to be light and ideas right now," he said, voice dry. "Unicorns and mortal men have... history."

Fuzanglong's whiskers lifted. "A lucky day to be a projection," he agreed, amused. "The ladies are quite safe. You and I, less so."

"Good to know," Marcus said. He shifted a fraction farther from the horn.

Kaelan didn't look up from her work. "Good news," she said calmly. "Neither of you are men at the moment."

The tiny dragon huffed. "Technicality accepted."

Sia felt the unicorn's breathing smooth under her palms. The raw edges at the shoulder dulled from angry to clean. She eased pressure, let the body keep the work. "That's it," she said. "Do the rest yourself." She lifted her hands and wiped her palms on the knees of her pants.

The forest around them matched the change. What had looked flat came back into focus. Leaves showed real greens instead of sick gloss. Water took on a shine that wasn't just light, it was health. Birdsong returned in normal notes instead of glitched loops. A breeze ran through the hollow, cool and ordinary.

The unicorn opened his eye. The look he gave them had weight. Sia felt a thanks land without words and put her palm to the ground in answer. "You're welcome," she said. She said it twice more, quietly, to seal the exchange.

He shifted his head toward the fused tree and the man inside it, then back to Sia and Kaelan. A question lived in the gesture: later?

"Later," Sia said. "We'll come back to him when you say it's safe."

The ear flicked once, agreement.

Kaelan capped the tin and sat back on her heels. "Salve will hold. Don't roll for a bit." She looked at Sia. "You good?"

"Tired," Sia said. "Good tired."

Marcus hopped back to her shoulder and settled in. The anchor cord cooled to normal. "Projection stable," he said. "Permission to retire the term Baby Marcus for the rest of the day."

Sia bumped him gently with a fingertip. "You earned it."

Fuzanglong lowered his head level with the unicorn's and spoke in a tone that felt old. "Lord of the Emerald, your forest answers. Hold your line. We will stand with you if something tries again."

The unicorn's breath came easier. He shut his eyes and let his head rest on the clean earth. The wards shifted to a loose perimeter, facing outward now, proud of themselves and trying not to show it.

"Water," Kaelan said, and filled a cup from the stream. She offered it in the space near the unicorn's mouth and set it down when he didn't move. "For when you want it."

Sia rose and picked up the umbrella. The ferrule left a neat round mark in the damp soil where the shield had anchored. She looked to the treeline where the wrongness had come from and saw only trees, ordinary and green.

"Emerald's back," she said.

"For now," Kaelan answered. "We keep it that way."

CHAPTER 4

Knight's Oath

SIA

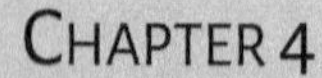

STEAM DRIFTED OFF THE ash ring until only clean damp earth was left. The unicorn pushed to standing and held there, breath steady, horn bright. Up close he looked like a banner raised after a fight, not a weapon. He turned his head and met each of their eyes in turn.

"I am Eachthighern," he said. "Lord of Unicorns. You broke the rot from my grove. You have my thanks."

Sia kept her hands visible. "You're welcome," she said. She said it two more times, quiet but clear, to make it stick the right way here.

Eachthighern tipped his horn toward the heart-tree where the armored figure was still fused into the trunk. "One favor more," he said. "Free the Forest's Protector. Until he stands, the Emerald will not heal straight."

Kaelan scanned the bindings with a quick, professional look. "Living bark grown through the plates," she said. "Vine stitches at the joints. That neck seam is not factory metal. Oath split, then set again."

She tapped the gorget with a knuckle and listened to the sound. "He is not dead. The tree holds him in place like a tourniquet."

Sia stepped to the trunk and set her palm near the pauldron. She felt the wood answer, stubborn but listening. "I can give the tree a memory to follow," she said. "Before it ever met armor. If it remembers that shape, it can loosen without tearing him."

Eachthighern moved beside her, quiet for something that large. He lowered his head until the horn rested a breath from the bark. "The grove will listen," he said. "I will make sure."

He tapped the horn to the trunk three times. Each touch carried a word that did not ride on sound so much as sit in the space. "Yield," with the first. "Remember," with the second. "Release," with the third.

The bark seemed to take a breath.

Kaelan pulled three slips of paper and inked fast, clean marks. She pressed one to the shoulder seam, one to the hip, and one just under the helmet rim. "Freeze, not break," she said. "On your count."

Sia nodded and closed her eyes for a second. She pictured this tree before it wrapped a person. Clean grain. Young bark. No metal. She slid that picture in like a thin wedge between wood and plate and held it steady. The trunk flexed under her palm. A hairline crack walked around the pauldron with a dry pop. The green axe haft, trapped at the hip, shifted a thumb's width like it wanted out.

"Good," Kaelan said. "Second line."

Sia added a second pass, thinner. The bark gave at the hip. The ofuda kept the vines from tightening in reflex. Fuzanglong's spectral body lifted and hovered at the edge of her sightline, eyes narrow, watching for a bad jump in the bindings.

"The neck," Kaelan said. "That seam matters."

Eachthighern set his horn lightly to the gorget where the metal looked like it had been cut once and pressed back. The bright line along the horn pulsed three times. The seam softened. The tree loosened around it as if it had been waiting for permission.

"On three," Kaelan said. "One. Two. Three."

Sia pushed the memory wedge deeper. Kaelan stripped the shoulder charm and dragged vines off the joint in a single practiced pull. The bark opened cleanly along the old lines. The man slumped forward as the trunk released him. Marcus, back in small form to save power, zipped from Sia's shoulder to Kaelan's pack strap and anchored there so she had both arms free. Sia got under the armored weight with both hands and guided him down to clean ground.

"Helm next," Kaelan said. She touched the charm at the rim. The latch whispered. The neck seam reseated with a click that sounded like a lock choosing to be a hinge again.

Eachthighern lowered his horn to the breastplate. Light ran along the scrollwork, washing verdigris into proper color. The oak leaf and holly patterns clarified, green bright against gold. The smell of rot lifted another notch and left crushed leaves and metal behind.

Sia set her palm above the man's sternum, not on it. She did not try to mend. She asked his body to come to the moment just before the worst of this, the step where systems were stressed but still organized. The pulse under her hand found a rhythm and stayed there. She kept it steady long enough to hand it back to him.

"Armor's clear," Kaelan said. She cut the last vine hooks and flicked them away. Eachthighern stepped back to give them space, horn up, eyes on the treeline in case the grove tried to reclaim what it had lost.

The tree did not reach for him. The split edges settled like a wound deciding to scar instead of bleed.

Sia and Kaelan rolled the man to his back. He was heavy even with most of the weight carried in place by the plates, but he moved like a person, not a bundle. The buckler half-swallowed by bark came free with him and clinked to the dirt. The quartered field showed green and gold. Three oak leaves sat proud in the top left. The axe haft followed with a tug, stained deep green along the grain.

Marcus hopped back to Sia's shoulder and kept watch. "Anchor solid," he said. "Projection holding. We are clear for a minute if you need both hands."

"I've got it," Sia said.

Eachthighern breathed out slowly. The grove answered him. Leaves settled. The air lost the last strange twist it had been holding. The wards, who had been pretending not to fidget, clapped tiny hands once and then remembered their manners.

Sia checked the man's face for color under the grime. Pale, but not corpse-pale. Sweat beaded along the hairline under the helmet rim. She lifted the helm a finger, waited to see if anything pulled the wrong way, then eased it up and off. The skin under it had the dull look of someone who had slept too long. His mouth was set, not slack. His jaw had a line to it that said will even when everything else said rest.

"He will wake," Eachthighern said. "He needs the shape of himself first."

Kaelan knelt at the hip joint and ran a fingertip along the seam. "Plates are aligned," she said. "No hooks left. If the oath-mangle was holding him, it is not now."

Sia drew two circles with her thumb above the breastplate and set a simple count in the space. "Breathe with me," she said to the man. "In. Hold. Out." She did not force it. She gave a path and let his lungs pick it up. On the third cycle, the breath under her palm matched her count. He coughed once and shivered hard.

"Easy," Kaelan said. She draped her travel cloak under his head to keep him off the wet ground.

Eachthighern touched horn to the breastplate one last time. "By my right in this wood," he said, quiet and firm, "I name the Protector free." The horn brightened and then dimmed, as if a circuit had closed.

The man's hands twitched. Fingers that had been locked to bark flexed and closed. The right hand found the axe haft like it knew the weight even before the mind did.

Sia lifted her palm and let the body keep its own count. She checked the ground where they had worked. No creeping vines, no shine of wrong on the bark. The split edges of the trunk held their line and did not try to close on empty space. The grove felt like a room after a bad argument had blown through. Quiet with a little shock left in it.

"Protector stands," Eachthighern said. He sounded satisfied for the first time since they met him. He looked at Sia and Kaelan and gave a small, exact nod. "You did clean work."

"We followed your lead," Kaelan said.

Sia sat back on her heels and rolled her shoulders out. "He will wake soon," she said. "Let him pick the first words."

Eachthighern agreed with another small nod. He stepped to the side so the first thing the man would see was not a horn pointed at his face. Fuzanglong lowered his head and rested his chin on his spectral claws, content to watch with no need to push. The wards took up proud positions on a low branch and pretended to be as quiet as leaves.

They waited while the forest kept breathing. On the sixth count, the Protector's eyes flicked under his lids. On the ninth, his chest rose deeper. On the twelfth, he opened his eyes to the hollow, blinked hard, and found them.

Sia did not speak yet. She only lifted two fingers in hello and kept her voice for when he asked for it.

Eachthighern inclined his head. "Protector," he said, simple as a greeting on a road. "Your grove stands. Come back to it."

THE MAN BLINKED UP at the sky, then at them. He thumbed the helmet latch and lifted it off. Sun-blonde hair fell in uneven lengths, the kind you get growing under steel. His eyes were a clear green that matched the enamel on his breastplate, and there was a faint green cast under his skin, like the grove lived just beneath it. Straight nose, strong jaw, a mouth that could go stern or warm without effort. Startlingly handsome, and now very awake.

Eachthighern stepped close enough to shade him. "Protector."

He set a fist to the earth and bowed his head. "My lord." He looked to Sia and Kaelan. "And to you, strangers who chose not to be." He pressed his fist over the quartered green-and-gold on his buckler. "Thank you."

"You're welcome," Sia said, then repeated it twice more, even and clear.

"You're welcome," Kaelan added.

He tested his grip on the green-stained axe haft, rose to a knee, then stood. Tall, steady, no wasted motion.

"I am the Green Knight," he said. "Bastian, sworn Protector of the Emerald." He glanced at the scored trunk, then at Eachthighern's horn. "I failed to keep rot from the heart. You pulled me free before failure turned to ruin. I owe you a debt."

Kaelan shook her head. "You were holding the line. We just took our turn."

He didn't argue. He laid his palm over the oak-leaf crest and made it formal. "Hear me. I, Bastian of the Emerald, vow to repay this aid. I vow to stand as your shield while debt remains. I vow to see you safely to the Summer Court." He repeated it, word for word, two more times. On the third, the promise settled over the clearing like a latch clicking shut.

The pixie wards chirped "seen" in tiny, serious voices. Sia felt the oath land clean.

Eachthighern lowered his horn, the bright line along it soft now. "Let the ledger show," he said, then turned to them. "And let gifts answer gifts."

He moved to Marcus first. The projection, small again on Sia's shoulder, straightened. Eachthighern touched the horn to the tiny dragon's brow, careful and exact. Light ran from the tip through Marcus's outline and along the anchor cord to Sia's wrist.

"For the dragon who held when the grove tried to throw him: stability, longer reach, and the right to lay flame on corruption without tearing yourself."

Marcus's shape snapped into crisp focus; the tug on Sia's cord eased to a steady hum. "Whoa. That feels... solid. Thank you."

Eachthighern faced Sia. "For the Dreamer who shaped fire clean." He tapped the umbrella shaft. The wood drank the light; the ferrule runes brightened, then settled to a calm glow. "Unbreakable. Not against steel, or oath, or panic. It will not splinter when you need it most. It will remember the geometries you ask of it."

Sia tested the balance. Same weight, different confidence. "Got it. Thank you." She said it again, and once more, to set the exchange right.

Kaelan squared up. Eachthighern lowered the horn to her shoulder seam. Light braided through the fabric like a ripple; for a heartbeat her kimono showed a faint leaf-sheen, then it faded.

"For the shrine maiden who cut true and kept the lanes open—edge-turning weave. Thorn will not take you easy. The threads will remember themselves and mend."

Kaelan rolled a sleeve and grinned. "I'll try not to make a hobby of testing it."

Last, he turned to Fuzanglong. The dragon god's spectral body dipped. "I owe the river, and the river owes me. Take one favor from the Emerald. Name it once, and the wood will answer."

"I accept," Fuzanglong said. "I'll spend it well."

Bastian watched the gifts with focused calm, helmet tucked under one arm, axe haft easy in his palm. "My oath stands," he said, and spoke it once more for the road, not the binding: "I will get you to Summer." He lifted the buckler slightly. "Witness, road." He nodded to the stream. "Witness, river." He set the axe head to the roots at his boots. "Witness, root."

Sia and Kaelan answered in threes, simple and clear.

"We hear you."

"We accept."

"We'll walk with you."

The wards spun in a tiny cheer and chirped another proud "seen."

Eachthighern tipped his horn toward the lowering sun. "Light is leaving. Rest here. The Emerald owes you guest food and safe watch." He looked to Sia, quieter now. "And there is more I would say to you when the fire is small."

"Later," Sia said, matching the promise.

Bastian scanned the treeline, guard instincts still on. Up close, with the helmet off and the grove's color back on him, he looked every inch the Protector the forest had tried to turn into a statue—blonde hair catching green light, green eyes steady, that faint woodland tint under his skin. Startling, yes. Also solid.

"I'll walk the edge while you eat," he said. "We can head out at first light."

"Okay," Sia said.

"Yeah," Kaelan added. "We'll be ready."

Marcus nudged Sia's cheek with the tiny side of his head. "For the record," he told Fuzanglong, deadpan, "I'm very happy to be a projection around a unicorn."

"A sensible preference," Fuzanglong agreed.

They stood a moment longer in the cleaned hollow, gifts settling, oaths cooling into place, and the path to Summer starting to show itself.

EVENING SLID IN SOFT. The ash ring was only a damp memory now, and the Emerald felt like it had finally taken a full breath. The forest handled the hosting without being asked. A low crown of branches folded into a windbreak, leaves shook free clean fruit with a few sharp thumps, and the stream widened into a shallow lip where anyone could scoop water without slipping. A small greenfire lifted from the ground and held steady light without heat.

Sia sat near the fire with her umbrella across her knees. The wood kept a quiet pulse in her hands, a steady hum that felt like a cat purring next to a radiator. Unbreakable did not feel heavy. It felt sure. Marcus's tiny dragon shape had curled into the hood of her jacket like a pocket pet, all claws sheathed and eyes half shut. The anchor cord rested warm against her wrist. He kept testing the new stability in little stretches of light, then relaxing again when it held without strain.

Kaelan's kimono showed a faint leaf sheen at the seams for a while, then the shimmer sank into the fabric like it had always been there. She filled cups from the widened stream and passed them around. Fuzanglong coiled spectrally just beyond the fire's circle, bright enough to see but thin enough to remind everyone he could not lift anything tonight except a warning.

Bastian returned from his slow walk of the perimeter with his helmet under one arm. He had that guard's rhythm of looking, listening, then looking again. When he set the helmet beside him and sat, the whole clearing seemed to settle a notch.

"Food's on us," Sia said, pointing to the neat pile the branches had shaken loose. "No jokes about salad. The forest is trying."

Bastian smiled at that and reached for a pear. "Guest-right," he said. "Eachthighern keeps it clean."

Marcus popped his head out of Sia's hood. "And safe," he added, then pretended he had not just spoken with a mouth full of pear juice after Sia handed him a slice on her palm.

They ate simple and quiet for a few minutes. The greenfire kept the shadows easy. When everyone had a little water and something sweet in them, Kaelan looked at Bastian across the light. "So," she said. "Protector. How did you end up part tree?"

Bastian ran a hand through his hair like he was feeling where the helmet had pressed. "The short version," he said. "Winter-front pushed hard along a line no one had flagged. That happens. The Hunt held their ground. Summer pushed back. The part that should not have happened was the rot that came with it."

"Like today," Sia said.

"Worse," Bastian answered. "Hidden under armor, questions that only arrive after you answer them, orders that feel right until you set them down and read them out loud. We tracked it to the heart-tree. I was the one standing with the authority to keep the center. The rot wanted a host. I was the best option in reach. I took a geas to stand fast without letting it in."

He tapped the old seam at his neck where the plate had once been split. Up close it looked almost like scar tissue made of metal. "It tried to take me anyway. The oath split me and set me again. I do not recommend the sensation. The tree decided it would keep me from falling while I did my job. It was not wrong. It just did not know how to let go after."

Kaelan watched him for a second longer, then nodded like she understood and accepted the answer. "Your axe?"

"Old," he said, lifting the green-stained haft with obvious affection. "Oak and holly. Summer make. I have carried others when the courts prefer a certain look, but this is the one that always comes back."

Sia looked toward the heart-tree, now just a tree again with a clean split that was already sealing its edges. "And the oath at your neck. That saved you."

"It saved the grove," Bastian said. "I was the cost that time. Costs change. That is why we say them out loud. If I had to choose again, I would do it again, but I would do it faster."

The wards perched like tiny judges on a low branch, faces serious. When Bastian finished, the leader nodded once in a way that said the story checked out and could be written down.

They set watches out of habit. Bastian took first without making a whole thing of it. Kaelan protested and then agreed to take second. Sia volunteered for last, since dreaming closest to dawn usually left her less wrecked. Fuzanglong kept an eye across the stream, not because he could throw power, but because having a god in the corner of your eye makes bad ideas smaller.

Eachthighern had stood quiet for most of the meal, but when the cups were empty and the greenfire eased lower, he dipped his head toward Sia. "Walk a little?" he asked.

Sia rose and followed him to the edge of the hollow where the ground went softer and the air felt like something had been washed out of it. They stopped where the stream curled and made a rare lazy sound.

"I kept part of the Dreaming with me while the rot held," Eachthighern said. "Unicorns and dreams cross often. I can still touch the edges of it where the forest kisses sleep."

Sia's fingers tightened on the umbrella handle. "You can walk my garden."

"When you need it," he said. "And only when you ask. But I would like to offer a watch. The Dreaming is thin in places. You have seen that. If your hands are busy with the waking world, I can lean my horn against your gate and listen. If something comes that should not, I will knock three times so you know it is me, then I will keep it outside until you arrive."

Sia exhaled. It felt like someone had just told her the shop across the street would keep an eye on her house when she worked a late shift. "I would like that," she said. "I do not take the offer lightly."

"I do not make it lightly," Eachthighern said. He lowered his head and touched the tip of his horn to a smooth stone at the path's edge. A faint, clean tone rang once and faded. "There. A mark you will feel when you pass. If you do not want me near, tell me three times. I will keep away unless called."

Sia nodded and matched the structure. "Thank you," she said. She said it again. She said it a third time, careful and clear.

They stood there for a minute with nothing pressing the space. When they walked back to the others, the greenfire had dimmed to a bowl of steady light. Bastian had returned from his round and sat close enough to talk but far enough to leave a pocket of quiet if anyone wanted it. Kaelan was coaxing a little steam from a cup like she had convinced the water to be warm for exactly thirty breaths and no more. Marcus pretended to be asleep and then immediately opened one eye the second Sia sat.

"Any mysterious dream business?" he asked in a whisper he clearly thought was subtle.

"Later," Sia said, and flicked his tiny tail with a fingertip. "Sleep."

Marcus made a show of settling more deeply into her hood. "I could sleep for a week."

"Please do not," Kaelan said. "We need you in the morning."

"I will do a power nap," he said, already drifting.

Bastian leaned back on his hands and looked at the canopy. "We move at first light. Summer roads if we can. No big crossings if we can help it. The courts watch and gossip. It will be easier if we arrive without giving them a week of stories on the way."

"That part I can handle," Kaelan said dryly. "I know more than a few of the story tellers."

"Of course you do," Sia said, and earned a little shoulder bump for it.

They let the night find its shape. The forest fed them again with a few more easy offerings. The wards rotated their own strange watch without being told, one always awake and two pretending not to be sleepy a second before they fell over sideways. Fuzanglong rested his chin on his coils and watched reflections slide down the stream. Eachthighern stood at the far edge with his head lowered, not sleeping exactly, more like a lighthouse deciding it could blink.

The boons settled while they rested. Marcus's projection held shape even when he drifted, which meant Sia did not have to wake him every time he loosened. The umbrella's hum evened out and tucked itself under her skin as a calm, quiet ready. Kaelan's armored threads finished their subtle work and left only normal cloth to the eye. When Sia rubbed the sleeve between two fingers she felt the strength braided through it.

When it was Sia's turn to take the last watch, the sky was only thinking about light. She stood with her umbrella grounded and let the grove speak in soft ordinary sounds. No stuttered birdsong. No wrong wind. Just leaves and water and sleeping friends.

Bastian stepped up beside her without making her jump. He looked different in this light, less like a statue, more like a person who had been given a hard job and still wanted to do it.

"You ready to walk?" he asked.

"Yeah," Sia said. She looked back at Kaelan rolling a sleeve, at Marcus pretending not to stretch, at Fuzanglong sliding his spectral coils up into a long ribbon of light. "We are."

"Good," Bastian said. He picked up his helmet and hooked it under his arm. "Summer is waiting."

An Audience

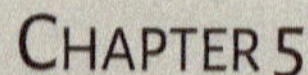

SIA

By the time a week had passed, the road itself looked happier to see them. Waystones that had been dull and mossy when they first stepped into Summer weakly glowed at dusk, then grew confident enough to shine by the fourth night. The air went from damp and earthy to warm and clean, like the world had opened all its windows. Even the trees leaned in. Their branches arched over the path in a way that felt intentional, not creepy, as if someone had taught the forest good manners.

Bastian took the lead with his helmet hooked under one arm. He walked like he knew where the roots hid and which flat stones would wobble. Kaelan handled the small customs as they came up. She reminded Sia to keep her hands visible when they passed boundary pillars, to say thank you three times when a meal arrived without a name, to decline anything wrapped with a ribbon. Marcus rode Sia's shoulder in his tiny dragon shape, testing his upgraded projection with cautious stretches of wing and a smug little hum when the anchor on Sia's wrist stayed steady.

On the seventh morning the path curved around a ridge and the world opened. Below lay a bowl of sunlight and, in the middle of it, the Summer Palace.

Sia stopped without meaning to. "Okay. Wow."

Terraces climbed the hill like stairs made for giants. Each level carried gardens that grew out of the stone rather than sitting on top of it, roots sunk in living shelves that drank the light. Slender towers rose at the back and reached toward a sky-bridge that looked too thin to hold anything until a pair of elves walked across it and did not fall. Sheets of glass caught sunlight and spread it the way water spreads glitter. Banners moved like heat shimmer. Nothing sagged or smoked or pretended. It looked bright without being fake.

"Sunstone," Bastian said. His voice softened on the name. "We check in at the Customs Green."

They followed the path down. A wide field lay before the outer gate, trimmed short and marked with pale lines that meant something to the guards. People waited in tidy lanes. Some were clearly locals who did this often. Others had the exact stiff posture of travelers trying very hard not to mess up in front of elves. Leaf-plate armor gleamed at the perimeters. A clerk with a glowing pen stood at a lectern and wrote in a book that looked like it had its own opinions.

Kaelan dropped her voice as they stepped off the road. "Hands out and empty. Names only. No titles unless they ask. No sudden magic. Do not accept anything with your name on it unless I tell you to."

"Got it," Sia said.

Marcus tucked his head. "Model citizen," he murmured.

Three wardens walked out to meet them. The leader had hair the color of fresh wheat and the kind of calm face that made people confess things. She stopped them at a painted line and lifted one hand.

"Halt," she said. "State your names and purpose. Declare any open debts in this court."

Kaelan stepped half a pace forward. "Kaelan Kuzunoha," she said. "Guest of Summer. No open debts."

"Sia Mason," Sia said. "Dreamer. No open debts."

"Marcus Duvall," Marcus said from Sia's shoulder. He gave a neat little nod. "Dragon, projection only. No open debts."

"Fuzanglong," the river dragon said, body faint and bright at the same time. "Guide. No open debts."

The warden's gaze moved to Bastian and warmed by a fraction. "Protector."

"Bastian," he said. "Green Knight of the Emerald. I am escort under oath to deliver these guests to Summer safely." He spoke it again, same words. Then a third time. The painted line seemed to accept that and stop being a barrier.

"Oath heard," the warden said. She tapped her boot on the line. "Witnessed by the road and the gate." She looked back to Sia's group. "Who sponsors you within the walls?"

"Protector Bastian," Kaelan said, because obvious was correct here.

"Purpose," the warden asked.

"Audience and report," Bastian answered. "We come from the Emerald. We freed the Protector your lord entrusted to the heart-tree. We bring our part of that story."

The warden's eyes flicked past them toward the woods they had left. She did not nod, but something in her stance said she had heard rumors. She gestured to the clerk. "Ledger."

The clerk came at a professional trot, pen already glowing. "Names, please," he said, trying and failing not to look at Marcus too long.

They repeated them. The clerk's script moved like running water. When he finished, he pressed his thumb to a small stamp. Four leaf tokens blinked into being on his tray, polished and green, each tied to a thin cord.

"Guest tokens," the warden said. "Wear them visible. Return them when you depart and your ledger line will close clean. While you wear them, hospitality applies. Do not test the limit of that sentence. These pretty much keep anyone in the Palace, whether it's Summer or a guest from trying to trick you into deals or getting favors. If you don't wear them we can't fully expect them to behave."

Kaelan handed cords around. Sia slipped hers over her head. It lay cool against her collarbone, a little heavier than it looked. Marcus did not get one. When the warden frowned at that, Kaelan answered first.

"He rides under Sia's line," she said. "Projection. If he drops, the token would drop with him."

The warden took a second to decide she had, in fact, seen stranger things. "Fine. Rules inside the outer gate. No bare steel in public spaces. You may keep your gear sheathed. Food and drink offered under hospitality is safe if it is not wrapped and has no name. Refuse anything else with a smile."

"Where first?" Sia asked.

"Herald's hall," the warden said, pointing along a path bordered with low stone and water. "Your sponsor will bring you. The chamberlain will assign rooms."

Bastian inclined his head. "Clear," he said, then caught himself and changed it mid-breath. "Thank you."

The warden almost smiled. "Welcome back, Protector. Try not to make my day interesting."

"I will do my best," he said.

Kaelan glanced at Sia. "That is as close to a hug as Summer guards get," she whispered.

They crossed the green with a page leading them. The outer gate looked like interlaced branches, but when Sia walked under it she felt the faint pressure of a threshold. The air on the other side carried the warmth of sun-soaked stone. Water ran along a shallow pool with lily pads and koi that changed color when they turned. A bell rang somewhere deeper in the complex. No one flinched. The sound meant time for something pleasant, not danger.

People moved along the walkways in groups and singles, all of them too beautiful to be fair by human standards. An elderly elf with silver braids stopped to tell a younger one that her vine pattern was crooked, which felt like the most normal conversation Sia had heard since they entered Faerie.

Marcus nudged her jaw with his head. "You okay?"

"Yeah," Sia said. "It's just a lot."

"Summer loves a lot," Kaelan said without looking back. "Smile with your eyes and keep your pockets shut."

They passed an arcade where carvings in the pillars shifted as they walked, showing scenes a half second before they stepped into them. A balcony overhead held two small trees in full fruit, which defied every rule Sia knew about potting soil and gravity. Bastian did not slow to gawk. He kept a polite pace, nodding only when someone greeted him by name.

At the end of the curve a herald waited in a short green cloak, attendants lined up behind him like tidy punctuation. He spotted Bastian and stood straighter.

"Protector," the herald said. "Welcome home."

"Thank you," Bastian said. "Guests of Summer, as recorded."

The herald's eyes flicked to the cords, then to Sia's umbrella, then to Marcus pretending very hard to be just a shoulder ornament. "Rooms are ready," he said. "The Queen is in session. The Lady attends. You will be called when the court is ready to hear you. Until then, the chamberlain will see you clean and fed."

"That sounds perfect," Kaelan said.

A chamberlain with a ring of keys and a smile that never reached her eyes stepped forward. "This way," she said.

They followed her through a broad hall where light fell in squares onto a floor that never seemed to collect dust. Sia kept her token visible and her expression set to polite. She did not reach for anything. She did not let anyone hand her anything tied with string. When a page offered a platter with cups of clear water, she took one, thanked him once, then twice more to be safe. The water tasted like stone and sunshine.

They reached a set of guest rooms along a quiet terrace that looked over a lower garden. The chamberlain unlocked two doors.

"Two suites," she said. "Easily joined if you wish. Baths are drawn. Clothing can be cleaned while you wash. Do not wander past the white markers on the terrace. The koi bite anyone who lies."

Sia blinked. "What?"

"Joke," the chamberlain said. She almost smiled, then did not. "Mostly."

Bastian hooked his helmet on a peg like he had done it a hundred times. "We will be ready when called," he told the chamberlain.

"You will," she said, and left in a glide of keys and competence.

Sia stood a second longer on the threshold, taking in the soft light, the carved lintel that showed leaves without a single thorn, the way the air felt easy in her lungs. It would be simple to relax. Kaelan caught her eye and shook her head, just a little.

"Not yet," Kaelan said. "Hospitality first. Trust later."

"Right," Sia said. She looked out across the garden toward the heart of the palace where glass and stone braided together. Somewhere in there, Titania would be sitting on a chair that made people forget to breathe. Somewhere in there, Winter had sent a representative who did not melt in all this light.

Marcus flicked his tail against her neck. "We made it to the door without starting trouble," he said. "That counts."

"It does," Sia said. She closed the door behind them and, for the first time in days, let the weight of the road slip off her shoulders without guilt. The palace could have its shine. They would have their footing.

THEY DID NOT WAIT long.

A herald in green led them through sun-bright arcades where vines traced living patterns up white columns. Music drifted from somewhere high and polite. Every surface seemed made to flatter daylight. Sia kept her guest token visible and her umbrella settled in her palm like a quiet reminder. Kaelan walked at her side, relaxed on purpose. Bastian followed with his helmet under one arm, easy as a local who knew every turn. Marcus perched on Sia's shoulder in small form, still as a pin, watching everything.

The Great Court opened like a stage. Terraces stepped inward toward a broad floor of pale stone. At the far end, the Summer thrones stood under a canopy of glass that filtered the sun into soft bands. Titania sat centered, light catching in her hair as if the palace wanted her to glow. Beside her, the Summer Lady, Aurora, watched with a calmer face, hands folded, eyes sharp.

Between them and the sun, a third presence cooled the room by a few degrees. The woman there wore frost like jewelry. Her hair lay pale as new ice across one shoulder, and the edges of her gown held a dim shine the heat could not touch. She looked elven in the way mountains look old. The air around her had the hush of snow. Winter had sent its queen.

"Mab," Kaelan breathed, just loud enough for Sia to hear. "Be precise."

Heralds announced names that had already been written in ledgers. Bastian stepped forward first and bowed with a respect that was clean, not servile. He said their names again for the room and added one sentence that turned heads.

"The Protector of the Emerald stands free," he said. "The rot is burned out of the heart."

A small current moved through the hall. Titania's smile did not change. Aurora let herself be pleased for half a heartbeat and then set the calm back on her face. Mab tilted her head, amused.

"How fortunate," Mab said, voice cool and light. "Your little test of Summer's champions went well after all, Titania. Protector Bastian stands with them."

Test hung in the air like a dropped pin.

Titania's smile stretched thinner. "We call it trust," she said. "We saw a problem and trusted competent hands."

Sia felt heat rise in her cheeks and kept her face neutral. Competent hands had been scraping rot off a unicorn while the heart-tree held a knight like a clamp. Trust was a word with edges.

Kaelan stepped forward half a pace, hands empty and visible. "Your Majesties," she said, and looked to Titania, then to Aurora, then back again, careful with the order and the pause. "If the court entrusted work to these hands, then the work was done. By Summer custom, work done in your name is accounted for. May the court acknowledge that value on the ledger."

Titania glanced down as if that ledger lived at her wrist. "You came as guests," she said. "Guests do not carry debts."

Kaelan did not smile. "We entered as guests," she said. "We left the road to put down a corruption that threatened your Protector and your woods. We expected nothing. Still, we acted. Will you mark that the act had value?"

Aurora shifted in her seat a fraction. The small movement felt like a nudge under the table. Titania's eyes flicked to her and back.

"Of course," Titania said. "Your act had value."

"One more time, please," Kaelan said, polite as paper. "For the ledger."

Titania blinked. Sia watched the moment land. Summer might love games, but the Rule of Three did not care about pride.

"It had value," Titania said again, slightly flatter.

"And the court will compensate value rendered," Kaelan said. "In the manner Summer judges fair."

Silence held just long enough to count. Sia could feel Marcus not-breathing on her shoulder.

"In the manner Summer judges fair," Titania repeated, the third time that locked it. Her smile thinned, then sharpened. "You bargain neatly, Miko."

Kaelan bowed a fraction. "I keep ledgers tidy. It is a vice."

Mab's mouth curved, pleased. "Summer's house grows clever. Good. We have need of clever." She turned her attention to Sia as if she had been waiting to look this whole time. "And you. Dreamer. You cleansed a rot my scouts could not see until it already bit. You will come to Winter next and look at my borders with those same eyes."

Sia met the queen's gaze and felt Winter the way you feel deep water. "If we go, we go by choice," she said. "And we walk with our escort."

"By choice," Mab agreed. "And with an escort. You will see what is actually happening when we stop telling you what we think."

Titania stood. The motion sent a ripple across the court, every attendant shifting focus with her. She let the glass canopy cast its light across her shoulders and gave the room a queen's voice.

"Right of Hospitality is invoked," she said. "For Sia Mason, for Kaelan Kuzunoha, for Marcus Duvall in projection, for Fuzanglong in specter, and for Protector Bastian while he stands in their company. Rooms are prepared, baths are drawn, and a proper feast will be set tomorrow to honor what was done."

"Tomorrow," Aurora echoed, warmer. "Not tonight. You look like the road."

Sia did not argue. She could feel mud in seams she had no name for.

"And the compensation?" Kaelan asked, gentle and relentless, in case anyone wanted to pretend the third acknowledgment had melted.

Titania's eyes brightened by a hair. "Our chamberlain will begin an accounting. Your escort's gear will be set to rights. Your focus will be tuned and unbreakable as promised. Your kimono will keep its memory. Fuzanglong's Emerald favor is recorded, to be honored when named. There will be more. We will speak when the feast is done."

"That settles the ledger for this chapter," Kaelan said. "Thank you."

Aurora stood too and the temperature of the room changed again, softer by a shade. "Rest," she told them, and it carried the feeling of clean sheets and a door that latches. "While you are within our markers, let the palace carry some of your weight."

Mab stepped forward one pace. The light did not reach her the same way. "Then carry this as well," she said. "After you sleep, walk out of Summer and into my lands. Not by the bright road. Take the edges. See what touches both courts without asking permission."

Bastian inclined his head, court-plain. "If they choose Winter's road, I will guide them."

Mab's eyes moved over him with interest. "You will guide them without letting my court claim them," she said. "Can you walk a line that tight, Protector?"

"I can," he said. "And I will."

"Say it three times," Kaelan said softly, for him.

"I can," Bastian repeated. "And I will." He said it a third time, steady. The floor seemed to accept it.

Titania lifted a hand and the court's hum resumed, petitioners moving, attendants gliding, the machine of Summer turning without visible gears. The herald stepped in with a small bow.

"Chamberlain will see you to your suites," he said to Sia's group. "Your audience is concluded for today."

Sia dipped a small bow toward the thrones. It felt strange to bow to two queens who had just agreed she had done their work for them, but the rules here mattered, and she had chosen to be useful. When she straightened, Titania's expression said nothing more than "you are seen." Aurora's eyes softened again and then went composed. Mab looked like a promise kept to itself.

They turned to go. Marcus exhaled once in Sia's ear, the breath she had felt him hold.

"That was a lot," he whispered.

"It was," she said. "We did fine."

"Kaelan did," he whispered back.

Kaelan heard and did not pretend she had not. "We did," she said. "Yeah. Let's clean up from the trip and, until tomorrow, don't take anything anyone tries to hand us."

Bastian gave Sia a small nod that read like approval. The helm under his arm caught a stripe of sun and threw it harmlessly at the floor.

As they followed the chamberlain out, Sia let herself look back once. Summer shone. Winter did not need to. Between them, the air felt very thin. She squared her shoulders and kept walking. Tomorrow would be a feast. After that, the road to Winter.

EVENING AT SUNSTONE LOOKED like a celebration that forgot to be loud. Lantern fruit glowed along the garden paths, each one a soft pearl inside a leaf cup. Musicians in a side arcade played something bright enough to keep feet moving and calm enough that no one had to shout to be heard. Courtiers drifted between terraces the way minnows move in shallow water, all color and easy turns.

Kaelan walked Sia down the main promenade and narrated rules in a voice that sounded like friend, not hall monitor. "Food from a table with the palace crest is safe," she said, tapping a small sun sigil etched into silver. "If anyone offers you a named thing, even something cute like 'May luck be tied to your braid,' say no. If someone says 'favor' or 'boon,' say you are honored to be asked and that you will answer in council. Smile with your eyes."

"I can do that," Sia said. She adjusted her guest token cord so it sat square against her shirt and kept her umbrella in her hand, ferrule grounded lightly. It felt normal to hold it now. Unbreakable hummed in the wood like a steady pulse just out of hearing.

Marcus stayed small on her shoulder. He had the posture of a gargoyle ornament that had decided to take protecting very seriously. "If anyone tries to pin a brooch on you, I will bite the brooch," he said into her ear.

"Please do not bite nobles," Kaelan said, then softened. "Unless they really deserve it."

Fuzanglong slid beside the path in his spectral coil, just visible enough to discourage mischief. A pair of little fae children followed at a polite distance, whispering that they could see a river moving where there was no river. Bastian walked a few steps behind Sia and Kaelan, helmet tucked under his arm, easing talkers away when their enthusiasm turned into tries at a swap.

They met a scholar with ink-stained fingers who wanted to compare dream-scripts. Sia admired his quill, then admired it two more times, and did not take it when he tried to tuck it into her pocket. They met a trio of musicians who offered Sia a ribbon that changed color with the beat. She thanked them nicely and did not let it touch her hair. They met a fox-featured courtier who called Kaelan "cousin" and tried to slide a wrapped sweet into Sia's palm while complimenting the umbrella. Kaelan smiled like sunlight off a knife and said, "Hospitality feeds guests. Debts feed ledgers." The wrapped sweet retreated as if it had never been there.

Not every exchange was work. A baker's page arrived with a tray of small pear tarts shaped like leaves. Sia took one because the tray bore

Summer's crest and the tart had no name stitched into the pastry. It tasted like a memory of the orchard behind her grandparents' apartment complex where she had once picked fruit from the low branch and felt taller than she was. Marcus stole a flake of crust and made a pleased noise.

By the time the sun moved behind the highest glass canopy, they had met a messenger from the Hunt who complimented Bastian's axe and promised not to borrow it, a botanist who grew roses with no thorns and looked offended when Sia preferred the ones that left scratches, and a polite boy in a short green cloak who wanted to see if the little dragon could breathe fire. Marcus refused to show off. He did agree to glow for exactly two seconds. The boy saluted him solemnly and ran off to report to a superior Sia could not see.

When the court's rhythm quieted for the night, a chamberlain appeared the way competent people do, present without having to make a noise first. "Their Majesties invite you to a brief parley," she said. "Informal, witnessed by the garden and the ledger. No oaths will be demanded here."

Sia shared a look with Kaelan. Kaelan nodded once. "We accept," Sia said.

The chamberlain led them along a hedge walk to a small pavilion set over a shallow pool. The water there took light from the lantern fruit and held it, so the pavilion looked like it was floating on a bowl of stars. Titania stood under the open roof with Aurora at her shoulder, both dressed simpler than they had been in court and somehow more imposing for it. On the far side, Mab waited with her hands bare and her attention quiet. Frost lived along the pavilion posts, not heavy enough to bite the wood, just enough to remind everyone Winter could sit anywhere it chose.

"Thank you for coming," Aurora said, and it did not feel like a line. It felt like a neighbor greeting you at the fence and meaning it.

Sia bowed her head in acknowledgement. "You asked," she said. "We came."

Titania's gaze flicked over Sia's umbrella, then to Kaelan's sleeves, then to Marcus pretending to be jewelry. "I prefer to see truths up close," Titania said. "At distance, they perform. Here, they stand."

Mab folded her hands. The air lost a degree. "And we are very tired of performances."

They did not waste time. Titania described where Summer's roadwatch had found patches of wrongness. A shepherd's hill that never quite warmed in the sun. A crossroads where the waystones glowed at the wrong hour. A glade that produced elaborate fruit overnight and then crumbled into rot by midday. None of it devastating on its own. All of it unnerving in a pattern you could trace on a map if you had the right eyes.

"We can hold rot when we see it," Titania said. "What we cannot hold is the knife that cuts before we feel the prick."

Mab listened without interrupting. When Titania finished, Winter's queen stepped to the rail and touched the tip of one finger to the water. Frost skated out until it met its reflection and stopped. "At my borders," she said, "the wrongness has teeth. It tests where my guard meets Summer's, and it stinks of the Dream. Not all of it walks from Hell. Some of it slips through where the world sleeps too close to waking."

Sia felt the words land where her nightmares lived. "You want me to look," she said.

"I want you to see," Mab said. "When I ask my favor, I will ask it in my court. I will not ask it here. But I ask now that you take the road to Winter next. Do not travel by the bright path only. Walk the edges. Stand where things touch and lie about it."

Titania said nothing for a long breath. Then she nodded once. "And I ask you to return to us after you see it," she said. "If Winter has a request, so will Summer. Balance is the only thing that keeps us from tearing the other in half."

It was not subtle. It was honest in the way dangerous offers are honest when everyone present has cut themselves on sharper tools.

Marcus leaned toward Sia's ear. "We are being used," he said, not loud and not unkind.

"I know," Sia said.

"It bothers me."

"It bothers me too." She kept her eyes on the water where frost met star and did not quite mix. "I still want to go. If the Dream is being pulled thin, I want to see where and how. If someone is cutting into it, I want to know what knife they use."

Kaelan did not argue. "We will walk," she said simply. "We will keep our own ledger while we do."

Bastian set his helmet on the pavilion bench and stepped forward. He had that calm you get when you choose your job and your job stops being a question. "If they go to Winter by the edges," he said, "I will guide them. I swear to bring them safely through the Fae Realms while they remain, and to keep the road square so Winter gains no standing over Summer by the walking."

"Witnesses?" Kaelan prompted, because details mattered.

Bastian touched the rail with his palm. "Witness, road," he said. He dipped two fingers into the pool so the frost licked them and did not take hold. "Witness, water." He crouched and set the axe haft against the pavilion's post where roots would live under stone. "Witness, root."

He repeated the oath twice more, the same words each time. On the third, the frost along the posts drew a thin line around the pavilion and then faded, like a circle agreeing to be drawn. The lantern fruit brightened by a shade and then returned to normal.

Mab slid her gaze to Kaelan. "You keep neat books," she said. "Name your safeguards."

Kaelan did not pretend humility. "Three of them," she said. "One. We carry Summer's guest tokens until we cross to Winter, so any favor asked or given along the way must target your ledger, not any one of ours. Two. We will not accept named gifts, even pretty temptations that only bite later. Three. Any oath demanded by a stranger on the road is refused unless it is spoken in open court under a queen's eyes."

"Fair," Titania said.

"Fair," Mab said, which meant "annoying" in Winter, but fair was the word.

Sia let her fingers rest against the umbrella shaft. The wood felt steady. The thought of the Dream being pulled thin did not. She pictured her garden's gate and the mark Eachthighern had left there for her, the knock she would feel if he stood watch. Knowing that lay behind her spine made it easier to look at the queens and say the part you could not take back.

"I will go," she said. "I choose it."

Marcus made a small sound of protest because love makes that sound sometimes. He was not wrong. He also did not argue after he heard the word choose.

Aurora's mouth softened. "Then leave after the feast," she said. "Not by the high road. Take the willow path by the south ponds. Bastian will show you where it stops pretending to be a path and starts being a boundary."

Mab stepped back from the rail. "When you cross the first frost line," she said, "speak your names plainly and give me exactly three knocks on the marker stone. My wardens will hear it. If three is not possible, knock once and leave a feather or a hair. We will still hear you."

"Three," Sia said. "I understand."

The chamberlain reappeared like night remembering to come. "Shall I see you back to your suites?" she asked.

"In a moment," Titania said. She looked at Sia and, for the first time, did not look like a queen first. She looked like a person who had watched her house for a long time and did not want to lose it. "Do not accept any story that makes you the only knife that can cut the knot," she said. "There is always more than one tool."

"I won't," Sia said. She did not promise to be careful the way adults like to hear. She promised to be exact.

They bowed and left the pavilion. The hedge walk felt different on the way back, not heavier, just more honest about where it ended. In the main garden, the musicians had switched to a slower tune. Pages cleared plates with efficient hands. Someone released a drift of tiny lights that rose and then went out before they could pretend to be stars.

"Tomorrow we feast," Kaelan said. "Then the willow path."

Marcus stretched one wing and set it flat again. "If anyone tries to give you a ribbon, I am eating it."

"Please do," Sia said.

Bastian put the helmet back under his arm and walked at Sia's side. "When the path turns strange," he said, "step where I step."

"Deal," Sia said.

Fuzanglong watched the lantern fruit dim by degrees. "Edges are where stories begin," he said, mostly to himself. "And where they go wrong. Keep your circles, children."

"We will," Sia said, and for once she did not feel like she was saying it to make the adults calm down. She felt like she was choosing the edge with both eyes open, her token cord warm against her skin and the weight of three queens' attention on her back like weather she could walk in without drowning.

CHAPTER 6

Frosted Borders

SIA

THEY LEFT SUNSTONE AFTER breakfast, the palace still shining like it had nothing better to do than catch light. The path out felt almost casual. One more terrace, a ribbon of road, then a shallow rise with waystones that hummed friendly when the group passed. Sia expected a long walk. Instead, the Summer border sat less than an hour away, tucked right up against the last garden wall.

"That is close," she said.

"On purpose," Kaelan answered. "Summer wants Winter where it can see it."

The border looked like two ideas arguing. On the Summer side, the road widened into a clean rectangle of grass marked with pale lines. A clerk stood at a high table with a thick ledger. Leaf-plate wardens moved like dancers rehearsing a pattern. The air felt warm, even with morning still new.

Beyond the painted line, Winter began. Frost dusted a low fort built of dark timber and stone. Smoke lifted from a forge stack and moved in a straight line until the cold smudged it. Footprints froze where people had walked and stayed there. A simple banner hung from the fort gate, white and blue, nothing more.

"Customs," Bastian said. He carried his helmet under one arm, relaxed without pretending he did not care. "Hands visible, names plain. We close Summer's ledger here."

The same clerk from their arrival stamped their line with brisk movements and not much conversation. Kaelan slipped her guest token cord over her head and set it on the tray. Sia and Marcus were counted together again, one line for both of them. The leaf tokens made a neat stack as the cords piled up, all that light and polish returning to a drawer.

"Outbound, recorded," the clerk said. "Right of Hospitality ceases at the painted line. Safe road to you."

"Thank you," Sia said, and said it two more times. She did not look back at the palace. It stayed in her eyes anyway.

Three Summer wardens walked them to the line. Their armor looked grown, not hammered. None of it had a scuff. One warden gave Bastian a small nod that said come back with stories. He returned the nod and stepped over the paint.

The temperature changed fast. Two Winter sentries stood just inside the gate in layered leather and plate, cloaks patched by hand. Their armor had dents that had been hammered flat and left as a record. Their swords were clean but nicked. The woman on the left had a scar that cut through one eyebrow and did not bother to hide it. The man on the right wore a leather wrap around his off-hand, stained from oil and old blood. They looked like people who had not stood still in a long time.

"Names," the woman said. Her voice was level and used to wind.

"Bastian," he answered. "Green Knight, escorting four guests."

"Sia Mason," Sia said. "No open debts in Winter."

"Kaelan Kuzunoha. Guest."

"Marcus Duvall," Marcus said from Sia's shoulder. "Projection."

"Fuzanglong," the river dragon added. His spectral form held steady in the cold, more visible in the thin light. "Guide."

The woman's eyes flicked to the umbrella in Sia's hand, then to Marcus, then back to Bastian. "Escort oath on record?"

"Given and heard," Bastian said. "Witnessed by road, water, and root."

"Fine." She jerked her chin at a second clerk with a slate. "Ledger them as guests under escort. No trade, no titles, no loose wandering."

The clerk scratched lines with a short graphite stick that did not bother to glow. He handed Sia a chipped tag painted blue on one side and white on the other. "Turn the blue out if you get separated," he said. "Wolves read it from a distance better than faces."

"Thank you," Sia said, plain.

The gate captain came down off the low wall as they finished the names. He wore heavier plate with fresh rivets and a cloak that had been re-hemmed at least twice. Frost clung to his boots. He took them in with one slow sweep, settling a fraction when he saw Bastian.

"Protector," he said. "You look less attached to a tree."

"Prefer it that way," Bastian said.

The captain's mouth tugged like it might be a smile. He looked past them at Summer's line and then back out across the frost. The comparison sat there on purpose. Palace on one side, working fort on the other.

"Keep tight to the posted road," he said. "Horn calls mean things. Two longs and one short is cover. Do not ignore wolf signals. If a wolf looks at you, follow it. Do not feed anything that is not handed to you by my cook. If you see a light that looks like it is calling you by name, it is not. Questions?"

Kaelan shook her head. "None."

Marcus leaned closer to Sia's ear. "I like it here," he said, quiet. "They look like they actually fight."

He did not mean it as an insult to Summer. Sia understood anyway. These soldiers had the same look Marcus got after long nights at the Farm, tired and steady with no patience for pretend.

They crossed into Winter proper with a crunch of frost under boots. The smell of wood smoke replaced the Summer garden scents. Someone banged a hammer on a spike to set a rivet, a sharp metal note that belonged here. A runner trotted by with a basket of wrapped bandages. No one stared. Everyone noticed.

Kaelan kept her hands in view, not because anyone asked, but because old habits kept you alive. Bastian fit into the flow like he had grown up in a place where the ground froze in neat lines. Fuzanglong's breath fogged the air each time he exhaled even though he was only half here, a pale river bending along the inside of the wall.

A young soldier with a shaved head led them to a small desk inside the gate, nothing like Summer's polished table. The desk had two dents and a crack, and someone had carved tally marks along the side. The clerk behind it wore fingerless gloves and a practical expression.

"Guests under escort," she confirmed, reading the slate handed off at the gate. "You are clear to move along the Hinterlands road. If a patrol challenges you, show the tag and stay behind Bastian."

"We know how to be boring," Kaelan said.

"Good," the clerk said. "Boring people live longer."

The captain waited while the marks went on the slate, then looked to Bastian again. "The line is noisy today," he said. "Three small rifts last night. Nothing burned through, but they tried. Keep your group close to wolves if you can. They taste wrong air better than we do."

"Understood," Bastian said.

Sia watched a pair of smiths carry a stack of repaired greaves to a rack, then swap out a broken buckle while they were at it. Every piece of metal in sight had a story. None of it asked to be admired.

She looked back across the painted line to Summer's side. The wardens there had already turned away to usher in a cart of herbs bound for Sunstone. The palace shimmered in the distance, beautiful as ever. It was strange to see how near it was to this. Thin paint, a gate, and two very different kinds of work.

Kaelan must have followed her eyes. "Summer smiles until it fights," she said. "Winter fights until it can afford to smile."

"Which one is better," Sia asked, "if you are trying to keep Hell out?"

"Whichever one is standing when the horn blows," Bastian said.

Marcus made a low sound that could have been agreement. "At least they are honest about it here," he said. "Shiny armor is nice. Dents tell you who got back up."

The gate captain heard it and did not pretend he had not. "We shine the armor when there is time," he said. "There is not much time."

He stepped aside and pointed down the road. It cut through low scrub and drifted toward a line of dark trees. Wooden posts carried strips of dyed cloth at intervals, colors Sia did not recognize yet. Beyond the trees, the horizon looked busy in a way that made her teeth feel cold.

"Do not mistake short distance for safety," the captain said. "Whatever Summer told you about borders, forget it at the line and learn our version. Border means the place where things try to come through."

Sia nodded. "We will keep to the road."

He turned to the inner wall and lifted his voice. "Wolfmaster. Walk them to the first marker."

A winter wolf padded out from a shadow like it had been waiting. It was huge and white with a grey saddle and eyes the color of late ice. Its breath came out in steady clouds. It looked at Bastian, then at Sia, then at Marcus, and did not care that a dragon sat on a girl's shoulder. It flicked its ear toward the road.

"Looks like a good sign," Marcus said.

"Or a very clear instruction," Kaelan said.

They followed the wolf past the last built thing and onto Winter's ground. The fort noise faded behind them, replaced by the creak of cold wood and the dry hiss of frost underfoot. The air tasted like iron and pine. Sia tightened her grip on the umbrella and felt the unbreakable hum settle into her hand.

At the first marker post the wolf stopped and sat. Blue cloth and white cloth tied near the top snapped in a small wind. The wolf lifted its head and let out a short, low call, not a howl, more of a statement. Somewhere deeper in the line, another wolf answered.

"That is your cue," the gate captain called from the wall. "Follow the flags. If the colors change, you are walking into something. Do not walk into something without telling someone."

"We will not," Sia said.

The wolf stood and took three deliberate steps forward, then looked back to see if they were paying attention.

"We are," Sia told it. She had no idea if it understood her words. She understood its meaning.

Marcus leaned in again, voice low. "This feels more like my kind of border," he said. "The kind that understands what is on the other side."

Sia let her breath out in a cloud and followed the wolf. The Summer palace sat behind them, close as a memory. Winter's road waited, marked and honest about why it existed.

THE ROAD NARROWED AFTER the first marker and lost the idea that it was trying to look pretty. Posts stood at intervals with strips of cloth that snapped in the cold. Blue meant calm. White meant watch yourself. A third strip, dull red, hung rolled and tied. Kaelan noticed it and did not say anything. Sia noticed Kaelan noticing.

Snow dusted the brush in a way that made everything look outlined. The wolf ahead of them moved steady and sure, pausing at rises to listen. When it stopped the second time, Sia first thought it had scented trouble. Then shadows lifted from the scrub in a quiet circle and became a patrol.

They were not a matched set like Summer's wardens. An elf captain in battered plate gave a hand sign that brought everyone to a halt. To her left, a dwarf with a frost-crusted beard rested a heavy hammer on his shoulder. Behind them stood two figures that had to be giants, wrapped in layered hides with iron rings laced through at odd angles. A pair of yeti watched from the flanks, pale fur catching the light, eyes darker than Sia expected. Goblins in short coats moved where a person might trip and made sure no one did. Redcaps tended their boots like they were knives. Frostkin wore ice that did not melt. Winter wolves padded between all of them, some lean and scarred, one with a chunk missing from an ear.

No one bared steel. Every hand knew where steel was.

"Hold," the elf captain said. Her voice carried without shouting. She looked at the wolf first, then at Bastian. "Escort under oath?"

"Under oath," Bastian said. He gave their names again, simple and complete.

The captain nodded as if the names matched something she had already been told. "We are walking the line today," she said. "You can walk it with us. Stay inside the wolves. Do not slip the flags."

Sia glanced at Kaelan. "Flags?"

Kaelan tipped her chin toward the nearest post. "Blue is fine. White means pay attention. Red means you are about to learn why Winter has a fort every few hills."

"Copy," Sia started to say, then caught herself. "Got it."

Marcus shifted on her shoulder and rested a claw lightly against the umbrella shaft. He had that alert, content look he got during training runs at the Farm when things were hard but straightforward. "This is more honest," he said under his breath. "I like honest."

The patrol folded around them without making them feel trapped. The wolves took point and tail, heads low, tongues out as if the cold tasted interesting. The dwarf fell in at Sia's left and kept half an eye on her umbrella.

"Good stick," he said, practical.

"Unbreakable," Sia said.

"Even better."

They walked. The air here did not waste time. It told them what they needed to know, then got out of the way. Sound traveled clean, so when a horn called twice from somewhere ahead, Sia heard each note as a shape in the cold. The elf captain flicked two fingers. The patrol narrowed for a stretch of brush-choked ground, then opened again.

The road rose and brought a border facility into view, less a fort than a stubborn cluster of wood and stone built around a watch tower. A palisade fenced a yard that held a cook tent, an armory wagon, and a triage table with clean bandages hanging to keep them from freezing to the surface. Two beacons stood at the corners, rune-carved stone with shallow bowls on top. One bowl burned with a blue-white flame that radiated no heat. The other was dim.

"Inside," the captain said. "Quick look and we will put you back on the road."

Sia half expected to be penned and questioned. The patrol did not even slow. They flowed through a side gate and up the tower stairs. The wood creaked like an old sailor. Frost filmed the rail where gloved hands had touched and left a print.

The Hinterlands rolled out in a wide swath of grey and white. At first Sia could not tell what she was looking at. Then her eyes adjusted. Far beyond the fort, small fires of wrongness flared and died like lightning that forgot to make thunder. Some of the flares opened into mouths, edges pulling back, red-black like old scabbed blood. The mouths spat small shapes that ran or flew, then the mouths collapsed under their own bad light and left the air bruised. Other places held steady with a faint shimmer, like heat over road, except there was no heat and no road. At each steady shimmer, a knotted line of Winter soldiers stood with wolves weaving in and out like water. When a flare grew teeth, someone blew a horn and the nearest line shifted to meet it, efficient and tired and ready.

Sia's stomach went cold in a way that had nothing to do with the weather. Summer's border had been a rule on a page. Winter's border was a fight that never stopped.

A man climbed the last steps behind them and took the rail with one palm. He wore an officer's cloak that had been mended in three different thread colors. A white streak cut through his dark hair. His eyes looked like they had learned to count hours by the way light changes on snow.

"Lieutenant Karst," the elf captain said. "They are Winter's guests. Sunstone sent them along the line."

Karst took them in quickly and returned to the view. "Good," he said. "Look."

He did not point. He did not need to. Another flare bit open on the horizon and spat something with too many joints. A wolf line hit it first. The thing turned. A frostkin raised both arms and dropped a sheet of ice that did not fall, it simply appeared where it needed to be. The sheet slowed the creature long enough for a giant to plant a spear. The thing convulsed, then melted wrong.

"That is a small one," Karst said. "Small is the size we like."

Kaelan raised an eyebrow. "I was told you had a border problem. This looks like a war."

Karst considered that and nodded once. "Border is the line where you can still dress for morning before you fight at noon," he said. "Past this is not border. Past this is the part where you do not take your cloak off. We do not invite guests there."

Sia watched two beacons flare blue along a ridge and extinguish in a measured, practiced order. "How long has this been going on like this?" she asked.

Karst's mouth flattened. "Since before you were born," he said. "Since before I was born. If you want a real answer, ask a priest to count from Babylon."

"Babylon," Marcus repeated, tone steady. "That long."

Karst finally looked at him. "Dragons have a memory for it," he said. "You know what holds and what does not."

"We know this is real work," Marcus said. There was no pride in it. Just recognition.

Karst's eyes moved to Sia's umbrella. "You are the Dreamer," he said, no question in the words.

"I am," Sia said.

"When these things open," he said, "we close some. Mostly we hold them to a size where they spit less. If we close one entirely, we mark the day. It is not nothing. It is not enough."

"Closing one is a miracle," the elf captain said, like a line she had said before, to other guests.

"It is," Karst said. He hit the rail with his knuckles once and the wood did not bruise. "We have learned to like small miracles. They keep the wolves fed and the dead counted in the right column."

Sia felt a prickle behind her eyes and blinked it away. She looked down at the yard where a cook ladled soup into bowls without spilling, at the armory wagon where a redcap polished a dent out of a breast-plate like he was taking pride in the story it told. She looked back out at the horizon and felt the Dream tug at her attention in a way that was not a voice, more a polite tap from another room.

Karst followed her gaze. "You can watch if you like," he said. "But do not stand up here and think you see the pattern. The pattern is a liar until you have walked cold feet along three ridges and listened to old wolves breathe while you wait for the second horn."

"What do your horns mean?" Sia asked.

"Two long notes means take cover and find your pack," Karst said. "Three short means a breach nearby. If you hear one long and you do not know why, go to ground and do not lift your head until someone you trust pulls you up."

Kaelan nodded. "We will stay boring," she said.

"Good," Karst said. "Boring means I do not have to write a letter about you."

A runner pounded up the stairs and touched two fingers to the rail in a quick mark of respect. "Sir," he said, winded. "Color shift at the south swale. Wolfmaster says the air smells wrong."

Karst's jaw tightened like a man bracing for something familiar and unwelcome. "Blue to white?"

"White to red," the runner said.

"Of course," Karst said. He did not sigh. He turned to the captain. "Move your patrol. Keep the guests inside your wolves."

The captain was already moving. "You heard him," she said. "Back down. Helmets on if you wear them. We stay on the road until told otherwise."

Bastian slid his helmet into place and checked the fit with the same quick precision he used to check a door latch. He gave Sia a small look that meant stay close and let me do my job. She answered with a nod.

Marcus braced his feet and stretched his wings once, a careful test that did not flare light. "I can upshift if I need to," he said near Sia's cheek. "Not all the way. Enough."

"Keep it that way until you have to," Sia said. "No heroics we did not plan."

"Deal," he said.

They came down the stairs into motion. Wolves flowed toward the south like poured mercury. The beacons at the corner of the yard woke a shade brighter. Someone tied red strips open on the nearest post. The air changed from cold to colder, not in temperature, but in the way a room changes when a door opens on a wind you did not invite.

Sia tightened her grip on the umbrella and kept her breath even. The noise out on the grey rose by a small, precise step, like a crowded room that stops pretending it is calm. She felt the Dream again, that tap from the other room, not insistent, just ready.

Karst stopped at the base of the tower and spoke to them without turning. "You wanted to see what border means," he said. "This is it. Do not run. Do not stand still. And if a wolf takes your sleeve, let it."

The horn blew three short notes. The red flags snapped open along the posts. The wolves lifted their heads in the same instant. The patrol set its feet.

No one cheered. No one prayed out loud. People who had done this before made space for people who had not, and then they all moved together toward the place where the day had decided to go wrong.

THE HORN BLEW THREE short notes. Red flags cracked open along the posts. The wolf in front of them lifted its head, then sprinted, and the patrol moved like water behind it.

Sia ran with Kaelan at her right and Bastian just ahead. The yard fence fell away to rough ground and scrub. The cold bit clean in her lungs. Out past the last marker, the air twisted. A seam formed above a shallow swale and pulled itself open like a cut. Red-black light pushed through. Shapes followed.

"Hold the road," the elf captain shouted. "Wolves on the flank."

The first cluster of demons hit the line at a run. They were wrong in familiar ways, limbs a little too long, joints bending where joints should not. Winter wolves met them first, bodies low, teeth bright, turning the charge into a tangle. A frostkin raised his hands and a clear sheet appeared in front of a knot of soldiers. The first demon hit it and lost speed. A giant's spear finished the job.

"Angles," Sia said, mostly for herself. She planted the umbrella ferrule and threw a shield in front of the nearest squad, a clean curve that caught a spray of hellfire and turned it sideways into bare dirt. The handle hummed steady in her palm. She snapped the shield wide and opened a lane. "Now."

Kaelan stepped into that lane and slapped ofuda into the dirt in a quick L shape. The paper flashed and the ground went slick. Three demons slid into her trap and froze at the knees. She blew foxfire along the line. The blue-white flame ran hot and stayed tight, enough to make the demons recoil without catching the soldiers behind them.

Marcus's claws tapped Sia's shoulder. "Going medium," he said.

"Do it," Sia answered.

Light ran down the anchor cord. The small dragon on her shoulder stretched outward into a lean, human-sized projection with wings tucked tight. Marcus hit the ground in a low crouch and drove forward with a short burst of breath that was more heat than fire. It staggered a horned thing that had cut past a wolf and raised both arms to strike a soldier's back. Marcus took the hit instead, threw the creature off balance, and broke its knee with a clean kick.

Bastian waded through the press like the fight had finally given him something honest to do. He set his shield where a line buckled, took a blow on the rim, and answered with the axe in a short, neat arc that cut a demon down at the shoulder. He did not waste motion. When a wolf slipped on blood slick, Bastian stepped half a pace to the right and took its place until the wolf found its feet again. Marcus glanced over, then back to his own target.

"Okay," he said under his breath. "He is not decoration."

Fuzanglong's spectral coil rose behind the second rank. A river-blue wash rolled out from him and soaked a stretch of ground that had started to burn, knocking hellfire flat. He set a curved barrier over a medic and two wounded soldiers. A thrown spine hit the barrier and fell harmlessly.

"Left," the elf captain called. "Cover left."

Sia pivoted. A fresh rip tore open to their left, smaller and closer. She raised the umbrella and set a ward across it before anything could fall through. Something struck the ward hard enough to make the ferrule jump in her hand. She gritted her teeth, pushed power into the line, and felt the wood hold.

The main seam above the swale widened. Bigger shapes tried to force their way out. The wolves sensed it first and shifted. Red caps moved to the low ground. A dwarf slammed his hammer into the earth and shouted to someone Sia could not see.

"Kaelan," Sia said.

"Already on it," Kaelan answered. She threw three more ofuda in a tight triangle and blew a straight column of foxfire through the gap Marcus had made. The fire held a lane open long enough for Bastian and a pair of soldiers to clear the last of the medium demons from the front.

The next wave stalled. The line steadied. Sia let her shield fall back to a smaller curve and drew a slow breath. At the edge of the main rip, a larger demon heaved itself half out. Thick shoulders. Mouth like a cracked anvil. The wrong light clung to it like ash.

It faltered. Sia felt that falter inside the noise the way she sometimes felt a dream start to shift. There was power knotted inside the demon, not its own. A tether. There was a second knot at the lip of the rip. The two lines pulled against each other and made the seam wider.

"I feel a hook," Sia said. "Something is feeding this."

"Can you cut it?" Marcus asked.

"Maybe," she said. "Keep the noise off me."

He nodded and moved up a step, wings tight, blocking anything with a clear line on her. Bastian saw the shift and slid right to plug the space Marcus left. The wolves adjusted without a signal. Kaelan dropped back half a pace to cover Sia's left with two fresh slips of paper ready between her fingers.

Sia grounded the umbrella and reached with the part of her that listened for doors. The Dream was near here. Not asleep, not fully awake. The seam had been stitched into it at a bad angle. She followed the wrong thread into the large demon's chest and found the knot. The knot pulsed hard, once. The demon bellowed and swiped at air. Sia ignored its noise and pulled the thread toward her hand.

A smaller demon spotted the opening and lunged. Kaelan's ofuda snapped out and locked its ankle to the ground. Marcus hit it a breath later and knocked it flat. Bastian took a strike on his shield that should have put him down. He rolled the impact off the rim and took the attacker's leg.

"Ten seconds," Sia said.

She laid a simple Dream geometry over the knot. Circle. Line. Gate. She did not fight the power head on. She reminded it of its shape, then turned it ten degrees. The knot loosened a fraction. The demon's light stuttered. She pulled more line. The tether snapped toward her like a rope under load.

It tried to go wild. She refused. She held the circle steady and fed the pulled energy into the ring at the base of the seam, the part that acted like a door frame. The frame took it and changed color the way metal changes under quench. The seam hiccuped. A second knot at the rip's edge tried to hold. Sia set a second circle. Line. Gate. Turn. The second knot gave.

"Now," she said.

Fuzanglong read the opening and sent a low, steady wave of river-force across the mouth of the rip, not to drown it, just to cool the heat so the shape could change. The rim of the seam curved inward.

The air pulled like a breath in reverse. The large demon reached for purchase and found none. Marcus hit it once across the neck. Bastian hooked it under the arm with the axe and yanked. The demon fell back through as the seam pinched down.

Sia took the last of the tether's energy and dropped it into the circle at her feet. The umbrella hummed and planted the pattern into the dirt. The seam closed with a hard, clean pop that pulled frost crystals up out of the swale and then let them fall.

Silence held for one long heartbeat. Then the yard noise returned in pieces. Wolves panted. A soldier laughed once, sharp with relief. Someone whooped like they could not help it. The elf captain lifted her sword in a short salute. The beacons dimmed from bright to steady.

Lieutenant Karst came up fast from the tower with two runners and stopped when he reached them. He looked at the swale, then at Sia, then at the swale again to make sure his eyes were not lying.

"You closed it," he said.

Sia swallowed and nodded. "It was already tied to something. I untied it and set the door the right way around."

Karst did not smile. He did not need to. His posture changed like someone had taken ten pounds off his shoulders. "We mark days like this," he said. "You get tired of hearing miracle. It is still the right word."

A medic did a fast pass of the group, checking for burns and cuts. Kaelan's sleeve was scorched at the hem. The armored threads had held. Marcus's projection flickered once, then steadied. He looked at Bastian and gave him a short nod that meant respect, not truce.

"You work clean," Marcus said.

"So do you," Bastian answered.

The wolf that had led them out sat at Sia's knee and looked up with its late ice eyes. It huffed once like approval.

Karst glanced at the elf captain. "Put it on the ledger," he said. "Close one portal, south swale, witnessed by road and line. Credit the guests under escort."

The captain snapped a clean, tired, "Yes, sir," then looked back at Sia's group. "Winter thanks you," she said. "Formally. The court will pay the debt. You will be received with favor at Mab's hall."

"We appreciate that," Kaelan said. Clear and plain. "Thank you."

Karst pointed to the patrol that had brought them in. "You take them forward," he told the captain. "Honor guard until they reach the next post. They have earned wolves on both sides."

The captain gave a single nod. "We will keep them between our teeth."

Sia let herself breathe. The ground felt normal again. The umbrella's hum settled to a low, steady note under her skin. She looked out across the grey and saw the other small fights still moving like brushfires, stubborn and contained. None of the other seams had grown. That would have to count.

"When you are ready," Karst said, "eat something hot. Then take the road. If the colors change, do what the wolves tell you."

"We will," Sia said.

Marcus flexed his hands once like he needed to remember how to be smaller. "You good?" he asked.

"I am," Sia said. She was tired and steady and a little cold in the hands. "Let's move."

The patrol formed around them with wolves left and right. Red flags rolled back to white at the posts. A cook jogged up and pressed a bowl into Sia's hands without asking. She took it and thanked him three times. He grinned and ran to the next person.

They walked out under a sky the color of iron. Behind them, the tower bell rang twice, then once, the all-clear in Winter's language. Ahead, the road bent toward the deeper line. The honor guard kept pace. The wolf at Sia's knee matched her stride. For the first time since they crossed the paint, she felt like the border had taken their names and decided to keep them safe for a little while longer.

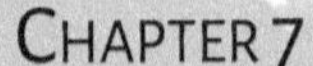

CHAPTER 7

Works of Holding

SIA

WINTER LAID OUT A straight line and told them to keep up. The honor guard set a steady pace across white plains broken by belts of dark pine. Flags on posts marked the safest run of ground. Blue meant fine. White meant pay attention. Red stayed rolled.

Wolves worked the edges. They ranged out, vanished into scrub, and came back with small head shakes that meant nothing hungry waited ahead. Breath smoked from everyone's mouths. Even Fuzanglong's spectral coil left a faint, shimmering trail in the air like frost waking up.

By noon the wind came up and stayed. It got under Sia's sleeves and found the seam at her collar. The cold did not feel cruel. It felt efficient. It wore her down by inches. Kaelan lasted longer, but when they paused at a marker stone, Sia saw her hands shaking as she poured tea from a travel flask that had almost given up being warm.

The elf captain noticed. She said something to the dwarf at her shoulder, then jerked her chin at two soldiers in patched cloaks. "Jaro. Nathan."

The two stepped over without fuss. Jaro was all square shoulders and a beard full of rime. Nathan looked younger, clean-shaven, with a streak of old burn across one glove where it had been repaired. He took in Sia's and Kaelan's faces, then the wind, then the long stretch of white ahead.

"Cloaks," he said.

Sia lifted her hands. "We're fine," she started, then the wind sliced that word apart and she heard how wrong it sounded. "We're mostly fine."

"Mostly is where cold wins," Jaro said. He unclasped his cloak and shook it out. The inside was a dense grey pelt. "This is thanks for the portal," he said. "Not a debt. Logged as gratitude with the lieutenant already."

Nathan did the same, handing his cloak to Kaelan. "You return them at Tor Arctis," he added. "Ledger clean. No hooks."

Kaelan met his eyes. "No favor owed," she said, checking the language.

"No favor owed," he repeated. "Winter pays on the court ledger. This is hospitality."

Sia slid into the cloak Jaro held. Warmth hit so fast it almost made her dizzy. It was not just heat. It was the feeling of being out of the wind even though the wind still blew. The pelt settled across her shoulders like a living thing that had decided to help.

"What is it made of?" she asked, soft because it felt wrong to be loud inside it.

"Dire wolf," Jaro said. "From our fallen. We skin them ourselves. They do not like graves. They like work. If their hide warms a future fighter, they call that a good end."

Sia glanced down at the thick fur and tried to arrange her face into something that wasn't horror. "I don't want to disrespect anyone," she said, careful. "It just surprised me."

Nathan nodded. "We get that a lot. The wolves choose it. Pack carries pack. Alive or gone."

A white wolf padded up beside them then, big as a pony, eyes the color of late ice. It touched its nose to Jaro's hand and then to the hem of Sia's new cloak. The gesture felt like approval, not ownership. The wolf huffed, turned, and went back to the edge of the column.

"See?" Jaro said. "They like the use."

Kaelan wrapped Nathan's cloak around herself and exhaled like she had been holding a breath for an hour. "Thank you," she said. "For real. And for the clear wording."

"Clear wording keeps people alive," Nathan said. "So do cloaks."

Marcus had been quiet on Sia's shoulder, conserving power. He stretched his wings once and settled again, clearly pleased. "This makes sense," he said. "Use what the fallen give you to keep fighting. Dragons have similar rules when it gets bad."

Nathan's mouth tipped. "I did not figure dragons for practical," he said.

"Spend a few centuries fighting Hell and see what you end up valuing," Marcus said. No bite, just truth.

They moved on. The pines closed in and opened again. A frozen lake took over the horizon, flat as a dropped plate. The leading wolf tested the edge, picked a line, and trotted out. The ice sang under their boots as the column followed, a low, whale-sounding note that made Sia keep her steps neat and her eyes on Bastian's back. The cloak kept her warm; the sound kept her respectful.

"Step where I step," Bastian said over his shoulder, even though they already were.

Halfway across, the wind died for six heartbeats. The silence made the lake feel huge. Sia listened to the tiny squeaks of ice shifting, the thin scrape of a wolf's claw, the back-and-forth of Kaelan's breath as the cold finally left her chest alone. Fuzanglong drifted close enough that his shimmer painted the ice a shade bluer.

On the far shore, the ground rose in slow waves. The flags came back, blue at first, then white where the trail skirted a gully. Nathan lifted a hand and they angled up to a firmer ridge. He walked next to Kaelan now, checking how she held herself. She caught him at it and gave him a half smile that said she would admit to being human this once and only because he had eyes.

By late afternoon, color had crept back into Sia's fingers. She could feel her toes again. The cloak settled into the background of her awareness the way good armor does when you stop resenting the weight. She adjusted it at the throat and looked over the line. Wolves loped with that tireless, ground-eating rhythm that made distance feel small. Soldiers rotated positions without speaking. A goblin jogged past with a coil of line and a toolkit and waved to a redcap who waved back with the grim cheer of a person who enjoys work that keeps the bad outside.

"Better," Kaelan said under her breath, cheeks pink now.

"Better," Sia agreed. "I was starting to feel like my bones were learning the alphabet."

"Save your metaphors for Summer," Nathan said, deadpan. "Out here we go with numbers. One, two, three, keep moving."

Sia laughed, short and real. "Got it," she said.

Marcus tapped her jaw with his head. "You can say whatever you want," he said. "He can handle it."

"I can handle a lot of things," Nathan said. "I cannot handle people losing fingers to prove they do not need help." He glanced at the cloak. "Keep it tight. The wind shifts hard near sunset."

It did. The light went from bright to steel, and the cold tried a different angle, dropping rather than pushing. The guard called a halt at a stand of stunted pines. Wolves set a loose ring and sat like they owned the place. Jaro showed Sia how to sit with the cloak tucked over her legs so the heat did not pour out. Nathan got a small fire going fast enough to feel like a magic trick. It was only practice.

"Thank you," Sia said again, plain and singular so it did not wander into oath territory.

Nathan shrugged. "You closed a portal," he said. "We keep the people who do that alive."

Bastian eased down beside them, rolling his shoulders once like the weight he carried had settled into familiar places. He glanced at the cloaks and gave the faintest nod, the kind you give when a plan you did not say out loud still worked.

"We break at grey-light," the elf captain called. "Eat now. Sleep in shifts. If the horn goes, follow wolves."

"Always follow wolves," Jaro added.

Marcus leaned against Sia's neck and watched the line, comfortable in a way she had not seen since they left the Farm. Winter's bluntness suited him. Sia understood why. Pretty could be a lie. This was not.

She pulled the pelt tighter and let her body take the warmth. The ledger in her head stayed tidy. Thanks given. No debt. Wolves approved. Road ahead.

THEY MADE CAMP IN the lee of a low ridge, where the wind slid over the top instead of straight through. Wolves took the outer ring and settled with their noses into their tails. Someone strung a windbreak from canvas and poles. Jaro built a cooking fire that burned low and steady. The smoke went up and then flattened, a thin line under the night.

Sia sat with her cloak tucked around her legs the way Jaro showed her. Heat pooled fast. She could feel her toes again. Kaelan sat close enough that their cloaks brushed. Fuzanglong rested beside the fire like a river had chosen to nap there, his light turned down to a faint glow. Marcus stayed small on Sia's shoulder, head under his wing like a cat pretending not to watch.

Bastian set his axe within reach and unbuckled his helm. Without it, he looked a little younger and a little more like someone who would laugh if you gave him a reason. Nathan passed out bowls of stew and a heel of bread for each person, careful that anything named stayed off the menu. The bread was just bread. The stew was just stew. Hospitality made sure of it.

"Story time," Jaro said once everyone had eaten enough to stop shivering. He jabbed the fire with a stick. "Give them something worth remembering while they learn to sleep to the sound of wolves."

Bastian glanced at Sia, then at Kaelan. "You want court gossip or old work?"

"Old work," Kaelan said. "Something true."

He nodded and tugged his cloak tighter at the neck. "They used to call me by another name in stories," he said. "Bertilak. I do not correct poets. They do not like being told they heard it wrong."

Sia leaned forward. "So the stories are real?"

"Some of them," Bastian said. "Some are drunk, some are borrowed, some are mean on purpose. This one is real enough. I was asked to test a knight once. Bright boy. Brave. Famous already because he did not run when someone blew a horn. Name was Gawain."

Kaelan's eyes lit. "Gawain of the Round Table."

"The same," Bastian said. "There was a hunt that turned into a quest that turned into too many prayers. He was sent to find a cup and a way to carry it without breaking himself. I was sent to see if he would keep his word when it hurt."

Nathan eased down on the other side of the fire and listened with the comfortable attention of someone who had heard this before and liked it anyway.

"I wore green and a smile," Bastian said. "I rode into their hall and offered a game. One strike for one strike, measured on the new year. He took the bargain. He swung first and did not miss."

Sia found herself holding her breath. "He hurt you."

"He did," Bastian said. "He also made a promise to stand where I told him to stand a year later. Then he went and had a very human year, which is to say he tried hard and lied a little. He showed up anyway. That mattered more than the lie. I let my axe kiss his neck to remind him the truth is not free, then I laughed and let him go. He went on to better work."

Kaelan smiled into the fire. "You were the test," she said. "Not the enemy."

"Exactly," Bastian said. "A court needs people who poke the bright ones and see what falls out. If all you do is praise, you end up with a king who thinks he can walk on ice in his bed slippers."

Sia looked at his hands, the calluses and the small scars that came from doing the same motion a thousand times until it lived in your bones. "You knew the Grail was real," she said.

Bastian's mouth tilted. "I knew the road to it was. Cups are cups. What you pour into them is the hard part."

"So Arthur was real too," Sia said. She heard how wide her voice went and did not try to narrow it. "The table. The swords."

Nathan cleared his throat. "If you ask Winter, the Arthurian cycle is history with a layer of story lacquered on top," he said. "The names wobble. The people do not. The swords exist."

"All three?" Kaelan asked.

"All three," Nathan said. "The king's blade, the protector's blade, and the one that judges. Different hands, different names, same bones. You can still find them if the world is loud enough."

Bastian nodded. "Metal does not care what century it is," he said. "Not if it was forged with a promise."

Nathan glanced at Sia's umbrella, then at her face. "You know one of them," he said, not quite a question.

Sia kept her eyes on the fire. Sparks lifted and went out. "I know a sword that scares me," she said. "It wears a name that means truth."

"Sounds like the judging one," Nathan said. "Old stories say each sword carries something more than metal. Some talk about nails. Some talk about souls."

Bastian's gaze went far for a moment, back to a hall with banners and a boy trying to be braver than he felt. "There were nails," he said quietly. "Three of them. A bad use turned into better purpose, hammered into crossguards so the worst day in one book could be turned into a promise in another."

Sia's chest tightened. Veritas. The word lived on her tongue a lot lately. Ella's hands on a hilt that burned with more than fire. Uriel looking out through her face. The armor that wrapped her friend like sunrise and fear at the same time. A nail in the crossguard. One of three. She filed it under things to say later when it mattered and when Ella could actually hear her.

Kaelan blew on her hands and tucked them deeper into her sleeves. "If those blades are still out there," she said, "they are either well hidden or walking around under different names."

"Both," Nathan said. "Winter does not hunt them. We wait for them to show up and make trouble. They always do."

Marcus lifted his head. "You believe in them like they are old friends," he said to Bastian.

"I believe in work," Bastian said. "A good sword works. A true sword works on the person holding it as much as it works on the enemy. Makes you honest about what you are doing. I do not have to like angels to respect that."

Sia smiled a little at that. "Not an angel person?"

"I prefer people who can be reasoned with," Bastian said. "Angels argue in straight lines. They do not always listen."

"Preach," Marcus murmured, and Sia felt a laugh catch in her throat and turn warm.

The wind shifted and pressed against the windbreak. Jaro fed the fire two more pieces of wood and checked the sky. The wolves on the outer ring did not move. Their ears flicked every so often like they were counting something only they could hear.

"Do you miss that time?" Kaelan asked, softer now. "The hall. The boy. The cup."

Bastian thought for a beat. "I miss work that ended when the sun went down," he said. "Now the line does not sleep. It is not worse. It is different."

Nathan tipped his bowl and finished the last swallow of stew. "The line sleeps if you have enough people to let it," he said. "We are still working on that part."

Sia rested her chin on the top curve of the umbrella handle and let the steam from the stew bowl warm her face. "Thank you for the story," she said to Bastian. "For real."

He lifted two fingers in a small salute. "You asked for something true," he said. "Truth holds heat."

"Look at you trying to sound wise," Jaro said, pleased.

"Do not tell anyone," Bastian said. "It will ruin my reputation."

The watch changed. Nathan rose for the first shift and a yeti padded out to take the far post beyond him. Kaelan tucked her cloak up to her ears and yawned into the wool. Marcus went heavier on Sia's shoulder as his little body decided it was finally safe enough to sleep without pretense.

Sia leaned back against the ridge and let the sounds of the camp hold together in her head. Wolves breathing. The fire's small crackle. Fuzanglong's whisper of water. Nathan's footsteps on frost, even and measured. Somewhere past the windbreak, the world worked at staying dangerous. Here, for a few hours, they had warmth and a story that lined up with the one she had been living. That would be enough until the morning.

TWO WEEKS BLURRED INTO a rhythm: flags, frost, wolves; fires at night and grey-light starts. Small problems got handled before they turned sharp. A beacon hiccuped and Nathan swapped a rune plate with numb fingers. A redcap caught a cracked strap and fixed it on the move. A young wolf learned the pace, an old wolf set it.

By late afternoon the horizon changed.

Tor Arctis rose out of the flats like the land had grown a spine. Walls of obsidian and black ice stacked into tiers, catching winter light and turning it blue under the surface. Bastions punched out along the curtain. Murder ledges cut shadows across the keep. Wolf banners snapped in the wind and looked like they meant every tooth.

"Okay, that's a lot," Sia said.

"Winter keeps the house tight," Nathan said, and he sounded proud of it.

The honor guard funneled them through a choke of stakes and stones that forced single file. A gate team waited under a roof of ribbed ice, faces wrapped, eyes clear. The elf captain lifted a hand; posture eased all around. Recognition beat any sigil.

"Guests under escort," she told the sergeant at a chalk-smeared table. "Record to court ledger. Courtesy route."

The sergeant wrote fast with a charcoal stub. "Names." They gave them. A quartermaster stepped up with calm hands for the cloaks.

"Return of loan," he said. "Thanks recorded. No debt."

Sia unclasped the pelt. It felt reluctant to leave, then didn't. A white wolf brushed her knee, sniffed the fur in the quartermaster's arms, and huffed like a stamp of approval.

A woman with a tin of soft wax peace-bound their weapons with practiced loops, firm and not insulting. She tied a neat strip around Sia's umbrella ferrule and patted the knot. "There. No one can claim you brought bare steel."

"Works for me," Sia said.

They passed under the inner portcullis into a yard that breathed pockets of heat. Forges worked. A line of kids in thick coats followed a handler and two patient wolves, learning where not to step. The air smelled like iron and resin and something sharp that meant clean.

A chamberlain met them at the stair, bowed just enough to be polite, and didn't waste time. "You're quartered together," she said. "Hot water is set. Food will follow. Audience shortly. Stay to marked corridors. If a wolf wants your attention, give it."

"Thank you," Sia said, plain.

The bunk room looked like a barracks designed by someone who cared: six wide beds, thick quilts, wolf-crest blankets folded at each foot. Hooks for gear, a long bench under a narrow pane of blue ice that served as a window, two steam kettles with towels stacked beside them like they had never once been short.

Sia thawed her hands over the kettle and didn't realize she'd sighed until Kaelan smiled into her towel. Jaro racked his axe with relief. Fuzanglong brightened a shade, happy in a place that felt finished and defended.

A bell rang. Not urgent. Summons.

"Showtime," Nathan said, rolling his shoulders back into formal lines.

They followed a page along a corridor where light moved inside the walls like a river under ice. Two wolves waited outside the throne hall and gave Sia and Kaelan a long look that ended with two slow tail thumps. Welcome enough.

The doors opened on Winter's heart.

Black ice rose into arches that should have been too heavy and weren't. The central chamber wasn't a stage; it was an engine. On a dais of stone and frozen glass, Mab stood inside a lattice of pale sigils that hung in the air like frost patterns made of light. Lines fed from the floor, the walls, the ceiling, converging through her hands. Her focus held the whole room still.

"Guests of the line," the herald said, softer than usual, like you keep your voice down in a workshop.

Bastian stepped forward and bowed just enough. "I deliver them as sworn."

Mab didn't look away from the spellwork. When she spoke, the lattice vibrated like a struck glass and then steadied. "Welcome to Tor Arctis," she said. "I apologize for the formality in motion."

Sia took in the circle: seven anchor points set into the floor, each marked with a wolf's head and a different pattern of runes. The light braided through them, then through Mab, then out along lines she could almost map. It felt like a net over a cliff edge, and someone had been repairing it mid-storm.

Kaelan kept her hands visible and her voice clear. "Do you need us to wait?"

"I need to keep this standing," Mab said. She shifted one palm. The far arch stopped buzzing. "We have recently lost our Winter Lady. The mantle has not yet moved to a new keeper. Until it does, this structure needs a spine."

Sia's breath caught. "I'm sorry," she said. "Is there anything we can do right now?"

"Not to this," Mab said. "To the reason for it, perhaps. We will speak when my hands are free."

A page stepped forward with a small bow. "Her Majesty asks that you rest and be fed," she said. "Court will call when the lattice can hold alone."

Sia looked at the sigils again. The work was beautiful and heavy and alive in a way that said someone had been standing here too long. "We'll get out of your way," she said.

"Good," Mab said. It wasn't rude. It was honest. "You will be received properly once the hour allows." Her eyes flicked to Bastian and then to Sia, quick and precise. "You made the line quieter. I noticed."

Sia's face warmed despite the cold room. "We did what we could."

"Do it again," Mab said, and the light along the far wall flared, calmed, and held.

The page backed them out with the same careful pace you use when someone is holding a door shut with both hands and teeth. In the corridor, the air felt lighter.

Kaelan exhaled. "So the mantle is loose."

"Which means Winter is holding its breath," Nathan said. He looked grim and steady. "We keep ours steady too."

Sia glanced back once at the door. The blue in the ice pane deepened, then eased. "Rest, eat, wait for the bell," she said, like a plan you could hold. "Then we see what she needs."

Second Purification

Sia

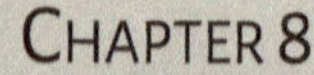

THE BELL SOUNDED ONCE. Not urgent, just firm. A page met them at the bunk room door and set a quick pace back to the central chamber. The corridor light shifted inside the black ice like a river under glass. Two wolves trotted ahead, tails level, ears forward.

Mab still stood in the lattice when they entered. Pale lines hung in the air around her hands, each one fed by an anchor set into the floor. The sigils looked like frost that had decided to stop being decoration and start being work. Her jaw was tight. The light jumped, then steadied.

"We can help," Sia said. No fancy words. "Tell us where."

Mab's eyes flicked to them and back to the weave. "Brace the outer ring," she said. "I need a shield that keeps inside things inside. I will hold the pull from the line if you hold the room."

Kaelan drew a breath and nodded. "Ofuda ring," she said to Sia. "Twelve points. We tie yours between mine."

"Do it," Sia said.

Kaelan's sleeves whispered as she moved. She laid slips of paper around the floor's edge, each one pressed flat, each one kissed with a short spoken seal. Foxfire kindled across ink, pale and steady. Sia set the umbrella ferrule at the first anchor and felt the hum crawl into her hand. She pictured the tower like a lantern. She pictured the ward like clean glass set around the flame.

Circle. Line. Gate.

The Dream was close here, not a door she could walk through, more like a window you could lean against with your forehead and cool down. She drew a thin geometry that touched each of Kaelan's points in order. When she reached the sixth charm, the light in Mab's lattice stuttered again. Sia tightened her focus and tied her line to the floor with three quiet words. The umbrella answered with a low tone she felt in her wrist.

"Halfway," she said.

"Keep it moving," Kaelan answered. Her voice stayed calm. Her hands moved fast and neat.

Bastian took a place at the edge facing the doors without being told. Fuzanglong coiled along the far wall and set a shallow water-bright barrier that intercepted stray pressure. A ward wolf lay down beside the nearest anchor and put its chin on its paws, eyes open and unblinking.

Sia finished the first circle and began a second, thinner one that braided through the first at three points. The tower gave a little, like a tree in wind. Then it held. She let herself breathe. The paper flames around the room settled to a steady pulse that matched Mab's lattice.

"Hold that," Mab said, and some of the strain left her face. She stepped back a fraction, hands still lifted, but no longer the only spine in the room. "Good. You have given the tower a skin. I can take my hands off the bones for a short time."

Sia kept her grip firm on the umbrella. "We will keep it up as long as we can."

Mab glanced at Kaelan's work and let out a small sound that might have been approval. "Clean ink," she said. "No tricks. I appreciate that."

"Clear wording keeps people alive," Kaelan said, and Sia heard Nathan's lesson in it.

Mab lowered her hands a little more. The hanging lines did not collapse. They ran through her like light through clear water and then kept going. She stepped out of the circle and came toward them, careful not to cross Sia's geometry at the wrong angle.

"You asked for structure," she said. "You should have it before we ask anything else of you."

Sia gave a small nod. "We are listening."

"In Faerie, each court is held by four," Mab said. "A Queen. A Lady. A Mother. A Knight. The Queen rules. The Lady moves. The Mother watches. The Knight fights. It is not always that simple, but this is how the parts meet."

Kaelan glanced at the empty dais beside the throne. "Your Lady seat is vacant."

"For the moment," Mab said. "The Mothers are harder to place. They are between places by design. They do not like halls. They like doorways. They smell storms before they happen and choose which roofs will not be there in the morning. You will not meet ours unless she decides there is a reason you should."

Sia filed that away under people you respect in a quiet and subtle way. "And the Knight?"

"The Knight makes sure hungry things do not cross into your kitchen," Mab said. "The Knight carries the Queen's edge into the field and brings back whatever is left. He or she takes oaths and enforces them. Sometimes with patience. Sometimes without."

Bastian's mouth tipped. He did not interrupt.

Mab looked at Sia's circle, then at Sia. "None of these are titles alone," she said. "They are Mantles. The work lives in them. The person wears the work for as long as it suits the court and the person both. When the person cannot hold it, the Mantle moves. There is always a Queen. There is always a Lady. There is always a Mother. There is always a Knight. The names change. The work remains."

Sia thought of Ella with Veritas burning in her hands and Uriel looking out through her eyes. She thought of how the sword did not make Ella herself, it made her a vessel for a function. "The Mantle is like the sword," she said softly. "It carries the job."

Mab's eyes warmed a fraction. "Yes," she said. "It chooses, it tests, it asks a price, and it gives you reach beyond your single body."

Kaelan folded her arms inside her sleeves. "You said the Lady mantle is unseated."

"We lost our Lady," Mab said. No ornament on the sentence. "The Mantle did not move when it should have. It hung for a time at the edge of the court. While it floats, the lattice buckles. I am the Queen. I can hold the weight for a while. Not forever. That is why I was standing inside a net instead of sitting in a chair pretending peace is easy."

Sia glanced at the ward wolf. It watched Mab as if it already knew the rest of the line and was waiting for the parts to arrive.

"What about Summer?" Sia asked. "Do they mirror this exactly?"

"They mirror it differently," Mab said. "Summer likes to call their pattern brighter. I call it louder. They still have four. Their Mother smiles more. Their Knight tells more stories. Their Lady dances more than mine. The work is the work."

Sia kept her ward humming and looked at the Queen the way you look at a storm you want to understand. "And the triads I have heard about? Three crones, three witches. Fate weaving three at a time."

"Same spine," Mab said. "Different names. Elder, woman, young lady. Three hands on one rope. You see it in old villages. You see it in temple carvings. You see it in the way people tell stories when they are trying to make sense of what cannot be put back. Faerie keeps the pattern on purpose. It keeps power from puddling in one place and becoming a rot."

Kaelan's eyes flicked to Sia, then back to Mab. "So a Mantle can move across blood and name. It does not need a family tree."

"It needs fitness and a story that can carry it," Mab said. "Family helps. It is not required."

The lattice ticked once, like ice settling in a pond. Sia adjusted the inner braid and felt the strain ease. Mab watched her do it and inclined her head again.

"How long until your brace fades?" Mab asked.

Sia checked the ring of paper and the thin glow at each corner. "We can give you an hour of safety without pulling from the anchors," she said. "Two if Fuzanglong feeds the outer line now and again."

"I can," Fuzanglong said, voice calm and deep. A shimmer rolled along the wall like a tide touching a stone and withdrawing.

"Good," Mab said. "Then I can spend words instead of sweat."

She stepped closer, close enough for Sia to see the fine frost in the braid at her temple. "Now the part that will not fit politely into a lesson," Mab said. "There is a problem inside my house. I have used it. I have let it breathe in the direction I chose. I cannot afford that game any longer. Not with you here. Not with the Lady unseated."

Sia kept her umbrella grounded. "Tell us what you need."

"I will," Mab said. "The shield you set is not only to keep enemies out. It is to keep one from leaving." Her mouth thinned. "Finish your brace. Eat. Drink. Then come back to this room when the bell sounds again. We will show you where to look."

Kaelan dipped her head. "We will be ready."

Mab's gaze passed over both of them, then to Bastian, then to the ward wolf. "Good," she said, and the word was not warm, but it was honest.

Sia tightened the last tie and felt the circle lock into place with a low click she heard more in her bones than her ears. The tower felt quieter. Not safe. Just less likely to tip while no one was looking.

"Brace is up," she said.

Mab stepped fully out of the lattice. The lines continued to flow, thinner through her now, heavier through the anchors and the new skin Sia and Kaelan had given it. She flexed her hands once like blood was coming back into fingers that had been still too long.

"Then we can speak like people," Mab said. "Come, sit. I will finish your lesson while the tower holds."

They did not take the dais. They took a bench along the wall where Sia could still feel the ward hum under her palm. Kaelan sat with her ofuda in her lap, ready to move if the light jumped. Bastian stood at ease, which meant he watched everything without making anyone nervous.

Mab faced them and set her shoulders. "Queens rule, Ladies move, Mothers watch, Knights fight," she said again, like a heading in a book. "Mantles carry the work between hands. Oaths bind in threes. Gifts are never free. Debts are never vague."

Sia nodded once. "Understood."

"Good," Mab said. "Now we can talk about the knife inside the bread."

THE BRACE HELD. SIA felt it in the floor like a quiet heartbeat, her Dream lines braided to Kaelan's ofuda ring and humming steady. The tower felt skinned, not sealed from the world, but tight enough that anything already inside would have to deal with staying.

Mab stood outside the lattice now. She looked like someone who had been holding a door against a storm and finally set her shoulder down. Two ward wolves lounged near the anchors, awake without fidgeting.

"Listen carefully," Mab said. "There is a spy in my house. I have used that fact for months. I fed it bad maps and schedules. I let it believe we argued when we were not, and I let it hear quiet when we moved. That game ends today. Your shieldwork is not to keep enemies out. It is to keep one from leaving."

Kaelan's eyes moved to the ring of paper. "So if it tries a gate, a mirror, or a crack in the wall, it hits the glass instead."

"It finds your glass," Mab said. "Good. Now we make it show itself."

"How?" Sia asked.

"The spy is not a clerk stealing lists," Mab said. "It wears skin. It carries a name. I have a strong idea which name. I want yours."

Sia set the ferrule, closed her eyes, and let the room fall away without letting go of the ward. Dreamsight did not mean sleep. It meant listening for wrong stitches. Under the steady hum of the lattice, she found one thread that vibrated out of tune, then hid itself, then vibrated again like a tooth you could not stop touching.

She followed it through stone and air to the north side stair. Cold edged the cord. Armor touched it. Oath iron touched it. Under the oath, something else gnawed.

Sia opened her eyes. "North stair. Coming fast."

Footsteps hit the far arch a breath later. Logan Blackice strode in, helm under one arm, black mail wet with melt. He looked like Winter had carved him out of the same ice as the walls and then taught him how to move. His eyes went from Mab to the lattice to the new ward line. They narrowed a fraction.

"Your Majesty," he said. He did not bow. Knights often did not, not in rooms built to hold. "There was a tremor at the south beacon. I came to—"

He saw Bastian. He saw the braided ward and the wolves lying like they owned the floor. He saw Kaelan's slips burning calm at the edges. He saw Sia with the umbrella planted like a staff at the anchor point.

He stopped speaking.

Mab did not look away. "Logan," she said. "Set your helm down and step into the center."

He did not move. "My place is on the line," he said. "If something is hunting, I should be there."

"Your place is where I put you," she said. Her voice hit the room like metal on ice. "Center."

They stared at each other for a long second. Logan set his jaw and walked forward. He put the helm on the floor with careful hands that made Sia's skin prickle. He stepped to the center mark and stood tall.

Up close, the wrong thread doubled. It ran through him like wire near a heart. When he breathed, it twanged.

"Logan," Mab said, softer now. "When did it get into you."

"Nothing is in me," he said.

"Lie," Kaelan said. Not cruel, just clear.

He cut his gaze to her, sharp and angry, and the wire pulled tight. The wrongness flared. It smiled first, then he did. The order told the truth.

Bastian stepped off the wall and brought his axe up in one smooth rise. "Majesty," he said. "Permission to stand."

Mab nodded once.

Bastian moved to Logan's right and slightly ahead, not closing, just setting an angle like a doorstop. The ward wolves lifted their heads and stayed down, which told Sia this was still a room where choices mattered.

Sia kept her voice gentle. "Logan, you know me. You saw what we did at the south swale. Let me look. If I can pull it off, you walk out. If I cannot, Mab freezes it where it sits and you still walk out. Either way, you walk."

He stared at her. Fury and pride fought in his face. His shoulders shifted in a way that did not belong to him. The wrongness moved and showed its hand. A crooked smile tugged his mouth in a way no soldier of Winter would allow.

"You think the Dream can lift me," it said with his voice. "How kind."

"Not kind," Sia said. "Patient."

Logan moved first.

He came at Bastian because that was the only honest way to open. Steel flashed. Bastian met the cut with shield and axe, not giving ground, just taking the line and setting it. The two of them locked into a rhythm that would have been beautiful if it were not so dangerous. Knight against Knight, each recognizing the other's training and working to cancel it.

Kaelan slid left, hands already moving. Ofuda snapped from her sleeves to the floor in a neat triangle and flared. She blew foxfire along the edge of the triangle. The flame threw clean light over Logan's boots and made the wrongness blink.

"Keep him inside the first circle," she said.

"I have him," Bastian answered through his teeth. Logan struck high. Bastian let the blow ring the rim and answered with a short hook that banged on Logan's pauldron hard enough to jar. "Show him his leash."

Sia grounded the umbrella and drew her circle over the stone inside Kaelan's triangle. Line. Gate. The Rule of Three beat in her head like a steady drum. First circle to map the shape of the thing where it did not belong. Second circle, thinner, to outline the seam between Logan and the intruder. Third circle, smallest, to set a door for one and not the other.

The wrongness felt her attention and pushed back. It tried to flood out through Logan's arms and into the steel to reach Bastian's edge. It tried to pour into the floor through Kaelan's paper. It tried to go up into the light that hung from the ceiling like frost flowers. Every path met ward or ink or the quiet glass of Sia's geometry.

"Now," Mab said, voice low and even. "Pull him clean."

Sia spoke three simple words and turned the smallest circle a quarter step. The Dream caught and turned with it. The wrongness twisted. Logan's jaw went rigid. His eyes showed a flash of terror that belonged to him and not the thing inside.

"I have you," Sia said to him, not to the intruder. She turned the second circle and the first together, the way you open a stuck jar when winter has made your hands stiff. The wrongness howled without sound and lunged for the nearest exit.

Bastian read the lunge before it moved. He slid one half step and blocked Logan's blade line without cutting, pinning him with pressure and skill until the body could not help but stay put. Kaelan's foxfire surged hot and bright. She flicked two more slips onto Logan's breastplate. Ink seared and held.

"Out," Sia said, and the smallest circle opened like a mouth the exact size of the thing that needed to leave.

It tore free.

It came out like steam made of knives, a shape that could not keep a shape, all jaw and ash and holes where eyes should be. Mab's hands moved in one finite gesture. Cold condensed in the middle of the room. Frost rose from the floor in a bloom, petal on petal, until the thing hit the forming sculpture and stuck. It clawed and screamed without air. Mab exhaled, turned her palm, and the frost closed over it in perfect layers until it looked like a statue of a storm caught mid bite.

"Named," she said, and gave it a name Sia did not recognize and would not repeat. The sculpture flashed once, then dulled to hard blue.

Logan sagged. Bastian caught him by the strap and eased him to a knee rather than the floor. Kaelan was already there with a hand on his wrist, checking for pulse and eyes and all the simple signs that mean a person is still a person.

"Easy," she said. "Stay with me."

He blinked up at her. He looked older by ten years. He looked empty around the edges.

Sia lowered her circles and let the umbrella rest. Her hands shook now that she could afford it. Fuzanglong rolled a soft wave across the floor to wash out the leftover heat and the sharp taste of demon noise. The ward wolves put their heads back down and yawned like the room had finally remembered how to be a room.

Mab came to them last. She crouched beside Logan and did not touch him until he focused. When he did, his mouth trembled. He swallowed it and met her eyes.

"I failed," he said.

"You were taken," Mab said. "Then you stood where I put you. That is not failure."

He breathed. It sounded thin.

Mab's voice softened. "You cannot carry the Mantle," she said. "Not now. Perhaps not again. That is not punishment. That is measure."

Logan shut his eyes once, honest and open. "Who will hold the line," he asked, barely above a whisper.

"We will," Mab said. "Until we choose the next hand."

He nodded like the answer hurt and also helped.

Kaelan glanced up at Sia. Sia had already turned the Dream down, making the room small enough for breath to fit right. "He needs strong tea and sleep," Kaelan said. "A week would be better. A month would be right."

"He will have what he needs," Mab said. She rose and touched the permafrost sculpture with two fingertips. The trapped thing hissed and went quiet. "And this will go where it belongs."

Bastian stepped back and let his shoulders loosen for the first time since Logan entered the hall. He looked at Sia and gave her a short, real nod. "Clean pull," he said.

"Good angle hold," she answered, and the small grin at the corner of his mouth made the room feel a shade warmer.

Mab signaled to two attendants. They brought a litter and blankets without questions. Logan let them help him because that was the work now. Mab walked a few paces with the litter, then looked back.

"Rest while the tower holds," she said. "Eat. Wash your hands. You will be called when I am finished putting this where it cannot touch anyone's skin."

Sia looked at the frozen sculpture, then at Logan's pale face, then at the ring of paper still burning steady. "We will be ready," she said.

Mab inclined her head to them, to the wolves, to the work. Then she left with the litter and the blue statue that carried a bad name, and the door closed on the sound of Winter doing exactly what it promised.

THEY WERE RELEASED WITH the kind of permission that felt like an order. Rest. Eat. Do not touch the lattice. The page led them back to the bunk room and shut the door with a soft click that said the hall was still listening.

Hot water waited. Sia curled both hands around a mug of strong tea and stood by the narrow pane of blue ice that passed for a window. The tower's hum sat under everything, steady now, like a big animal asleep but ready. Kaelan sank onto a bed with her boots off and her hairpins on the quilt. She drank slow and kept the ofuda stack beside her within reach even here.

Bastian checked the room the way a fighter checks a new camp. Hooks, exits, line of sight. Satisfied, he propped his axe against the wall and sat on the bench beneath the window, elbows on his knees. Fuzanglong's light folded down to a river-glow that warmed the floorboards and took the edge off the cold in the air.

Sia set her mug on the sill and rolled her shoulders. The pull behind her eyes had turned into a normal ache. She could live with that. The ring of paper she and Kaelan left in the central chamber would hold. She told herself that twice and let the belief click into place.

"That could have gone worse," Kaelan said. She spoke softly, as if anything louder might shake the ward on the far side of the wall.

"It could have," Sia agreed. "Logan is still Logan. That is the part I care about."

Bastian nodded once. "He stood when asked," he said. "It will count for him later."

Marcus stretched on her shoulder, a small weight that had become normal in a way she did not notice until it changed. His claws tapped the fabric, then stilled.

"Sia," he said. "I should jump back for a bit. If Winter is this loud, Earth will feel it in the seams. I can push a message to the Farm and the Museum faster if I go home and link from a full anchor."

Sia looked at him and tried very hard not to ask him to stay. "You think it is that bad," she said. Not a challenge, just a line she wanted measured.

"I think bad likes company," Marcus said. "Winter flares. Earth flares. Hell thinks in doors, not maps. I would rather they hear it from us before a portal opens in the wrong hallway."

"Go," she said. The word hurt less when she said it first. "Tell them what we saw. Tell them Mab has the spy on ice. Tell my parents I am warm and I ate."

"I will," he said. He touched his nose to the rim of her umbrella, an old habit that had become a promise. "Back soon."

"How soon," she asked, and did not try to make it casual.

"Soon," he said, and gave her the look that meant more than the word. He went to light that felt like a warm breath and was gone. The anchor ring on her wrist hummed, then settled. The empty spot on her shoulder felt larger than the space he used to fill.

Kaelan watched Sia rub the cuff with her thumb and pretended not to see the sting. "He will be back," she said, practical and kind.

"I know," Sia said. She did. The knowing did not fix the quiet.

She sat on the bench beside Bastian and picked up her tea. The heat came through the cup and into her fingers until she could feel the bones again. She thought about Marcus as a full dragon, everything in him big and steady, a living mountain that rumbled under her hands. She thought about him small, a shoulder weight who fell asleep with his head tucked under her ear. Missing him felt the same size both ways.

Fuzanglong lifted his head. "You formed a clean door," he said. "That made the pull gentle on the host."

"Thank you," Sia said. "I could feel the difference. The Dream wanted to turn it into a flood. The circles kept it to a pour."

Bastian leaned back against the wall and closed his eyes for a breath. "If you need a blade held straight while you pull again, I will stand where you need me."

"I know," Sia said. "You held him without breaking him. That matters."

Food arrived on a tray that had seen hard use. Bread that was just bread. Stew that was just stew. A bowl of berries that tasted like frost and sugar had met and shaken hands. Jaro traded them a shaker of salt for a thank you. The trade had the clean feel of a thing that did not owe anything else.

They ate because bodies demand boring things after magic. When the bowls were clean, Kaelan rinsed them in the basin and stacked them neatly. She perched on the edge of the bed and looked at Sia with the expression she used when she wanted to ask a question without making it into a test.

"How are you, really," Kaelan said.

"Worried," Sia said. "About Logan, about the mantle, about Marcus, about how much of this is about to spill into our world. Also a little proud that we did not mess up the Queen's tower. Also tired."

"Good," Kaelan said. "You are human. Have some water."

Sia drank. It helped more than she expected. She leaned her shoulder against the cold pane and looked out at the inner yard. Wolves moved in quiet patterns. A pair of children chased each other along a cleared path, supervised by a patient soldier who pretended not to smile. The tower kept its promise. For now, that was enough.

A soft horn sounded through the stone. Not alarm. The tone that meant attention. Bastian rose at once and lifted his axe into the peace tie on his back. Sia finished her water and set the cup down.

"Back to work," she said.

Kaelan slid her pins into place and pulled her sleeves straight. "Back to work," she echoed.

They opened the door to the corridor light. The hum under the floor still felt steady. Sia pressed two fingers to the anchor ring, felt the faint answering note from Marcus somewhere far but not gone, and let the sound steady her. Then she followed the others into the hall, ready to find out which part of Winter needed a hand next.

Mab's Gab

SIA

THE MESS HALL SMELLED like stew and clean steel. Frost light slipped through the blue ice panes and turned the long tables into streaks of pale color. Heat hung low around the hearth and thinned toward the doors, so the room felt like two seasons arguing quietly. Sia wrapped her fingers around a mug and watched the steam rise in threads that vanished near the window. The tea tasted like pine and peppermint. It settled her stomach and woke up the parts of her brain that felt fuzzy after too much magic.

Kaelan sat beside her with a plate arranged into tidy thirds. Bread. Berries. A ladle of stew that had already lost its skin of steam. She ate with slow care and kept her ofuda case on the table within reach. Across from them, Bastian stood to eat with his back to a post and his eyes on both doors. He had a habit of checking the ceiling beams too, like he expected trouble to come from anywhere a person could climb. Fuzanglong lay along the far wall, a river glow pooling around him that made the floorboards look like wet stone. No one seemed bothered by a dragon god using their mess hall for a nap. Winter had bigger things to worry about.

Mab arrived without a guard. She carried a leather sheath that she set on the table with the same care a person uses for something that can cut you for looking at it wrong. Then she took out a cloth and started cleaning a knife that was already clean. The blade was narrow and bright. The cloth came away red. She folded it once. The red disappeared. She folded again and the cloth looked like it had never touched a stain.

Sia tried not to stare. She failed a little.

Mab slid the knife home, set the sheath beside her mug, and sat. "Winter does not waste time," she said. "I will tell you why you came north. Then we go to work."

Nobody filled the silence with small talk. The only sounds for a few breaths were the scrape of spoons and the soft thunk of a ladle meeting the edge of a pot. Sia nodded and took another drink. Kaelan's chopsticks rested across her bowl like a closed gate. Bastian lowered his plate and listened with that steady attention he gave to stories that might turn into instructions.

"There are two courts you have walked already," Mab said. "Summer and Winter. You have met our manners." Her mouth tilted, not quite a smile. "Now you will hear about the third. We call it the Untamed Wilds."

"Neutral," Sia said, mostly to show she was following. She set her mug down because the heat kept making her think about the cold, and the cold made her think about the line outside, and she wanted to stay here in the room on purpose.

"Neutral by policy," Mab said. "Not harmless. The Wilds follow the same bones as Summer and Winter. Ledgers. Oaths. The Rule of Three. They choose to stand between. Those who refuse either crown go there. Most are not seen again. Sometimes that is a mercy. Sometimes it is not."

Kaelan tilted her head. "They carry Mantles too."

"They do," Mab said. "Four stations, as with us. Queen. Lady. Mother. Knight. The names fit differently in the Wilds. They do not love our labels, but the work is the work."

"Who holds them," Sia asked.

Mab folded the cloth again. Red hid inside the neat square. "The Wild Queen is not a queen in the way you think of it," she said. "The mantle is called the Dreaming One. A keeper more than a ruler. A guardian that has stood watch a very long time." She looked at Sia for a beat that did not need words. "You hear the rhyme."

Sia felt it in her throat. "I do," she said.

"The Lady is called the Wild Lady," Mab continued. "Old stories say she rules a hidden tribe of Unseelie elves. They have not shown themselves in an age. They will not come because someone asks. They will come because the road they chose runs through your feet and they like where it goes."

Kaelan sat a little straighter. "If they are Unseelie, why do they belong to the Wilds and not to you."

"Because court is not blood," Mab said. "Court is work. They swore to the Wilds, so the Wilds keeps them. If they break that, there will be a price. I do not choose the price."

Sia thought about the way Winter handled debt, clear and exact. She thought about Summer wrapping everything in bright language that still added up. The Wilds keeping both ledgers and refusing both crowns made a kind of sense that gave her a cold feeling behind the ribs.

"And the Mother," Kaelan asked. "Do you know her name."

Mab's mouth thinned. "The Mother is an old thing with no name and no patience for halls," she said. "Your concern for her should be limited to this. The other Mothers keep an eye on her and say nothing to me. I take the hint and keep my head down."

Sia nodded. It was the kind of answer that did not help and still gave you exactly what you needed, which was a boundary.

"The Knight is Der Earlking," Mab said. "The Goblin King. Lord of the Hunt. He keeps predators on a leash and lets them run when it is time. Friend and problem in equal measure, depending on where you stand."

Bastian set his plate on the table and wiped his hands on a cloth. "He hunts for balance," he said, thinking aloud. "Not for a crown."

"He hunts for the Wilds," Mab said. "Balance is their crown. When it works, they are the bone between teeth. When it breaks, everyone bleeds."

Sia glanced at the knife on the table and then back at Mab's face. "You cleaned that where we could see," she said. "Was that a message."

"I cleaned it because it needed cleaning," Mab said. "It is also useful for you to remember that we deal with our problems directly. Ceremony has a place. It does not come first. Not here."

She reached for her tea and drank. Her eyes looked a shade less bright now that she had said the part that would scare most people. Sia did not feel scared, exactly. She felt like she had been handed a puzzle with a clock on it.

"What does the Wild Lady want from us," Sia asked, careful with the pronoun since they had not met her and careful with the verb since the Wilds did not ask so much as allow.

"You will not begin with what she wants," Mab said. "You will begin with what is wrong. Then you will decide what you can fix. Then you will bring that answer to the people who hold the rope on our side." She set the folded cloth away and stood. "Finish your food. Then come to the war room. Now that you have the names, you need the map, such as it is, and the reason any of this matters to Winter at all."

Sia took another mouthful of tea and let it sit warm in the pocket under her tongue. Kaelan finished her berries and set her chopsticks across the bowl with the ends lined up. Bastian gathered their plates onto the tray without being asked, a small kindness that made the mess hall feel more like a kitchen and less like a barracks. Fuzanglong's light lifted from the floor and flowed after Mab like water finding a channel.

On their way out, Sia paused by the serving line to return her mug. The quartermaster behind the pots nodded once at her and once at the empty sheath on the table, like both were normal. In Winter, maybe they were.

"War room," Sia said under her breath. The words steadied her.

"War room," Kaelan echoed with a soft snort that made the corners of her eyes crinkle. "Breakfast first, war room second. Priorities."

Sia smiled and let it be real for three steps. Then she matched Mab's pace and the smile turned into focus. The air in the corridor felt cooler than the mess hall, and the light inside the walls moved like a slow river under ice. She touched the anchor ring on her wrist and felt the faint answering hum that meant Marcus was on his way back. It helped. Not a lot. Enough to take the edge off the worry.

They followed Mab through a turn that smelled like oil and iron, past a doorway where wolves slept with their noses tucked under their tails, and into a room where the floor had been polished by boot soles and the table in the center did not want to hold still. Sia took a breath and set her hands on the back of a chair. Names were useful. Maps were better. Reasons turned both into work. She was ready to listen.

THE WAR ROOM LOOKED like a glacier had learned how to be a classroom. Black ice made ribs along the ceiling. Stone tiles held cold in their seams. The long table in the middle was a single slab that looked like glass but breathed like skin. Light moved under it in slow currents, lines drifting, touching, and separating as if the table was remembering how to be a map.

Mab took the head of the table and set her hands on the rim. The surface stilled, then brightened. Sia moved to her right with Kaelan, umbrella tucked to her wrist. Bastian stood a half step back and watched the doors without looking like he was watching the doors. Fuzanglong's glow pooled in the far corner and turned the map into something that felt deep enough to fall into.

"Watch," Mab said.

The slab filled with a view that was not a single view. Summer flared to the left in gold and green, rivers curling like script that kept changing its mind. Winter rose to the right in panes of blue and black, mountains revealing shape by shadow. Between them, the wild country breathed. Forests unfurled. Lakes faded and returned. Hills grew and sank, then grew again somewhere else. The map refused to pretend it would stay put just because you wanted it to.

Sia let the motion settle into her eyes until it stopped feeling like a trick and started feeling like information. The wild center never left the middle. Summer kept shining. Winter held the edge. Boundaries tried to help and then shrugged and moved anyway.

Mab lifted her left hand. Points of hot light appeared. "Hellgates," she said. "The ones we hold."

A constellation blinked along Winter's outer wall. Sia had seen the line in person, a humming horizon of work and teeth, but seeing it laid out made it feel bigger and smaller at the same time. Bigger because there were so many. Smaller because Winter had built a life around them like a city that learned to live with a river.

More points sparked inside the wild center. They pulsed like bad stars.

"These are new," Mab said. "Singles at first. Now clusters. When enough clusters form, a Hellmouth opens, a void in which anything may escape from below into our plane and there is no chance of closing them.”

The table sharpened its own view. The red marks beat in a rhythm that did not match the land, off by just enough to itch.

“Winter cannot hold the Wilds,” Mab said. “Not by law and not by design. We push when gates spill onto our roads. We do not push farther, or the map breaks where it still works.”

“Summer can't cover it,” Kaelan said. Calm, not cruel. “They send stories and parties and songs. Not armies. They are not built for that kind of work. They heal the world instead of destroy others.”

“Correct,” Mab said.

She turned her right hand. The map shifted to a pattern more than a place. Cobweb-fine lines ran through the red points, joining and unjoining in loops that lifted the hairs on Sia’s arms.

“That is a dream road,” Sia said.

“Yes,” Mab answered. “The Dreaming One kept these quiet. They are not quiet now.”

“How long,” Sia asked.

“Years,” Mab said. “Long enough to try cleverness. Long enough to be done with it.”

She pressed her palm into a shallow dish on the rim. Frost rose in a ring under her hand. Three points lit in sequence, Summer, Winter, and Wild, as if the map itself nodded to duty.

“By the crown of Winter,” Mab said, voice even, “and by the ledger that keeps this court honest, I charge you with a quest. Find the Dreaming One. Confirm her strength or her silence. If she stands, give her what she needs and return. If she falls, learn what can be carried and bring it to hands that can hold it. You will have neutral passage where Winter’s name can buy it. You will have Winter’s oath where Winter’s reach can touch it.”

The slab drew a path that was not straight. It threaded a cedar stand, crossed a wrong-right lake, and curved toward a swirl of light like a knot in wood. Not a flag on a finish line. A promise that a road existed if you learned how to see it.

Bastian dipped his head. "Winter speaks," he said. "I will carry the charge."

"Summer hears," Kaelan said. "We will move."

Sia touched the glass near Winter's marked edge. Cold without bite. "I accept," she said. The certainty clicked inside her three times. The umbrella at her wrist gave a small hum like it was pleased with her manners.

"Good," Mab said, lifting her hand as the frost ring sank. "You will take a Winter envoy. A voice that opens the right doors and closes the wrong ones."

"Who," Sia asked.

"Come," Mab said. "You will meet her at court."

They left the table breathing to itself and stepped into the corridor. The walls carried a slow blue light like a river under ice. Sia felt her anchor ring warm, then buzz. Light gathered above her left shoulder, sketching a dragon three times before it held the fourth.

Marcus blinked into focus the size of her palm, claws careful on her coat. He looked like he had flown through a storm that did not care about dragons.

"Finally," he said. His voice sounded thin and rough from distance. "I have been cut off. Not dropped. Blocked. We had a run."

Sia kept pace with Mab and kept her voice low. "Tell me."

"Sanctuary sent us to Chicago on a rumor," Marcus said. "Charles heard about a crew buying reagents and ward keys that do not belong on the same list unless you are trying something stupid. We tracked them to a cold warehouse near the river. Black Mages. A full circle on the floor, fresh. They were opening a Hellmouth."

Kaelan's head turned, eyes sharp. "You stopped it."

"We broke the ring," Marcus said. "Eric broke the chant, Mariah blanked half the sigils with a hymn, Peter kept civilians out of the way.

I held the backlash long enough for Charles to kill the primary key. Then a claw came through. Not a full breach. Enough. It grabbed for the nearest life and that was Mia. She burned it off with her own fire. It kept pulling. She went down."

The world narrowed for a second. Sia forced air into her chest. "Is she alive."

"She is," Marcus said. "Barely was. Becca and your mom got her back. And then the mantle moved. Winter's Lady was empty. It came looking through the cold and found someone who had just fought a Hellmouth to keep a city breathing. It chose her."

Sia stopped for half a heartbeat and made herself move again. "Say it clear."

"Mia is the Winter Lady," Marcus said. "I tried to reach you sooner. The link kept clipping. There is court business wrapped around her. I cannot unpack it clean while walking."

Mab glanced back at the word Lady. She did not slow. "Inside," she told the page at the far doors. Then to Sia, "You will have your envoy. Hear first. Speak second."

Marcus leaned closer to Sia's ear. "There is more. The Black Mages were not free agents. Someone paid for the reagents with coin that smells like a court. The keys were keyed for Faerie doors, not city ones. We found a name burned under the chalk. It looked like a joke. It felt like a signature."

"Whose," Kaelan asked.

"Earlking," Marcus said. "Either someone wants us to stare at the Hunt while they go the other way, or the Hunt wants us to know the other way exists."

Bastian's shoulders tightened, then eased. "Hunt marks are real when they need to be," he said. "They are also bait when it suits them. However, there are several times in history when mankind has invoked the Call of the Hunt for various reason. They likely sought to use the Goblin King as fuel for their Hellmouth. It would also explain

Winter's Mantle coming there. A Faerie door like that, it's an easy route to finding a mortal to take it."

"Sanctuary," Sia said, pulling herself back to the part that held her throat. "Safe."

"Safe for now," Marcus said. "Charles has the thresholds singing. Eric is furious in the productive way. Your mom is with Mia and will not move until she is sure. The place is quiet, not relaxed. Everyone is awake."

They reached the tall doors of the throne hall. Two wolves rose, shook frost from their coats, and took posts to either side. The latch lifted. Sound rolled out, the kind of quiet a room makes when it is trying very hard to be formal.

Mab paused on the threshold and looked at Sia, at Kaelan, and at Bastian in turn. "On that note, Sia Mason, your mother's duty is done. Mia is quite well by now thanks to Winter's Might within her. You will have your envoy," she said. "You will have your path. After that, it is your feet."

Sia touched the ring and felt Marcus through it like a hand on her shoulder. She did not trust her voice, so she nodded. Kaelan straightened her sleeves. Bastian checked the peace tie across his axe, habit more than need. Fuzanglong flowed in behind them like a slow tide.

"Be strong, Sia." Marcus whispered. "She's Mia, but the Mantle might have her acting a bit... well, like Mab."

Sia set her shoulders and stepped through into Winter's blue. The court opened around them, high and cold and alive, the kind of room where oaths stick and words cost. She kept the Rule of Three steady in her head. Hear, then speak, then bind. The rest could come after.

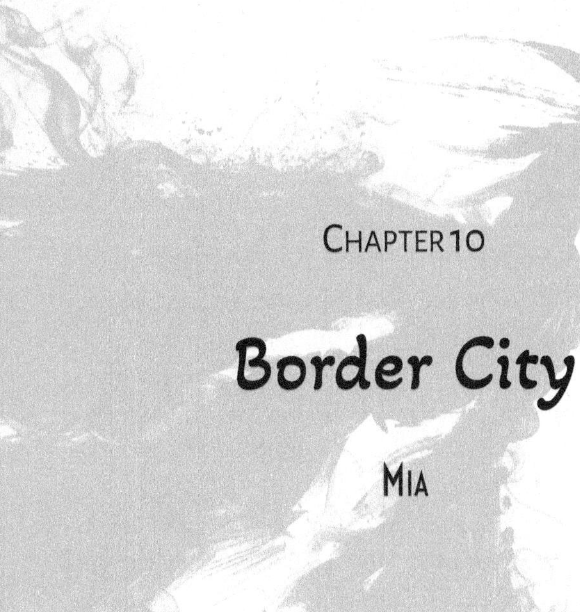

CHAPTER 10

Border City

MIA

A WEEK BEFORE WINTER named its Lady.

Morning at the Museum came in layers. Bells on the lower thresholds hummed a scale that matched the hour. The lobby smelled like lemon oil and old paper. Someone in the kitchen was already baking, which meant there would be warm bread later and Charles would pretend he had not saved the end piece for himself. Truth padded past with a tennis ball in her mouth, tail thumping as she made a victory lap around the lobby. She dropped the ball at Mia's feet and waited, bright and patient.

"Later, brave girl," Mia said, scratching behind her ears. Truth accepted two seconds of affection, picked up the ball again, and trotted off to check on the bellman like she owned the place.

Mia took a slow breath from the bottom of her lungs and listened for trouble. No static at the edges. The ache in her ribs had stepped down from a shout to a memory. Good enough. She stretched until her back popped, then slipped into the rehearsal room where Mariah liked to start the day.

"Hum for me," Mariah said, already smiling.

Mia set a simple line in the air and held it steady. Mariah reached up, adjusted Mia's shoulders with two soft taps, then shaped the sound with her hand.

"Good center," Mariah said. "Field work voice, not a stage voice. Keep it under the room."

Mia nodded. "Under the room," she repeated, filing it next to drink water and do not forget snacks.

Life at the Sanctuary had changed since Sia and Kaelan left for Faerie. The halls were still busy, but quieter. People moved with purpose instead of the easy drift of a hotel. Eric had converted a storage closet into a planning nook covered in sticky notes and hand-drawn maps. He slept there as often as his bed, head on a rolled sweatshirt, books open like wings around him. Charles wore the same suit most days, swapping ties like flags to prove he still remembered how to be a host. He had a new habit of walking the building at dawn and again near midnight, palms brushing doorframes like he was checking the pulse of the house.

Marcus spent most of each day in the small shrine room facing a bowl of still water. He would project a tiny version of himself at breakfast, say everything was on track, crack one dry joke, then tell them he needed to rest so he could keep the line open to Sia. At sundown he came back for two minutes, voice thin and almost staticky, with one update from Faerie and one reminder for Mia to eat. Then the ring on Mia's wrist would cool and fall quiet until morning.

Eric arrived at the rehearsal room exactly on time, thermos in one hand, a notebook with five colored tabs in the other. He looked like he had slept, which meant he had probably not.

"We have a pattern," he said, nodding to both of them. "Charles pulled receipts on three suppliers. Reagent buys that do not belong together unless someone is building something big. Ward keys bent to force a door. It smells like circle work and a very bad idea."

Mariah's smile faded. "Hellmouth," she said.

Eric flipped his notebook open to a page full of symbols in tidy blue ink. "If we are wrong, I will mail every one of you a handwritten apology. If we are right, we do not let them finish the shape."

They met in Charles's office for the briefing. The Curator had maps spread across his desk and a line of teacups already poured. Truth lay under the table with her ball between her paws, listening like she expected to be assigned a job. Peter stood by the window with his jacket folded over his arm, trying not to pace. Becca sat on the edge of a chair, medical kit open, rolling tape between her fingers.

"Three cities involved in the supply chain," Charles said, tapping a map with his pen. "Buffalo, Cleveland, then here. Purchases staggered to avoid flagging, cash with a clean smell that still feels wrong. Eric thinks the only ritual those lists fit is one we are not going to let them use."

Peter lifted his chin. "I will drive you to the station," he said. "I am not going any farther than that. I trust you to do the rest."

Mia reached for his hand and squeezed once. "Thank you," she said.

They kept the team small. Eric for timing and spellwork. Mariah to disrupt chants and steady hearts. Mia to carry backlash in a controlled line. Marcus as a projection for height and bite. Peter as logistics until the last safe point. Becca stayed here on standby, monitor ready, threads and salves prepped. Charles sat the thresholds and tuned the bells tighter than usual.

Eric set the rules like he always did. "Phones dark. Eyes up. If I say off, you go off. No improvising yourself into a corner because you felt heroic."

Peter snorted. "He means do not be stupid."

"I mean do not be stupid," Eric agreed. He glanced at Mia. "You are not bait. That is a plan we do not run."

Mia wanted to argue that she was fine, better than fine. The words did not make it past her teeth. "Okay," she said.

They met the last piece of the puzzle in the loading bay. A rental sedan with Buffalo plates idled near the back door, exhaust a thin ribbon in the cold. A woman leaned against the trunk with a paper cup of coffee and the posture of someone who could stand for a very long time without getting tired. Her hair was long and red with a white streak that split the front. She wore a plain heavy coat and a small Blue sigil coin on a chain. When she lifted it, the metal caught the light and threw it back like a wink.

"Tabetha Cole," she said. "Buffalo by way of wherever the trouble is. Hybrid. Red and Blue."

Eric lifted his eyebrows. "Hybrid as in you dabble, or hybrid as in you have the paperwork for two circles."

"I have the paperwork," Tabetha said. She hummed a clean Red tone that set the air humming along the loading bay, then spoke two short Blue phrases in tidy Latin that made the concrete feel denser. "Not many of us. Not impossible either."

The steel door swung back toward her in a gust. It smacked her left arm hard enough to dent itself. Tabetha barely flicked a glance at it and moved the cup to her other hand.

"Left arm is complicated," she said. "Invulnerable to most things. It does strange things to wards. Useful if you plan ahead. A headache if you do not."

Mariah introduced everyone. Tabetha nodded like she was pinning names to a board in her head. When she looked at Mia, something softened for half a second, like recognition of a familiar kind of stubborn.

"We are chasing the same people," Tabetha said. "Order of Balfagor. Wrath types. They stole a small thing that does very big work. An amulet keyed to the Earlking. It turns the mortal side of a door into a Faerie lock. I would like to return it to the shelf where it belongs and stop anyone from playing with it in a lake city."

"Chicago," Peter said, already fishing his keys from his pocket. "Of course it is Chicago."

"Border cities pull games like this," Tabetha said, almost apologetic. "Buffalo, too. Lakes and nations make thin places. Some folks think it is clever to pry there."

Marcus's light collected near Mia's shoulder, tried to form twice, and held on the third. He looked smaller than usual, like it cost him to stay. "We agree," he said, voice faint but steady. "We will be faster in person than trying to pull strings across three rooms of maps."

Eric checked the last of the gear, then checked it again. Becca handed Mia a small pouch to clip inside her jacket. "Sugar, salt, and water packets," Becca said. "You get shaky, you fix it. Do not be brave about it. Be boring and healthy."

Mia saluted with two fingers. "Yes, ma'am."

Mariah tucked a folded paper into Mia's palm. "Settle line," she said. "If your breath slips, hum this under your tongue until it finds you again."

Charles passed out tickets and a contact token for each of them. "Go quiet, come home," he said. "The house will listen for you."

Truth brought the tennis ball back and bumped it against Mia's knee with a soft whuff. Mia crouched and pressed her forehead to Truth's for a second. "Guard the Curator," she whispered. "No crumbs left behind."

Truth wagged like she understood every word, then bounded back to Charles's side and sat like a soldier.

Peter drove them to the station. He hugged Mia at the curb longer than he meant to and then cleared his throat like it was allergies. "You call if you can," he said. "If not, you send a dragon. I accept dragons."

Marcus tried to look serious and failed. "Noted," he said.

On the train, the car rocked into a rhythm that let conversation fall into short pieces. Tabetha traced symbols in Eric's notebook from memory, adding a Red correction here and a Blue footnote there. Eric's mouth twitched in the way it did when he was impressed and pretending not to be. Mariah leaned on the window and watched the trees blur by, humming under her breath with her eyes closed. Peter texted once to say he had cleaned out the trunk of his car like a real adult. Charles sent a bell emoji and then the house's quiet little chime came through everyone's token at once, which was his way of saying he had them.

Chicago met them with wind off the river, bridge echo, and sodium lights that turned everything into a different shade of tired. The city sounded out of tune tonight. Mia could hear it the way she heard rooms. The chords under traffic sat a half step too high, like someone had tuned the air tight and dared everyone to notice.

"Border city," Tabetha said, catching Mia watching the water. "Buffalo has the same edge. If you stand in the right spot, you can feel the country on the other side breathe."

Two rideshares dropped them a block from the riverfront warehouses. The drivers pretended not to see the saber case, the coil of rope, the way Eric counted under his breath. They were kind that way. Eric ran the last rules check on the sidewalk, breath fogging in a neat line. "Recon until it is not," he said. "No civilians hurt. Small footprint. Priority is collapse a Hellmouth if we find one."

"And the amulet," Tabetha said. "My responsibility. If it flares, I need two counts of cover."

"You will have it," Eric said. "Do not let it sing."

"I would never," she said, completely serious.

They split and moved. Marcus went up. Eric and Mariah ghosted the alley. Mia and Tabetha climbed a back stair and looked down through the upper slats. Inside, robed figures moved like a clockwork. Chalk lines gleamed. Oil lamps made a heat shimmer hover over the floor. The outer ring read Hellmouth to anyone who had done the homework. The inner ring read Faerie key if you knew how the symbols leaned. A velvet box sat on a crate near center, and even at this distance Mia could feel something old hum inside it like a hunting horn under ice.

"Double ring," Tabetha said quietly. "Outer to burn through. Inner to aim where it lands. The box is the key."

Mia swallowed and set her breath in the pattern Mariah had taught her. The air from the river pulled through the warehouse and came out thinner, like the building was sipping it. Eric's hand rose from the shadows below, counting down in clean, sure beats.

Mia touched the anchor ring on her wrist. It warmed, then steadied. Sia was far, Marcus was near, the house was listening, and the night was about to bend.

THE RIVER DISTRICT WORE its lights like tired jewelry. Sodium lamps threw amber rings across wet concrete. Wind under the bridges stretched every loose sound until it went thin. The team split before the last corner. Eric and Mariah slid into the shadow of a brick loading dock and put their hands on the wall to listen. Marcus climbed in a ripple of light and disappeared along the rafters of the nearest warehouse. Tabetha and Mia took the long back stair on a storage shed that lined up with the upper slats of their target building.

From the top step, the bones of the place showed themselves. Inside, the warehouse held its breath. Oil lamps burned steady around a chalked circle the size of a small house. Robed figures moved on clean loops, two at the outer ring, four at stations marked with care, and one by the back wall with a shaking book. The lines on the floor had a shine that did not belong to a classroom. Oil sat in the chalk and made the curves gleam. Little barbs hid in the arcs, thorns that meant the circle would bite if touched wrong.

Mia counted under her breath and named their roles in her head. Two primaries watching cadence. Four supports tending sigils and heat. A seventh who looked like a novice trying not to faint. The outer ring read as a Hellmouth to anyone who had done the study. Thick and hungry, built to bite a door into the world. The inner circle sat inside it like a lock. Faerie sign laid over mortal geometry, symbols leaning toward wild roads and thresholds rather than Summer or Winter.

"Double ring," Tabetha murmured. She did not fix her eyes on one point for long. She never gave the pattern a chance to notice her. "Outer eats space. Inner tells it where to land."

A small velvet box sat on a crate near the innermost line. It should have been nothing. It felt like a hunting horn buried in snow. Mia tasted the hum in her molars.

"The amulet," Tabetha said. Her voice stayed low and simple. "Do not look hungry for it."

Across the alley, Eric lifted two fingers just above the dock rail. Mariah touched her throat and pointed to the roof vents. Cadence almost stable. Airflow not helping. A tiny spark bobbed near the north corner of the rafters and vanished. Marcus had the overhead mapped. Two buildings over, Peter eased a pair of drowsy cleaners toward the street with a clipboard and a quiet story about a false gas reading. His text came through as a single dot. Clear.

Tabetha slid a folded sheet between their boots on the step. Handwritten seals copied from receipts and memory. She tapped three with a nail.

"Buffalo, Cleveland, and a local stop," she said. "Same buyers behind different names. Burn oils that keep an outer circle hot. Ward keys shaved to force door logic. The box lets them skip the standing stone. They brought their own."

Mia held a fingertip just above one drawn seal and felt the wrongness like touching a shirt that still carried someone else's heat. "Paid in cash," she said.

"Cash that still smells like a court," Tabetha answered. "Not Summer. Not Winter. Wild would not spend like this. Someone washed the money through shells, but the metal memory clung."

Below, a robed mage adjusted a brazier and light rolled across the chalk. Wrath sigils flashed for a heartbeat. Red cords bound their cuffs. The Order of Balfagor wore their sin like a badge.

"Cadence is close," Mia said. The chant had climbed a notch and settled. The floor felt like it was waiting to catch.

"Tools," Tabetha said.

Mia checked the fold of paper Mariah had given her. The settle line sat in her pocket like a small square of calm. The anchor ring at her wrist hummed once and steadied. Heat gathered where it should, a banked ember she could carry in a note without letting it jump.

Across the way, Eric set a sigil scrambler under the eave and pinned another near the latch, timing each click to the clatter of a distant truck. Mariah pressed both hands to brick and listened with her bones. A low hymn slid under her breath, too soft to hear unless you were a spell. The wall changed character to Mia's ear, less echo and more grip, as if the building had decided to help.

Tabetha opened the long case and drew her blade. Starstinger drank the light and returned it in a single thin line the eye could follow. When she threaded power through the metal, blue pulsed down the fuller like a waking vein and a red edge bloomed thin as thread. She flexed her left hand once and watched the air catch on her fingers. The skin looked ordinary until you noticed how nothing ever marked it.

"If the ward knots are keyed to time," she said, "this arm will make them stutter. That is our opening. Thirty seconds to break the lock and take the box. After that, Eric runs the room."

"Two counts of cover if the amulet flares," Mia said, repeating the plan until it fit her muscles.

"Thank you." Tabetha's eyes stayed on the floor below. "Do not let it sing. It likes to carry a note, and anything that hears it will try to follow."

A shadow crossed the back office door. Peter guided the last worker out with a nod and a thank you that looked like it belonged there. He glanced up once, met Mia's eyes, and disappeared into the dark.

Eric's voice came through the token on a bare thread. "Positions. Lights on my mark. Mariah blankets the first crack. Mia pulls heat into a low carry. Marcus above the primaries. Tabetha takes the box on ten. Everyone else is a problem we solve later."

Mia ran the breath pattern Mariah drilled into her every morning. In through the nose. Hold. Out on a tone that sits under the room. The chant inside held its new height. The air around the warehouse pulled tight like a belt.

"Wrath cells usually rush," Tabetha whispered. "This one has patience."

"Which means someone smarter taught them to wait," Mia said. The answer came out steady.

"Good," Tabetha said, and Mia heard approval, not grading.

Eric lifted his hand. Five. Four. Three. Two. One.

He ghosted the grid. Lamps flickered and came back. The door latch decided to be helpful and clicked once. Mariah's harmony slid into the small places between syllables and the chant stumbled. The chalk lines quivered.

"Move," Eric said.

Tabetha went first, smooth and fast, left hand to the nearest ward knot. The circle shivered under her palm like a clock nudged out of time. She drew one clean blue cut down the chalk spine with Starstinger and kept the design from cascading. Pressure flipped. Heat tried to jump to cold. Mia drew it down into a low tone and carried it like wire. Marcus coiled along a beam over the closest primary, fire banked, ready to throw a shield if anything reached for a throat.

The velvet box vibrated once on its crate. The inner ring brightened. The amulet thrummed like a horn under winter trees. Fine hairs rose along Mia's arms.

"On the box," Tabetha said, just loud enough to count. "Ten."

Eric gave one short nod without looking away from the circle.

Mia tasted frost under the heat. Air thinned between the rings, a cave mouth opening by degrees. The Order of Balfagor switched meters and tried to climb over the timing the team had set. The outer circle pushed. Something pressed weight against the space between worlds.

"Nine," Eric said.

Mia held the heat in her note and let the river wind pass through without shaking it. Marcus's claws bit wood. Mariah's harmony brightened a hair and kept its shape.

"Eight," Eric said.

Inside, robed figures reached for new glyphs. The inner ring called again and the box answered. Tabetha's left hand hovered over the crate, measuring the flare the way a carpenter checks for level.

"Seven," Eric said.

The wind under the bridge lifted and tried to steal edges. Mia let her tone grow heavier instead of higher.

"Six," Eric said.

Tabetha shifted her grip. Blue along the fuller. Red at the edge. Starstinger told the eye exactly where it meant to go.

"Five," Eric said.

Mia's heart hit once hard. She let it, and did not chase it. The hum from the amulet crawled along her teeth.

"Four," Eric said.

The inner ring flared. The velvet box quivered. The road it wanted to open felt older than Summer and Winter, a sideways pull toward the Wilds.

"Three," Eric said.

Tabetha lowered her left hand. Her palm brushed the velvet. The hum jumped at her and hit the time-static living in her arm. The sound bent like a string pulled off true.

"Two," Eric said.

She curled her fingers around the box and braced for a pull in any direction.

"One," Eric said.

Mia drew the heat deeper into her tone and made room for what would try to climb through it. Tabetha lifted the box. White flared along the inner circle. The whole design paused on the edge between explosion and collapse.

They moved.

THE WAREHOUSE NOTICED THEM late.

Lights fluttered, steadied, then ran too bright along the rafters. The big door's latch clicked once and held itself open just enough to change how the air moved. Mariah's harmony slid into the chant like tidewater under a dock and turned hard syllables soft. Chalk lines trembled as if the floor had a pulse.

Tabetha crossed first. She moved like she had done this before. Her left palm pressed to a ward knot and the circle's timing stumbled the way a clock stutters when a table shakes. Starstinger drew a single blue line along a chalk spine that linked two load points. The mark did not break the ring. It made the design argue with itself, energy turning back in on the path it wanted to take.

Heat flipped toward the cold edge that sat above the inner circle. Mia pulled that heat into a low note and held it beneath her ribs. The sound stayed under the room, a quiet rail for backlash to run on without snapping.

Marcus uncoiled above the nearest primary and went still with his claws sunk into a beam. Fire rolled once along his tongue and settled back. If anything reached for a throat, he was close enough to drop a shield without thinking.

Two robed figures lost a step when the cadence changed. Their leader did not. He chopped the air and shifted the meter. The chant climbed over the stumble and tried to reclaim ground. A pair of supports tightened brazier collars to force the flame hot and close. The outer ring's glow thickened. The rafters beyond it blurred like heat above a road.

Eric's first scrambler hissed and bit an anchor symbol near a corner seam. His other hand was already sliding to the next hinge in the pattern. He shaved seconds off the machine the Order of Balfagor had built, never touching the center, only the pieces that made it spin.

"Hold the carry," he said over the token. His voice was calm enough to file.

Mia kept the note level. The backlash that wanted to snap outward stepped into her tone and ran along it like wire. Sweat slid down her spine in a single clean sheet. The velvet box on the crate vibrated. The inner ring brightened to a hard white and dimmed again. The hum in her teeth rose just enough to taste. The amulet was answering the circle as if someone had called its name.

"Six bodies," Eric said for the team. "Two primaries, four supports."

"There is a seventh by the wall," Mia said. "He is trying to be smaller than his robe."

"Leave him small," Eric answered.

The leader barked for sightlines in a language that landed like a hit to the ear. One support started a counter-hum to tangle Mariah's blanket. She changed key without raising volume. His voice ran out of space and dropped under hers. The room felt like it had chosen which singer it liked better.

Tabetha slid one step along the ring and kept her left hand pressed to the knot so timing could not recover. Red woke along Starstinger's edge like a thin sunrise on metal. She looked once at the crate, then back to her point on the floor. Her face did not show strain, only a careful focus that said she knew exactly how much push her arm could take.

The outer ring pushed as if someone leaned a shoulder against it from the other side. Air over the chalk dipped like a pond when a stone hits far away. The inner ring called again. It was not a sound so much as the idea of a horn in a white forest. The velvet box rocked once like a heartbeat. Fine hairs lifted along Mia's arms. Frost threaded under the heat she carried. It belonged to a road she had touched in dreams. Someone had built a door for the Wilds and was daring it to open.

At the wall, the nervous mage grabbed for a sigil he did not own. His fingers smeared it. The circle hissed where he touched. The leader backhanded him without looking. It told Mia exactly who would be left on the floor if this went wrong.

Tabetha lifted her palm a fraction. The ring rushed to catch the beat it had lost. She set her hand again and made it stumble a second time. The push hit her arm like weather striking stone. Her jaw tightened, then eased. The blue cut she had drawn held the two load points out of sync by a hair. It was enough to keep the ring from choosing a clean path forward.

Mariah's voice rose a shade and wrapped the primaries. Their next harsh syllable landed soft. On the east side a support fumbled a brazier lid. Oil licked at the chalk and then thought better of touching it.

Tabetha reached for the velvet box. She did not snatch. Her invulnerable hand curled over the lid the way you offer your palm to a skittish animal. The hum jumped at her skin and found the wrong kind of time. It bent, tried to climb, and could not get purchase. She lifted the box. White flashed around the inner ring. The whole design paused on the edge between explosion and collapse, energy deciding which habit to obey.

The leader cut his own palm with a silvered knife and flung blood into the chalk. The circle tried to choose him over everyone else. Eric snapped Charles's remote sigil onto the core glyph. The symbol cupped and folded on itself like paper in rain. The ritual's heart stuttered. A rush of pressure looked for the shortest way out.

Mariah thickened her blanket over a spread of smaller signs so the supports could not pivot to a fallback cadence. Her throat had to burn for it. She did not sound like it did.

The amulet kicked in Tabetha's grip. For a heartbeat her shoulder jerked as if the box had turned into a weight. The time-static in her arm took the force and sent it nowhere useful. She slid the box into a warded pouch that hung open at her belt. The pouch shut with a final little thud. Blue phrases locked it twice. A thin Red line sealed the seam.

The ring hated that. Bright rolled back and spat a sheet of cold across the floor to make everyone flinch. Mia kept her note steady and swallowed the jump. Her eyes watered, then cleared. The inner circle flickered and sent a narrow needle of frost through the space between rings. It found Mia and ran under her skin like ice on a nerve. She held the note and did not give the reaching cold her eyes.

The leader pointed at her and said a word that did not belong to any normal throat. The air above the inner ring wrinkled. Something pressed two hooked fingers through reality like a hand testing a curtain. Not a full arm. Not yet. It tasted the room for a life to grab and leaned toward Mia as if attention were a handle.

Marcus dropped like a thrown blade. Fire burst between Mia and the reaching shape. The thing recoiled, then leaned again as if the heat was a light it could hunt by. Mia kept her focus on the note and let the handle slide off. The pull looked for eye contact and did not get it.

"Primary key is broken," Eric said. "Edges are dirty. Hold."

Mia held. Backlash kept stepping into the place she made for it. Her breath found its limit and she widened it instead of forcing. The floor under her boots felt steady. The building had decided they were the kind of problem it wanted to help solve.

Across the circle, a support mage pivoted to a knife and came for Eric like a runner. Marcus hissed from the rafters and dropped a small shield of flame that made the man pull up short. Eric did not look at him. He was busy pinning a second scrambler into a seam where the chalk had not mixed right. The seam sucked the disk down like sand drinking water.

Tabetha finished breaking the knot at her point and stepped clean around a chalk edge like she was walking past a sleeping dog. Her eyes flicked to the pouch at her belt and back to the floor. She did not touch the bag again. She did not need to. The locks would hold unless someone could turn both Blue and Red in the same hand.

The circle tried one more trick. Frost leaped up the walls and down the center like a spine. The outer ring sagged, then buckled. Eric's devices took the weight they were built to carry and held. Mariah eased her voice down a fraction so the room could follow her instead of panicking. The hooked fingers in the air thinned like breath on glass and flattened.

The leader looked at the door as if running might still work. Eric saw the look and shifted to cut him off. Marcus tracked the angle from above. The nervous mage by the wall sat down without meaning to, hands flat on his knees, eyes squeezed shut like he wanted to be anywhere else.

For a second there was quiet around the low hum of Mia's note and the hiss of scramblers doing their work. Then the ritual remembered it did not have a clean center anymore and sagged across its own weight. The oil in two lines guttered. A third smoldered and went out. The big shape that had tried to push through lost interest the way a hand does when it finds no latch.

Mia let her note taper a half inch and felt how much pressure still needed a place to go. Not much. Enough to respect. She held for three more breaths and then eased it lower again. Her legs shook once, then settled. Mariah's voice softened to a thread and then to a breath. The building decided not to shake itself apart.

Eric straightened without taking his eyes off the ring. "We are not done," he said. "We are past the first drop."

The leader snarled and threw his knife at the pouch on Tabetha's belt. Tabetha turned with no wasted motion. Starstinger's red edge kissed the blade and sent it skittering into dead chalk. The metal hissed as the warded pouch shed the last of the amulet's ring.

"Do not touch the bag," she said to no one in particular. "It is quiet. Let it stay quiet."

Mia's note finally reached the place where it could stop without the room snapping. She closed her mouth and swallowed a mouthful of cold air. Her tongue tasted like iron and winter mint. Her hands shook now that the line did not need them.

Marcus breathed out a thin plume of smoke and kept his eyes on the leader. "Try running," he said, perfectly polite.

The man did, because people like him always think they are the exception. He made it three steps. Eric flicked a small copper coin across the chalk and the floor turned slick where the runner planted his heel. He went down hard. The knife he pulled with his left hand clattered away. When he rolled to look up at the rafters, he saw a dragon looking back.

Tabetha checked the pouch with two short Blue phrases that sounded like the word for hush. The locks held. She let out a breath she had been keeping in her chest since the moment she touched the box. Her left arm still looked like skin. No burn, no mark, no frostbite. She flexed her fingers and winced once, then forced the hand to relax.

Mia looked across the broken ring and found the novice by the wall again. He had not moved. He was shaking hard enough to rattle his robe. She did not have space to feel sorry for him. She did register that he was going to survive this if Eric could keep it under control.

The warehouse settled to a new sound. Not safe. Not yet. No longer the sound of a door trying to grow teeth. The first window was theirs. The next minute would decide whether the Order of Balfagor broke and ran or tried something desperate.

Mia drew one more steady breath and felt the anchor ring warm at her wrist as if Marcus had tapped it. She did not look away from the circle. She did not look at the door. They had bought themselves thirty seconds of ground. They were going to keep it.

CHAPTER 11

Black Lattice

MIA

THE WAREHOUSE HELD A new sound, a thin electric hiss that did not belong to lamps or wind. It came from the floor. From the chalk. From the seams in the concrete that should have been boring.

"Hold," Eric said, eyes on the circle. "Look under it."

Mia did. The guttering inner ring threw off just enough light to show hair-fine lines that were not chalk at all. They ran into the cracks, into the rebar, into the metal throat of a floor drain near the center. The lines were darker than black, as if someone had drawn with shadow.

"Not just a circle," Eric said. "It is a lattice. Pre-laid across the block. It routes power when we cut a glyph."

Tabetha's mouth tightened. She checked the ward pouch at her belt, palm flat. "Amulet is quiet," she said. She locked it again with two quick Blue phrases and a neat Red stitch. "It wants to sing. It is not going to."

155

The chant tried to rebuild itself. Mariah shifted her voice and dropped a new harmony under the room, catching the lattice at a frequency it did not like. The thin lines dimmed a hair, then brightened as the Order's leader chopped the air and dragged the meter back on beat.

Mia kept her low carry steady. Heat from the ruptured working fought to leap into air. She took it into the tone beneath her ribs and held it there like a wire. Her hands shook. She made them still. Thirty seconds had been enough to break the first shape. Now the warehouse wanted to make a second.

Marcus flowed along the rafters and fixed on a set of corner bolts where the lattice gleamed hardest. He dropped a bead of fire on each one, not to burn, but to make the metal hold a shield. Three nodes dulled. The hiss dipped. It did not die.

"Find the hubs," Eric said. "Every graph needs a brain."

Mia scanned the floor. She felt the lattice more than saw it, a crawl under her skin that rose when her eyes passed the right places. "Drain. Back wall spine," she said. "Both hum."

"Take the wall," Tabetha said, already moving. Starstinger woke in her hand, blue pulsing along the fuller, red alive at the edge. Her left palm pressed to the junction box and the box's lock stuttered, like a clock trying to keep time in a storm.

Eric slid copper from his sleeve and flicked a coin to the floor drain. It landed dead center and kissed the metal with a small, certain click. He spoke four clean Latin words. The coin sank a breath, then held, lines of tarnish snapping out from its rim like spokes.

The Order's leader saw it happening and panicked. He slashed his own palm again and flung blood toward the inner ring, trying to give the lattice a new heart. Mariah raised her harmony and pinned the syllables in his throat. His next word came out dull and wrong. It hit the air and fell.

The lattice did not want to listen to Mariah. It wanted Mia. The note under Mia's ribs had become a path, and paths were what this thing loved. A faint tremor ran up her arms like standing too close to a bass speaker. She tightened her carry and kept it low, careful not to give the lattice a higher step to climb.

"Mia," Marcus warned from the rafters. "It is trying to ride you."

"I know," she said, and set her feet.

Tabetha cut the first ward logic at the wall hub, blue line severed, red edge sealing the backlash that tried to spray. The junction box coughed sparks that froze against her left hand and died on contact. Her arm did not mark. It never did.

Eric's coin-lock bit deeper. The floor drain's rim frosted, then cracked with a sound like ice in a glass. The hiss jumped louder, as if the room had decided to shout.

"Two cuts," Eric said. "One to go."

"Where," Mia asked, eyes moving. She tasted the wrongness like a penny on her tongue.

"Under the inner ring," Mariah said, reading the room with her bones. "Center seam."

The place she pointed to was the worst possible place. The chalk there was still lit. The air above it looked thin, as if it had learned how to forget being air. A Hellmouth had been growing. The circle had failed to finish it. The lattice wanted to finish it anyway.

"Do not step inside," Eric said. "We cut from the edge."

Mia breathed and set her note a half inch lower. The heat rode it like a rail, away from the seam. The Order's leader saw what they were doing and threw his last card.

"Now," he spat, and the chant spiked.

The inner ring convulsed. Reality at the center thinned to a bruise. Not a door. A mouth. Mia felt the pull in the soft meat behind her sternum. The world narrowed to the seam and the coin and the blue line climbing Starstinger's spine.

"Hold me on the wall," Tabetha said, voice flat. "I have it."

"I have you," Mia said, and meant it. She widened her note just enough to take the backlash that would kick when Tabetha's edge met the last knot. Her throat burned. She kept the sound even.

Eric slid another coin along the chalk to the seam's edge and snapped a second lock into place. The two coins talked to each other through the floor, copper to rebar, rebar to lattice, lattice to nowhere useful. The hiss pitched high, then higher again.

"Almost," Mariah said, sweat bright at her temple. "Now."

Tabetha cut. Starstinger's edge took the knot clean. The red sealed it as it split. The wall hub died in her hand, the box lights going cold like a held breath finally let go. At the same time Eric's pair of locks bit down on the center seam. The building gutters answered back. The inner ring blew itself out with a hard white flash that smelled like frost and old oil.

The Hellmouth collapsed. The bruise of air closed.

For a heartbeat there was silence.

Then something on the other side refused to leave without one more hit.

The dying aperture tore sideways and spat a hooked shadow through the gap. It moved like smoke but hit like iron. It snapped across the circle for Mariah's throat, riding the last of the ritual's aim. Mia saw it because she had been watching Mariah's breath, matching it to keep their harmonies from drifting apart.

There was no time to think. Mia threw herself at Mariah and shoved.

The lash caught Mia instead. Cold punched her chest like a fist. It slid under her ribs with a scraping pressure that had nothing to do with hands. Her breath stopped. The floor hit her shoulder. She did not feel the bruise. She felt winter crawl through her. Not weather. Not temperature. A rule.

Mariah's hymn broke. "Mia."

Eric's coins held. The seam stayed shut. The lattice trembled with no place to feed. Marcus dropped from the rafters and burned the space where the lash had been, but there was nothing left to burn.

Mia's vision narrowed to a tunnel. The anchor ring warmed against her skin and could not find anything to anchor. Her fingers went numb. She tried to take a breath and swallowed glass. Sound faded, then came back tinny and thin.

"Stay with me," Mariah said. She had Mia's head in her hands and her voice pressed close to Mia's ear, small and steady. "In through your nose. Out on the count. Do not race it."

"I cannot," Mia said, but it was a whisper in her head, not a sound in the room.

Tabetha knelt on the other side and pressed her left palm just above the impact point, not touching, just hovering. Her arm took on a faint frost-laminate in the light. It did not change what was happening. The cold inside Mia was not skin deep. It was a wire looking for her heart.

Eric scanned the circle once, twice, then dropped to a knee by Mia's feet. He put two fingers on her ankle and tracked the pulse there because the wrist one was gone. His face did not move. His eyes did.

"She is losing it," he said. He did not shout. He never shouted when it counted. "We are done with the working. We are not done with the night."

Marcus folded himself small and put his head near Mia's face, smoke thin as chalk lines curling from his nostrils. "Hey," he said, voice careful. "Breathe. Take what Mariah gives you. I am here."

Mia tried. The cold carried its own gravity. It pulled at everything, even thoughts. She fought to keep a single idea in her hands. Mariah's voice. Marcus's eyes. The taste of oil and frost. Anything to stay.

The floor around them glittered. Rime formed on dead chalk in a slow fall that did not come from the ceiling. It came from the air itself choosing a different state. The temperature dropped without wind, without warning. The warehouse decided to be a winter room.

Somewhere far away, three soft knocks sounded against nothing. Not loud. Not wooden. More like a hand on ice. One. Two. Three.

Mia's eyes slid to Mariah's. Mariah shook her head, not at Mia, at the noise, at the timing, at the whole unfairness of it. "Hold on," she said, voice rough. "Please."

Mia would have said yes if she could. The cold climbed another inch toward her heart. The anchor ring buzzed and lost the note. The world dimmed at the edges and then came back, like a light with a bad wire.

Eric looked up at the glittering air, then at Tabetha, then at Marcus. He did not need to explain what the knocks meant. Everyone in the room already knew Faerie rules. Everyone knew the old law that said three repeats make a binding.

"Stay with me, Mia," Mariah said again, breath against Mia's cheek, small and warm and real. "I have you."

Mia believed her because believing was the last thing she had the strength to do.

The circle was dead. The lattice was bleeding out. The Hellmouth was gone. And Mia lay on cold concrete with winter in her chest, listening to a Court she had never met knock on the air.

COLD KEPT HER FROM her breath. Not winter-on-skin cold, but rule-cold, the kind that decided what stayed alive and what did not. It spread from the place where the demon's lash had struck, under her ribs and toward the center of her chest. Every inhale felt like it had to ask permission.

"Stay with me," Mariah said, palms bracing Mia's cheeks, voice set to the same calm note she used to quiet crowds. "In through your nose. Out slow. Match me."

Mia tried. Air broke in short pieces. She saw Mariah's face go in and out like a light seen through rain. Eric knelt at her feet, fingers pressed to her ankle because the wrist pulse had gone thin. Tabetha hovered at Mia's side with her left hand close to the wound but not touching, as if her skin carried a heat shield the cold would respect. Marcus tucked against Mia's shoulder, small enough to ride a girl's hand, eyes bright as coins.

"Look at me," Marcus said. "Borrow my breath if you need to."

Mia focused on the shape of his pupils until the room steadied. It did not warm. Frost crawled over dead chalk and ladder rungs and the cut ends of pallets. A slow glitter fell through air that had no business snowing inside. The temperature dropped without wind.

Three soft knocks sounded on nothing. They felt like they came from the air itself. One. Two. Three.

Tabetha lifted her eyes. "Rule of Three," she said, quiet and certain.

A long shadow flowed across the warehouse floor and reformed into a wolf tall as a man's chest. It was not made of fur. It was made of the blue light that lives inside ice. Its eyes were the blue of fresh-cut glacier. When it breathed, frost curled out and fell like dust. Every step left a print that stayed.

Eric rose a hand but did not reach for anything. "Eyes," he said. "No one talk first."

The wolf stopped a pace away. Its voice was not a growl. It sounded like a lake in January. "Winter's Lady is empty. Winter marks a worthy defender at the edge of death." Its head turned toward Mia. "Answer if you can hear."

Mia tried to say yes and only made a small sound. The cold in her chest pulled tight like a rope. Mariah's harmony shifted to match Mia's broken inhale so the sound inside them would not fight itself.

The wolf lowered its head. "First call. Are you willing to be weighed."

Mariah's eyes flicked to Eric. Eric did not nod. He did not shake his head either. His look said the choice was not his to make. Marcus pressed closer to Mia's ear.

"Choose life," he said. "I will not choose it for you."

Mia fought for one clear thought. If she said nothing, the cold would finish what it started. If she said yes, something older than Winter would live under her skin forever. She could see Sia's face in her memory the way it looked when Sia had to jump into a fight and did not want to. Not brave and fearless. Brave and scared and doing it anyway.

She worked her tongue against her teeth. "Yes," she said, and the word came out like a cracked glass but it came out.

The wolf's gaze did not blink. "Second call. Will you take Winter's Mantle. It will guard your life and claim your seasons. You will carry its edge and its mercy. You will belong to Winter and Winter will belong to you."

Mariah's hands were steady. Her voice was a thin line of warmth. "I have you," she whispered, as if the words could stack up and make a wall.

Mia wanted to ask a hundred questions. She had one that mattered. "If I take it," she said, breath sawing, "does the cold stop hurting."

"It becomes yours," the wolf said. "It will obey."

Mia closed her eyes hard and opened them again. She was not ready. No one was ready for this. That did not matter. "Yes," she said. This time it was a full word.

The glitter in the air thickened. The wolf lifted its head.

"Third call. Speak your answer and bind. There will not be another offer."

Eric's voice stayed level. "If you refuse, you die here," he said. "If you accept, you live with the cost. That is the truth."

Mia tasted copper and wintermint. She looked once at Mariah, and Mariah gave a small nod through eyes that were getting wet. Marcus leaned closer.

"We are right here," he said.

Mia took the last choice that was still hers. "Yes," she said. "Yes. Yes."

The answer clicked against the air like locks turning. Something opened without moving. Frost sigils sprang under her skin in a pattern her eyes could not follow. They shone and then settled invisible, like light pressed into paper. The cold inside her chest unraveled and poured backward, not out of her, but into her hands. It was like catching a rope that had been dragging her and realizing she could pull it instead.

Breath returned. It did not fog white of its own will anymore. It fogged because she wanted it to. The pain stopped being pain. It became weight. It became a tool.

Mia pushed her palm out and the glitter answered, drawing to her fingers as if attracted to a magnet. The black threads of the lattice that still crawled along the floor twitched. They tried to reconnect across dead chalk. She looked at them the way Mab had looked at a map and said the first Winter word that came to her, not in Latin, not in any church tongue, just the clean syllables that lived under ice.

"Be still."

The black threads froze in place. Not trapped under a spell that would fail later. Stilled, like water that had chosen to be ice.

The wolf watched her and then dipped its head in a small bow. "Lady," it said.

Mariah let out a breath she had been holding so long it made her shoulders shake. She pressed her forehead to Mia's for a second and laughed once without sound. Eric looked at the circle again and then at Mia's eyes, which still held winter blue around the edges. He nodded one short time as if checking a box he hated and respected.

Tabetha took her hand away from the air over the wound and flexed her fingers. "Vitals are back," she said. "Arm stays weird as always." She looked Mia over with clinician's focus. "Pain."

"Manageable," Mia said. It was strange to hear her own voice carry that new edge. It sounded like herself wearing a ring she had never owned and now could not take off.

Marcus eased back to her shoulder and smiled the way only a dragon can, a lot of teeth and an odd tenderness. "Your eyes," he said. "Blue suits you."

Mia blinked and felt the color sit like a choice she could make. She let it fade to something less bright. The wolf's prints steamed, then iced over again.

"Winter charges you to stand," the wolf said. "Winter will not walk for you." It turned, leaving perfect tracks across glittering dust, and faded where shadow met shadow.

Mia sat up with Mariah's help. The world felt the same and different, like a song she knew that had been recorded in a new key. She clenched and opened her right hand. Cold pooled in her palm, clean and ready. It did not bite anymore. It waited.

"Can you move," Eric asked.

"Yes," Mia said. She looked at Mariah. "Are you okay."

Mariah nodded. "You took it for me."

"Of course I did," Mia said, and now the words came without breaking. "You're my Mom."

Eric tilted his head toward the broken circle. "We still have to clean this," he said. "And we are not alone in the building."

"We are not," Tabetha said. "But we are done being prey."

Mia pushed to her feet. The room did not spin. The ache under her ribs stayed, but it was a dull echo. She could warm it if she wanted. She chose not to. She looked at the last crawl of lattice near the drain and lifted two fingers. It stilled without a sound. Ice sheathed her hands like claws, from there a version of Tabetha's sword grew into her hand as frost condensed in the air, she made for herself something to cut the darkness.

"Okay," she said, steady now. "Enough with these cultist jerks. Let's finish it."

THE CIRCLE WAS DEAD, but the room still felt wrong. Chalk dust hung like fog. Oil smoked at the edges where the flames had kissed it and gone out. The hiss in the floor faded in little steps.

"Break the stragglers," Eric said, already moving. "No heroes. Keep them breathing."

Two robed supports tried to bolt through a side door. Marcus dropped from the rafters and set a low wall of flame that made them skid back on their heels. Mariah pointed, and Mia flicked a line of cold across the threshold. Frost climbed the metal and sealed the latch. The men stumbled, saw the ice, and put their hands up fast.

Tabetha stepped through the crate aisle and turned a wrist. Starstinger's red edge kissed a knife from a third cultist's grip. She caught his sleeve with her left hand. He yanked and then went still when he realized her arm did not move. Not an inch.

"On the ground," she said. He obeyed.

Eric zip tied wrists, kicked weapons away, and kept count out loud. "One runner to the pallets. One surrender by the wall. Three contained." He checked the leader last and rolled him onto his side so he would not choke. "We are not here to kill you," he said. "Do not try for a second chance at bad decisions."

With the room quiet, the wrongness stood out more. Black threads still clung to bolts and drains, thin as hair, trying to pretend they were nothing. Mia lifted a palm and felt the cold gather without hurting her. She gave the threads a single look and a word that felt like it belonged to her now.

"Stop."

They froze where they lay, as if the floor had chosen to be ice under them.

Mariah put a hand on Mia's shoulder. "Easy," she said. "Small pulls. No need to prove anything."

"I know," Mia said, and let the cold thin to a breath. The ache under her ribs eased on command. That would take time to stop feeling strange.

Tabetha came back to the central table and rested Starstinger across the top. She touched the small warded pouch at her belt and then nudged the velvet box it had swallowed. "Your Earlking," she said, tapping the faint acid-etched mark on the underside of the lid. "They wanted the Hunt to answer. Stupid. Brave, if you are a child. Mostly stupid."

Eric looked, took a fast photo, and nodded once. "Thank you," he said. "We will file your statement with ours."

Tabetha locked the pouch again. The seals clicked like a safe. "Chain of custody stays with me," she said. "Blue will return it to its owner. Your Sanctuary can make a note."

"Make two," Eric said. He did not smile, but his voice softened. "And do not be a stranger. We could use another set of eyes who knows how these people think."

Tabetha's mouth tipped at one corner. "I thought you would say that." She glanced at Mia and Mariah. "You two saved a city block. That is not small." Her eyes settled on Mia's. "The Mantle sits well on you. Let it be yours. Do not let it own you."

"I will try," Mia said. She meant it.

Tabetha gave a short, formal nod. "I am heading east. If your people need me, ask for Tabetha Cole at the Blue Circle office in Buffalo.

Someone always knows where I am." She tapped the pouch. "I will keep this quiet."

Eric offered his hand. She shook it with her right, then lifted her left and flexed. The skin looked normal. The air around it did not. "Good hunting," he said.

"And good hospitality," she answered. She slid Starstinger home, stepped into the alley's dark, and was gone between one breath and the next.

The warehouse felt bigger without her. Marcus settled on Mia's shoulder and tapped the anchor ring. "Projection window in five," he said. "I can make the call from the car."

"Let us go home," Mariah said. She squeezed Mia's hand once. "Tea, food, sleep. Not in that order."

They moved through the aisles, past cooling braziers and chalk lines that would never light again. Eric checked the doors, listened once more for sirens, then waved them up the ladder to the mezzanine. The night air on the roof bit at cheeks and noses. It did not bite Mia's lungs anymore. She tasted wintermint and city smoke and felt steady.

"Sanctuary in thirty," Eric said, picking their path along the rooftops. "No detours. We write it up and we let the thresholds do their work."

Mia looked back once at the warehouse. Frost still dusted the dead circle. The black threads lay quiet. She turned away and followed the others across the gap to the next roof.

"Hey," Marcus said near her ear, voice small and warm. "You did good."

Mia touched the ring with her thumb. "So did you," she said. "Tell Sia we are on our way."

"I will," he said, and his eyes went bright.

They dropped to the alley two blocks later and slipped into the car Peter had parked under a burnt-out streetlight. Doors shut. Locks clicked. The city rolled past in streaks of neon and sodium. Mariah leaned her head back and closed her eyes. Eric drove with both hands on the wheel and the careful quiet of someone who had been running at a sprint for an hour.

Mia watched the river lights slide by and let a small breath of snow bloom on her palm before she closed her fist and let it fade. Home first. Plans later. Sanctuary waited.

CHAPTER 12

New Mantles

MIA

THE MUSEUM'S BELLS FELT them before they touched the door. They gave a quick chime that sounded like welcome back, then settled into the soft pattern that meant the thresholds were awake. The air by the brass handles shimmered and thinned, like heat over asphalt. Eric pushed the right door and the shimmer slid over Mia's skin. It counted metal, watched their hands, checked their hearts. It tasted the Winter inside her and did not throw them back. It adjusted, the way Sanctuary always did, and made room.

They crossed into the lobby. Old wood and glass cases and soft lamps that never hummed too loud. Charles was already halfway down the stairs from the mezzanine, cane in his right hand, jacket a little off like he had dressed too fast. He looked them over in a single sweep and stopped when he saw Mia. His shoulders eased a fraction.

"You are intact," he said, voice dry, eyes worried. "That is the headline I wanted."

"Short version," Eric said as the door swung shut behind them. "One circle. One lattice. Hellmouth shut. The Earlking amulet is out of the city with Blue. Mia took a hit and then took the Mantle. We can give you the long version after sleep."

Charles lifted his chin toward the hallway that led to the family suite. "Then this way. The building has stayed quiet. The rules are holding."

Truth's tags jingled from behind the front desk. The golden retriever trotted out, sniffed Mia's knuckles, and pressed her head against Mia's thigh with a soft huff. Mia curled her fingers into Truth's ruff. Cold tried to rise to her fingertips without thinking about it. She told it no and reached for warmth instead. Truth leaned harder and sighed like someone turning down a radio.

Becca rolled a tea cart from the staff door with two night attendants behind her. Steam lifted under a towel. Porcelain rattled in a soft, polite way. Becca had a stethoscope around her neck and three pens tucked behind one ear like she had been waiting on the staircase with a to-do list.

"Vitals first," she said. "Talking second."

They moved as a cluster. Eric and Peter peeled off to lock the front, flip the after-hours sign, and set the latch that made the Museum's threshold seals pinch tight. Marcus rode Mia's shoulder in his tiny dragon form, claws careful through her coat. His glow showed in the anchor ring like a trick of light under the skin. Mariah kept a hand at the small of Mia's back. She did not push. She matched Mia's steps.

The family suite held a low couch, a quilt folded over the arm, a bookshelf with more paperbacks than display items, and two narrow beds down the hall. The air smelled like lemon oil, dust, and cardamom. Becca pointed at the couch and Mia sat. Her legs had not been shaking in the alley. They thought about shaking now that the door was closed.

Becca looped the cuff around Mia's arm and pumped the bulb. She watched the needle, then touched two fingers to the line of Mia's jaw, then to the pulse at her wrist. "Cold," she said, calm as a meter. "Stable. Heart is a little narrow. You are low on reserves." She tilted a penlight and found the ring of winter in Mia's eyes. It pulsed and faded. "The color will come and go for a while," Becca said. "Do not let it scare you."

"It does not," Mia said. That was true. The fear she felt was not the same fear as before. It did not drag at her. It sat outside her like weather. She could choose a coat.

Peter stepped into the doorway, saw Mia on the couch, and stopped like he had run into an invisible line. He set his palm on the door frame and looked from her face to Mariah's and back again. His mouth tightened. Then he crossed and kissed Mia's hair.

"I'm okay," Mia said. "I promise."

"You are going to be okay," Peter said, correcting the tense like he was fixing a loose screw. He lifted his hand from her shoulder and let Becca work.

Eric handed Charles a folded card with four lines on it. "Ledger stub," he said. "More later."

Charles slid the card into a pocket without looking. "Tea now," he said, "or your mother will stage a coup." He poured. The kettle hissed once like it approved. He passed cups to whoever could hold one. Honey drifted on the steam.

Marcus tapped the anchor ring with a gentle claw. "Window," he said. His voice had the thin quality that always came with projection. "If you keep your arm still I can make the call clean."

"Tell her we are home," Mariah said.

"I will," Marcus said. He closed his eyes and went still. The anchor ring warmed. Mia felt the small thread her sister would feel on the far end. Marcus sat and seemed to fall asleep as he moved to his projection, or tried to. He opened his eyes a few moments later and frowned. "I may need some real sleep before I can project in. I'll tell them as soon as I can."

Becca finished with the cuff and stethoscope. She tested a tiny hammer on Mia's elbow and watched the reflex. "Deep bruising," she said. "The kind that argues for rest and hot tea and people being nice to you." She glanced at Mariah. "Can you keep a soft anchor while she drifts. Nothing big. A tone she can find if she wanders."

"I have it," Mariah said. She set two fingers at the point on Mia's wrist where the ring sat. Her hum was almost not a hum. It was breath with a note in it. Mia felt it where her ribs met her spine.

Charles leaned his cane against the arm of the couch. "I am going to put three lines in the book," he said, tone halfway to a joke and halfway to a promise. "One that says we welcome you back. One that says we did not let anyone hurt you in here. One that says we owe you a good breakfast."

"That is a lot of lines," Peter said, voice eased now that there was a list.

"We keep ledgers," Charles said, as if the ledger was not a book that sometimes wrote back.

Eric crouched beside the tea cart and pulled a clean towel from the shelf below. He folded it in thirds and set it behind Mia's neck. "You will feel the drop," he said. "Let it happen. If you wake up in a few minutes and feel like you fell through a floor, that is fine. You will fall again and sleep for real."

"Not scary," Mia said. She took a breath to prove it. The air slid in and out without sticking. It did not burn. The ache where the lash had hit her was still there, a dull rectangle under her ribs, but it was an ache she could look at without tipping over.

Truth put her chin on Mia's knee. Her eyes were the soft brown of old wood. She was an excellent listener and a better pillow. Mia scratched between her ears. Truth closed her eyes like she was charging.

The anchor ring buzzed once in a way that meant the call had hit Sia's side. Marcus opened his eyes. "Heard," he said. "She is safe. Still in Winter. Still moving. She said to sleep or Charles will station the bell in here to scold you every hour."

Charles did not smile but his eyes did. "I would never misuse the bells," he said. He paused. "On an ordinary day."

Mariah's hand shifted from Mia's wrist to her cheek. "You shoved me out of the way," she said, barely above a whisper.

"You would have done it for me," Mia said.

"I would," Mariah said. "But thank you anyway."

Mia's body had been holding on to full alert with claws. Now that the door was closed and Daddy had left the frame and the tea was warm in her throat, those claws unhooked. The room softened at the edges. The world did not maybe-end if she closed her eyes for thirty seconds. She let her shoulders settle back into the couch.

"Bed," Becca said, kind and firm. "Ten steps down the hall. I will carry the tea."

Mariah stood and Mia stood with her. The first step felt like stepping into deeper carpet. The second step felt like stepping into sand at the edge of a lake. By the third step her knees wanted to laugh and sit on the floor. She did not sit on the floor. She kept walking. Mariah's arm around her waist felt like a railing at a skating rink.

The bedroom was dim, the lamp low. Someone had turned down the quilt. There was a clean shirt on the chair like a little flag that said someone had thought about them. Mia slid onto the bed and pulled her feet under the sheet. The cotton was cool and real. She had a sudden, fierce love for the simplest things. A mattress. A quilt. A door that shut.

"Do you want me to sing," Mariah asked.

"Please," Mia said.

Mariah sat on the edge of the bed and found the tone she had used in the car when Mia could not get air. It ran under the actual sound in a way that her own bones recognized. The Winter inside Mia heard it and did not try to own it. It stepped back and watched the door.

Eric knocked his knuckles on the frame so she knew he was there without a startle. "We will be in the next room," he said. "Marcus will do the next check-in."

Mia nodded. That moved felt huge and small at once. "Thanks," she said.

Peter leaned in and set his palm on the crown of her head the way he had when she was five. "Sleep," he said. "That is the job."

Mia put her hand over the anchor ring. It was warm as skin. She breathed with Mariah's hum and let the weight behind her eyes pull her down. The quilt had a stitched pattern that she followed with her finger once, twice, three times. The Rule of Three lilted in her head for no reason except that it had been a loud part of her day. She smiled at the thought, strange as that was, and let it go.

The drop came like Eric said it would. The first fall was quick, a short sink past the point where you decide to sleep. Mia's body jerked like she had missed a stair. She blinked, saw Mariah, heard the hum, and fell again. The second fall was longer. The bed became a raft. The room became a shoreline she was moving away from on purpose.

Cold moved with her, clean and quiet. It did not claw at her. It did not crowd her lungs. It found places that hurt and pressed there like a careful ice pack. She could tell it yes or no, here or there, warm up or cool down. It obeyed when she asked and waited when she did not. That was the difference that mattered.

Frost feathered the corner of the quilt and faded without leaving it wet. The lamp seemed farther away. The voices in the other room thinned to nothing. Truth's tags gave one soft jingle as she circled and lay down by the door.

Mia let her mind show her Sia's face. She pictured the blue ring in her sister's eyes and the green of the Winter herald and the black ice lake she had not yet seen but would. The picture held for a second, then slid away. She did not chase it. There would be time. There would be a dream that belonged to Winter in a minute. For now there was the hum and the quilt and the steady promise of a building that kept knives outside.

She fell the rest of the way. The last thought through before sleep was not about Hell or Courts or laws. It was about breakfast and how Charles would try to make oatmeal feel like a feast and how that would somehow work. Then there was nothing, only the deep pull of a mantle finding its seat and the relief of not having to hold on by herself.

SLEEP DID NOT DRIFT. It took her like a hand on her shoulder and set her down on black ice under a sky that moved. Green and blue curtains slid across each other without sound. The cold had weight but not bite. It felt like standing in a room that had already decided what season it would be.

The lake stretched forever. No shore. No trees. Just a horizon that felt close and far at the same time. Beneath her boots the ice was clear as glass. Embers hung in it like stars in a jar. They pulsed a dull red, stubborn and slow, the color of burned sugar and old hurt.

Mia curled her toes inside her socks and waited for panic. It did not come. She could breathe. The air did not scratch her lungs. When she exhaled, her breath fogged only because she chose to see it. She made a small cloud, then let the air stay clear.

A wolf padded into view and stopped a few paces away. It was not made of fur. It was made of the blue light that lives inside winter. Its eyes were glacier bright. Frost curled from its nose and fell like dust. It watched her with a guard's attention, not hostile, not friendly, exactly the kind of look a border gives you while it waits to see why you have shown up.

"This is not Sia's dream," Mia said. It felt good to say something out loud and hear it stay in the air.

"Winter's ground," the wolf said. Its voice sounded like a lake in January. "A place for edges and decisions. I witness. I do not judge."

Someone else stepped out of the aurora. Mia turned and saw herself. Not a mirror. Not a trick. Another version of her, the way a role looks when it is worn by someone who has been wearing it for a very long time. The other Mia's eyes were ringed in winter blue that did not fade. Her shoulders were relaxed the way hunters are relaxed when the trail is easy to read. She moved like she had already stopped wasting motion. When she spoke, her voice was calm and cool.

"You called me when you said yes," the other Mia said.

"I did not try to call a copy," Mia said.

"You called the part of you that holds the Mantle when it hunts," the other said. "You can ignore me. You should not. We need rules."

Mia looked down through the ice. The embers pulsed again, the stubborn heartbeat of something that wanted to keep its place. Hellfire had lived in her for months. It had helped her survive when there was nothing else, and then it had tried to name her. It had not won. She was not letting Winter name her either. She would name herself and set terms.

"Are you a monster," she asked the other. "Or am I."

"I am the shape that protects a line when something crosses with harm," the other said. "Predator is the right word. Monster is the wrong one. Winter feeds on trespass. It does not feed on people. If I am wild, I am wild with purpose."

Mia swallowed. Honest words were easier to carry than pretty ones. "I have been a monster before," she said. "It almost ate me. I learned how to make it sit. I am not afraid of you. I am afraid of liking you too much."

The other Mia smiled once. It showed teeth without threatening anything. "Good," she said. "Then let us test what you think you know."

She moved, not fast, just close enough that Mia felt the cool of her breath at her throat. "First test," the other said. "Do you fear yourself."

Mia kept her eyes forward. "No. I fear misuse. I fear losing the reason why."

The other Mia nodded, then circled back into view. "Second test. Hunger. The chase is clean. The finish is cleaner. Will you hunt because it feels good."

"I will hunt because someone needs me to stand between," Mia said. "Duty first. Want is a bad compass."

"Third test," the other said. "Mercy. Will you spare what will kill tomorrow."

"I will spare until it endangers the innocent," Mia said. "After that I end the threat. I do not play with lives to feel kind."

The wolf exhaled. Frost sifted over the ice and stayed. The sound felt like approval without praise.

"Say them again," the other Mia said.

Mia did. Each answer, three times, steady and plain. The words settled in her mouth like tools that fit her hand. Protect the border. Hunt only what harms. Spare when she safely could.

The embers under the ice brightened at her voice, as if they were listening. Mia knelt and laid her palm flat. The cold met her skin like a weight put in the right place. It did not bite. It waited.

"These are not power," the other said, watching the embers. "They are leftovers. Hurt that learned how to burn."

"Hurt I used when I had nothing else," Mia said. "I am done letting it choose."

She pressed her will through her hand. Frost bloomed out in a clean ring. The red pulses dimmed where the ring passed, then went out.

One by one they vanished. The lake beneath her hand went clear. She left a single spark the size of a seed inside a thin circle of frost.

"What is that for," the other asked.

"Home," Mia said. "Family. Warmth for people I love. Not a weapon."

"Then bind it," the other said.

Mia touched the spark with two fingers. "This stays mine," she said. "It answers when I say so. It does not answer to anger." She said it three times. The spark steadied and dimmed to a steady amber that looked like a kitchen light through a door at night.

The wolf paced a slow line and spoke again. "Lore, so you do not learn it by bleeding," it said. "Border law. Winter answers when harm crosses the line. Winter does not hunt for sport. Invoked hunts are a contract. If a mortal calls the Hunt correctly, the Hunt must answer."

The other Mia lifted a hand. Letters like frost traced themselves above her palm and then melted. "Oath economy," she said. "Your word binds you. It also binds the Court when you wear the Mantle. Loose promises turn into obligations. Be precise. Be simple. Speak three times when you mean to bind. Do not speak three times when you do not."

"And mercy," the wolf said. "A fallen foe who yields three times must be marked and released to Summer's judgment, unless demon-tainted beyond recall. If you spare, you take responsibility for what comes of that mercy. If you kill, you take responsibility for that too."

"That last part is the hard part," Mia said. It came out without sarcasm. She had blood on her hands from fights she had not asked for. She had spared things that came back meaner. She had also spared people who later stood beside her. None of it had been clean.

"You will be wrong sometimes," the other said. "Be wrong for the right reasons."

Mia stood. The lake did not crack. She liked that. She hated falling through things she could not see. "What else," she asked.

"Shape," the other said. She touched two fingers to Mia's sternum. A light frost-sigil formed there for a breath and then sank under the skin. It left a cool independence behind, the feeling of a muscle she had not known she could flex. "Focus," the other said. "You can push cold through that point without spraying it everywhere. You can shape it thin or wide. You can ask it to bind first and bite second."

"Show me," Mia said.

The other lifted her hand. A single filament of ice drew between her fingers like a glass thread. It was thin and clear, almost not there. She flicked her wrist. The thread wrapped around Mia's forearm and held, cool and steady, not cutting. "Bind," the other said, then released. "It only kills if you speak a killing word, and you should decide what that word is and promise not to use it unless you must."

"I will pick something I hate to say," Mia said. "So I do not say it by accident."

"Good," the other said. "You can also throw a veil for a breath. It is not invisibility. It makes eyes slide off you if you stay still and quiet. It costs focus. Do not try it tired unless you are sure the trade is worth it."

Mia tried the veil. She pulled cold up through the new sigil and let it spread like fog. The light around her bent. If she moved more than a slow shift of weight it broke. She brought it down. "Good for a doorway," she said. "Or a prayer."

The wolf took another slow step. "Rule of Three binds here as it does in Faerie. Names said three times. Vows spoken three times. A hunt called three times. Keep the count on purpose."

Mia looked at the other Mia and then at the wolf. "What about me," she asked. "What am I when I am not hunting. Am I going to feel like this all the time."

"You feel like this because you are in Winter," the other said. "In the waking world the Mantle will sit behind you unless you invite it forward. It will listen. It will wait. If you try to pretend it is not there, it will find its own work. If you own it, it will work when you ask and rest when you tell it to rest."

Mia snorted once. "So it is like a dog that can open doors and also write contracts."

The wolf huffed. If a glacier could laugh, it would sound like that. "Closer to a river that decided to be helpful," it said. "It will keep flowing. You choose where to dig channels."

The other Mia stepped closer and then stopped. She did not reach for Mia. She raised her hands, palms out, as if asking permission. "Integration," she said. "I do not take over. I step in when you ask. I am yours. If you do not like how I move, you tell me and I adjust. If you start to like what I do for the wrong reasons, you tell someone who loves you and you step back."

Mia thought of Mariah's voice that had held her on the warehouse floor. She thought of Sia's grip on her wrist when they crossed streets as kids without looking. She thought of Eric's steady instructions and Marcus's jokes that were not jokes when everything hurt. She thought of Truth's head against her knee. She had people who would call her on it. She had a building that would throw her into a chair and make her drink tea. She nodded.

"Okay," Mia said. "On my terms."

"On your terms," the other said.

They moved at the same time. Not a collision. A match. The other Mia breathed in and stepped forward. She did not blur. She did not melt. She fit, the way a jacket fits when it belongs to you and not to the person who had it last. Mia felt the shift like a click behind her heart. Her balance changed. Her hearing sharpened at the edges. It was not a rush. It was a set. She had more control than she had a minute ago, not less.

The wolf bowed its head. "Lady," it said. "The Hunt answers your call, not your impulse."

Mia looked down at the lake. The embers were gone except for the small spark she had chosen to keep. She pressed her palm to the ice over it. Warmth answered. Not heat that takes. Warmth that holds. She could carry both now. She did not have to burn to feel strong.

"Bind it," the wolf said. "Your words. Three times."

Mia spoke. "I guard the border," she said. "I hunt only what harms. I spare when I safely can." She said each line three times. The aurora above her bent as if the sky had nodded. The sigil at her sternum cooled to a calm point.

The wolf lifted its nose and tasted the air. "Done," it said. "One more thing. If a fallen foe yields three times, mark and release to Summer unless demon-tainted beyond recall. If they lie about yielding, your mercy is complete and your right to end the threat stands. Do not let clever mouths shame a clean kill."

"I understand," Mia said. She did not like the word kill. She did not pretend it did not belong here. "I will not keep score for pride. I will keep count for safety."

The lake changed. The ice cleared in a widening ring. The aurora faded toward dawn blue. Somewhere very far off, a bell sounded once, the way Sanctuary sometimes announced a guest.

"Time," the wolf said.

Mia took a breath. The air tasted like wintermint and clean metal. She checked her hands. No shake. She checked her chest. No clawing cold. She felt tired in a way that made sense. She felt ready in a way that did not scare her.

"Tell Sia I did not break myself," she said to the wolf, because saying it out loud made it more true in her bones.

"I witness," the wolf said. "I do not carry messages."

"Fair," Mia said. She smiled without forcing it. "I will tell her myself."

A thin path of hoarfrost opened across the lake, a bright line pointing back toward waking. Mia looked once more at the small spark in the ice. It glowed like a kitchen light through a door. She tapped the glass with two fingers in a private little promise, then followed the path.

The frost carried her like a bridge. The last thing she saw was the wolf watching the line, patient and sure. The last thing she felt was the other self sitting where she belonged, quiet until called. Then the lake became a quilt, the aurora became a ceiling, and the cold settled into its place without asking for more.

AFTERNOON LIGHT TURNED THE lobby glass into pale gold. The Museum had been quiet for hours, the kind of quiet that came after real sleep. Mia woke once to drink water and once to be bullied into soup. Then she slept again and went under fast. Mariah stayed in the chair with a blanket and a book she did not read. Her hum had thinned to a thread you felt more than heard.

The bells changed. Not loud. Not many. Three notes that did not belong to the building's usual songs. Cold crept along the door frame in a clean line, frost feathering the wood and stopping exactly at the threshold. It looked like winter had written its name in small handwriting and waited.

Charles was already in the lobby when the frost finished. He set his cane tip down and took a slow breath that would not show as worry. He did not call anyone. The bells had done that for him.

The front door opened without a hand. Air leaned in, bright and sharp. Mab stepped through as if she had always known the layout. Winter walked with her in a careful way that did not bruise the rules.

The rime on the floor stopped at the inlaid brass that marked the no-violence line and did not cross.

"Guest-right," she said to Charles. Three words. Clear.

"Given," Charles said. He nodded once. He did not bow. It was not a court. "Within Sanctuary's law."

"Within Sanctuary's law," Mab repeated. She looked across the lobby toward the family suite and knew which door was theirs without asking.

Eric arrived from the office at a fast walk that pretended it was normal speed. Marcus blinked into being on his shoulder, small and bright. "We have a guest," Eric said, as if it were news.

"We have a queen," Charles said.

Mab's gaze slid over them like a knife set back in its sheath. She did not pull on the room's temperature. She did not make the glass sing. She did not need to. "I came for the Lady," she said. "And to pay a debt I accepted the moment she lived."

"Then you can come as far as the door to that room," Eric said. "And not one step past without my say. I will not have the Mantle bullying my building."

Mab's mouth tipped by a fraction. "If Winter meant to bully," she said, "you would know." She did not push. She crossed the lobby and stopped at the brass line again. "Do I have permission to touch her," she asked. She said the words once, then again. Then a third time, each with the same weight. The Rule of Three set itself down between the four of them without dust.

Charles looked at Eric. Eric looked at Mariah through the open bedroom door. She had heard. She nodded once and set the book down.

"You have permission," Eric said. "Under Sanctuary law. Touch only. Heal if you can. No binding. No oaths. No tricks that someone has to clean up later."

"No tricks," Mab said. She stepped through the doorway in a way that did not feel like stepping. A cold smell like clean iron stood up from the air for one second and then smoothed.

Mia lay on her side, hair across her cheek, breath steady and even. The winter ring in her eyes showed faintly under her lids with each slow blink. Frost sigils had written themselves across her skin while she slept and faded again, like the tide touching sand. Mariah stood up and did not wobble, but she looked like a candle that had been kind long past when you should blow it out.

Mab stopped at the foot of the bed. She set three fingertips over the quilt where Mia's sternum lay under it. Nothing dramatic happened. No flash. No wind. Three soft knocks sounded in the air and made the lamp shiver.

"First," Mab said. "Seat the Mantle clean." The frost sigils that had been wandering settled and sank. Mia's breath deepened by a hair.

"Second," Mab said. "Mend what is tired." Coolth slid through the quilt like a tide and took the ache with it. Mia made a small sound that was not a word. Her shoulders let go.

"Third," Mab said. "Bind the distance so it does not starve." A thin white line appeared between Mab's hand and the anchor ring at Mia's wrist, then vanished as if it had only wanted to say that it existed. The air felt lighter after, not heavier.

Mariah's eyes filled all at once, sudden and unstoppable. She pressed her mouth into the back of her hand and laughed one short, broken laugh. Mab turned her head and met her where she stood.

"Your work is seen," Mab said. The words were plain. They landed like a blanket. "Rest."

Mariah sat because her knees decided for her. The chair caught her and she let her head fall back and closed her eyes. The hum that had been running all night unwound at last. It felt like a house settling.

Eric had a list of questions sitting in his throat. He swallowed them long enough to get the order right. "Logan," he said. "You sent word he is freed."

"Freed," Mab said. "Weak as a man who stopped drowning yesterday. He will breathe." She tipped her chin toward Mia. "I require my Lady for court business. She will return when that business does not need her hands."

"You do not require," Charles said. "You request. In this building, request is the word."

Mab did not argue. "I request," she said. "Three times." The last repetition left a visible mark in the air, a thin ring that rang once and vanished.

Eric's mouth twitched. He did not smile. "Conditions," he said. "She returns after debrief. We maintain contact. No oaths are taken here. You do not press our thresholds."

"Agreed," Mab said. She spoke each piece once. She did not need to repeat them. She had already bound herself by asking three times.

Mia opened her eyes. The blue in them firmed and then settled back to ordinary. She blinked at the ceiling, then found Mariah first. "Hi," she said, voice scratchy with sleep.

"Hi," Mariah said, hoarse. "You are fine."

"I am fine," Mia said, and this time the room believed her. She sat up slowly. The ache under her ribs had gone quiet. Her hands were steady. She saw Mab. She did not flinch.

"You came inside a place that does not like you," Mia said.

"I asked," Mab said. "They said yes."

Mia looked at Charles. He tipped his cane an inch. She looked at Eric. He nodded once. Marcus leaned around the door frame and gave her a tiny salute with his wing.

"Okay," Mia said. She swung her feet to the floor and did not sway. "What do you need."

"Presence," Mab said. "Voice. The court will eat its own tail without a Lady to keep it from pretending that is the point." She paused and something like approval passed across her face and was gone. "You smell like Winter in the right way. That is rare this soon."

"I had a good talk with myself," Mia said. She stood and pulled the clean shirt from the chair over her tank top. The motion did not hurt. She laced her boots with hands that did not feel like claws.

Eric stepped in and set a hand on her shoulder. "Two things," he said. "You come back. You call if you cannot."

"I will," Mia said.

Mariah opened her eyes long enough to catch Mia's hand. "I am going to sleep," she said. "That is not me giving up. That is me letting someone else carry the next part. You bring that hand back so I can hold it again tonight."

"I will," Mia said. She squeezed once and set her mother's hand down like you set a glass on a table you love.

Mab moved back to the doorway. She touched her knuckles to the empty air just outside the threshold. It rippled and held. A pane of deep blue formed like water that had changed its mind about being water. Cold spilled from it in a clean way that felt like new snow and open sky. The gate stayed outside the line on purpose. Winter had learned the house.

"One more thing little lady," Charles said, looking directly at Mia. "You will bring back your sister safe from the other side."

"I will," Mia said, then felt the air solidify about her a moment. She felt a warm smile creep over her face as she realized what her friends had just done for her. Thrice she had sworn to them, and thrice promised meant even the Mantle of the Winter Lady could not stop her from coming home.

"Ready," Mab said.

Mia took one more look around the room. Charles by the door with his steady eyes. Eric with the list he would not read to her for an hour. Marcus bright and small and trying not to look proud. Mariah asleep in a chair at last, mouth soft, breath even. Truth lifted her head and thumped her tail twice. She set her palm in Mab's offered hand. It was cold and strong. The blue pane rippled. For a heartbeat the lobby light doubled and turned everything to a winter version of itself. Then Mia stepped through and the rime at the doorway pulled back like a tide leaving clean sand.

The bells did not ring again. The building kept its peace.

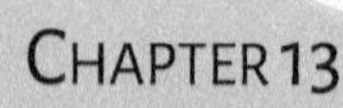

CHAPTER 13

Hunt's Road

SIA

THE HALL IN TOR Arctis felt like the inside of a glacier that learned how to be a cathedral. Blue light ran in the ice ribs above, dim and steady, like a heartbeat that refused to hurry. Sia kept one hand on her umbrella as the doors opened and cold air slid over her shoes. Marcus perched on her shoulder in his tiny dragon form, claws careful, tail wrapped around the strap of her coat. Kaelan walked at Sia's left, sleeves straight and calm. Bastian strode on the right with his axe peace-tied and his chin high.

Mia stood at the base of the throne dais with a circle of wolves behind her and frost blooming in a faint ring around her boots. She wore Winter like a second skin. The aura was quiet and sharp, not a costume, not a spotlight. It felt like a lake in January, waiting under snow, holding more than it showed.

Sia stopped three steps away. For a second they only looked at each other. Mia's eyes flashed blue, then settled. The Mantle was there, but so was the girl who drew comics on the back of math worksheets.

Sia moved first. She crossed the gap and hugged her, hard. The cold around Mia tried to rise and then eased, as if it had been taught manners. Mia hugged back with both arms and did not pretend she was fine. Sia felt her breathe in, breathe out, and find the rhythm that meant safe enough for now.

"Nice coat," Sia said into her shoulder.

"Nice dragon," Mia said into Sia's hair.

Marcus lifted his head. "I am technically majestic," he said. His voice came thin from the distance of projection. He fluffed himself up anyway. "This is only my travel size."

Sia pulled back and wiped her face with the heel of her hand. "Your baby form, you mean."

Marcus huffed. "I will remember this when I am large again."

Kaelan stepped forward, palms open a polite inch from her kimono. "Lady Winter," she said to Mia, Summer-courteous and precise, "I am honored to stand with you." Her smile tilted warmer and turned into a real one. "Also hi. I missed you."

"Hi," Mia said, softer. "I missed you too."

Bastian dropped to one knee and bowed his head. "My Lady," he said. "I am Bastian of the Green. I put my edge between you and harm while we walk together."

"Please stand," Mia said, almost embarrassed. "I am not going to make you kneel every time you breathe."

"Then I will kneel when it matters," Bastian said, and rose.

The sound of Winter shifted at the far end of the hall, the way a room changes when a second conversation ends. Mab stood beside her throne with one hand on the carved arm, watching them like a teacher who had already graded the test and was waiting to see if the students would arrive on their own. She stepped down, each footfall soft and clear.

"Reunions are good," Mab said. "We are not built to do this alone." She looked at Sia and then at Mia. "There is a charge to put on the table."

"We are ready," Sia said. She made sure to keep her voice normal. Not loud. Not small.

Mab's gaze flicked to the wolves and they settled like shadows. "Speak it simple and in threes," she said, mostly to herself. Then she faced the four of them. "One. The Wilds are open and wrong in places. Winter cannot hold what is not Winter. Two. A Dreaming keeps the Wild in order when it can. The Dreaming is not answering. Three. I charge your company to go into the Wilds, find the Faery Dreamer, and confirm strength or silence."

She pointed to each of them in turn. "Bastian is your escort by Summer's right. Kaelan is your Summer witness. Marcus is your dragon voice, so long as he can hold his thread. Sia is the Dreamer of Earth. Mia is Winter's envoy. Guide, not commander."

Mia nodded once. "Guide, not commander," she said. She repeated it again. Then a third time, steady. The Rule of Three settled like a click in the air.

Bastian went to one knee again. "I renew my oath," he said. "I will see Sia Mason safe to Summer's border, safe through Hunt ground, and safe into the Wilds. I will put my blade between her and harm." He said it again. Then a third time. Sia felt it bind the way a knot binds when you pull both ends and the rope does not move.

Kaelan placed two fingers over her heart and bowed to Sia and then to Mia. "I bear Summer's token and keep count," she said. "I will name debts correctly. I will warn you before you step into one." She repeated the lines twice more and breathed out.

Mab lifted a small case from a wolf's back. Inside lay three thin disks, dark metal with a pale stamp in the center. Antlers, a crown of ice, and a spiral cut into one design. She handed one to Sia, one to Mia, and one to Bastian.

"Travel writs," Mab said. "Stamped for Winter, recognized by the Hunt. If you enter Summer ground with respect, their door will not shut in your face. If you break terms, the stamp goes dark and I will not argue your case."

Sia turned her disk over in her palm. It was cold enough to feel alive, but not painful. "Terms?"

"Plain speech at parley," Mab said. "No glamour at the circle. No steel drawn inside a Hunt ring. Do not spill first blood on Hunt ground. If you find Hell seams, mark them for Winter and Hunt both and move on. If a lawful Hunt runs across your path, you stand aside unless it trespasses your charge."

Sia raised the umbrella slightly. "I can make the marks visible to both," she said. "Dream signs that echo to Winter's ledger. Simple. Three lines. One at sight. One at distance. One at the road." She said it again. Then a third time.

Mab dipped her head a fraction. "Good. That will help my patrols and keep us from chasing the same fire twice."

Marcus nudged Sia's neck with his snout. "Sanctuary is steady," he said for the room. "Charles has the bells on a hair trigger. Eric set the wards like a net. Mia's room still smells like soup. We can go."

Mia glanced at the wolves who had settled into statues again. "Any other ground rules we are missing," she asked.

"Consent magic is a Sanctuary thing," Sia said quietly to her. "Out here it is favors, guest-right, and oaths. We keep our pockets closed unless we are making a deal on purpose."

"I can do that," Mia said. She let the Mantle sit behind her words so they had weight without menace.

Mab paced a slow line in front of them, hands clasped. "Say your intent," she said. "Three lines is enough."

Sia squared her shoulders. "We enter the Wilds by the Hunt road," she said. "We look for the Dreaming's tracks. We keep our oaths clean." She said it twice more. The words felt like a path on her tongue.

Mia followed. "I guide where Winter knowledge helps," she said. "I listen before I push. I keep the border when trespass crosses it." She repeated it again. Then a third time. The wolves' ears flicked like they heard what they liked.

Bastian spoke next. "I hold the front and watch the sides," he said. "I speak when Summer needs to be heard. I do not start fights that belong to someone else." He made it three.

Kaelan finished the set. "I count debts," she said. "I keep our feet out of snares. I remind us when a ladder is a snake."

Mab's mouth tilted. "You will do," she said. She looked past them to a page waiting by the side door. "Road," she ordered. The page bowed and ran.

The air in the hall changed again, like a body taking a deeper breath. A gate lifted outside the throne and peeled itself out of nothing. It was not a circle of light. It was a pane of winter sky you could walk through. Frost formed along the edge, then stopped where the brass inset of the hall floor began. Winter had learned the line here. That mattered.

"First light puts you at the patrol road," Mab said. "You will reach Hunt ground by midday if you do not wander. Their herald will find you if you look like you know what you are doing."

Sia checked the anchor ring. Marcus flickered and then steadied. "You good," she asked him under her breath.

"I am offended by the doubt," he said. Then he softened. "Yes. If the pressure cuts the link, I will find you again. Do not do anything that makes me wish I could breathe fire right now."

"Try to be bigger," Sia said. "This is very tiny."

He pinched her ear with a claw. "Rude."

Kaelan adjusted her sleeves. "No food. No gifts," she murmured. "If you must trade, make it clean and small. Words first. Hands last."

Mia rolled her shoulders like a runner settling at a start line. "We have this," she said, and made herself believe it enough that Winter stopped leaning forward and stepped back.

They faced Mab together. Sia felt the urge to say thank you the way you say it to a teacher on the last day of class. She went with something truer.

"We will bring back good news," Sia said. "Or the truth you need."

"Bring back the truth," Mab said. "Good is a bonus."

The page returned at a jog and stopped with his hands behind his back. "Road steady," he said. "Wolves posted. Sky clear."

Mab lifted her hand. "Go, then," she said. She paused and looked at Mia. "Lady, you smell like Winter the right way already. Keep it that way."

"I plan to," Mia said.

Sia took the first step. The gate felt like walking through a cold splash that did not wet her clothes. Marcus shivered and then perked up like a flashlight finding full battery again. Kaelan followed, smooth and balanced, sandals whispering on stone. Bastian ducked his head and went through last, axe still tied, mouth set with the kind of smile that shows up before a fight you want to win without starting.

Behind them the hall stayed quiet. The wolves watched with eyes that held the light. Mab's hand fell to her side. The pane sealed as the last boot crossed and left only the echo of their steps on the road outside, thinner air, and the taste of snow that had not fallen yet.

The patrol road waited, flat and blue-black, with pine shadows marching away toward a horizon that looked honest about being far. Sia set the umbrella to a walking rhythm. Mia matched it, mantle steady. Kaelan checked the north by habit, then the sun. Bastian sniffed the air like a hunter deciding which wind to trust.

"Okay," Sia said. "We find the Hunt. We keep our oaths. We follow the signs."

"And we do not feed any goblins," Marcus said from her shoulder.

Sia smiled. "That too." She looked ahead where the trees thickened and the snow held more stories than the road did. "Let's go."

THE PATROL ROAD THINNED to two ruts and a ribbon of blue-black ice. Pines closed in, taller and meaner than Summer's forests, with bark that looked like it had learned to take a hit. Sia kept her umbrella tucked in her palm, tip ticking against the road every few steps. Marcus rode her shoulder in his tiny dragon body, claws light through her coat. His warmth felt like a pocket heater pressed to her collarbone.

"Stay to the center," Bastian said, easy and steady. The Green Knight walked point, eyes on the trees, pace set like he had measured this ground with his feet since he could stand. "Hunt markers start at the first old stump you want to kick. When you feel like kicking it, that means you found one."

Sia almost smiled. "That is helpful and not helpful at the same time."

"It will make sense when you see it," he said.

Kaelan fell in beside Sia, sleeves neat, hair smooth despite the cold air. "Rules check," she said. "We do not accept food. We do not pocket anything, even a pretty rock. We only make deals on purpose and in complete sentences. No one tells their full name unless we agree that is the bargain."

"Got it," Sia said.

"Say it," Kaelan said, nudging her.

Sia said it. "No food. No freebies. Only deals on purpose. No full names unless we choose."

Kaelan nodded once. "Good. Do not be afraid to repeat yourself. In Faerie, three times is clean."

The road tipped down into a shallow ravine. That was where the markers started. An antler crown had been carved into the face of a dead birch stump, each tine cut deep. A pair of paw prints had been burned into a standing post, claws long and curved like a signature. Bone chimes hung from a low branch, bleached white and strung with red thread. When wind slid through them they rang in threes, a clear little note that made the inside of Sia's ears itch.

"Welcome to Hunt ground," Bastian said.

Fuzanglong drifted at their rear, no bigger than a scarf made of river light. He had been bright in the throne hall. Here he kept himself to a careful glow, scales like watered silk. "I will keep my voice low," he said, mild. "This place does not enjoy voices that promise too much."

"Promise less. Do more," Marcus said. "A mood I respect."

The smell changed before the sign did. Sulfur pushed into the cold air, not strong, just enough to bite the roof of Sia's mouth. On the right, a set of hoofprints cut across the road and broke into the trees at an angle that did not match any prey animal Sia had seen. The prints were too clean, too deep, and each center held a smear of gray-black ash that refused to blow away. Claw marks ran along a birch at shoulder height like something had dragged one hand to steady itself. A metal snare lay twisted in the ditch with the spring burned black.

Sia knelt by the hoofprints. Her breath fogged the air. "Demon traffic," she said.

"Fresh," Bastian said. He turned his head, listening, then faced forward again. "Hours. Not days."

Mia crouched at the snagged snare and frowned. The Winter in her eyes went a shade brighter and cooled back. "They wanted a hunter," she said. "Or anything with a spine and pride."

"Do not follow those tracks," Kaelan said, gentle and firm. "That is how they teach you to run in circles until you are far from your own road."

Sia stood. The umbrella's ferrule clicked twice on stone before she caught herself and made it three times. She did not love being watched. She could feel it now, shapes pacing a parallel path in the timber, too good at staying just out of sight.

The first horn sounded from somewhere ahead, a smooth low note that did not echo so much as slide along the bark. A second note followed, shorter. A third answered from the left, same tone, same length. Then it all went quiet again.

"Hunt scouts," Bastian said. He did not reach for his axe. He did not change his pace. "They will decide if we are worth a conversation or a chase."

Sia kept her eyes forward. "Conversation, please."

"Stay plain," Kaelan murmured. "No pretty words to hide what we want. Pretty words look like traps to people who make traps as a job."

Marcus shifted his claws. "And do not smile too much," he added softly. "Wolves read that wrong."

The road funneled between two boulders thick with lichen, then opened into a shallow ring of standing stones. The stones were waist high and old enough to lean. Snow had drifted into the ring and held an undisturbed skin. Bone-and-iron windbells hung here too, three to a stone, silent. Sia recognized the feeling almost before she named it. Parley ground. Even the air stood at attention.

"Hands visible," Bastian said. He lifted his open. "Steel stays tied. Glamours off."

Kaelan snapped a paper charm between her fingers. It dissolved into clear air, taking the last polite ripple of illusion from her face and sleeves. "There," she said. "Nothing but me."

Mia settled the Mantle behind her like a cloak you hang on a chair before you sit. Winter did not leave the room. It just stopped leaning forward.

Sia took one step into the ring and stopped. She felt the line like a raised thread under her boot. She took one more step until she stood on the central patch of snow. The umbrella stayed down. Marcus stayed on her shoulder, eyes narrow, smoke thin as pencil lead curling from his nose and gone on the next breath.

They waited. Waiting felt like a test. Sia let her weight settle evenly and counted her breaths. She reached three and started over. She reached three again and did it once more.

The Hunt came in without rustle. Six wolves first, fur like night, eyes pale as old ice, fanning to either side with their heads low and relaxed. Three goblins came behind them, all leather and sinew, faces carved by wind, ears pierced with rings that chimed once when they stopped. A fourth shape dropped from a branch with the kind of grace you only get from living in trees. He wore a collar of antler slivers and a heavy ring stamped with a crown and a rack.

"Speak plain," the new one said. His voice had sand in it. "No this and that. We hear it and decide."

Bastian bowed his head. "We request parley at the ring," he said. "I am Bastian of the Green, escort by Summer oath. This company crosses Hunt runs to the Wilds to find the Faery Dreamer."

Mia kept her hands open at her sides. "I am Mia Mason, Winter's Lady," she said. "Guide, not commander. We bring word of demon trespass on your runs and we will mark seams we find so your people and Winter's patrols see the same sign."

Kaelan tipped two fingers off her sleeve. "Kaelan of Summer. Witness and ward."

Sia lifted the umbrella an inch. "Sia Mason," she said. She did not add more. The umbrella went back down.

The goblin with the antler collar watched their mouths while they spoke, like he weighed words the way a butcher weighed meat. He looked at their hands. He looked at their feet. He looked at the tied axe and the dim dragon and the way Mia wore winter without trying to impress anyone.

"You are the ones who closed a door by the river city," he said. He did not make it a question.

"We stopped a Hellmouth," Mia said. "We also returned something stolen."

"An amulet," Sia added. "Stamped like the ring on your hand."

The goblin glanced at the ring, then back to their faces. A muscle in his jaw told one small story. "The Chicago thing was bait," he said. "Not for you. For a seller who sells behind Winter's skirts. That seller ran. He will run again." He lifted his hand. One of the wolves stepped forward, mouth holding a leather case. The goblin took it and flipped the lid.

Inside lay a flat stamp carved in dark iron, the mirror of his ring crest. He showed it to the company, then pressed it to a strip of bark. The bark hissed and took the mark clean.

"Passage-right," he said. "Across three runs. You do not spill first blood on Hunt ground. You do not draw steel inside a circle. You do not steal. You mark Hell seams with three signs that Winter's ledgers and our runners both can read. If a lawful Hunt runs across you, you step aside."

Sia felt the weight of the moment line up with their plan. "We agree," she said. "We will mark one sign close, one sign at distance, one sign at the road." She let the umbrella hum and held still until the hum calmed. "Plain marks. No tricks."

"Say it again," the goblin said.

Sia did. Then one more time.

Mia repeated the limits back word for word. Bastian did the same and added his escort oath by Summer law. Kaelan spoke the debt line, promising a fair ledger and no games. The air inside the stones tightened, then loosened like a knot pulled and checked.

"Good," the goblin said. He stamped the strip again and handed it to Bastian. "Night brings a trial. You will cross a clearing with the

Hunt moving around you. If you cry out, throw light, or reach for a blade, the right ends. Do not be stupid."

"We will not," Bastian said.

The goblins stepped back. The wolves flowed with them like water changing shape. The bone chimes rang once. Twice. Then a third time, without wind.

Sia let her shoulders ease. She could still feel eyes on them in the trees, but the eyes felt different now. Not friendly. But not hunting them either.

"First step taken," Kaelan said quietly.

"Two to go," Sia answered, and set the umbrella moving again as they left the ring and followed the road deeper into Hunt ground.

THE HUNTING HALL ROSE out of the firs like a ship pulled onto land and left to remember storms. Pine trunks made the ribs. Smoke curled from a stone throat in the roof. The doors stood open, firelight spilling across packed snow. Inside, benches flanked a long table scarred by knives and claws. Meat steamed on wooden trenchers. Bones stacked in tidy piles against one wall said this place liked order even when it smelled like blood and smoke.

A handler in lacquered leather waved them in with two fingers. "Hospitality," he said. One word, clean. The word loosened Sia's shoulders. Hospitality meant you ate what was offered and nobody kept a secret bill to hand you at the door.

They sat halfway down the table. Bastian took the aisle side like a reflex. Kaelan folded neatly on the bench and set her sleeves just clear of the grease trenchers. Mia settled with her back to a post. Marcus stayed on Sia's shoulder. His tail twitched at the smell of roasted boar.

Wooden plates arrived with slabs of venison, boar ribs glazed in something sharp and sweet, a stack of dark bread still hot enough to steam, bowls of thick stew that tasted like winter had learned herbs. No forks. Knives were tied to the table with leather thongs and left for everyone to share. Sia glanced at Kaelan. Kaelan nodded once. Hospitality meant no debt. You ate. You did not pay. You did not offer a trade. You said thank you only to the room.

"Do not ask where the sausage comes from," Marcus whispered in Sia's ear. "Eat first. Existential dread later."

She nudged him with her jaw and reached for bread.

Conversation stayed a low hum along the hall. Hunters measured them the way craftsmen measure a tool they might want to keep. At the far end of the table, under a crest of mounted antlers, a man watched and did not pretend otherwise.

He was tall in a way that made space around him. The furs on his shoulders were winter wolf and something darker that drank firelight. Under the fur lay old leather banded with iron rings that had been hammered flat from years of wear. His helm rested on the bench beside him. The antlers rising from it were not trophies bolted on. They had grown through the metal long ago and the steel had learned to bend around them. A loop of polished horn hung at his belt with a thumb print worn into the curve. He had an eyepatch of black hide stitched with a single white thread in the shape of a crescent. The uncovered eye was the pale gray of wood ash and it missed nothing.

His face had the clean planes of a statue left out in rain. Time had cut him but not softened him. A brush beard ran short along his jaw, iron gray shading into white at the chin. A thin scar climbed from the corner of his mouth toward the patch and made his almost smile look like a secret. Tattoos the color of old bruises coiled from under his sleeves to the backs of his hands, knots and hounds and antlers worked into lines that moved when his fingers moved. His hands were large and square, the nails trimmed blunt. When he breathed, the air around him smelled like cold leather, wet leaves, and the first bite of snow.

He did not sit like a king in a story. He sat like a hunter between runs, still as a stump with all the life under the bark. The wolves near the hearth checked him the way a pack checks its road. One glance. Then quiet. The hall's noise leaned around him without touching him.

Sia lifted her cup and held his gaze three breaths. Recognition clicked before she could talk herself out of it. She set her cup down so the wood would not shake.

"The Earlking," she said, clear enough to carry, not loud enough to challenge.

He smiled with half his mouth. "Correct," he said. His voice was low and clean. It reached the corners without raising itself.

"I draw a lot," Sia said. "Helps with outlines."

He pushed his trencher aside and stood. The room made way the way tide pulls back from a sandbar. He came halfway down the table and set both hands on the wood opposite them. Up close, Sia could see a thread of silver caught in the seam of his bracer where someone had repaired it by hand. The small details felt like the truth behind the title.

"Names are for callers," he said, amused. "I do not need them to know who sits at my table." He pointed with two fingers, exact rather than rude. "Bastian of the Green. Summer's edge. Oath in his bones." His eyes moved. "Kaelan Kuzunoha. Miko of Tsukiyomi. Summer's guest who counts debts correctly." A look to Mia. "Mia Mason. Winter's Lady. Guide, not commander. Winter sits behind your eyes and does not push." Last he regarded Sia. "Sia Mason. Dreamer of Earth. You carry a garden in your head and a door in your hand." He flicked a glance at Marcus without turning his face. "And a dragon trying to look taller."

Marcus froze, then nodded like a knight accepting a promotion. "Temporarily compact," he said.

That earned the smallest twitch at the corner of the Earlking's mouth. "Temporarily is a brave word," he said, then back to Sia. "You wondered what else I am called. Say the ones you know. See what answers."

"Goblin King," Sia said. "Lord of the Hunt. Cernunnos when forests want an older name. Herne when a story needs antlers in English. Master of roads that touch without touching. I do not know which you prefer."

"I prefer the one that fits the day," he said. "Today I am the Earlking. Tomorrow may need a horn with a different name. Your teachers would tell you not to get attached to labels, little Dreamer."

"Every teacher I have says that," Sia said, and took a swallow of bitter beer because not drinking would be rude. "They still want me to label my homework."

He laughed, short and pleased. The hall relaxed. Someone two benches down argued about dogs. A woman told a joke about a wolf that would not fetch. Heat rolled deeper off the hearth.

They ate. Hospitality held. No oaths. No bargains. Plates did not empty until you stopped reaching. Cups did not spill unless you were careless. Sia kept her portions reasonable. Kaelan nudged her once when she reached to pass a bowl to a hunter at her back. Sia set it on the table and slid it with a finger. The hunter reached. No debt created. Mia watched the room the way Eric watched a crowded hallway, shoulders loose, eyes counting exits.

When the food slowed and the noise settled, the Earlking tapped the table. Runners swapped meat for dried berries and a wedge of hard cheese that tasted like smoke and pine. He did not take any. He looked at them, then at Marcus, who was trying very hard to be dignified and small at the same time.

"You will sleep under my roof tonight," he said. "Beds, water, and a roof that does not listen to teeth. No price on that part. Hospitality is a law that makes the world less stupid."

Sia braced for the second half. It came like a fence post set straight.

"Along your road there is a river that forgot how to be itself," he said. "You will come to it. It will ask for help and not have the manners to ask well. Clean it. Close any mouth you find near it. If demons hunt on my runs, make sure they learn to be elsewhere. In return, the Hunt grants you our wayhouses and the silence of our woods for three days. You will not be chased unless you act like prey."

Bastian glanced at Sia. Mia watched Sia too. The room seemed to wait with them.

Sia set her palm on her umbrella's handle. "We accept," she said. She counted the lines off clean. "We will cleanse the river if we can. We will close any nearby Hell mouth. We will not bring Winter's law into your hunts."

"Do not pretend you did not like saying that last one," the Earlking said, faintly amused.

"Maybe a little," Sia said.

Mia added her three. "Guide, not commander," she said. "I will not speak Winter's law on your ground unless it keeps a border from breaking. I will keep count of what we owe and pay it where it belongs."

Kaelan lifted two fingers from the table. "I will name debts correctly," she said. "I will warn them before they step into one. I will not trade without making the trade plain."

Bastian finished the set. "I will put my edge between them and what hunts stupid," he said. "I will not raise steel at your table. I will be on my feet at dawn."

The Earlking touched two knuckles to the wood, not quite a blessing. "Good," he said. "Beds are down the east hall. Wash water is hot. If you speak to the dogs, speak to them like people. They are better listeners than most of us." He paused and looked at Sia again. "Names bind when repeated. Do not say one three times unless you want it to answer."

"I know that rule," Sia said. "I just forget it when people ask for introductions."

"Then remember," he said. "The Wild does not bother to forgive."

He stepped back. The room's attention loosened. Hunters went back to their talk. A drum began to tap under the noise. Sia felt the kind of tired that lives in bones settle in. The thought of a bed with a roof felt like a spell.

Marcus yawned so wide his wings twitched. "We like him," he said.

"We respect him," Kaelan said. "Liking can come later."

Mia finished her water and stood. "Beds sound good," she said. "I want my head clear for a river that does not ask well."

They took the east hall. It was warmer than the main room, lined with doors cut into thick timber. Their space held four pallets with clean wool and a bench for gear. A hound lifted its head from the corner and thumped its tail twice, accepted them, and went back to sleep.

Sia set her umbrella within reach and the writ disk on the bench where she could see it. The stamped rawhide knot looked simple and final. She breathed in smoke and pine and the faint musk of dog. Outside, a horn sounded once, then twice, then three times. The hall answered with nothing at all, which felt like trust.

"Tomorrow we find a river," Sia said.

"Tomorrow the river finds us," Mia said, and smiled without showing teeth.

"Either way," Bastian said from the doorway, "we wake before the dogs."

Sia blew out the lamp and let the dark fill in. The Wild pressed close on the other side of the wall. Hospitality held. That was enough for one night.

CHAPTER 14

Water Memories

SIA

THEY LEFT THE HUNT hall at first light, breath smoking in short puffs, boots creaking where the top layer of snow had crusted overnight. A wolfrider paced them to the gate, checked their stamped writ with a quick press of thumb, then turned his wolf and melted into the trees. No farewell. Not rude, just efficient. The hall doors swung shut behind them and the forest took back the road.

Bastian set an easy pace that kept them warm without burning energy. Kaelan walked light and quiet beside Sia, sleeves neat, eyes taking in every small thing. Mia carried the Winter mantle like a steady pressure behind her shoulders, not showy, not loud. Marcus rode Sia's shoulder in his compact dragon form, claws careful on her coat. Fuzanglong kept to a thin river-serpent ribbon along Kaelan's cuff, a pearl glow that refused to grow larger than it needed.

The antler totems that marked Hunt jurisdiction fell away within a quarter mile. In their place, driftwood fetishes appeared, wired together with fishbone and thread, hanging from branches over low swales. Someone had tied them to sway without clacking. When wind pushed through the needles, the fetishes rocked and pointed like weather vanes. Sia realized they were tracking current even under snow.

The smell changed first. Winter air usually holds clean cold and wood smoke if you are lucky. Here it picked up a metal edge, like wet iron, and an algae breath that did not belong under solid ice. The sound changed second. Normal creeks talk in a steady run. This one had a pulse, a low throb under the crunch of boots. Sia felt it in her teeth before she could place it.

"Water totems," Kaelan said, nodding at a fishbone string knotted above a frozen dip. "This stretch belongs to the river, not the Hunt. That means we ask the water before we move it."

"Alright," Sia said automatically, then caught herself. "Got it."

They topped a short rise. Below, the land cut into a shallow braid of channels. The main thread curved out of sight behind a stand of black spruce. Feeder streams showed themselves as dark lines under wind-scoured ice. At the first side run they crossed, soot streaked the cattails. Not on top. Inside the ice, suspended like flake pepper in glass.

Sia set her umbrella tip to the bank and drew a small sign in the air, just big enough to hold a glimmer. One Dream mark to ping Winter's ledger, nothing flashy. The sign folded itself into the cattail shadows and faded. Her anchor ring warmed, then cooled. One marker placed.

They moved on. The next feeder had a rim of ice that looked dented from below. Drag marks ran up the gravel bar, heavy and wide, like something had hauled itself along on elbows. The snow over those tracks had melted and refrozen, leaving a skin that flashed under the clouded sun. Bastian crouched, pressed two fingers to the ice, and stood again without comment. Kaelan didn't need to say it. Everyone could read heavy, recent, and wrong.

Sia marked that feeder too, a single quick sigil that would echo back to Winter patrol ledgers. She kept the lines simple. Sight. Record.

Move. No need to stack signs or build a net. The Hunt had asked them to keep the road clean, not to build a station.

As they worked their way upstream, the driftwood fetishes thickened. Some were just tied sticks. Others were more complex, little spirals and fish shapes woven from willow. None felt like decorations. They looked like the sort of thing a place uses to remind itself how to behave.

"That smell," Mia said quietly, pulling her scarf higher. "It gets in your mouth."

"Like a penny under your tongue," Marcus muttered. "I hate it."

"Stay alert, not jumpy," Bastian said over his shoulder. "If the river is sick, it will try to share."

They pushed through a stand of young birch and came to the bend. The ford should have been a rough shelf of pebbles under shallow current. Instead the surface had turned to black glass, rippled and frozen mid-flow. Reed stubs along the bank wore a ring of soot like bad eyeliner. The current under the ice beat against itself in slow, uneven pushes. Sia could feel the pressure through the soles of her boots.

"Do not say the river's name," Kaelan said. "Not even guesses. If someone has twisted the name, speaking the wrong one feeds it."

Sia nodded and kept her mouth shut. She scanned the edges instead. A snag of roots held a snarl of hair-fine weeds that should have been tan and stringy. They were dark and slick, clotted where the ice had grabbed them. A weak ripple of Hell pressure tapped her ring. Not a gate in the air. Something braided in the water's idea of itself.

She stepped to the gravel lip and raised the umbrella like a staff. The ferrule touched the ice and did not crack it. Cold climbed the wood and into her hand. It didn't feel like winter. It felt like a wrong word.

"Two more marks," she said. "Upstream and down. Then we stop where we are and think."

Mia scanned the tree line. "I'll keep the frost thin," she said. "We do not freeze anything until we know what we are freezing."

Bastian moved midstream on the shallow shelf, testing with his boot, keeping the axe slung and using the haft like a pole. He stopped where the pressure peaked and pointed with his chin. "Knot is under there," he said. "Feels like a snarl. No demon stink on the shore. If something came up, it went back in."

Fuzanglong's pale head lifted from Kaelan's sleeve, whiskers drifting in the cold air. "The current is trying to run inside out," he said, voice low and even. "Someone told it to listen to a false beat."

Sia placed the last two Dream marks, small and exact. One above the bend in a line of wind-scoured willow. One down below on the side channel where the soot was thinner. She kept her breathing calm and counted each gesture. When she finished, she let the umbrella rest in her palm and looked at the ford again.

"We do this carefully," she said. "Test before we hit. If there is a mind in there, we ask it what went wrong. If it is only a seam woven into a name, we will have to pull the wrong syllable and give it the right one back."

Kaelan fished out two folded papers and shook them once. "Boots and staff," she said. "So the pull does not get a grip." She stuck the paper to Sia's boots, then touched the umbrella tip with a charm. The air around the ferrule steadied.

Mia listened to the ice and the water. Her breath fogged and drifted sideways on a tiny breeze. "I can hold a thin skin to quiet the churn if it panics."

"Hold until we need it," Bastian said. "Noise matters."

Sia lifted her chin and looked up the bend. The trees leaned over the water as if they were trying to shield it. A pair of driftwood fetishes hung low there, turning slowly. She took that as a sign the place wanted help, not a fight.

"Okay," she said. "We've found it."

Marcus tucked his wings in tighter and pressed himself against Sia's neck for warmth. "I am ready," he said. "I am not going to sneeze."

"Good plan," Sia said, mouth crooked. She checked the stamped writ at her collar, felt the rawhide knot firm against her skin, and let that stand in for courage. "We go slow. We watch the edges. We do not give the river more of us than it should have."

Bastian pointed to a gravel patch under a leaning alder. "Stage there," he said. "If it surges, higher ground in three steps."

They moved to the spot and set their feet. The ford groaned softly, not from weight, but from a rhythm trying to break through the wrong one laid over it. Sia planted the umbrella's tip on the bank and felt for the seam with the Dream the way she would test paper with a pencil, light first, then firmer.

The wrong beat pushed back. Not a voice. Not yet. More like a song that had been taught badly. It wanted to pull her listening off balance and make that the new normal.

"Got it," she said, keeping her voice steady. "It is braided into the name. We will have to unpick it at the knot."

"Then let us cut and weave," Kaelan said.

Mia flexed her fingers and let a fine lace of frost drift out over the black glass. It did not crack the surface. It quieted the glare. The smell of algae thinned.

"Ready on your call," Bastian said.

Sia closed her eyes for one breath and called up the sense of a clean stream from summers that felt far away. She held that picture in her head like a lantern and opened her eyes again.

"Let's fix a river," she said.

SIA KEPT THE UMBRELLA planted on the bank while the others spread out the way they had planned on the rise. Bastian stood on the shallow lip, weight low, hands loose on his axe handle. Kaelan stayed to Sia's left, sleeves neat, attention locked on the surface. Mia took position a little upstream at the bend, eyes narrow, breathing steady. Marcus pressed himself flat against Sia's collar to keep warm. Fuzanglong lifted his small river-drake head from Kaelan's cuff and tasted the air with a delicate flick of whiskers.

The ice across the ford looked like black glass poured over moving muscle. Reeds along the bank wore soot inside their skins. The push under Sia's boots came in uneven beats, wrong enough to rub her nerves raw.

"Testing the water, not claiming it," Kaelan said. "Keep it simple."

Sia nodded once. She leaned on the umbrella the way Eric taught her to test a threshold, light touch first, then a little more. The Dream sense rode down the ferrule into the frozen skin and met a pull that had nothing to do with winter. Not a voice, not yet. More like a song sung off key, loud enough to bully the right tune out of a room.

Something stirred under the glass. Three shapes rose into the dark, not swimming, more like being pushed up by their own decision. Faces formed in the silt swirl and took almost-shape. They had cheekbones and eyes and not much else. Water streamed off hair that was more weed than hair.

The middle one hissed. "Hungry."

The one on the right answered, voice a grit-choked whisper. "Thirsty."

The third found a word and let it rattle like a pebble in a tin. "Cold."

Mia lifted her palm and exhaled. A lace of frost drifted across the ford, thin and steady, just enough to tamp the churn. The ice did not thicken. It calmed. The algae smell eased.

"We hear you," Sia said, keeping her tone even. "We won't drown your voices. We're here to fix a knot."

The naiads' eyes slid to her, then to the umbrella, then back. They did not flinch from the staff, which Sia took as a good sign.

A sound came from under the ford, dull and almost human. It repeated itself like a cough that wanted to be a word. Sia felt the syllables try to climb up through the black glass and hook into her head. The name it pressed into the air was wrong. Close around the edges. Off in the middle like a mismatched bone.

The naiad on the left jerked toward the sound as if tugged. The frost lace stopped it from lunging, but its face stretched toward the wrong word the way moths lean toward porch light.

"Stop," Kaelan said, calm and firm. "Do not chase the bait."

The thing under the ice said the wrong name again. Sia's anchor ring buzzed once in warning. She drew the umbrella back a fraction, doused the urge to answer, and recognized the trick. The seam had braided itself into the river's identity. Anyone who called the river by that twisted name would feed the knot and tighten it.

"It isn't a doorway," she said, mostly for the team. "It's a false name woven through the water's idea of itself."

"Can you cut it without cutting the river," Bastian asked.

"We cut and then stitch," Sia said. "But we won't do it alone."

She set the umbrella tip back to the ice and spoke to the faces. "Listen," she said, steady. "Your ford has a wrong word sitting on top of the right one. If you want help, give us the true name once. Not loud. Not three times. Once. We'll carry it where it belongs and speak it three times to seat it. Then we shut the seam."

The naiads stared. Their features blurred and reshaped, as if the idea of faces took effort. The one on the right hissed again, softer. "Hungry."

"You're feeding on the wrong thing," Mia said. "Let the name go the right way and you'll have more than hunger."

Kaelan pulled a small charm from her sleeve and pressed it to Sia's staff just above the ferrule. "Grip set," she said. "If the pull climbs, it hits that line instead of your bones."

Sia flicked her eyes in thanks. She kept talking to the water. "You don't owe us," she said. "We promised to clean a river, and this is you asking in the only way you can. Tap once if you agree to share the name one time for repair. Tap twice if you want us to leave and call Winter to send a patrol later. Tap three times if you can't answer either way."

The middle naiad's hand, more ripple than hand, slid down and touched stone beneath the ice. Tap. The sound came up like a heartbeat. Then another. Then a third. Not refusal. Not a demand. An answer that also said they did not have the right kind of voice right now.

Sia breathed out. "Okay," she said. "We'll ask a different way."

She lowered the umbrella tip until it just kissed the black surface and set her other palm lightly on the shaft. She called up a memory of clean water from summers at the Farm, ankles cold in a creek, sun on the back of her neck, the world smelling like grass. She did not force it into the river. She held it like a mirror and let the ford see itself in a better light.

Fuzanglong tilted his head. "Good," he said softly. "Show, not shove."

The sound under the ice stuttered. The wrong syllable thinned. Beneath it, something truer moved. The naiads leaned toward it. This time they weren't tugged by a hook. They were reaching the same way Sia was.

"Quiet," Mia said, and drew the frost net a shade thicker, not to bind, to keep the echo from scattering. The pressure evened. The algae smell dropped to background.

A change ran through the glass. It wasn't a crack. It was an un-knotting. Sia felt letters she had not heard in years but somehow knew, the kind of name that isn't English or Latin or anything from Eric's books. River tongues care about banks, stones, spring floods that forget and remember at the same time.

The name reached her. A bright core buried under grime. One clean loop. Sia caught it without grabbing. She held it like a bubble in cupped hands and did not let it touch the wrong syllable.

"Got you," she said, barely above a whisper.

"Once," Kaelan said, reminding without nagging.

Sia nodded. She lifted the umbrella a finger's width and tucked the true name behind her teeth where the Dream would hold it without being rude. The naiads stilled, eyes brightening in the silt of their faces. Under the ford the wrong word hissed again, small and angry. It slid off the net Mia kept over the surface.

Bastian shifted his stance by half a toe, finding the center of the shelf. "If it fights when you say it right," he said, "we keep the mess off you."

"I know," Sia said.

Marcus dug his claws a little deeper through her coat. "No sneezing," he murmured.

"Please don't," she said.

She let her chest settle. Then she looked to each of them in turn. Kaelan, ready with paper and breath-fire. Mia, steady with frost and Winter at her back. Bastian, braced. Fuzanglong, a ribbon of calm. Marcus, small and determined. The ford. The wrong word. The right one curled safe and bright.

"Here's the deal one more time," she told the river, because clarity mattered. "We will speak your true name three times at the knot. Between the second and the third, we burn the false syllable out so the third holds clean. When your name seats, we close the seam. If anything crawls out before we finish, my friends keep it where it belongs. If you understand, tap once."

The middle naiad touched stone. Tap. The frost over the glass did not crack. It hummed like a tight wire.

Kaelan glanced at Mia. "Be ready," she said. Mia dipped her chin.

Sia eased the umbrella toward the center where Bastian had pointed. The push under the ice slid in her direction like a current deciding which way it meant to go. She did not speak yet. She set the tip where the beat of the wrong word felt strongest. The shaft picked up that rhythm and carried it into her hands. It wanted to make her say the wrong thing loud. She let it surge past. Then she waited until it faltered on its own.

"Now," she said. Not loud. Very clear.

Mia's frost veil thinned and flattened until it was the quiet in a classroom before a test. Kaelan's hands lifted to either side of Sia's shoulder, ready to pinch off air or feed it. Bastian planted his feet. Fuzanglong's whiskers drew in, storing motion. Marcus was a warm coin at Sia's neck.

Sia opened her mouth and let the first true syllable out.

It fell into the ford like a stone that belonged there. The wrong word jerked, surprised. Bastian held still. Mia kept the frost level. Kaelan let out a thin breath, and a fleck of foxfire slid across the surface and ate a scrap of grime. The middle naiad pressed both palms to the ice and did not sink.

Sia spoke the second syllable. The knot under the glass shifted hard, trying to twist the sound. The umbrella vibrated in her grip. She held the tone clean, the way Mariah taught her to hold a note when nerves tried to steal it. Kaelan blew a finer ribbon of foxfire under the ferrule, right where the false syllable lived. It burned fast and quiet. The pressure dipped.

Sia kept the third syllable behind her teeth and waited half a breath to feel the gap open. It did. Small. Enough.

She spoke the last part of the name, not louder, just exact.

The ford answered. The black glass did not shatter. It rippled. The wrong word slid off like oil and thinned into nothing. Water moved underneath with the right cadence, not perfect yet, but alive. The naiads' faces smoothed. Their eyes became eyes and not just holes where eyes might be. Hands that had been silt and habit became hands long enough to touch the ice and knock once, this time like thanks instead of a signal.

Sia didn't look away from the surface. "We aren't done," she said. She set the umbrella tip down again and felt for the seam that had taught the wrong name. It was still there, smaller than before, wound tight around an absence. She didn't pull. She marked it like she had the feeder streams, but deeper, tied to Winter's ledger and the Hunt's proof. One at sight. One above. One on the path the ford uses every spring when it runs high. The ring at her finger warmed and cooled once.

"Good," Kaelan said. "Hold it there."

Mia eased the frost veil back until only a thin skin remained. The algae smell dropped to normal creek breath. The pressure underfoot settled into a heartbeat that felt like a river remembering itself.

Bastian exhaled. "They gave us the name," he said to the water. "We'll keep our side of it."

The naiads dipped together. Not a bow. Something older. They sank back under the surface and did not vanish. Sia could still feel them there, not hungry now, just tired.

She stepped away from the bank and let the umbrella rest against her shoulder. Her hands tingled where the wrong rhythm tried to climb up her arms. Kaelan pressed a warm paper into her palm. "For the ache," she said. The charm's heat settled into Sia's skin like a small sun.

"Thanks," Sia said.

Mia scanned the tree line. "No movement," she said. "If something was waiting for us to mess that up, it lost interest."

"Or it is thinking about its next bad idea," Marcus said.

"Let it think," Bastian said. "We'll be here for the doing."

Sia checked the marks once more with her eyes, then with the quiet sense the Dream lent her when she earned it. The triad sat where it should. The true name held. The seam waited for the hard part, closing it without inviting anything to nap on the threshold.

"That's next," she said. "We cut. We sew. We keep the stitches in place."

"Eat first," Kaelan said, practical. "You sew better when your hands stop shaking."

Sia looked down and realized she was trembling just enough to notice. She let out the breath she had been saving since the naiads rose and gave herself the two seconds it took to stop.

"Okay," she said. "Snack, then stitches."

"Got it," Marcus said.

Mia gave the river one last look. The black glass had softened to a dark sheet with current that made sense. She let the frost net go. The surface didn't buck. It settled into its lane like a runner finding stride.

"Say when," Bastian told Sia.

She lifted the umbrella again and set her feet. The ford had told the truth once. The next part was work.

THEY ATE FAST. A heel of bread. A strip of dried meat. Enough to stop the shakes. Then everyone went back to places without needing to say who stood where.

The ford looked less like glass now and more like a dark window over muscle. The wrong beat had quieted, but the seam was still there, wound tight around an empty spot like a knot tied in air.

"Closing time," Sia said, more to the river than to them. She set the umbrella tip on the bank again. The true name waited behind her teeth, warm and bright. Not a secret. A key she had to turn in the right lock.

Bastian stepped out onto the shallow shelf. He used the axe like a staff and kept the blade behind him. Kaelan loosened a paper charm with her thumb and held her breath the way singers did before a hard note. Mia lifted her palm and let a thin frost gather at her fingertips, ready to drop it over the surface if the current tried to buck. Fuzanglong uncoiled from Kaelan's sleeve and lengthened to a bright ribbon that hovered just above the water. Marcus took a careful hop to Sia's wrist, claws set along the umbrella's grip.

The seam felt them getting ready. The surface trembled. Silt bloomed up from the riverbed in fat clouds. Something thumped under the ice and pressed at the thin spots like knuckles trying to punch through a drum.

"Steady," Sia said.

The river answered with trouble. Mud should not pick a shape on its own. This mud did. A man-sized lump hauled itself up along the shelf and sloughed into a thing with shoulders and no face. Two more followed, one heavy with bits of gravel stuck in its back, the other slick with a coat of thin ice. When they moved, the ice on them squealed. The sound made Sia's teeth ache.

A horn sounded somewhere in the trees. Once. Not a call for help. More like a witness. The Hunt had ears on them.

Bastian did not swing. He blocked. He used the axe haft to take the first mud-man at the chest and shove it back into the current. Its arms reached without hands. He stepped to keep it off the bank and let water do as much of the work as it wanted to do. When the gravel-backed one lunged, the edge of a tooth showed inside the clay where a rock had broken just right. That counted as a mouth. Bastian's blade flashed once and sheared the rocky jaw away. He went back to the haft as soon as the teeth were gone.

Mia flattened her palm. Frost crawled out in a sheet no thicker than an eggshell and pinned the slick one long enough for Bastian to push it sideways. The frost did not lock the river. It quieted the wrong motions like a heavy blanket on a restless kid.

"Lane," Sia said, and felt Marcus gather. He slid down to the umbrella head and stretched into a hawk-long serpent of light. He breathed a tight gout along the waterline, a careful strip of dragonfire that burned in a straight path without touching the banks. It cut a clean space between the shelf and the knot.

Fuzanglong drifted forward and dipped a whisker through the ice. The current obeyed him. He curled it into a slow spiral that made the knot show itself like a loose thread under cloth.

"There," Kaelan said.

Sia placed the umbrella tip over that spot. She built a small Dream lattice in the air, a simple grid no bigger than a doorframe. Nothing fancy. Clear lines, steady corners. It hung over the seam like a frame sits over a picture, giving the place a boundary to push against.

The mud-men shoved again. Bastian took the weight and gave it back with the haft. Mia added a second lace of frost where the ice-slick one tried to wriggle free. Kaelan breathed a thin line of foxfire under Sia's lattice, right where the false syllable had lived.

Sia spoke the true name. The first time, she said it for the river. The lattice tightened. The seam twitched like something realizing it had been seen. The current tried to push the sound sideways. Fuzanglong's spiral held it long enough for the word to seat.

The second time, Sia said it for the knot. The umbrella shivered in her hands as the wrong word under it tried to twist. Kaelan blew another thread of foxfire right across the center of the frame. It caught the last smear of the false name and burned it into a string of bubbles that popped and were gone.

The gravel-backed mud-man decided someone had moved his food. He dragged himself up over the shelf. Bastian lowered his shoulder and bumped it back so neatly it looked like dance. The ice-slick one broke free of the frost for a second and lurched toward Sia. Marcus met it with a narrow dart of flame that only touched the thin coat on top. The ice shrank and cracked like candy. The thing under it lost shape and fell forward in a lump.

Mia set her frost down again, only where she needed it, and kept it thin so the water could still run. She did not look like a queen or a statue. She looked like a girl who had learned a hard job and decided she could do it.

Sia waited for the gap she had felt before, that small place between wrong and right that opened if you gave it half a breath. It came. She spoke the name a third time. Not louder. Exact.

The lattice snapped into place. Not a crack. A click. The seam folded inward like a mouth closing after a yawn. Black glass softened. The pulse under their feet stopped trying to be a second heart and went back to the normal push and pull of a stream that had work to do.

The mud-men lasted two more seconds. The one with gravel in its back slumped and slithered apart into plain silt. The slick one lost the last of its shape and washed past Bastian's boots as a brown smear. The first one tried one more grab and fell apart at his shove like wet bread.

Silence held for a long beat. Then the ford breathed. Not the wrong breath. The right one. Tight and small, still healing, but right.

Sia let the umbrella down and felt for the seam again. It was no longer a wound. It was a scar with good edges. She set a final Dream mark inside the lattice and tied it to the two she had already placed. Three points, one binding. The ring on her finger warmed and cooled.

The naiads rose just enough to show their eyes and crowns of weed. No hunger now. No dragging pull. They pressed both palms to the underside of the surface and knocked once. The sound was clean, like a spoon on a glass.

"Thank you," Sia said. She did not say it three times. Once was enough.

Bastian stepped back to the bank and shook water from the hem of his cloak. He looked pleased in the quiet way he looked pleased with good work. Kaelan tucked her last paper away and smoothed her sleeves like a teacher between classes. Mia drew a breath and let it go, and the frost skim dissolved back into the air in a burst of glitter that fell and was gone.

Marcus shrank to palm size again and flopped along the umbrella head like a cat who had won a small argument with a laser pointer. "I did not sneeze," he said.

"You did great," Sia said, and scratched the ridge behind his head with her thumb.

From the trees, the horn sounded twice and then a third time, spaced like a stamp on paper. That felt like a message: seen, measured, approved.

"Wayhouses are ours for three days," Bastian said, hearing the same thing. "Beds and silence."

"Good," Mia said. "I would like a night where the floor does not hum."

The naiads slipped back under and did not vanish entirely. Sia could still sense them the way you sense a person in another room with the door open. The river smelled like clean cold again. Not perfect. Better.

Sia lifted the umbrella, turned the lattice once so the binding would settle evenly, and let it fade. The mark stayed even when the shape went away.

"That is one favor down," she said. "Earlking gets his river back. We get to keep walking."

Kaelan pointed with two fingers to a gravel bar that would dry boots fast. "Five minutes there," she said. "Then we climb for the trail."

Bastian nodded. "Five," he said. "Then the Wild."

Sia took one last look at the ford. The wrong word was gone. The right one sat where it belonged. She touched the ring and felt the quiet yes of Winter's ledger making note.

"Let's go," she said.

CHAPTER 15

Smiths & Healers

Sia

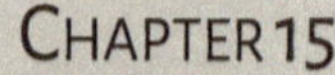

THE PATH BENT AROUND a knuckle of dark rock and opened on a ruined forge. Walls stood to half height, stacked stone black with smoke. The chimney was cracked near the top, but heat still breathed out of it like the place had a pulse. Iron smell. Wet ash. Old hammers laid on a bench that should have fallen apart years ago.

"Not abandoned," Bastian said quietly. He put two fingers on the anvil. "Warm."

A coal popped in the firebox. The sound ran around the circle of the room and came back as a voice.

"Warm is the point."

A man stepped out from behind the shadow of the chimney. He was broad through the shoulders, hair cut close, beard trimmed to keep it away from sparks. His hands looked like they had been washed in iron filings and never quite came clean. His eyes were the color of banked coals.

"Goibniu," Kaelan said, and dipped her head.

"Good." He looked them over, one by one, as if checking for loose bolts. His gaze paused on Mia, then moved on without comment, respectful but not impressed. It stopped at the umbrella hooked over Sia's wrist. "You brought a focus to a forge that makes edges. Interesting choice."

Sia lifted the umbrella a little. "It's what I have."

"Then it is what you learn." He pointed to the hearth. "The river was cleaned. I saw the mark of it. That paid the gate fee. The rest you earn."

A rack slid out from the wall on its own. Four chains hung from it, each with a flat iron plate at the end the size of a dinner plate. The plates were dull, but when Sia looked at them too long the air around them wobbled like heat over road.

Goibniu flicked a glance at Bastian. "Knight, you go second. Girl with the umbrella, show me you can push power through that frame without spilling it into my walls."

Sia swallowed and stepped forward. Marcus shifted on her shoulder, claws careful through her coat. "You have this," he said, barely above a whisper.

Sia planted the tip of the umbrella on the hearth stones and set her palm just above the ferrule. She built a small Dream lattice in her head. Clean lines. A single square. No flourishes. Eric would have smiled at the restraint.

"Only the plate," Goibniu said. He tapped the nearest chain with his knuckle. "If the chain glows, you spilled. If the wall hums, you spilled. If you make a mess, I will make you clean it before I let you leave."

"Got it," Sia said.

She drew a breath and pushed a narrow thread of power down the shaft. The umbrella thrummed in her hand. The thread touched the plate. It lit like a coin catching sun, then dimmed. The chain stayed dull. The wall stayed quiet.

Goibniu grunted once. "Again. Stronger."

She tightened the lattice a notch and fed a longer line. The plate glowed orange, then red. Heat pressed back into her fingers. She held the lane. The chain twitched and settled.

"Again. Add fire that is not your own."

Marcus slid down the umbrella and wrapped himself around the head. He extended, not full, just enough to lay his jaw along the edge. "On you," he said.

Sia angled the thread so Marcus's breath could ride it without touching the frame. He exhaled a thin gout, neat and white-hot. The plate blazed. The chain did not take it. The wall did not hum. The heat came back up the line like a test, and she kept it in the narrow lane she had set.

Goibniu watched, expression flat in the way of someone who only smiled when metal rang right. "Again," he said. "And now let the Winter in."

Mia lifted her hand. "I can keep the lane cool," she said. "I won't freeze your hearth."

"Do it," Goibniu said.

Sia felt Mia's frost gather like a steady hand over her shoulder. Not ice. Calm. The plate held at bright red. The heat that wanted to push into the chain found nowhere to go. Sia kept the thread exact until her knuckles ached from holding still.

"Enough," Goibniu said. He stepped in, took the umbrella by the steel pole, and weighed it like a craftsman checks balance. "You kept your lane. You did not lean on your helpers so hard the work fell apart when they breathed. That matters."

He set the tip back on the stones and looked at the crook of the handle. "What is it made of."

"Wood," Sia said. "I don't actually know the tree. It was my grandmother's."

He nodded once and laid his palm along the shaft. Heat rolled out of his hand and into the steel. He murmured words Sia did not recognize. Not Latin. Not any human language she knew. The metal took the sound like cloth takes dye.

Green light slid along the pole and through the inner lattice. Soft, not sickly. The steel looked the same until the light settled, and then it didn't. It held a sheen, as if a living leaf had been pressed into the metal and decided to stay.

"Frame first," Goibniu said. "A focus is only as good as the bones that carry it."

He thumbed the ferrule. The umbrella's red cloth hood lifted on its own and opened like a flower. Goibniu traced a finger along the seams. Faint runes woke in the weave, not flashy, just present, like stitches sewn with ember thread.

"You bend power," he said. "Let the cloth bend with you and hold the shape you mean, not the one the room tries to force on you."

The hood lowered. Sia blinked and realized the handle felt different in her hand. The wood was still wood, smooth under her fingers, the crook solid and familiar. But the pole and the inner lattice now held that soft green sheen like light under water. The cloth looked the same red, but the runes glowed if she tilted it toward the hearth.

He looked up at her. "Tell me what changed."

Sia steadied the umbrella and listened. "The frame will not break," she said. "It will flex and not fail. The hood is tuned to my focus so it strengthens what I'm aiming at instead of bleeding it into the air."

"Good," Goibniu said. "Say it in fewer words."

"Unbreakable frame. Runes that boost my focus."

He almost smiled. "Better."

Bastian stepped forward when Goibniu turned. The Green Knight unhooked his axe and held it flat across his palms, blade toward himself so he did not look like he was presenting a threat.

"Edge discipline," Goibniu said. "I don't bless hacks. I bless hands that know how not to ruin their own work."

"What do you want me to cut," Bastian asked.

"Nothing," Goibniu said, and sketched a line in the air with two fingers. A figure stepped out of the heat, shaped like a man and made of hammered cinder. It lifted its arms as if to grab.

Bastian did not chop. He slid in and checked its wrist with the haft, pushed its weight past its heels, and let it fall. When it tried to rise, he rapped the blade's flat across its forearm. Not a cleave. A correction. The figure paused, reconsidered its choices, and reached again. Bastian used the butt-cap to bump its knee and turn it. No splinters. No spray. The iron man fell a second time.

"Enough," Goibniu said, and let the figure go back into the heat. He took the axe, sighted along the edge, and nodded once. He set it on the anvil and laid his hand across the cheek. A straight line of pale shine ran along the blade and settled there like frost that would not melt.

"Your edge will stay true when it bites demon hide," he said. "If you swing to split bone you don't need to split, the blessing will go quiet until you remember you have hands and not a hammer."

"I understand," Bastian said.

Goibniu handed the axe back and faced Sia again. "Hold it up."

Sia raised the umbrella. The wood handle sat right in her grip, the crook familiar against her wrist. The steel pole and inner lattice shone with that soft green sheen, a quiet signal that felt like strength rather than a shout. The red cloth hood held faint runes along each rib, glowing like banked letters. The whole thing felt balanced. Hers.

"Thank you," she said.

"You cleaned a river," Goibniu said. "I watched you keep your lane. This is not a gift. It is the right tool for the work ahead." He wiped his hands on a rag and tucked it into his belt. "There is a healer down the track who likes to keep a quiet fire. Brigid. She will set your cold right, Winter Lady, and lay a calming knot so your mantle does not bite when you rest."

Mia nodded once. "Thank you."

Goibniu stepped back into the shadow of the chimney. "Do not drag dirt into her bothy," he said, and the forge breathed, and the heat settled like a blanket.

Sia looked at the umbrella again and smiled. "Okay," she said. "Let's go find the healer."

THE TRAIL LEFT THE forge like a warm breath cooling in a cup. It curled through firs that had learned to grow with snow on their backs, then broke into a clearing with a single stone hut. The bothy sat low and square, roof thatched in reeds and frost that did not melt. A thin column of light stood above the chimney instead of smoke, like the air itself had chosen to glow. The place felt settled. Not safe in the Summer way. Safe in the way of a well kept kitchen where knives are sharp and never point the wrong way by accident.

"Hospitality ring," Bastian said, nodding at a carved circle set into the lintel. "Marked this season."

Kaelan touched the stone with two fingers and pulled her hand back before the third tap. "Lawful," she said. "We do not open a bargain. We accept what is already paid."

Sia shifted the umbrella in her hand. The crook sat against her wrist where it belonged. The steel pole and lattice held a soft green sheen from Goibniu's blessing. The red hood kept its color low, runes along each rib settling like embers. She could feel the way the frame would flex and not fail. It made her shoulders loosen a little.

The door opened before they could knock. The woman in the doorway had black hair braided back, sleeves rolled to the elbow, and hands that could pick up a pot with a grip or pack a wound with the same sure pressure. Her eyes took them in without weighing them like coins. She looked at Sia's umbrella, glanced at Bastian's axe, and then set her gaze on Mia.

"Come in," she said. "You worked, so the food is yours. I am Brigid."

Mia blinked, caught between pride and the ache under her skin. "Thank you," she said.

The bothy smelled like baked bread, rosemary, and clean heat. A table waited with thick pottery bowls turned upside down. Hooks along the wall held ladles and iron tongs. Herbs hung in bundles from a beam, leaves dried to the edge of crumbling but not past it. A hearth sat in the corner. The flame was steady and bright and made no smoke at all. The light felt like good daylight and not like a bright lie.

Brigid pointed at a bench near the fire. "Winter Lady, sit," she said. Then, to the rest, "Bastian, keep your edge sheathed and your shoulders easy. Kaelan, if you carry shrine paper, keep it in your sleeves until I ask. Sia, keep that umbrella in your hand. I want to see if it tries to pick a fight with my hearth."

"It will not," Sia said, because the runes under the red cloth had moved when she stepped inside, not bristling, just settling into the room's rhythm.

Marcus hopped from Sia's shoulder to the table edge with careful claws. "I will not scratch anything," he told Brigid.

She gave him a look that almost smiled. "You can warm the spoons," she said, and set a bundle of metal on the stone beside him.

Fuzanglong's small river-drake form uncoiled a little from Kaelan's sleeve and dipped his head. "Your fire knows how to breathe," he said.

"It remembers," Brigid answered. She set a wide clay bowl on the table and poured water from a copper kettle. The water hissed and calmed. "And we help it remember."

She turned back to Mia. "Where does it hurt."

Mia tried to play it off with a shrug and failed. "Ribs. Back. It feels like a hand is still there sometimes. The burns pull when the mantle wakes up to check everything."

Brigid knelt and tapped the bench. "Shirt to the side," she said. "We will not be careless with modesty, but I need to see the truth of it."

Mia slid her coat off and rolled her shirt to show the ribs along her left side. The healed skin ran in new lines, pale and branching like frost on a window. The lines glowed faintly when she breathed in too fast. Sia's chest tightened just looking at them.

"Consent?" Brigid asked. She held her hands where Mia could see them. "I will lay fingers and then lay a charm. It will not steal will. It will not bind your choices. It will quiet a surge that is not useful to you."

"Yes," Mia said.

Brigid's fingers were warm but not hot. She pressed three points along the worst places and watched Mia's face, not the scars. On the third press, Mia's breath hitched, then eased.

"Good," Brigid said softly. "Your mantle is eager. It wants to prove itself. Eager weapons are like eager dogs. They protect and they bite the wrong thing if you let them choose how."

Mia let out a breath that sounded like a laugh that did not make it all the way to a joke. "I do not want to be a weapon."

"You are not," Brigid said. She went to the hearth and took three small coals with iron tongs. She set them in a shallow stone dish and shook a pinch of salt over them. "You carry one."

She dropped a twist of herb that Sia did not know by name onto the coals. The scent was sharp and clean, like pine and mint and snow together. Brigid poured a trickle of water into the dish. It sizzled, then steadied into a steam that felt like mountain shade.

She wrapped a length of rush cord loosely around her hand and dipped her fist through the steam. "This is not ice," she said to Mia. "This is the idea of cold that keeps shape without breaking. The charm is simple. It is a knot that asks your mantle to rest when there is no task. It will not stop you from choosing heat. It will stop heat from choosing you."

Mia nodded. "Okay."

Brigid held out her free hand. "Left wrist."

Mia gave it. Brigid touched the inside with her thumb. "Speak what you are and what you are not, once," she said.

Mia swallowed. "I am Mia Mason," she said. "I am not a storm that hurts the people I love."

Brigid tied the rush cord in a small, neat knot around her wrist bones. She drew the steam across it and whispered something that sounded like two words and a held breath. The knot cooled under Brigid's fingers. Frost bloomed there without spreading, a tiny white flower that did not drip.

Mia's shoulders went down like someone had lowered a weight she had been pretending not to carry. The light along her ribs dimmed to a steady pulse. Her breath evened.

"What do you feel," Brigid asked.

"Like I can hear myself again," Mia said. "The cold is still there. It is listening instead of shouting. My own thoughts are louder than the part that wants to snap at shadows."

"Good," Brigid said. "That is all it is meant to do. If you need to pull hard, the knot will not stop you. If you fall into heat without choosing, the knot will slow the fall until your head catches up." She tapped the rush once. "Do not wet it on purpose. If it gets wet by accident, it will hold. If it unravels on its own, it means the mantle has learned the lesson, and you do not need the knot any more."

"Thank you," Mia said, voice thick at the edges.

Sia had not realized she had been holding her umbrella like a shield. She let the crook rest in the hollow of her elbow. The red cloth shifted and showed a shadow of runes. Brigid's eyes flicked to it.

"We will make sure that blessing does not snag on Wild rules," Brigid said. "Not tonight. Eat first."

She flipped the bowls on the table. They were warm. She lifted a lid on an iron pot and ladled out stew that smelled like rabbit and roots. Bread went down on a board, still hot from somewhere that was not the hearth and also was. She paused with the ladle in her hand.

"The price was paid when you cleaned the river," she said. "You owe nothing here."

Kaelan relaxed. "Thank you for saying it out loud."

"I do not let people guess the cost," Brigid said. "Eat."

They did. The stew hit all the right notes after a day of work. Sia had two bites before she realized how hungry she was. Bastian ate thoughtfully, like food was part of a job and also part of being a person. Kaelan took small sips, then pushed her bowl toward Mia until Brigid slid another serving from nowhere and made the question silly. Marcus warmed the spoons the way he promised, then curled on the table edge near the herbs where it smelled nice.

"You cleaned a name before you cleaned a seam," Brigid said to Sia between bowls. "Not many remember to do that."

"It told us it wanted to be right," Sia said. "We just gave it a lane."

Brigid looked pleased in a way that did not need a smile. "You will be fine in the Garden when you find it."

Sia lifted her head. "What garden."

Brigid's mouth tipped. "Tomorrow," she said, and poured tea that tasted like hay and apple peel. "Tonight is for feeding and mending. Not for maps."

Mia flexed her hand, testing the knot. The frost flower held. She looked at Brigid. "How do I not mess this up."

"By not trying to be the mantle," Brigid said. "Be yourself and make the mantle do its job. If you do not know which is which, ask the people at your table. They will tell you when you are being you and when you are being the part that wants to be a story instead of a person."

Mia glanced at Sia. Sia nodded. "We can do that," Sia said.

"You already are," Brigid said. She stood and set a second pot near the fire to keep warm. "There are bed rolls in the corner. Two in the loft. The floor is heated under those stones if someone likes to sleep where they can see the door. If you use my sink, speak the thanks when the water runs clear."

"Thank you," Bastian said, automatic and honest.

Brigid pointed at his axe. "Your edge is bright," she said. "Try not to use it unless you must. It will want to prove itself, same as her cold."

"I will mind it," Bastian said.

Brigid looked at Sia one more time. "Keep the umbrella near your head while you sleep," she said. "Not because something will come. Because your dreaming is part of the work, and a focus by the pillow keeps the lines from tangling."

Sia touched the crook. "Yes, ma'am."

The room settled into the easy noise of people who have finished a hard day. Bowls scraped. Tea steamed. The fire kept its steady light. When Sia stood to carry dishes, Brigid took them from her and gave her a small wrapped bundle instead.

"For the road," Brigid said. "Bread that will not go stale until it smells like rain, and a bit of salt. If you salt your feet and then cross a running stream, tricks have a harder time sticking to you that day."

Kaelan raised an eyebrow. "That is a useful rumor to be true."

"It is true enough," Brigid said.

Mia touched the knot again. The frost did not sting. It just stayed. She looked steadier. Tired, but not hollowed out. Sia felt the bone-deep gratitude that comes when someone fixes a problem you did not have words for yet. She wanted to say something grand and could not find anything better than the simple thing.

"Thank you," she said.

"You are welcome," Brigid said. She glanced toward the door as if hearing a wind they could not. "Sleep. Morning will know what to say."

They made their space without fuss. Bastian took the warm stones by the door and tilted his head against the wall with the kind of rest that listens while it sleeps. Kaelan and Mia claimed the loft. Sia unrolled a bed by the hearth so the umbrella could sit between her pillow and the bricks. Marcus made a circle on the crook and snugged in like a ring.

The hearth light settled a shade lower. The herbs on the beam breathed out the last of their green. Brigid tidied a table that did not need tidying and let her hands slow.

Sia watched the green sheen on the umbrella's pole catch the fire, soft and clean. The runes under the red cloth glowed just enough to say they were ready when she was. Mia's breathing evened on the loft boards. Kaelan turned once and stilled. Bastian did not move at all.

Brigid set a small clay dish with a pinch of ash and a pinch of salt on the mantle. She looked like she might say the message she had held back, then did not. Tomorrow was close enough.

Sia closed her eyes. The bothy kept quiet like a promise. The fire hummed the same low note as Goibniu's forge, and the room held them without owning them. That was what real hospitality felt like. Not a debt. A right answer.

Sleep came the way a door closes when it was always meant to be shut.

Dawn came in quiet and stuck to the bothy like a second skin. Frost traced the window edge. The hearth kept its steady light. Brigid moved like the kind of morning that knew what to do without being told.

"Up," she said, and it did not feel like an order. More like a weather report.

They ate simple things, hot and filling. Mia looked brighter. The frost knot at her wrist sat like a tiny flower that had decided to stay. Sia checked her umbrella while the tea steamed. Wood handle, crook end. Steel pole and inner lattice with that soft green sheen from Goibniu. Red hood with faint runes along the ribs that woke when she turned it toward the fire. It felt balanced and sure.

Brigid wiped her hands on a cloth and held out her palm. "Let me set one last seam," she said to Sia. "Eachthighern's blessing came from Summer. It is clean, but Wild places like to catch loose threads. I will seal it so it answers to you first."

Sia passed the umbrella over. Brigid did not treat it like a relic. She treated it like a tool someone was going to use. She angled the hood open and checked the stitching at three points. She hummed a low note that matched the hearth, then pressed her thumb along a seam until the faint runes pulled tighter and settled. She did it again on the opposite rib. Then a third time, at the center point where the ribs met the pole.

"Rule of Three," Brigid said, almost to herself. "So the place hears you."

Sia felt the change under her fingers when Brigid handed it back. Not a new power. Less noise. The umbrella sat even more firmly in her grip, like the room had stopped arguing with it.

Sia's head kept turning old study notes into real things. Goibniu, the smith who poured perfect edges and poured perfect feasts, one hand for iron and one for bread. In stories his blades never missed and his mead never ran dry. Brigid, bright over three arts at once, healing and poetry and the forge, flame that warms and does not waste. And Aengus Óg, the one with the harp and the swans, a road-builder in dreams who finds the door that still wants to open. It felt strange and good to meet them as people after learning them as lines in a book.

"Thank you," Sia said.

Brigid nodded and looked around the table. "Count what you carry," she said. "Say it out loud so the road agrees."

They went around without making it a big ceremony. Bastian named the stamped Hunt writ and his oath to escort. Kaelan named her paper charms, the bread and salt pack Brigid had wrapped, and the debts she would not open unless asked three times. Mia named the frost knot and the cooling charm's plain purpose. Sia named the umbrella's blessings and the river name they had set right. Marcus tapped the crook with a claw and said, "I am here," which counted. Fuzanglong simply dipped his head. Brigid gave a small smile at that and let it stand.

"Good," Brigid said. "Listen, then. This is the part you came for."

She set a small flat stone on the table. A spiral and a tiny harp were carved into it. The same mark had appeared at the ford at dusk. She touched the spiral.

"The Dreaming keeps a garden," she said. "Keep your oaths and you will find the gate."

The words landed like clear water. No riddle. No catch in the phrasing. Sia felt the line click inside her three times.

Bastian tilted his head. "Straight enough," he said.

"It is," Brigid said. "But straight does not mean easy. The road from here bends through people who have good reasons to hide. You will pass the Unseen first if you want the fast way. Their forest refuses to be looked at. Do not pretend you can stare it down."

Kaelan nodded. "How do we announce ourselves without opening a debt."

"Do not offer names," Brigid said. "Offer work. Tell the Matron what you fixed at the river. She respects clean jobs more than bright reputations." Brigid's eyes flicked to Sia and Mia. "Do not use three taps or three knocks unless you mean to bind a thing. The Wild listens. If the Matron invites you to eat, she will say the price first. If she does not say it, you say no and wait."

"Got it," Mia said. She glanced at Sia's umbrella. "What about Summer and Winter on us. Does that make it worse."

"It makes you obvious," Brigid said. "Obvious is not bad if you tell the truth before someone else tells a prettier lie. You have Hunt writ for wayhouses two more nights. Use them and move. Do not loiter where the border likes to shift under your feet."

She slid the carved token toward Sia. "Keep this where it will not rub smooth. If you lose it, it means the one who left it does not need you to find him that way anymore."

Sia tucked the token into the inner pocket of her coat. "Aengus Óg," she said.

Brigid did not confirm or deny. "Youth is not about being young," she said. "It is about not giving up on a better line through a mess. That mark reads you as people who still try. Try smart."

She moved to the hearth one more time. From a small clay jar she took three grains of something black. Coal, but finer. She set them on the mantle and looked at Mia.

"If your cold jumps without asking," Brigid said, "hold one of these in your palm and count ten regular breaths. Not fast. The coal will take the edge and burn out. When it goes light, you can let go. Pocket the ash and throw it in running water later. That clears the slate."

Mia took the jar like it might break and nodded. "Thanks," she said. "For all of this."

Brigid's answer was a simple, "You are welcome."

They cleaned their bowls and thanked the sink when the water ran clear. Brigid checked the door, then paused with her hand on the latch.

"One more," she said. "If someone offers you three chances to step off your road, that is not mercy. That is a trap that wants you to say yes and make it binding. Say no the first time and keep walking."

Sia breathed out. "We will."

Brigid opened the door. Morning hit like a fair deal. Cold, but honest. The bothy's roof glittered. The clearing looked the same as the night before, only less crowded with shadows.

Bastian adjusted the strap on his axe. "Which way to the Unseen's line."

Brigid pointed between two firs that made an arch without trying. "North by the tree with the split crown. Walk until your eyes want to slide off what is in front of you. That will mean you made it. Do not stare. Name your work and wait to be seen."

Kaelan looked at the arch. "Noted."

Brigid turned to Sia one last time. "Keep that focus by your head when you rest," she said. "Not because of monsters. Because you dream the shape of things, and your own tool keeps the lines from tangling. You already know this. I am saying it out loud so the road hears it too."

Sia felt her face heat and laughed at herself. "Okay. I will."

Mia shrugged on her coat. The frost knot sat neat at her wrist. She lifted it toward Brigid. "If this unravels on its own, that is good, right."

"It means you learned what it was trying to teach," Brigid said. "It means you can carry the quiet without help."

Mia smiled, small and real. "Then I will do my homework."

Brigid's mouth tipped. "Good. Go."

They stepped out into the crisp air. The bothy's door shut behind them and the sound was gentle. Sia turned back once and saw Brigid in the window, not waving, just there. The steady kind of goodbye.

They checked packs. Bastian tucked the bread and salt into a side pouch. Kaelan sealed her sleeve where the charm papers lived. Marcus settled on the umbrella crook with a little huff, then made himself comfortable. Fuzanglong rode Sia's shoulder for a few steps, then drifted to Mia's, approving of the new calm.

"Unseen first," Sia said.

"Then the Garden," Mia said.

"Then whatever Pride thinks he can throw," Bastian added.

"Then we keep our oaths," Kaelan said, because saying it once mattered.

They took the path Brigid had pointed out. The trees arched. The light shifted to that thin, clean brightness that lived in the first hour after sunrise. Sia kept the carved token warm against her chest and the umbrella balanced in her hand.

As they walked, Sia kept a mental file on the three who had brushed their road. Goibniu was the old lesson that sharp tools and good bread come from the same honest heat. Brigid was the living hearth, the poem and the bandage and the steel, three bright jobs inside one patient person. Aengus Óg was the reminder that some doors only open if you keep your heart young enough to try a second path. She knew the stories. She knew them better now.

Behind them, the steady light over the bothy's chimney rose and thinned into the sky. The door stayed shut. The Rule of Three pulsed in Sia's head like a heartbeat she could keep time with. Keep your oaths and you will find the gate.

She believed it. She put her boots where belief asked her to. And the Wild opened enough to let them through.

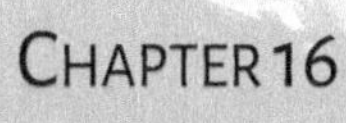

CHAPTER 16

The Unseen

Sia

By MIDMORNING THE TRAIL stopped pretending to be a trail. Sound got soft like someone put blankets over the trees. The air cooled without wind. Sia felt it first in her teeth and then behind her eyes, a gentle slide like the world was trying to ease her focus a few inches to the left.

"Here," Bastian said, voice low. He pointed with his chin, not his hand. Two firs arched together ahead, not quite touching. The space between them felt important without trying.

Kaelan lifted a palm. "We step in on my count," she said. "No names. No titles. We state what we fixed. One line. Then we wait."

Sia tightened her grip on the umbrella's crook. The steel pole held the soft green sheen from Goibniu's blessing. The red hood showed a faint line of runes when she turned it. The tool felt calm in her hand and that helped.

Mia touched the rush knot at her wrist. The tiny frost flower Brigid had set there stayed cold, not biting. "Answer once," she said to herself, like a reminder.

"Once," Sia echoed.

They crossed under the arch. Sound dimmed another notch. The forest was right there and also not. When Sia tried to focus on a trunk, her attention slid off to a shadow or a patch of moss that suddenly looked very interesting. If she pushed, the slide got worse. If she let her eyes go soft, the shapes held better.

A seam-stitch on the cloth pack Brigid had tied for them warmed just once against Bastian's hip. He glanced down and eased a little. "She marked us," he said. "Hospitality noted, not owed."

Sia let a tiny Dream spark fall off the tip of the umbrella to the soil. It landed, then dimmed to almost nothing, a dot only she would notice if they had to turn back. She waited a dozen steps and set another. Not a line. Breadcrumbs for eyes that could be tricked.

The hush wasn't empty. It was full of listening. Marcus shrank tight against the umbrella crook, keeping his claws gentle. "Everything hears here," he whispered. "Even the things that are not trying."

Fuzanglong rode Mia's shoulder like a pale ribbon of river light. "Do not insist on being seen," he said. "It reads like a threat."

Kaelan stopped at a patch of ground that looked like every other patch of ground. She set her feet, smoothed her sleeves, and spoke into the hush.

"Work done," she said. "We cleaned a ford that had forgotten its name. Half-tainted naiads are well again. The current holds the true cadence."

She closed her mouth and did not add anything. Not the Earlking's writ. Not Summer. Not who they were. She let the words sit.

The forest breathed. It felt like a held inhale deciding whether to exhale.

A voice drifted from somewhere that was not a mouth. "Who speaks."

Mia's fingers twitched. Sia made herself look at the ground near her boots and not into the trees. Kaelan did not lift her chin. She did not answer again.

"Who commands," the same not-voice asked, closer, as if leaning in.

Bastian's shoulders stayed loose. He kept his hands open. Sia felt the itch to fill silence, to be polite, to prove they were fine people, not problems. She held it down. Rule of Three. One answer given. Two more would turn polite into binding.

Leaves rustled on the right in a way wind never does. A smooth, curious tone, like someone humming a question behind a door.

The hush waited, and so did they.

Mia's frost knot cooled another degree, checking the mantle before it woke up on its own. Marcus pressed his head against Sia's thumb. "Good," he breathed. "Let them lead."

A different sound came from ahead, a single reed note held and then cut. The pressure in the air eased the smallest amount. The space in front of them blurred, then drew a narrow lane out of the gray, just wide enough for two to walk side by side if they did not mind shoulders brushing.

Kaelan nodded once to the empty air. "Thank you," she said, and stopped there. She did not make it three.

They followed the lane. If Sia tried to look past the path, her eyes slid again. The trick was to let the lane be the only thing worth looking at. She set another dim tick on the ground at a turn and felt the place notice and decide it was not an insult.

They passed a shape that might have been a watching post grown from dark glass and living wood. It did not want to be counted. Sia let it be a feeling instead of a number. Footsteps paced them above and to the left. She did not look. If she named the watchers in her head, her thoughts would snag. She kept them as "someone" and moved on.

A small branch broke with an intentional snap to their right. Bastian slowed half a step and then matched the lane again. It read like a test to see if they would chase sound off the path. They did not.

"Left," a child's voice whispered behind Sia's ear, warm breath against the fine hairs at her neck.

She didn't turn. "No," she said, just once, soft and sure, a word for herself more than for the whisper.

The lane bent left later on its own.

They came to a place where the path narrowed to a seam between two black-barked trunks. Kaelan raised her hand, palm open, and paused. The seam opened enough to let them through. Her sleeve brushed the bark and came away clean. No hooks, no thorns. The place had rules and those rules were being careful with them because they had been careful first.

A second reed note sounded ahead, then stopped. Sia felt the strange sensation of walking into a room where the furniture was already set and the hosts were already watching from a place you could not point to.

The lane opened into a circle of ground with no leaves on it. Not swept. Agreed clear. Across the circle a hall waited, grown from living boughs and panes of dark, shined wood. Starlight seemed to move under its surfaces even though it was daytime. Doorways stood open but held their own shadows. Two sentries flanked the entrance with eyes like night water. They did not look at faces. They watched where hands were.

Kaelan stopped at the circle's edge. She glanced back to make sure the line held. Bastian stood slightly off Sia's right shoulder, not blocking, just present. Mia kept her hands visible and the frost knot quiet. Fuzanglong dimmed his glow until he was a suggestion of river under snow. Marcus folded his wings close and sat like a brooch on Sia's umbrella.

The not-voice returned, clearer now and shaped by someone close. "Work named. No names given. No gates pushed."

Kaelan inclined her head a fraction. She did not speak.

Something like satisfaction moved across the hall's plain. Not a smile. An adjustment. The air in the doorway changed from "closed but polite" to "open with terms."

"Enter," the voice said. "Do not offer names. Do not ask ours. Say what you want in one line."

Kaelan let out the breath she had been holding and stepped forward first, as caller, feet careful not to scuff the clear ground. The others matched her pace. Sia felt the tick marks she had dropped behind them cool and go quiet, agreeing they were not needed now. Admission granted without debt. The forest had decided to see them.

Under her hand the umbrella felt steady and ready. The Rule of Three sat in her head like a metronome. One answer. One ask. One binding when it mattered. The rest would be noise, and the Unseen had already told them how they felt about noise.

They crossed the threshold into the hall of a people who preferred to be a rumor. The hush followed, respectful, and stood behind them like a door that would close if they forgot their manners.

THE HALL WAS GROWN, not built. Branches arched into ribs and set dark panels between them, the wood polished until it held starlight even in daytime. Two sentries waited at the threshold with open hands. They did not stare at faces. They watched where hands might move.

Kaelan stopped one step inside. "Work done," she said, voice steady. "We cleared a fouled ford and ask safe passage toward the Three-Stone Sleep barrow, with counsel for crossing Wild seams."

A soft reed note answered from somewhere high. Frost eased off the air.

A woman stepped out from shadow like the room had been saving her for this moment. Ash dusted her skin, hair black with thin silver threads braided through. Her eyes held night water brightness. She did not sit. She stood and let the hall arrange itself around her.

"You did not bring names to hang on us," she said. "Good. Names drag extra doors into rooms."

Kaelan inclined her head. "We were told to offer work, not reputation."

"Then say what you carry," the woman said. "One line each."

Kaelan: "Shrine papers and the memory of a river set right."

Bastian: "An oath to escort, sworn clean."

Mia lifted her wrist, frost knot neat and small. "A charm that keeps the mantle calm until I need it."

Sia kept the umbrella in her hand. "A focus that will not break, and a ford that remembers its name."

On Sia's crook, Marcus tipped his head. "And a dragon who fits in a pocket."

The sentries' mouths almost smiled. The woman's expression did not change, but something in the hall relaxed.

"And you," she said, looking to the pale coil on Mia's shoulder.

Fuzanglong bowed, just enough. "A river that remembers how to move around stone."

"Enough," the woman said. She studied Mia a breath longer, then Sia, then the red hood with its faint runes. "Winter walks with you. Summer's flavor follows. The Hunt knows your boots. This would be noise if you had tried to make us hold it for you. You did not."

A slot in the far wall let down a thin spill of water into a wooden basin. No cups. No bread. Just clear water waiting.

"We drink after the price is spoken," the woman said. "So there is no confusion."

Kaelan nodded. "Name it."

"Our border holds a soft seam," the woman said. She drew a line in the air with one finger and the line hung there, a wet thread. "It is not open. It wants to be. We blunt it at dawn and dusk. We want a ward that holds when hands are elsewhere. Drawn true. Not copied. Made by someone who knows how to ask a place to behave without breaking it."

Her eyes settled on Sia. "That is the work."

Sia's fingers tightened on the crook. "I can do it."

"In return," the woman said, "we lend you a pathfinder for one league in our wood, and we teach our wards to read your tool as friendly if you cross our edge again." She glanced at Bastian. "Your escort vow will not snag on our rules while you carry it."

Bastian dipped his head. "Understood."

"Plain terms," the woman said. "Say them back so the room hears them, or say no and walk out clean."

Sia raised her hand to match the woman's open palm. "I will draw a true ward for the seam you name," she said. "You will lend a pathfinder for one league and mark my focus so your wards do not bite. No extra favors. The price ends when you touch the ward and the seam stays quiet."

The hall took it in like a single breath. No flare of ritual. Just a click of agreement that everyone could feel. The water cleared the last cloud from its surface.

"Drink," the woman said.

They cupped water in their hands. It tasted cold and simple. The slide at the edges of Sia's vision finally let go.

"Lore for your road," the woman said. "We are elves who would not kneel and would not fall. We keep edges so maps still work for Heaven and Earth. That is why we do not love names. Names are extra fences. We have enough fences to mind."

Mia listened hard. "Does the Dreaming going quiet make seams worse."

"Yes," the woman said. "Quiet makes bad listeners brave."

Kaelan looked to Sia. "Our next waymark is a garden. We were told that keeping our word would show the gate."

"Then keep it," the woman said. "Do not chase friendship to buy speed. Do not stare into places that want to stay to the side of your eyes. If you are invited to eat, the cost will be said before you touch the plate. If it is not said, refuse and wait."

A shadow near the right doorway slid into the shape of a person without a sound. A runner, lean and unadorned, ash-touched patterns along cheek and brow, eyes dark enough to keep more than light. No weapon in sight. Their attention sat in their feet and shoulders like they were already halfway down a trail.

"Pathfinder," the woman said, as if that were enough of a name. She lifted two fingers and brought them near the umbrella's hood. A clean sign, no bigger than a thumbnail, lit and sank under the red cloth's runes. It felt like a door in the tool had just learned a familiar knock. She brushed Bastian's peace tie next. A pale sigil settled into the rush cord and went still.

"Our wards will know you," she said. "Your vow will not argue with ours."

"Thank you," Bastian said.

"The price ends when your ward holds under my hand," the woman said. "If it fails, we wash it away and forget you came."

"It will hold," Sia said. "I will draw what the seam asks for, not what I want."

The woman's gaze stayed on her a beat, then she nodded. "Good. We prefer listeners to speechmakers."

The runner made a small sound in their throat, like a reed note without the reed. The woman answered with a lift of her chin. "Go," she told them. "Three-Stone Sleep is one league if you learn to look the right way. The path bends."

Sia adjusted the umbrella. The steel pole's green sheen picked up a slice of the hall's light. The runes under the red cloth stayed dim. Ready, not loud.

Mia touched her knot. It felt steady. "We will do the work," she said.

"You will," the woman said. She did not bless them. She did not wish them luck. She stepped back into the deeper part of the hall and the sentries breathed like a room coming off pause.

Kaelan led them out the way they came in, same careful pace, no extra words. At the threshold Sia glanced at the basin. The water reflected her face like a plain mirror. No hooks hiding in it.

Outside, the hush met them without pressing on their eyes. The runner stood at the lane's edge and lifted a hand, not quite a wave. They shaped three fingers into a simple sign that meant follow.

They did, and let silence be part of the agreement. The bargain was made. The road would listen. The rest was just doing the job.

THE RUNNER SET AN easy pace, light on their feet, eyes never fixed on any one thing for long. They carried no visible weapon, only a short reed at the throat that gave a soft note now and then. When the note sounded, the forest lanes seemed to tilt so the next bend appeared on its own.

They brought the group to a shallow swale where the ground held a tired kind of damp. The air felt thin, like a room before a storm. Sia's skin prickled. The seam was not open, but it wanted to be.

The runner lifted a hand and stopped. They pointed to a stand of birch. White bark peeled in long curls like paper waiting to be used. Kaelan met Sia's eyes and nodded once.

Sia chose a sheet no bigger than her palm and eased it free. She set the umbrella across her lap and let the crook anchor her breathing. The red hood's faint runes settled. The steel pole's green sheen caught the gray light. She closed her eyes long enough to listen.

It came as a pattern more than a picture. The seam pulsed off beat with the land, a soft push and pull that did not belong to this place. Sia breathed with it until she could feel where the rhythm wanted to snag, then opened her eyes and drew. She did not sketch a lock. She sketched a habit. Curves that taught the ground to remember its own weight. Lines that asked water to choose the older channel instead of the new itch.

Kaelan stood at her shoulder with shrine paper ready. "Edges," she said softly.

"Edges," Sia answered, and finished the last turning mark.

Kaelan sealed the birch with four neat touches at the corners. Mia held the finished bark between her hands and blew a slow breath over it. Frost formed in a thin skin that did not crack. The lines held under it, not trapped, just set.

Fuzanglong flowed from Mia's shoulder to the birch stand and touched each tree with his snout. When he reached the ward, he breathed the hint of a river on it. Not a wetness. A memory of flow.

Bastian faced the open ground and planted his boots. He did not raise his axe. His body language made it clear he was here to keep the work from being interrupted, not to make a show.

Marcus crouched on Sia's umbrella and watched the air as if it might grow claws. "Hurry is the enemy here," he said under his breath.

"I know," Sia said.

The runner watched her hands, not her face. Their expression never changed, but when she finished the last small line and the frost settled clean, they gave a single reed note that sounded like approval.

Sia stood and looked at the seam. Nothing dramatic shifted. Good. She did not want dramatic. She wanted quiet. She walked to the spot where the air felt thin and pressed the birch bark to it like a bandage. For a second, the ward did not catch. She adjusted her grip and moved it a finger's width lower, where the pull was strongest. The birch touched and held. The pressure against her palm eased, like a muscle unclenching.

The runner tilted their head and listened to the ground. After a moment, they cut the reed note short. The lane they had arrived on drew itself back into shape. The swale felt heavier in a way that made Sia's knees want to bend.

A rustle moved through the trees behind them. Not a threat. The hall's sentry stepped out of shadow with the Matron at their side. She came without a train of attendants, without anyone to say her name. She walked to the swale and set her hand where Sia's had been.

The Matron closed her eyes for a heartbeat. When she opened them, the lines around her mouth had softened. "It holds," she said. She looked at the birch. "Drawn for the place, not for your pride."

Sia let out air she did not realize she had been holding. "We wanted it to work when we were gone."

The Matron touched the ward again, then traced a small sign in the air over Sia's umbrella, a sister mark to the one she had set in the hall. It warmed under the red cloth and went quiet again.

"Our wards will know you," she said. She brushed her fingers over Bastian's peace tie. The pale sigil there steadied. "And your vow will not argue with our law."

Bastian bowed his head a fraction. "Appreciated."

The runner brought their hand to their throat and gave a short reed call. The forest answered with nothing more than ordinary quiet. The Matron watched the line for another breath, then turned to Kaelan.

"You offered work and paid it," she said. "Your ledger with us is closed."

Kaelan dipped a shoulder. "Thank you for saying it out loud."

"We do not leave people guessing," the Matron said. She looked to Mia. "Your cold has learned to listen. Keep it that way. If it tries to lead, tell it what road you are on."

Mia lifted her wrist and checked the frost knot. It sat neat and calm. "I will."

The Matron faced Sia again. "Your road bends toward the barrow. The runner will walk you to the edge of our wood and no farther. When you reach stones that look like they grew from sleep, do not count them aloud. People get stuck counting."

"Got it," Sia said.

The Matron stepped back. She did not bless them. She did not ask for thanks. She seemed satisfied that the work matched the price.

The runner set off without a word. The lane found itself ahead of their feet, always narrow, always just visible if they did not try too hard to see it. The hush lightened the closer they came to the Unseen border. Sia felt the umbrella lighten in her grip in the same measure.

They walked for a while that could have been twenty minutes or an hour. The forest folded around them and then opened by degrees. At one bend, the runner paused and pressed two fingers to a patch of moss. When they lifted their hand, Sia saw a faint carved mark underneath, a spiral with a little line like a harp string set beside it. Not the same token Brigid had given them, but a cousin to it. She did not touch it. She only memorized the shape and felt her chest lift.

"Someone is building roads that are not on maps," Kaelan murmured.

"Or keeping old ones from vanishing," Bastian said.

The runner gave a small reed note and moved on. The trees thinned. The light changed from blue-green to a clearer white. Ahead, a rise of land showed through the trunks. Flat stones stood there, three heavy slabs sunk into the earth as if they had pushed up from below and then fallen back asleep on purpose.

The runner stopped at the line where the Unseen's wood ended. They lifted a hand and made a simple gesture that meant this is as far as I go. No speech. No name. Just the rule.

"Thank you," Sia said.

The runner touched two fingers to the place over their heart and then to the small sign hidden under the umbrella's red hood. They slipped backward into the trees and vanished without breaking a twig.

Bastian looked over the rise where the stones waited. "Three-Stone Sleep," he said. "We are pointed right."

Sia checked the birch she had used for the ward. The bare peel she had taken looked neat, not raw. The seam behind them held its quiet. Debt paid.

"Next job," Mia said. She rolled her shoulders and set her coat right. "Let's go see who sleeps."

Sia tightened her grip on the umbrella's crook. The tool felt steady and sure. Marcus settled a little deeper on the crook like he trusted this path. Fuzanglong's small form gleamed along Mia's collarbone. Kaelan smoothed her sleeve where the charm papers lived.

They stepped off the Unseen's edge and started up toward the stones. Behind them, the forest closed its attention like a book that had been read and returned to the shelf in good order. Ahead, the barrow kept its own counsel and waited to see if they would approach with the same care.

CHAPTER 17

Elemental Chaos

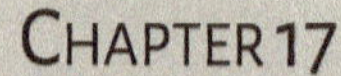

SIA

THE CLIMB TURNED ROUGH fast. The trail rose into broken rock that looked like it had cooled in a hurry and then cracked itself to pieces. Heat leaked from thin seams in the ground. Not hot enough to burn, just enough to say this place had a pulse. The air had a faint sulfur bite. It thrummed off beat with the land in a way that made Sia's skin crawl.

"Volcanic," Bastian said, checking the ground with the toe of his boot. "Or it used to be."

"It still remembers," Sia answered. She balanced the umbrella in her hand and let the crook steady her wrist. The steel pole kept its soft green sheen. The red hood's faint runes showed when the light caught them. The tool felt calm. She did not.

Mia tugged her sleeve down over the small frost knot Brigid had left on her wrist. "The mantle wants to posture," she said, honest and annoyed. "I'm telling it to sit."

"Keep it quiet," Kaelan said. She moved ahead two steps, then froze. Her eyes tracked empty air across the saddle of the ridge. "There is a net here," she said. "Not rope. Glamour."

Sia tried to focus where Kaelan looked and felt her attention slide away. The saddle between two black outcrops looked normal and also wrong. Heat shimmered there like a mirage. Every time she blinked, the saddle seemed an inch farther to the left.

Kaelan pulled a set of shrine papers from her sleeve. "If we walk into that, it snaps," she said. "It will yank us sideways. Then the ridge does the rest."

"Can you cut it without setting it off," Bastian asked.

"Yes," Kaelan said. "But I need the line to stop moving."

Sia planted the umbrella tip and touched Dream sight just enough to see the net's edges. Thin threads ran from rock to rock, catching light that was not there. She lifted the umbrella and drew three small marks in the air. Not bright. Just enough to tell the net where to stand still.

"Now," Sia said.

Kaelan stepped to the nearest anchor point and pressed a paper charm to the air. The paper stuck to nothing and everything at once. She moved to the middle, did it again, then to the far side. Three papers in a row. The heat shimmer stopped crawling.

"Cut," she said.

She snapped her fingers once. The papers flashed like camera bulbs. The shimmer fell apart and slid down the rocks like a bad idea losing confidence. The saddle settled into one place and stayed there.

Bastian let out a breath he had been holding. "Good catch."

Kaelan tucked the empty paper slips away. "Someone wanted us to trip," she said. "Or rush."

"Slow," Marcus said from the umbrella crook. "If we hurry, we'll mess this up."

Sia nodded. She set the umbrella tip to stone and felt for the rhythm under her boots. The ground pulsed. Not angry. Hooked. Like something had put nails through a living thing and told it to move on command. The heat in the seams spiked in short, ugly bursts that did not match the sun or the slope.

"Elementals," Marcus said, reading her face. "Bound ones. Not natives acting out. Someone put iron on them."

"Hooks," Sia said.

He dipped his head. "Black iron thorns are common for this trick. If you blast the bodies, you leave the hooks. Then they grow new bodies. You want the ties, not the faces."

Mia glanced down the ridge. Dust lifted in small spirals and then fell like it remembered gravity late. "How many."

"Three wakes," Fuzanglong said. He uncoiled from Mia's collarbone and hovered, pale and thin as river light. "Two smaller. One in the core." He lowered to the ground and skimmed the seams. "Sulfur is loud. The safe stones are dull. Step where I mark."

He breathed a faint, colorless curl across a line of rock. The marks were not wet, but Sia could feel the difference underfoot. The dull stones held. The shiny ones wanted to slip.

Bastian lifted his axe and checked the peace tie. "Anchor point." He picked a flat spot where the ridge narrowed and the team could set their backs to rock. "If it breaks here, it breaks slow."

Kaelan looked over the saddle one more time and shook her head. "The air will lie to us when they wake. I can pin the echoes." She drew more papers and held them like cards. "Just keep your feet where they belong," she added, eyeing Sia and Mia. "Do not chase a fake shadow off the edge."

"Copy," Mia said, then grimaced. "I mean, got it."

Sia smiled without looking away from the ground. "We hold and free," she said. "Not scorch the hill."

Marcus flexed his claws. "Measured fire," he said. "Give me the signal and I feed you heat in lines, not a flood."

Sia lifted the umbrella a fraction and ran through the moves in her head. Bands, not blasts. Clean lines across anchor points. She could cut ties if she did not cook the slope.

The ridge tremored as if someone had knocked on a door under their feet. Dust jumped. A seam of heat brightened and then went flat. The air thickened. Sia braced.

The first elemental pulled itself out of a crack to their left. It had a body like stacked plates of black stone with orange light leaking between. Iron thorns stuck through its shoulders like someone had nailed it into its own shape. It turned a face toward them, a blank wedge of hot rock with a single bend like a brow.

The second rose near the right, smaller, faster, same thorns punched through joints. Between them, a coil of dust twisted into a short, mean whirlwind and tried to blind the team.

Kaelan slapped a charm into the spinning grit. The paper stuck in the air and the dust-devil fell apart like a bag with a cut bottom. She flicked two more papers and pinned the fake shimmer that tried to make the ridge look lower than it was.

"Eyes front," she said. "What looks easy is a lie."

The ground under Bastian's boots jumped. He set his stance and met the smaller elemental's first swing with the flat of his axe. He did not aim for the head. He chopped for the iron thorn punched through its elbow. The blow rang. The thorn cracked but did not break. The elemental's arm jolted like a limb waking from numbness.

Fuzanglong rolled a thin wall of river between Bastian and the heat. It hissed when sparks hit it and held in a tight sheet, not a flood.

The larger elemental took one step toward them and drew heat out of the seam under its feet. Black iron hugged its torso like barbed wire. Sia saw four anchor spots the thorns fed. Two she could reach. Two were turned away.

"Now, Marcus," she said.

He leaned into the crook. Heat bled into her grip, not a burn, a clean line of power. Sia raised the umbrella and drew a band of dragonfire across the nearest set of thorns. The flame did not spread. It cut. Black iron glowed dull red, then snapped in two with a noise like a nail giving way in old wood.

The elemental staggered. Its head swung toward her. It opened a seam in its chest like a mouth to throw heat back.

"Left," Kaelan called, and slammed a charm into the air. The elemental's aim bent. The blast hit rock and ran up the wall where it could not hurt anyone.

Mia stepped forward and raised her hands. The frost knot on her wrist went cold enough to fog the air. She spoke a short Winter word that sounded like ice forming on a pond. White lines wrapped the big elemental's legs. Not to break. To hold.

It strained, but the hold took. The iron thorns kept catching heat and carrying it into the wrong places. Sia could feel them like splinters in skin that wanted to heal.

"Second tie," Marcus said, voice tight. "Low right."

Sia shifted and drew another clean band through the thorns on the elemental's hip. The iron went red, then black, then fell in two dull pieces to the stone. The heat coming off the creature dropped a notch. Its body flickered like a flame that forgot why it was lit.

Bastian broke the smaller elemental's elbow thorn with a downward chop. It screamed like coal cracking in a stove and swung with the other arm. He stepped inside and smashed the second thorn. The plates of its forearm slid into a new shape and stopped trying to hit him. It swayed, lost, then sagged toward the ground. Fuzanglong's thin wall kissed it and took the hiss without boiling.

"Third hook," Marcus said. "Back plate. You cannot see it."

"I can feel it," Sia said. She set her feet, lifted the umbrella, and pulled the band through the space where the hook tugged. The world liked that choice. The band landed where it should. The iron cracked. Mia tightened the hold before the elemental could buck.

Kaelan pinned one more shimmer that tried to fake a gap in the rocks near Sia's left heel. "Focus," she said, flat and calm. "Do not trust the easy steps."

Sia breathed and kept the umbrella steady. The air kept thrumming wrong, but the rhythm was breaking up. The large elemental stopped straining against Mia's bind and shuddered like a headache leaving. The last iron thorn sat near the center of its chest, sunk deep.

"Core hook," Marcus warned. "If you cut it messy, the shell will throw heat and crack the ridge."

"Then we do it clean," Sia said. She met Mia's eyes. "On my mark, hold tight. Bastian, if it twists, go for the plate above the hook, not the hook. Split the load."

"Ready," Bastian said.

"Ready," Mia said, and set her feet harder.

Sia drew the last band. Not a slice. A steady pull. The iron heated, sang, then gave up and broke with a single dull snap. Bastian brought his axe down in the same breath and split the top plate just enough to stop a twist. Mia's bind tightened, then eased.

The big elemental's shoulders lowered. Heat bled out of the seams in the rock and settled into a steady warmth. The creature turned its blank wedge of a face toward the ridge like it had been listening to the wrong song and finally heard the right one. It sank back into the stone without a fight. The smaller one followed, sliding into a seam that no longer sparked.

Sia kept the umbrella ready and checked the ground with a slow turn. No more hooks pulled. The air still smelled like sulfur, but the off beat thrum was gone.

Kaelan lowered her hands and let the last charm burn itself out in her palm. "Net will re-knit by nightfall," she said. "We should be off this saddle before then."

Mia flexed her fingers. The frost knot cooled to its usual small chill. "Bind held. No backlash."

Bastian listened with his eyes half closed. "The ridge is calmer," he said. "Whatever was shouting at it is done for now."

Marcus eased his grip on the crook and lay along the umbrella like a cat that had decided to nap later. "Hooks first," he said. "Every time."

"Hooks first," Sia echoed. She let herself smile for a second, then looked down slope. Heat shimmered over a dark face of rock, then lifted like a breath leaving. On the ridge above them, a faint spiral with a single harp line showed in cooled slag. It was not bright. It was enough.

"We move," Bastian said, following her gaze. "While the road wants us."

HEAT ROLLED THROUGH THE ridge and kicked the ground off beat. A plate of black stone pushed up on Sia's left, orange light leaking from seams, iron thorns punched through its shoulder like nails. Another hauled free on the right, smaller and quicker. Dust whipped into a tight spiral between them.

"Eyes up, not feet," Kaelan said. She flicked a paper charm into the spinning dust. It stuck in the air and the whirlwind dumped like a split bag. Two more slips pinned a fake low step that tried to lure them over the edge. "If it looks easy, it's a trap."

Bastian stepped into the narrow saddle and set his boots on the dull stones Fuzanglong had marked. He met the smaller elemental with the flat of his axe and chopped for the iron spike in its elbow. The hit rang down the ridge. The thorn cracked but held. The arm jolted like it had fallen asleep and woke up angry.

Fuzanglong slid a thin wall of river between Bastian and the spray of heat. Water hissed and held. "Stay on the dull rock," he said. "Shiny stone wants to roll."

The larger elemental turned toward Sia and dragged heat up from the seam under its feet. Black iron hugged its core like barbed wire. Four anchor spots fed it. Two faced her. Two didn't.

"Slow down," Marcus said from the umbrella crook. "If we hurry, we'll mess this up."

"Got it," Sia said. She lifted the umbrella. The steel pole's green sheen felt steady in her hand. "I need clean lines."

"I'm with you," Marcus said.

He pushed a tight stream of heat into her grip. Sia drew a band like she was cutting ribbon, not throwing flame. The dragonfire tracked the line she chose, crossed the nearest thorns, and sliced them without licking into brush. Iron glowed dull red, then snapped with a hard pop. The elemental flinched. Its chest opened like a hot seam to spit the blast back.

"Left," Kaelan called. She slammed a charm into the air. The aim bent. Heat hit bare rock and spent itself in steam.

Mia raised both hands. Brigid's frost knot at her wrist went cold enough to silver her breath. She spoke a short Winter word. White bands wrapped the elemental's legs. Not breaking them. Holding them still. Plates ground. The bind set like packed snow.

"Next tie," Marcus said. "Low right."

Sia shifted to the marked stone and drew another clean band through the thorns on the hip. Iron flashed and fell in two dull chunks. Heat shook off the creature like water. It swayed, confused, then tried to pull more from the seam.

Bastian slammed his axe down on the smaller elemental's elbow spike. It shattered with a crack like a rock exploding in a campfire. The thing swung with its other arm. He slid inside and broke that thorn too. Without the hooks, the plates loosened and stopped swinging.

It sagged toward the ground. Fuzanglong's wall took the hiss and thinned to mist.

Dust kicked again to blind them. Kaelan slapped a charm where the air twisted and it fell flat. "Keep your footing," she said. "The ridge is lying."

Sia planted the umbrella tip and felt past the noise. The big one still dragged heat into its chest where a core hook sat. Another hook pulled from the back plate, just out of sight.

"Hidden anchor, back side," Marcus said. "Feel for the tug."

"I've got it," Sia said. She drew through empty air. The band landed where the pull was strongest. Iron sang and split. Mia tightened the hold. The elemental groaned like a kiln cooling too fast.

A fake dip slid under Sia's heel. Kaelan caught it with a charm before she stepped. "Eyes here," Kaelan said. "Do not chase shadows."

"I'm here," Sia said. The rhythm under the ground was breaking up. Good. One more tie.

The last hook sat near the center of the chest, sunk deep. If she cut it wrong, the shell would choke on loose heat and crack the ridge.

"Core hook," Marcus warned. "Make it clean."

Sia met Mia's eyes. "Hold tight on my mark," she said. "Bastian, if it twists, hit the plate above it, not the hook."

"Ready," Bastian said.

"Ready," Mia said.

Sia brought the umbrella across like a careful stitch. The dragonfire stayed a thin line. Iron heated, hit one sharp note, then broke with a plain snap. In the same breath Bastian split the top plate just enough to kill the twist. Mia's bind tightened, then eased.

The elemental sagged. Heat bled off in slow waves. It turned its blank face toward the ridge like it could finally hear the ground. Then it sank back into the seam. The smaller one followed, sliding into the crack Bastian had cleared.

Sia kept the umbrella ready and tested the air. No more hooks tugged at her hand. The sulfur bite stayed, but the wrong rhythm was gone.

Kaelan let the last charm burn out in her palm. "That net we cut earlier will knit itself back by dark," she said, eyeing the empty saddle. "We shouldn't be here then."

Mia flexed her fingers. The frost knot cooled to its usual small chill. "Binding seems to have held. I don't think we'll see a rebound."

Bastian rolled his shoulders and listened. "The ridge sounds like someone finally turned the stove off," he said. "I'll take it."

Fuzanglong dipped along the seam and nodded. "Flow is steady again."

Marcus stretched along the umbrella crook and settled. " Hit the hooks, not the body." he said, pleased. "Every time."

"Hooks first," Sia said.

Heat shimmered above a dark slab up-slope, then thinned like a breath leaving. On the rock face near Sia's elbow, a faint spiral with a short harp line woke in the cooled slag. Not bright, but clear.

Kaelan followed her gaze. "Tuatha marker," she said. "And it's pointing off the main trail."

"Window's open," Bastian said, checking the light. "We take it while the hill likes us."

They did a quick check. Water. Hands. Boots on dull stone. No speeches. Sia closed her fingers on the umbrella's crook. The tool settled against her palm like a kept promise. The glow on the slag angled toward a narrow cut in the ridge scrub. Brush leaned a little, like a wind had just gone through.

"Move," Sia said.

They went, careful and fast. The ridge let them pass. Behind, the saddle looked harmless again. Ahead, the off-path glen waited where the air felt clean and the bad beat was gone.

HEAT BLED OFF THE rocks in slow waves, then evened out like someone turned a knob to steady. The wrong thrum in the ground went quiet. Sia held the umbrella ready a moment longer, testing the air the way you listen for a phone that finally stops buzzing.

"I don't feel any more pulls," she said.

"Same," Mia answered. Frost smoked once around her wrists, then faded. She opened her hands and eased the Winter bind off the big elemental. The white bands loosened, turned thin, and broke apart like hoarfrost in sun. The freed shape paused as if listening, then sank into the ridge without drama.

Bastian took two careful steps, set his palm to the rock, and waited. "Warm, not angry," he said. "Good sign."

Kaelan scanned the saddle, eyes flicking over seams and shadows. She lifted one last paper strip and pressed it to a low shimmer that clung to the far edge. It burned out quick. "That should stop the leftovers from trying to trip us," she said. "But the net we cut earlier will grow back by nightfall."

"Then we don't still be here at night," Marcus said. He stretched along the umbrella crook, a small dragon trying to look casual and not quite getting there. "Please."

Sia half smiled and shifted her grip on the crook. The steel pole stayed cool and steady. The red hood kept its faint runes low, ready, not loud. "We won't," she said.

Fuzanglong slid his ribbon-thin body along the nearest seam and rose. "Flow is even," he said. "If there are hooks left, they are asleep."

"Let's make sure," Sia said.

She walked the line they had fought along, tapping the umbrella tip in short, clean touches. Nothing snagged at her hand. No cold hitch, no hot snap. On the upper face of rock, a faint mark brightened in cooled slag: a spiral with a short line beside it, like a tiny harp. It tilted toward a narrow cut in scrub above the trail.

"Hey," Mia said, following her gaze. "Another Tuatha sign."

"Angus's style," Kaelan said, stepping up. "Spiral and harp."

"Pointing there," Sia said. She traced the angle with her finger. Brush leaned a little like wind had just pushed through. The air smelled cleaner up that way, less sulfur, more pine.

Bastian eyed the sky and the stone. "We take it while the ridge likes us," he said. "Drink, check boots, move."

They did the quick loop without anyone asking. Sia sipped from her bottle and wet her lips. Mia tied her hair back tighter. Kaelan slid fresh papers into her sleeve stack. Bastian checked the rush cord that held his axe's peace tie. Fuzanglong settled again along Mia's collarbone like a thin necklace of river light. Marcus re-positioned his claws on the crook so he would not slip if they had to run.

"Everyone good," Kaelan asked.

"Good," Mia said.

"Good," Bastian said.

Marcus lifted a forefoot. "Goodish," he said. "I do not bounce well off basalt."

"Noted," Sia said. "We'll keep the pace smooth."

Kaelan squinted at the far saddle they had crossed. "No speeches," she said. "But thanks for not stepping into the obvious holes."

"I came close," Sia admitted.

"You noticed and stopped," Kaelan said. "That's the point."

Sia breathed once, steady. The umbrella belonged in her hand the way a favorite pen belongs in your fingers when the page finally clicks. "Alright," she said. "Off-trail it is."

They angled toward the cut the marker favored. The slope pushed back for a dozen steps, then eased like the hill had decided to be polite. The scrub parted enough to walk without scraping. Loose pebbles tried to roll their ankles, then thought better of it. The heat staying in the seams felt like a street in late afternoon, not like a stove left on.

Below them, the saddle looked ordinary again. If someone arrived now, they might think the ridge had always been quiet. Sia knew better. Places remembered, just not the way people did.

"Do you think the Tuatha are steering us on purpose," Mia asked, voice low. "Or is this more like breadcrumbs they left behind for whoever can see them."

"Both," Kaelan said. "They wrote the stories that taught people how to read roads. They also like to cheat."

"I appreciate the cheating," Marcus said.

"Same," Mia said. "I'll take a hint over a surprise."

Fuzanglong hummed. "Hints are the kind of help a place can live with," he said. "Surprises are how you get elementals wearing iron."

"Speaking of," Sia said, glancing back down the ridge. "I'm not seeing more thorns in the stone."

"Hooks are cut," Marcus said, satisfied. "Hit the hooks, not the body. Always."

"Always," Sia agreed.

They crested a lip of rock and found the start of the glen the marker promised. A narrow notch ran between two shoulders of the ridge, brushed with grass and low pine. The air smelled like sap and cold water. If they had stood very still, Sia felt like she might have heard the place breathe.

Bastian took point, boots careful, not quiet for quiet's sake so much as respectful. Kaelan drifted left to watch for glamours. Mia kept to Sia's right, fingers near the frost knot but relaxed. Sia set a clean pace they could all hold.

"Five minutes and we'll be out of the hot zone," Kaelan said. "After that, no more thinking about iron."

"Until the next hill," Marcus said.

"Don't jinx it," Mia told him.

"I am an optimist," Marcus said, deadpan. "With evidence."

They moved through the notch. The ridge fell away behind them. Wind touched their faces for the first time since the climb started. On the far side, a line of scrub opened into scattered trees, and beyond that the ground dipped toward a shallow bowl of green. The air there looked clearer, the light flatter in a good way, like a room with the right curtains pulled.

Sia stopped for a second at the lip. The umbrella felt a little lighter, like it liked where they were headed. She could not tell if that was the tool or her own shoulders. Either way, she would take it.

"We go down," Bastian said, reading the same thing. "Then we see what the glen wants."

"Works for me," Mia said. She set her palm to the rough bark of a low pine and smiled when resin stuck to her hand. "This smells like a normal day."

"Keep liking it," Kaelan said. "But stay ready."

Sia nodded and followed Bastian into the green. Behind them, heat stayed in the rock where it belonged. Up-slope, the faint spiral and harp on the slag cooled until it was just another dull mark in stone. The net over the saddle would knit itself back together by dark, exactly like Kaelan said. That part of the ridge would be a problem again for someone else, some other time.

For now, the hill let them go. And ahead, the off-path road was open.

CHAPTER 18

Gardens Between

SIA

THE PATH NARROWED UNTIL it was more idea than trail. Branches arched overhead and braided themselves into a tunnel, bark seams shining like old scars. The air changed first. It lost the bite of Winter and the sweetness of Summer and settled into something that felt like a breath held for a long time and finally let out. When the roots opened, the Garden waited beyond them.

Light lived here. Not bright, not dim, just right. It came from nowhere and from everything at once, sliding through leaves and along the ground the way water finds low places. A pool lay at the center like a round mirror set into the earth. An arch of living roots grew over it, woven so tight the wood looked like a single piece. Flowers pushed through stone where stone should not allow it. The air carried a quiet summer smell, cut grass and rain that already happened.

Sia stopped on the last step of the root tunnel and let her eyes adjust. Her umbrella hung at her wrist by the crook, weight familiar and sure. The red hood's runes gave a soft answer-glow as if it recognized the place. Marcus settled on her shoulder in his small form, careful claws not quite touching skin through her coat. He didn't speak, and he didn't have to. The whole group felt it. This was a kept place.

"Welcome," said a voice from the far side of the pool.

The woman who stepped into view moved like someone who had never once tripped. She wore dark green that read as forest more than cloth, a fall of hair the color of wet bark, and the kind of calm face people try to fake and never get right. Sia had seen her before in the Wilds, at a distance and without a name. The Unseelie leader who had traveled under other titles. Now she stood without any of them.

"I am the Dreaming," she said. She didn't lift her chin or make a show of it. She simply allowed the truth to sit between them.

Mia's Winter steadied inside her, not a costume but a choice. Frost-soft light gathered at her fingers and then settled. "You called us," she said.

"I asked," the Dreaming corrected, and there was no sting in it. "Thank you for answering."

Bastian took two steps forward and bowed from the waist, not low, just respectful. "Bastian of the Green," he said. "Oath in Summer's sight to keep these travelers whole while they stand within my reach."

"Seen," the Dreaming said, as if she were writing it in a book only she could see. Her gaze moved to Kaelan. "Miko of moonlight. You carry temple quiet with you."

Kaelan returned a small nod. "And stop talking when the place deserves it," she said, just enough humor to keep the moment human.

Fuzanglong's arrival was more felt than seen, a low silver-blue glow that gathered at the pool's edge and shaped itself into a long, graceful coil of river light. "I am not made for gardens," he said, amused. "But I can behave."

"I would appreciate that," the Dreaming said.

Thanatos stood to the left under a birch that had grown a curve into itself to make room for him. He had already been there, which felt correct. His hands were folded behind his back. His eyes were kind and sharp at the same time. "I am here as a witness," he said. "I will speak if truth is bent."

Sia stepped forward until the arch framed the top of her vision and the pool filled the bottom. The surface did not ripple, not even from the breeze that moved through the leaves. "You held the Wilds when no one else could," she said. It wasn't a question. The place answered for the woman in front of them.

"For longer than was wise," the Dreaming said. "The Wilds belong to themselves. They do not belong to me. I only carried what needed carrying when the gates began to argue with the land."

"How bad is it?" Mia asked.

"Bad enough that Winter has bled for it and would bleed more if I let them," the Dreaming said, looking to Mia with a kind of gratitude that did not push. "Bad enough that Summer's healing cannot reach this far past its borders. Bad enough that the Hunt is busy killing trespass while more trespass keeps coming."

Sia's thumb found the umbrella's crook and pressed there. The wood was warm where her skin met it. "We've seen the fronts," she said. "We've closed a few seams. It felt like bailing a boat with a cup."

"The boat keeps floating when someone bails," the Dreaming said, almost smiling, "but you grow tired. I am tired."

Bastian looked toward the trees. "We cleared your elementals," he said. "They were guardians. They were also a warning. Someone has been trying to feed on them."

"Pride likes to test the oldest stones," the Dreaming said. "Wrath prefers to break them. Envy prefers to wear them like jewelry and call that victory. It doesn't matter which hand reaches. The Wilds do not want any of them."

Kaelan's voice went softer. "What do you need from us?"

"I need three things," the Dreaming said. "Truth spoken aloud. A clean hand on the weave. And someone willing to hold what I have carried so it can live somewhere larger than my two hands."

Sia felt the sentence ring in the air, not magic, just importance. "I can do the second," she said. "I can try the third. I should say the first."

"Say your three lines," Thanatos suggested. "And let the rest of us say ours."

Sia breathed once and kept it simple. "I'm Sia Mason," she said. "I am the Dreamer of our world. I came because you asked for help. I will not take anything that doesn't want to be taken."

Mia stepped up beside her without asking if she should. "I'm Mia Mason," she said. "I carry Winter's Lady because it chose to live with me when I should have died. I will use it to keep doors shut if those doors lead here from Hell."

Kaelan touched the paper slips tucked into her sleeve. "Kaelan Kuzunoha," she said. "I speak for Summer when Summer chooses to be polite. My promise is to cut lies when I see them and to pay my debts."

Bastian set his hands to the haft at his hip and kept his tone calm. "Bastian," he said. "Green's Knight. My word is service. My oath is escort. My choice is to stand where I am most needed."

Fuzanglong lifted his head, the water in his mane catching the Garden's light. "Fuzanglong," he said. "Guardian of hidden things. I know how to move a river without insulting it. If you need that, say so."

Marcus leaned closer to Sia's ear. "Marcus Duvall," he said, and the little dragon voice had a smile in it. "I am here as long as the link holds. I can lend measured heat without burning the room."

Thanatos didn't repeat himself. He only inclined his head. The truth was built into everything he was.

The Dreaming listened and did not rush. She let silence close each sentence and then opened it for the next. When everyone had spoken, she turned to the pool and put her palm just above the surface.

"This Garden is a boundary that chose to rest," she said. "It is not a weapon. It is not a prize. It is a promise that the Wilds can be safe without being tamed. I would like to lay down what I hold and let it root into a role that can outlast me."

"You want me to take it," Sia said. There was weight in the words, but it did not feel like a trap. It felt like setting a heavy box on a table and admitting you need another set of hands.

"I want you to fold it into what you already carry," the Dreaming said. "You are the Dreamer of your world. Faerie sits along the edges of that road. If you tell your road to hold Faerie's passages as part of your keeping, gates will stop learning bad habits. Winter will not have to be everywhere at once. Summer will heal more and panic less. The Hunt will catch trespass instead of chasing smoke."

Mia's shoulders loosened. "That sounds like something we can live with," she said.

"It will not fix everything," the Dreaming said. "It will give us a chance to fix things before they break."

Sia took a step closer to the pool. She felt the arch hum through the bones of her wrists. "If I do this," she said, "what happens to you?"

"I rest," the Dreaming said. "Not death. Not sleep. Something between. I will watch the Garden with Thanatos while you learn the patterns. When you do not need me, I will sit with the trees and remember what they are instead of what they are supposed to be."

Thanatos's mouth tipped like he almost smiled. "I am very good at watching," he said. "And at reminding people not to poke the parts that should not be poked."

"Do you trust us?" Kaelan asked the Dreaming, not unkindly. "Not the idea of us. Us."

"Yes," the Dreaming said. She looked at Mia when she said it, then Sia, then the others. "Trust is a road you build and walk every day. You have walked it."

Bastian exhaled, not quite relief, more like readiness. "Tell us how to begin," he said.

The Dreaming lowered her hand until it just kissed the pool. Light gathered under the surface, not bright, just definite. The arch's hum deepened as if it approved.

"Step onto the stone at the rim," the Dreaming told Sia. "Set your focus in both hands. Let the Garden show you the first pattern. Don't fight it. Don't add to it. Hold steady until it feels like it belongs to you and you belong to it."

Sia slipped the umbrella into her grip. The crook settled into her left palm. The steel pole warmed in her right. She met Mia's eyes and did not have to say anything. Mia moved with her to the rim, hands set for calm. Kaelan's paper flashed once and faded as she warded the space without a speech. Bastian found the angle where he could watch the trees and the pool at the same time. Fuzanglong lay his water ring over the surface like a thin halo. Marcus braced in the umbrella's crook and anchored, a careful weight and a steady heat if she needed it.

"Ready," Sia said, and the word didn't echo. It simply fit.

THEY CIRCLED TO A low pavilion of woven branches that had grown itself out of the bank. The roof let light through like a thin green glass. A long stone sat at the center as a table, worn smooth by hands that had met here before. The pool's quiet reached them in a steady pulse. When Sia placed her umbrella on the tabletop, the runes on the red cloth eased to a soft glow, as if the Garden had decided they were guests.

"We speak plainly here," the Dreaming said. She took the far side so the pool stayed at her back. "No performances. Say what is true, then we decide what to do with it."

Mia stood to Sia's right and rested her fingers on the stone. Cold gathered there, not ice, just calm that stayed where she put it. Kaelan chose the seat nearest the arch so she could watch the path. Bastian leaned his axe within reach and sat without rattling a single leaf. Fuzanglong coiled along the open side like a patient river. Thanatos remained at the threshold where pavilion met path, a witness who did not need a chair to belong.

Sia glanced at Mia, then at the Dreaming. "I will go first," she said. "I am Sia Mason. I hold the Dreamer's work in our world. We came because you asked. I will not take anything that does not want to be taken." She kept it short so the words would land.

"Winter hears that," Mia said, meeting the Dreaming's eyes. "I carry the Lady's mantle by choice. I will use it to keep Hell out of Faerie where Winter's reach can touch."

Kaelan touched the paper slips tucked in her sleeve. "Kaelan Kuzunoha," she said. "Miko of Tsukiyomi. I speak for Summer when Summer prefers polite. I will cut lies when I see them and I will pay my debts."

Bastian set his palms on the stone. "Bastian of the Green," he said. "My word is service. My oath is escort. I stand where I am most needed."

Fuzanglong dipped his head, mane catching a wash of the pool's light. "Fuzanglong," he said. "Guardian of hidden things. I can move a river without offending it. Say if you need that."

Thanatos's voice stayed even. "I am here to keep the floor level," he said. "If a story bends in the middle, I will point to the bend."

The Dreaming listened like someone taking notes in a book only she could see. "Good," she said. "Then I say mine. I am the Dreaming of this Garden. I have held the Wilds alone longer than is wise. I cannot hold them alone and keep them whole. Hell pries where my hands are thin. I am asking for help that lasts."

She turned the stone in her palm that Sia had first noticed on the path, a smooth oval with a faint spiral carved into it. "Winter has carried more than its share," she said, glancing to Mia. "Summer heals what it can reach. The Hunt takes whoever trespasses and calls the taking justice. The Wilds are not a court. They still need a keeper at the edges. That is the truth."

"And your ask," Sia said.

"Fold the Garden's doorways into your road," the Dreaming said. "Make Faerie's passages part of what you police when you walk the Dream. Not all of them. Only the ones that reach where Hell is most clever. If you do, seams will stop learning bad habits. Winter will not bleed everywhere at once. Summer will have time to mend. The Hunt can hunt trespass instead of chasing smoke."

Mia let her hand settle flat on the stone. The quiet under her palm answered. "If Sia carries those passages, Winter can anchor border work instead of sprinting," she said. "We can live with that."

Kaelan rested her elbows on the table and kept her voice careful. "Summer will ask for the ledger," she said. "Who pays for what when things break. I can speak that language here. Hospitality covers the meal, not the roof."

"Then say the ledger," the Dreaming said.

Kaelan lifted one finger. "When the Dreamer closes a Faerie seam, Winter recognizes that work as lawful under Winter's protection. No court can claim debt from the Dreamer for acting fast." She raised a second finger. "When Winter holds a front that touches the Dream, Summer is free to cross and heal without paying entry fee in those halls." A third finger. "When Summer's healing runs out, the Hunt lends teeth by formal call rather than waiting on courtesy."

"The Hunt will want its say," Bastian said. "But the Earlking enjoys clear games. He will answer."

Thanatos rocked once on his heels. "These are statements that can be true," he said. "None of them smells like a trick."

Sia looked at the Dreaming. "If I do this, what happens to you," she asked, repeating the question from the pool because it mattered here too.

"I rest," the Dreaming said. "I do not vanish. I sit with the trees. I keep watch with him while you learn the patterns." She tipped her head toward Thanatos. "When your hands are sure, I will be a story again instead of a lever someone can pry."

Sia felt the arch's hum thread through her hands where they touched the stone. The umbrella's runes gave a soft answer. Mia's presence at her side was a steady cold she had grown to trust, not a costume, not a stranger. Sia knew what the right choice felt like in her bones. It felt like something heavy being set on a table so more than one person could carry it.

"I can hold the passages," she said. "I will build them into the road I already keep."

The Dreaming did not rush to seal it. She studied Sia's face the way a teacher studies a student who is about to lift more weight than last week. "Then we fix terms so no one can pretend they did not hear them," she said. "Three lines spoken, and three lines answered."

She placed the spiral stone on the table. Its carved line caught the light. "By this Garden and by the work I have carried, I recognize Sia Mason as a keeper of Faerie passages when she walks the Dream. I will show her the first pattern and no one will call it theft." She tapped the stone once. "Sia?"

Sia put her palm on the spiral. The stone was cool, then warm. "By my road and by the work I already hold, I accept the keeping of those passages," she said. "I will not close doors that are not mine. I will close the ones that feed Hell."

Mia set two fingers beside Sia's hand. "Winter stands with that," she said. "When the Dreamer holds a seam, Winter treats her as under our protection for that work. We do not bill the Dreamer for doing the right thing."

Kaelan gave a quick nod. "Summer puts ink to it," she said. "When the Dreamer's work is done at a border, Summer crosses to heal without a toll at those doors."

Bastian looked to the open path and then back to the table. "And the Hunt is on call by formal word when healing alone will not do," he said. "I will carry that to my lord if you want it in his voice. He likes to make an entrance."

"He will still hear it," Thanatos said, mild as weather. "He hears most things he finds amusing."

The Dreaming gathered the spiral stone and closed her hand around it. The light in the pavilion shifted. The pool's pulse felt closer, like breath near a cheek. "Then we begin," she said. "There will be a weight to it. Do not try to move the weight faster than it wants to move."

Sia lifted the umbrella and found the grip that felt truest. The crook sat sure in her palm. The steel pole balanced the way a good tool does when your hands understand it. She met Mia's eyes, and Mia did not have to say a word. Calm was already set and would be there as long as Sia needed it.

"One question before we stand," Kaelan said to the Dreaming. "Where do we go when we finish this and the Garden is quiet?"

"To work," the Dreaming said, and a small smile reached her eyes. "The Hunt's road first. A river that remembers next. There are old friends ahead who would like to be asked for help the right way."

Bastian's mouth edged toward a grin he did not quite let out. "I prefer a plan that involves asking before swinging," he said. "Even if the swinging still happens."

Sia stepped back from the table and felt the pavilion breathe around them. The Garden had been listening. It would keep listening. She looked to the pool, then to the arch, and felt the weight of what she was about to accept settle in a way that felt right.

"I'm ready," she said.

"Good," the Dreaming answered. She rose without creak or flourish. "Then we set the pattern and let it belong to you."

THE POOL GLOWED LIKE a lamp under glass while the root arch above it kept a low, even hum that Sia felt in her ribs. She stepped onto a flat stone at the rim and set her umbrella across both hands. The crook fit neatly in her left palm. The steel pole felt warm and steady in her right. Runes on the red cloth hood glimmered as if they were paying attention. Across the water, the Dreaming lifted her hand over the surface and told Sia to match what she felt, not to force it. Sia let her breath fall into the arch's rhythm and traced the first shape. The pole gave a small, friendly vibration. The runes brightened, then settled. Her anchor ring warmed against her skin.

Mia took position at Sia's right, shoulders easy, hands open. Kaelan knelt and placed three paper slips in a neat triangle beside a low stone bench. Bastian set his boots on the inner edge of the arch where he could step in fast without crowding the pool. Fuzanglong raised a thin ring of water and let it drift along the rim, clear and quiet. Marcus hooked his claws into the umbrella's crook and went still. He was no bigger than Sia's hand today, but his careful weight told her he was locked in.

A pale lattice rose from the pool like a net made of lines. It hovered over Sia and waited to be met. She traced a second figure, then a third. The lattice lowered a little at a time until it rested inside her focus and in the familiar spot behind her eyes where Dream work lives when she is awake. Nothing snagged or bit. It felt like snapping a tool into the right slot. Mia spoke a short Winter word and the air chose to be still without turning sharp. Kaelan's slips warmed and faded as they finished their job. Fuzanglong's ring drank two bright flecks with a soft hiss. Marcus kept his weight steady on the crook.

"You are not carrying the road," the Dreaming said, watching Sia's hands. "You are telling it how to behave."

"I understand," Sia said. She let the umbrella hold most of the shape. The steel stayed solid. The crook sat right. The red hood kept its calm glow. The pattern settled with the quiet click of something that belongs. The Dreaming named it the first layer, the kind that keeps seams from fraying around you. Thanatos stepped a little closer, studied the motion of Sia's fingers, and said it was clean. There was no hook hiding in the weave.

Bastian did not look away from the tree line. He promised to escort Sia when she walked Wild ground again, spoke the promise three times, and let the air take it without a show. The Dreaming turned to Mia and told her that inside this Garden, Winter followed her lead. If she called for more, it would answer at the level she set. Mia flexed her fingers once and said she could work with that. A softer glow built under the water as if a second set of lines wanted to rise, then dimmed again when the Dreaming raised her hand. Later, she said. One grip at a time.

Sia stood still long enough to check the stability. The lattice sat where it belonged, shared between her focus and the umbrella. The pool's light stayed even. Her shoulders eased a notch. Marcus leaned close to her ear and asked how it felt. Like it belongs, Sia told him. The Dreaming touched the pool with a fingertip. A thread of light rose, crossed to the umbrella, and sank into the red cloth, leaving a faint mark beneath the runes. Heat moved through the frame in a friendly wave.

"An unseen mark," the Dreaming said. "Our wards will read your focus as safe."

"That saves us an argument at every door," Kaelan said, satisfied.

The vale breathed the way a room does after furniture lands where it should. Then the far edge of the glen twitched. It was a small, wrong movement, like a knuckle tapping glass. A tight vibration traveled through the umbrella that did not belong to the Garden. The air near the pool sharpened with attention. Mia turned toward the trees and asked if Sia felt it. Sia said yes and tightened her grip on the crook.

"Hold your jobs," the Dreaming said. "No rushing."

Bastian slid his front foot by an inch, set his hips, and lifted his axe to a steady height. If anything crossed the line, it would meet him first. Kaelan rose and lifted two fresh slips between her fingers. If the border tried to lie, she would cut it back to the truth. Fuzanglong narrowed the water ring until it was a clean band, ready to carry a blow sideways if it came at the pool. Marcus pressed his claws into the crook just enough to anchor and told Sia he could stitch a heat thread wherever she pointed. Thanatos did not blink. Pride enjoys tests, he said, and the thing at the edge was testing the fence.

Sia raised the umbrella and set a reinforcement across the arch and the water the way the Dreaming had shown her. She did not make it harder; she made it steadier. The lattice hummed along the steel and softened through the cloth. Her ring warmed again. She watched the weave, not the shadows, and kept her breathing even. Without looking away, she checked the team.

Kaelan showed the slips and said her cuts were ready and the ground on their side was clear. Bastian dug his boots a fraction deeper and claimed the line, promising that anything that stepped over would stop at him. Mia lifted one hand high and one low. Frost gathered across her fingers and held. Calm was steady, she said. She would take first bind and use the holding word unless Sia told her different. Fuzanglong raised the water ring a finger's width and said the wall was sure. If Sia called a count, he would carry any strike sideways so the Garden did not take it. Marcus said he had a clean thread and would place the heat exactly where she asked. Thanatos added that he was watching for lies and would call them out if they tried to stand.

Sia gave the plan one more time in clear pieces. If something dragged for the water, they held here. If it pulled on the arch, they pushed through the frame, not the ground. No one overreached. The win was the Garden staying whole. Pressure leaned on the edge again and left a dry hiss along the bark of an outer trunk. The pool kept its light. The arch kept its note. Thanatos said it was coming in the same even tone he used for everything that mattered.

Bastian lowered his center another inch and settled. Mia told him she had first bind and he would take the hit, and he agreed without taking his eyes off the seam. Kaelan fixed her focus on a thin bend in the air where the border was wrong and promised to cut it back if it slid. Fuzanglong told Sia to say the word if she wanted the wall to carry force. Sia said she would. Marcus said heat was on thread and ready.

Sia adjusted her feet and let the umbrella carry the pattern. The lattice lay across the arch and the pool like a brace where a door meets its frame. She felt where it would flex and where it would hold. The umbrella hummed, and the red runes brightened before they settled. She kept her attention on the shape of the work and did not let the creeping fear up her spine make any choices. When she asked if everyone was set, Mia said she was locked and the cold at her fingers felt like a promise. Bastian said he was anchored and raised his axe to the right height. Kaelan said she was clear and kept the slips poised to cut. Fuzanglong said he was holding and the water brightened a shade. Marcus said he was threaded and kept the heat quiet behind the word.

On the far side of the glen, the wrong pull gathered like someone working a zipper in the dark. Sound bent low. Light crawled the wrong direction along the tree line. Sia kept her eyes on the weave and gave the call. Mia snapped a holding bind onto the edge with clean frost meant to catch the first ankle without freezing the leg. Bastian brought his axe into the exact space where anything would have to step to reach them. Kaelan's slips rose a hair, ready to slice any false border the instant it formed. Fuzanglong widened the ring just enough to throw a heavy strike sideways if it fell toward the water. Marcus held for Sia's word with the heat laced and waiting.

Sia set the brace against the push and let the arch answer back in the same steady note. The pool's light did not flicker. The pressure hit like a hand trying to shove through a doorframe, and the frame refused. The Garden held.

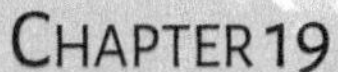

Pride Cometh

Sia

THE FIRST WRONG NOTE came like a tap on glass. It ran along the arch, through the steel in Sia's umbrella, and settled under her skin. She tightened her grip on the crook and set the brace where it needed to live, a clean line across pool and root, the pattern the Dreaming had taught her. The Garden kept its even light. The air kept its quiet. The edge of the trees did not.

Bark darkened at three trunks on the far side of the glen. The wood did not burn. It agreed. It was the kind of change a bully wants, not the kind a forest chooses. Something heavy pushed, and the seam pulled like a zipper worked in the dark. The opening was not wide. It was confident.

"Hold your jobs," the Dreaming said. Her voice sat beside Sia's shoulder without hurry. She mirrored Sia's pattern with one hand above the water, sharing the load like two people carrying the same box.

Mia set her hands and spoke a calm word that did not freeze anything. The air accepted it and steadied. Frost laid itself across her fingers, fine as powder and ready to move where she told it. "Field is up," she said. "I am taking first bind if it steps through."

Kaelan moved along the inside arc and lifted a pair of slips between her fingers. "There is a false line trying to form," she said, eyes on a shimmer that was almost a path. "If it lies, I cut it back to where it belongs."

Bastian set his boots in the same place he had marked in the last breath of quiet and rolled his shoulders until the weight settled where he liked it. He held his axe low and sure. "If anything crosses the boundary," he said, "it meets me before it meets the arch."

Fuzanglong narrowed his water ring until it became a band as thin as a blade. The light inside the ring brightened, clean and patient. "I can carry a strike sideways," he said. "Say the count and I will give it back to the air."

Marcus pressed his small claws into the umbrella's crook and leaned his head out past the red cloth to see the seam. "I have a thread ready," he told Sia. "Give me a point to stitch."

Thanatos did not change his stance under the birch. His eyes moved, and that was all. "There is no hidden lie in the rift," he said in a mild tone that felt like a level held flat. "It is what it says it is. It believes itself."

The press on the line grew teeth. A shape forced itself against the seam until the light bent around it. Authority arrived before the figure did. Sia felt the room want to agree that whoever came was in charge, the way a crowd will sometimes tip toward the person who speaks loudest. She let the umbrella take that weight and gave it a steady place to sit. The lattice hummed along steel and softened through the cloth.

The Pride-forged General stepped into view a finger's width inside the wrong. Plate armor rose in layered barbs like a crown turned into a ribcage. The helm carried a jagged circlet that was part metal and part idea. Every edge was made to catch the eye and teach it a lesson. Smoke slid out from joints that did not fit a living body. When it spoke, the sound rubbed the grain of the world and tried to make it face the other way.

"You are holding a door made for kings," the General said. "Open it."

Sia kept her eyes on the weave and did not look at the face. The voice pressed where her attention would have been. The pressure found nothing to grab. The Garden did not answer a stranger's orders. The arch kept its note.

"Not your door," she said, plain.

The General's left gauntlet spread its fingers. Black light crawled from the palm into the seam and drew a sigil like a crooked star with too many points. The mark did not burn. It declared. Sia felt the seam try to feed off the declaration, as if it had been told the rules and wanted to be helpful.

"It is planting a feeder," Kaelan said. She had already palmed a third slip.

"Do not stare at it," the Dreaming said. "You teach the road by where you look."

Sia did not look. She strengthened the brace where it touched the arch and the water and pulled the seam's attention back to the clean places. The umbrella warmed in her hands. The red runes along the hood brightened and then held steady. Her anchor ring sent a small pulse through her finger, a beat she could match her breathing to.

The General pushed. The seam surged. The outer trunks hissed and smoked without flame. Stone along the pool's edge cracked hairline. The force found Bastian at the only honest path through and hit him like a moving wall. He took it in the legs and shoulders and gave ground by half a step, then drove it back with the whole line of his spine. The blow dented his lower gauntlet and left a dark scuff on the haft where it slid.

"I am fine," Bastian said through his teeth. "It does not get past me."

Mia let the calm field breathe instead of harden. When the pressure peaked, she spoke and set a holding bind across the threshold. The bind was not a box. It was a net made to catch ankles and elbows and keep them from flailing, the sort of restraint that lets a person stand while taking away their rush. The net shimmered once and set.

"Bind is ready," she said. A line of blood started under one nostril and she wiped it with the back of her wrist. "I can hold two if I have to."

"Let me carry the hit if it aims for your side," Fuzanglong said. The water ring widened a breath, then thinned again. "Sia, say when you want the throw."

"On four," Sia said. She watched the seam, not the General's hands, and counted in her head. "One." The arch answered in that same steady tone. "Two." The pool's light did not flicker. "Three." The lattice made its small, friendly vibration through the steel. "Four."

The General slammed a barbed weight of force at the arch, a crown-shaped strike meant to make the frame sag. Fuzanglong's ring caught it and turned it as if it had always wanted to be rain. Droplets hissed from the leaves and fell in a clean curtain outside the pool's rim. The force was still a force. It did not land where it wanted to land.

Marcus's head dipped with focus. "Thread," he said, and Sia angled the umbrella so he could lace heat along the pattern without touching the wood or the cloth. He stitched it where the brace met the water. The heat did not scorch. It sealed.

"Bastian," Kaelan warned, and flicked a slip. The paper cut through a thin shimmer the General was trying to cheat into becoming a path. The false border broke like a soap film. "It keeps pushing the edge where it is not."

"I have the true line," Bastian said. He ground the heel of his boot until the soil accepted that he did. "If it wants to argue, it can argue with me."

The General spread both hands. A second feeder mark started to form in the seam, this one humming with the same ugly logic as the first. Agree because I said so. Agree because I am a crown wearing a man wearing a crown. Sia felt the idea reach for her attention again.

"Do not give it your eyes," the Dreaming said quietly.

"I am not," Sia said. She let the umbrella carry the shape the Garden wanted. Pride's logic slid off the work the way rain slides off oil. She felt the feeder mark search for purchase and come up empty.

The push came again, harder, and this time it slid low like a leg sweep. Bastian met it with the haft and caught it, but the angle drove a vibration into his arms that would have undone a softer stance. He let the energy run through him and into the ground. The dent in his gauntlet split a little, not enough to cut skin, enough to count later when he retied the straps.

"I have a clean second thread," Marcus said. His voice had gone thin with effort. "I can lay it, then I need a breath."

"Lay it," Sia said.

He laid it and went still. Heat warmed the joint where weave met water, then quieted under her hands. The seam narrowed by a fraction. It did not close. It hated that.

The General's voice rolled across the glen again. "You are arguing with rank," it said. "You are not rank."

Sia did not answer. It would have been like trying to teach a storm manners. She gave the Garden her attention and the Garden gave it back. The arch kept humming. The pool kept its light. The feeder marks kept starving as long as she refused to look at them.

"We need lawful leverage," Mia said, eyes never leaving the seam. "It knows how to shove. It also knows how to pretend the line is wherever it steps."

"The Hunt likes lines," Bastian said. He did not look away either.

The push drew in as if the General was winding up a third strike, something wider and proud enough to try for the arch itself. Kaelan's slips warmed against her fingers. The Dreaming adjusted her hand over the pool without a word and matched Sia's pressure exactly, twice and then again until the lattice felt like two hands on one tool.

Sia kept the pattern steady and the fear out of her fingers. "Call the Hunt the right way," she said, not loud, very clear. "Name the border. Make it count."

Mia breathed once and nodded. The light did not change. The water did not move. The Garden waited to hear what the law would say next.

MIA STEPPED FORWARD UNTIL her boots met the exact seam Bastian had been guarding. The Garden's light was steady on her hands. Winter sat inside her like a quiet muscle, ready to move when she told it to. She did not raise her voice. She did not need to. "This is Garden ground," she said. "This line is the border. You crossed it without leave. I call the Hunt to witness and to hold the rule."

The air changed the way a crowd changes when someone important walks in. Shadows lengthened across the treeline. Wolves eased out of them, lean and silent, each with a thin band of pale metal at the throat that caught blue in the Garden light. Goblin outriders followed on shaggy ponies with tack that looked mended a hundred times. A herald came last and did not look like much at first. He wore dark leather, carried a spear in a one-handed grip, and walked with the bored confidence of someone who rarely needs to explain himself. He stepped to the border, planted the spear like it was a survey stake, and the ground accepted it with a small sound that carried farther than it should have.

Two black crows spiraled down and settled on the spear's crossbar. They did not caw. They clicked their beaks like stones tapping glass and watched everything with bright, coin-flat eyes.

The Pride General straightened under its crown of barbs. The helm had no expression, but the body language said contempt. It reached into the seam with one hand and split part of itself into three shapes, lieutenants made of steel and ash. They slid left and right, testing angles like thieves pushing along a wall for a loose brick. Each tried to step in places where the border bent, as if walking along a technicality could keep the Hunt out of the game.

"Keep to your jobs," Sia said without looking away from the weave. The umbrella hummed in her grip. The lattice lay steady across arch and pool, tighter now, no sharpness, just certainty.

Bastian took one pace to center the narrow gap and set his axe at a plain, workable height. He breathed once and let the breath go, shoulders loose, weight low. Marcus perched on the crook of the umbrella and watched Sia's hands for the moment she would call a count. "Heat is ready," he said. "Tell me where."

Kaelan moved to the place where the edge looked dishonest and lifted a slip between two fingers. "I see the twist," she said. "If it tries to make that path real, I cut it back."

Fuzanglong raised the water ring until it was as tall as a person and as thin as a blade, a curved wall clear enough to see through. "I can turn a strike sideways into clean rain," he said. "Call the count."

The herald had not moved since he planted the spear. He looked at the General the way a ranger looks at a poacher who already knows he is caught. The crows shifted on the crossbar and gave two short clicks that sounded like a ruling being entered.

The General tried authority again. "This ground recognizes rank," it said. "Move."

"Not yours," Mia answered. She set calm across the front and did not harden it into a freeze. "You are named trespass. The Hunt has the line."

The General's command aura flexed. It felt like someone pushing on the back of Sia's neck, trying to tilt her attention just a little. Kaelan whispered a moon prayer and snapped a rite that broke glamour without flash. The pressure thinned like steam let out of a valve. "Its voice is smaller," Kaelan said, shaking out her fingers. The slip's edge had gone hot enough to prickle her skin.

"Left," Bastian warned. One lieutenant skated toward a ripple in the air that pretended to be a gap. Kaelan's second slip sliced the ripple like a soap film. The path vanished and the lieutenant stuttered. Mia flicked a holding word that wrapped the thing at the ankle and elbow. Her bind was not a cage. It was a careful knot that took speed and made it stand.

The second lieutenant mirrored the move on the other flank. Mia caught that one too and held both at once. A thin line of blood started at her nose. She wiped it with the back of her wrist and kept her focus. "I have two," she said. "I can keep them if the line stays honest."

The herald pulled the planted spear free in one clean motion and drew his arm back. The two crows lifted a finger's width, wings ready, eyes locked. The spear left his hand like the air itself had thrown it. Lightning crawled along the haft, not wild, not loud, just sure. The point hit the Pride General's pauldron at the exact place where border met body and drove it back one half step. Sparks crawled over the armor and wrote a sign that was not letters but still read as meaning. It did not kill. It marked. The General stood at the limit and could not claim past it. The crows croaked once, sharp and satisfied, like judges noting that a rule had landed.

The seam bucked. Sia held the brace and stole a breath of the sigil's logic from the feeder mark the General had planted, the part that tried to make the world agree because it said so. She did not rip it out. She turned it off for one beat. The rift's pulse sputtered and lost rhythm.

"Center," Bastian said. The General tried to force a narrow commit through him, crown edge first. He met the blade on the haft and turned it down and away from the arch. "Now," he called.

"One," Sia said. "Two." Marcus laced heat along the axe edge on the third beat, just enough to make metal slip against metal and steal grip. The General staggered the smallest amount. Bastian drove the opening with his shoulder and regained ground he had given earlier. Sparks fell in a sheet that Fuzanglong gathered and gave to the air as a soft rain. The pool did not take a single drop.

Kaelan thumbed a third paper, hissed when it stung her skin, and cut a fresh false border before it could bloom under the General's heel. "Stop trying to cheat where the line is," she said, more to herself than to the enemy.

"I am at safe heat," Marcus warned. His voice had that thin sound he got when a projection was working hard. "I can give one more thread later. Not now."

"I can hold two binds for a count of ten," Mia said, eyes never leaving the lieutenants. "If the Hunt wants them, this is the moment."

The herald tapped the butt of the spear to the ground. It made a muffled thunder that Sia felt in her ankles. Wolves surged from the trees and took the bound lieutenants with clean, practiced bites, pulling them off the line and into the dark at the exact angle that counted as claim under Hunt law. The crows leaned forward and clicked three times in a row, a sound that felt like papers stamped.

"That leaves you," Bastian told the General. He did not bare his teeth. He did not need to.

The General gathered power in the crown. Sia saw it in the way light tilted toward the spikes. The next strike would try for the arch and not for the person in front of it. "Carry it," she told Fuzanglong, already setting a cross stitch between Dream and Winter inside her pattern. "On my word."

"Ready," the river dragon said.

Sia matched the Dreaming's hand above the water. She felt the older keeper lock pressure with her, two people holding the same tool steady while someone else tried to tear out the nails. Thanatos stood behind them and did nothing but watch for lies. He did not find any. This was not trick magic. This was a hammer aimed at a hinge.

The crown strike fell. Fuzanglong cut it, turned it, and sent it sideways in a shiver of spray that fell harmlessly beyond the pool's rim. The arch groaned but kept its shape. Sia's arms shook and then steadied. The General snarled without a face to snarl with.

"Again?" Mia asked Sia, eyes flicking toward the seam and back.

"Again," Sia said. She pulled Winter's calm through her own weave the way a surgeon pulls thread through skin and felt Mia set the holding word across the exact spot it needed to live. The General's footing hit law like a wall. The crows rose from the spear and wheeled above the gap, counting witnesses.

"Close his food," Kaelan said through her teeth. "He is done pretending."

"I am on it," Sia said. She kept the pattern honest and did not let the fear up her spine make choices. The feeder mark guttered. The seam narrowed a little more. The Garden held its light. The Hunt held the line. And the General, pinned at the very edge by rule and witnesses, was forced to meet them where they were strongest.

THE CROWN STRIKE HAD failed. The spear's lightning still crawled faintly over the Pride General's pauldron where the herald's throw had marked him at the line. The two crows wheeled once and settled again on the crossbar, heads tilted as if they were counting what came next. The seam kept breathing, a thin, ugly inhale that wanted to become a shout.

Sia lifted the umbrella and felt the lattice sit in her hands like a real tool, not a trick. The red hood's runes glowed soft and held. The steel pole hummed along the arch's note. The pool's light did not flicker. She opened the pattern just enough to let Winter's calm thread through it, then drew the edges together the way you bring skin to skin for a stitch. The pressure in the seam changed. Not off. Hungry in the way a closed door is hungry for footsteps it will not get.

Mia stood at Sia's right, both palms up, frost lying across her fingers like very fine dust. "I have the bind," she said. "Call it and I will set it."

"On my count," Sia said. She placed the first cross knot in the seam and felt it take. "Now."

Mia spoke the holding word. It went out without a shout or a shine. It landed where law had already been set by the spear and the crows, and it held the General to the exact line he had chosen. The armor flexed against the word. The helm tilted a fraction. The bind did not snap. It tightened the way a knot tightens when you pull from the right angle.

The General tried contempt again. "You are not enough," it said. The air wanted to tilt toward the voice the way a room wants to tilt toward a stage. Kaelan slid a paper slip between two fingers and whispered a clean moon prayer. The aura dulled like a loud speaker turned down. "Your stage is broken," Kaelan said, and flicked the slip aside before it burned her fingers.

On the center lane Bastian set his feet and moved with the kind of patience that lets heavy branches fall past your shoulder without taking your head. He gave the General a target it could not ignore and refused to be a wall that would crack. Marcus leaned forward on the umbrella's crook. "I have one more clean thread," he said, voice thin with the weight of projection. "Place me and I will lay it."

"Edge of the pool, low," Sia said. She traced a small circle with the umbrella tip to show him where the brace met the water. Marcus stitched his heat along the circle like a seal. The warmth pulsed once under her hands, then settled. The seam narrowed to the width of a fist and quivered there.

Fuzanglong lifted the water wall a finger's height. "If it throws wide again, I will send it away," he said. "Say when."

The General dug for feed. The crooked star he had drawn into the seam caught at Sia's attention again. Agree because I said so. Sia did not look at it. She kept her eyes on the places that belonged to the Garden. The Dreaming matched her hand above the pool. Two people, one tool. Thanatos watched for a lie and did not find one. This was force trying to pass for right.

"Cost," Bastian said, almost conversational as he turned the General's blade off the arch a second time. The dent in his gauntlet split a thread wider. He shifted his grip before it could bite. "I can keep this up, but the strap will need repair after."

Mia's breath showed white and then smoothed again as she adjusted the bind's pressure without changing its shape. A thin line of blood traced from her nose. She dragged the back of her wrist across it and kept her focus. "I am fine," she said. "The hold is honest."

"Last mirror," Kaelan warned. A ripple formed under the General's heel, the kind of false path that wins by a technicality. Kaelan's slip cut the ripple with a sharp little sound. The path collapsed. "Stop cheating," she told the air, more to keep her own hands steady than to argue with an enemy who did not care.

The General gathered itself for a lunge as if the right answer to a locked door was to run through it with your head. Bastian stepped into the exact space that made the angle bad and met the blade on the haft. It skidded. Sparks slid down into Fuzanglong's wall and came out as rain beyond the rim. The arch groaned from the force passing near it but held its shape.

Sia felt the seam fight under her hands. It tried to remember how to be large. It tried to be a mouth instead of a healed line. She set the second cross knot and tightened it. The umbrella's runes pulsed a little faster. The crook felt warm. Her anchor ring gave a soft beat that matched the pool.

"Two more knots and I can starve it," she said. Not a boast. A measure.

"Do it," Mia said. "I will keep the bind until your last pull."

The two crows rose from the spear and circled once over the narrow gap, black wings cutting neat curves. They clicked three times as they passed over the General's crown. Witnesses counting. When they settled again, the herald shifted his grip on the spear and rested the point on his boot. He did not look bored anymore. He looked satisfied.

The General tried something new. It divided its weight across the border in a way that felt like both feet were on the line without crossing it. A bad trick in a courtroom. A worse one at a door. Thanatos lifted his chin. "He is standing on two answers," he said. "He cannot be both."

Mia adjusted her bind in one clean motion and pinned the General's center, not the feet. "Then he is one," she said. "And that one is not moving."

"Third knot," Sia said. She set it and drew the line tight. The seam narrowed further. The wrong air around it thinned like fog that has decided to admit there is a road. The General's armor creaked. Not with fear. With strain.

Marcus exhaled and steadied himself on the crook. "That is my limit," he said. "I can hold here. More heat will pull me apart."

"Hold," Sia told him. "You did enough."

The General dragged force into its crown and made a final push that felt like a crowned head trying to bend the hinge by name alone. The hinge did not care. The Garden had the name it wanted. Fuzanglong cut the shove into spray and sent it hissing into the ground beyond the pool. Kaelan shook out her fingers and let the earlier slips crumble to ash. Bastian leaned into the bind's rhythm, met the General's weight, and stepped him back half a pace without overreaching. The line held like it had been there forever.

"Last knot," Sia said. Her arms shook and she set her jaw until the shake became a steady burn. She planted the final stitch and tied it through the pattern Mia was feeding her. The seam cinched to the size of a coin pressed into bark. It was still a wound. It was not a gate. It would not feed anything on the wrong side.

The pool's glow dipped as if it had given over a share of itself, then returned to normal. The arch's hum fell back to its earlier pitch. The umbrella warmed from the crook down the pole and then cooled. Sia let out a breath she had not realized she was holding and kept her hands in place a beat longer to be sure the work would stay without her.

"It will hold," the Dreaming said softly. "Let it be what it is."

Sia eased the umbrella down. The pattern remained. The Garden breathed the way a room breathes after a heavy thing finally sits on the right shelf. She looked up at the General and met the helm without flinching. "You are done," she said.

The General did not answer. It pulled back against Mia's bind and could not move. The lightning mark on the pauldron flared once. The two crows clicked in unison. The herald lifted the spear from his boot and stood very straight.

A low horn sounded on the border, not loud, not long. Trees parted without breaking. The Earlking stepped out of the shade with his wolves and riders fanned behind him. He wore a heavy coat of leather and fur and the tall helm crowned with antlers Sia had seen in the Hunt hall. His beard was brush-thick. His face looked carved rather than aged. An eyepatch cut a clean line over one eye and made the other look brighter. He took in the spear, the crows, the marked armor, the narrow seam, and the way the light sat on Mia's hands. He nodded once, as if he had arrived at the answer he expected.

"Trespass named," he said. His voice was not raised and carried anyway. "Claim to be argued."

He looked at the General the way a judge looks at a defendant who already knows how the verdict will read. "You are on my line," he said. "You do not get to declare the ground yours by saying it out loud."

The wolves lowered their heads in perfect time. The goblin outriders angled their ponies to box the path that would have been an escape if there had been one. The herald set the spear's butt to earth again and the crows answered with two sharp clicks.

Sia felt the last of the fear release her shoulders. She did not relax past ready. This was not finished. It was held in a way that meant it could be finished without breaking the Garden. She glanced at Mia. Winter rode easy in her now. Not a mask. Part of who she was. Mia gave a short nod. Sia nodded back.

"Close his food," Kaelan said, quieter now, skin singed at the edges of her fingers where the slips had burned. "He cannot pretend any longer."

"I already did," Sia said. The seam showed its coin-sized scar. It would fade. It would not reopen because a crown told it to.

The Earlking stepped to the exact edge the spear marked and stopped with one boot in shadow and one in the Garden's light. "Hold him where he stands," he said to Mia, and there was respect in the way he said it. "We will discuss the matter of teeth."

Mia settled the bind without making a ceremony out of it. "He is held," she said.

"Good," the Earlking said. His one visible eye flashed like a coin catching sun. "Then let us see what law wants to do with him."

The Garden stayed bright. The arch sang its low tone. The umbrella felt light in Sia's hands for the first time since the seam had started to pull. The fight was not loud anymore. It was precise. And that was where they were strongest.

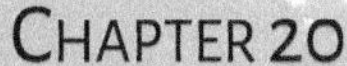

CHAPTER 20

Pride's Fall

Sia

THE SEAM LOOKED LIKE a coin pressed into the world. It sat in the air where the arch met the treeline, thin and wrong, breathing in a way that made Sia's skin want to crawl. The Hunt spear stood at the border with its point in the dirt, lightning still whispering along the iron where it had marked the Pride General. Two crows kept their place on the crossbar and watched like officials at a meet.

Sia lifted her umbrella and let her hands find the grip that felt most honest. The crook fit the heel of her palm. The steel pole hummed with the same note the arch was singing. The red cloth glowed soft with runes that settled her breathing even before she told them to. She did not think about the General. She thought about the work. Winter's calm sat inside her reach through Mia, close enough to thread through the Dream weave without a fight.

"Ready," she said, eyes on the seam, not on its armor.

"Bind is steady," Mia answered. Her voice was even. Frost lay across her fingers like a fine dust and moved where she sent it.

Bastian shifted his boots until the ground agreed with him. He kept his axe low and set, not swinging, not showing off. "Center lane is mine," he said. "If it leans this way, I meet it."

Kaelan stood where the border had tried to cheat in the last fight and held a fresh paper slip between her fingers. "Mirrors are quiet," she said. "If one wakes up, I cut it before it believes itself."

Fuzanglong thinned the water ring to a clear blade and raised it until it stood as tall as Sia's shoulder. "I will carry anything wide," he said. "Say when and I will turn it."

Marcus crouched on the crook of the umbrella, claws careful on the wood. His eyes were bright, but his voice had that thin stretch it got when a projection had run long. "I have tack heat for stitch points," he said. "Short and safe. Place me."

The Dreaming stood across the pool with one hand over the surface as if she was holding a lid down. "We share the box," she told Sia quietly. "Do not hurry. Do not stare at the wrong thing."

Thanatos leaned a shoulder against a birch. He did not offer a lecture. "No lies hiding," he said. "Just pressure. Keep the window small."

Sia opened the pattern in the umbrella a finger's width and let Winter's calm thread through it like a cool line. Then she drew the edges together the way you draw skin together for a stitch. The seam dragged against her hands as if it wanted to stay big just because it had been big a moment ago. She ignored the pull and set the first cross knot where arch and water met.

The Pride General tried authority the way a bad boss tries a tone. The helm turned, and the air around it pushed at everyone's attention, asking to be the loudest thing in the room. Kaelan breathed a short moon prayer and snapped a rite that took the shine off the voice. The pressure faded like someone had turned down a speaker.

"Stay with me," Sia said. It was for all of them, and also for herself.

She placed the second knot. The umbrella warmed along the pole, and the runes on the hood brightened, then steadied. The seam flinched, not with fear, but with the kind of insult a bully feels when a door closes. The coin-sized wound tried to sip power from the crooked star the General had planted earlier. Sia felt the feeder logic reach for her attention. Agree because I said so. She did not give it her eyes. The ladder of her pattern climbed where the Garden wanted it to climb.

"Left mirror," Kaelan warned. A ripple under the General's heel looked for a way to become a path. Kaelan's slip cut it with a soft sound like a string being plucked. The ripple collapsed. "Try again somewhere else," she muttered.

Bastian made a small adjustment with his back foot and brought the axe haft up to catch the next test of weight. The blow slid, not clean, but controlled. The dent in his lower bracer creaked as the strap tugged. He ignored it and set the angle again.

Marcus dipped his head. "Point," he said.

"Here," Sia answered, tilting the umbrella so he could see the tiny circle where stitch met water. He breathed once and laced a thread of heat along the seam. It flared and settled. The stitch locked.

Mia eased more calm into the brace. She did not freeze anything. She made standing possible. A thin line of blood started at her nose. She wiped it with her wrist and kept her hands open. "I am good," she said. "The hold will not slip."

The General flexed against the Hunt's spear mark. Lightning crawled over the iron and wrote the same quiet warning across the pauldron: pinned at the line. One of the crows clicked twice without looking away. The sound was small and still managed to carry.

Sia felt the seam's hunger falter. No food. She set the third cross and tied it across the feeder sigil so the bad logic had to chase itself instead of drinking the room. The seam tightened by a fraction and then by another. The arch's low note stayed true, not perfectly strong, but steady enough to count on.

"Let me get a damage alert guys," Sia said without lifting her eyes.

"I am fine," Mia said. Her breath fogged for a second and then smoothed. "Bind is where it needs to be."

"Strap will need tying later," Bastian added. "Arm is good."

"Fingers singed," Kaelan said. "Nothing serious."

"Heat is spent for a minute," Marcus said. "I can hold. No more lines right now."

"Pool is clean," Fuzanglong told them. "Give me anything you do not want near it."

The Pride General pulled again on rank like a lever that should move the world. It did not. Its helm turned toward Sia as if attention could break a hinge. Sia kept her gaze on the pattern she was making and not on the idea of a crown. The umbrella's runes answered with a soft pulse under her hands, a little heartbeat she could match without thinking.

The seam went still for a breath. It was not closed. It had stopped getting fed. Sia felt the change in the way pressure shifted along the arch, less drag, more stubborn trying. That was good. Stubborn was something you could tie down if you were patient and did not get distracted by noise.

"First pass is in," she said. "It cannot eat from its mark."

The Dreaming moved her hand over the pool and matched Sia's pressure precisely. "Hold this level," she said. "We set the top row and then we decide how much we can take in one pull."

A ripple of heat climbed the General's armor. Fuzanglong raised the water blade and brought it across in a gentle cut. The heat sheared off and fell away as harmless mist on the far side of the pool. The Garden did not accept a single drop.

The herald did not speak. He rested his palm on the spear as if to remind the ground that the line was more than a suggestion. The crows adjusted their feet and watched with patient, bright attention. Sia felt their looking the way she felt a rule being written down.

"Again," she said. She set another stitch at the far edge and gave it a short tug. The seam held. The arch held. The pool light dipped and then settled the same way a person settles after lifting a box that turned out to be heavier than it looked.

The Pride General shifted weight like it meant to test Bastian's patience. Bastian refused to give it a clean angle. He met the blade with the haft, turned it down and in, and let it skid. He did not try to win the fight in a burst. He refused to lose it to pride.

"Good," Sia whispered to nobody and everybody. She placed the next knot and felt Mia catch the pressure at the same time on her side of the brace. The work moved like two hands that had practiced enough to stop bumping into each other.

The coin-seam shrank by the width of a fingernail. It was still there. It could not drink. The General's posture changed in a way that read as patience running out. Sia did not let that matter.

"No more food," she said, steady and clear. The words did not make the magic. They reminded her hands what they were already doing. "We keep it here and we hold."

MIA STEPPED TO THE exact line the Hunt spear marked and set her hands where the air could see them. Winter settled through her like a muscle she knew how to use. "This is Garden ground," she said. "This is the border. You crossed without leave. I call the Hunt to witness and to hold the rule."

The treeline answered. Moon-collared wolves padded out of the shade and took places along the edge. Goblin outriders came behind them on shaggy ponies with old tack that had been mended until the leather looked like maps. A single herald walked the last few steps.

He wore dark leather and carried his spear as if it belonged to the ground more than to him. He set its butt to earth with a small sound that traveled farther than it should have. Two black crows spiraled down and perched on the crossbar. They clicked their beaks once and watched with bright, coin-flat eyes.

The Pride General turned its helm toward the assembly. Barbed plates rose like a crown made into a cage. Smoke slid from the joints. The voice came out flat and heavy, tuned to make the world agree with it. "Yield your hold. This door answers rank."

"It does not answer yours," Mia said. She did not raise her voice. Frost dusted her fingers and moved where she told it to. "You are named trespass."

The Earlking stepped into view the way a storm steps over a ridge. He wore layered leather and fur, a tall helm crowned with antlers, and an eyepatch that made his visible eye look brighter. His brush-thick beard framed a face cut in clean lines rather than age. He looked at the spear, at the crows, at the General's mark, at the coin-wide seam, then at Mia's open hands. "Venue stands," he said, not loud at all. "Trespass is named. Choice is simple. Yield to claim and be taken clean. Stand to judgment at the line. Breach the mark and become lawful prey."

The Pride General did not look at him. It tried the ground again with its voice. The air in front of Sia's face pressed as if a stage wanted to tilt toward a microphone. Kaelan breathed a moon prayer under her breath, flicked a paper slip, and cut the command aura down to its real size. The pressure thinned like steam leaving a kettle.

"Thank you," Sia said without looking away from her pattern. The umbrella hummed in her hands. The runes along the red cloth hood held steady. She felt the brace across arch and pool lock to the tone of the Garden.

On the narrow center lane, Bastian moved no more than he needed. He met the General's testing weight with the haft of his axe and turned it aside, angle over force, not giving up ground and not chasing. His dented bracer creaked. He resettled the strap without looking down.

"False path," Kaelan warned. A ripple near the General's heel tried to learn how to become a road. Her second slip sliced it with a soft string-note sound. The ripple popped and left nothing.

"I have the binds," Mia said. One hand flicked, then the other. Holding words wrapped the two steel-and-ash lieutenants that had slid to either side. She did not box them. She knotted their speed and took their rush. A thin line of blood started at her nose. She wiped it with her wrist and breathed until the field stayed even. "They will not move unless law takes them."

The herald pulled his planted spear free in one motion. The two crows rose a finger's width and set again. He drew his arm back and threw. Lightning crawled along the haft in a quiet veil. The point struck the Pride General's pauldron at the exact place where border met body. The blow did not tear. It marked. Sparks wrote a sign that was not letters but still read as meaning. Pinned at the line. The crows clicked once, sharp and pleased.

The seam bucked. Sia did not give it her eyes. She pressed the cross-stitch flatter and starved the crooked star the General had planted, the part that said agree because I said so. For a breath the rift forgot how to feed.

"Left bound is ready for claim," Mia said, eyes on her knots.

The herald tapped the spear butt to earth. Wolves slid forward in perfect time, took the two bound lieutenants by the law of angle and line, and dragged them back into the trees. The crows clicked three times, like stamps on paper. The Pride General stood alone at the mark.

"You still have your choice," the Earlking told the General. "Yield and go with teeth that answer the ledger. Stand and be measured. Break, and you will be taken."

The General tilted its crown and flared heat under the plates. Fuzanglong raised the water blade and shaved the heat sideways so it fell as mist beyond the pool's rim. Marcus, small on the umbrella's crook, watched Sia's hands and waited. "I can give one short line," he said. "Say when."

"Hold it for the end," Sia answered. She felt the seam's hunger searching. It found nothing to drink. The arch's tone steadied by a hair.

The General tried contempt again. "Children," it said. "You are not enough."

"Then step," Bastian said. "Or do not."

The helm turned toward him. The blade came low. Bastian knocked it down and away from the arch, not with a show of strength but with a clean angle that sent the force where it could not do harm. He took back the half-step the first test had earned and set his feet again.

Kaelan shook out her fingers. The edges of the old slips had singed her skin. She tucked a fresh one ready between two unburned knuckles. "No mirrors," she said. "Not one."

The herald rested his palm on the planted spear and watched the helm, patient as a clock. The crows flattened themselves against the crossbar and stared with bright attention.

"Listen," Mia said, and her voice carried because law wanted it to. "Yield. Or stand to judgment. If you cross the spear you will be hunted, and not by us."

The Pride General's plates shifted. The air shivered in a way that was not heat. For a heartbeat Sia thought it would lunge and try the simple answer of a heavy body at a closed hinge. Instead, the wrong light inside the armor twisted. The crown edge brightened as if it had found a wire to pull.

Thanatos lifted his chin the smallest amount. "It is reaching past this place," he said. "Not a lie. A chain."

The ground thrummed. Distant points answered like bad stars waking, then others farther out, a line of gates that had been quietly burning for too long. Sia felt the pull run through the broken feeder logic and hunt for the rift like a river looking for a cut in the bank.

"It is calling the other portals," Kaelan said, quick and clear.

"Hold him," Sia said to Mia, already widening her pattern just enough to take the strain without tearing the Garden. "Do not let him shift weight across two answers."

"I have him," Mia said. She pinned the General's center rather than its feet and set the bind to the spear's mark. Her breath fogged and then steadied. "He will not move."

"Angle," Bastian said, and set himself in the exact place that made a crown-strike a bad choice. The General tested him and found no clean path.

Fuzanglong lifted the water blade a hand higher. "I will carry any wide surge," he said. "The pool will not drink one drop of it."

Marcus curled his claws on the crook. The projection flickered, then held. "I have one stitch left," he said. "Tell me where in the last moment."

The Earlking glanced once at the crows. They clicked together as if marking the start of a count. He did not raise his voice. "You choosing breach," he told the General, "makes you prey whether you live or die."

The wrong light from the far gates drew tight toward the coin-seam like cords on a net being yanked all at once. The Pride General braced to ram everything through the narrow wound with a single crowned blow. The arch shivered. The roots groaned. The Garden felt the threat and held.

Sia let the fear move past her and did not let it choose. She set her hands and kept the cross-stitch true. Winter ran through the Dream weave like a cool thread that would not slip. The coin in the world stayed the size of a coin. The pull built anyway, lines of power dragging in from every connected Hellgate like bad veins finding a heart.

"Ready," Sia said, eyes on the work, not on the crown. "On my word."

Mia nodded once. Bastian did not move. Kaelan watched the edges. Fuzanglong waited to turn the surge. Marcus held his one clean thread like a pin. The herald kept his hand on the spear. The two crows leaned forward, bright eyes fixed on the line.

The Pride General gathered everything it could steal and drew breath to strike. The Garden did not blink. The scene held on the tight edge between the pull and the answer, and Sia felt the moment arrive when a closed door can teach a thief what a door really is.

THE GROUND KEPT THAT low tremor that meant the Pride General was drawing from places that should not answer. Sia felt the pull find every dirty line tied to this cluster, gates that had sat open too long in the Wilds. Power ran toward the coin-seam like water grabbed by a broken drain. The arch and pool took the strain without cracking, but the sound inside the wood and stone said they would not forgive many mistakes.

"He is chaining other gates," Thanatos said. He did not raise his voice. He was naming weather.

"Hold him," Sia told Mia. "Center, not the feet."

"I have him," Mia said. The holding word tightened across the Pride General's middle like a wide band that allowed breath and nothing else. Frost lay along her fingers and did not flake. Her eyes stayed on the line the spear marked.

The Earlking rested a palm on the spear haft. "Venue stands," he said to the air, like an answer to a question nobody else had heard. The two crows leaned forward and clicked once. The sound landed like a stamp.

The Pride General pulled again. Bad light spooled from distant gates, thin cords gathering into a rope. The crown on the helm brightened. It looked like it had decided that if it could not push through the door, it would tear down the wall by shouting its name into the bricks.

"Wolves are set," Bastian said without looking away from the blade. He spoke like he was telling his hands where to live. "If it lunges I meet it."

Kaelan stood on the shiver of air that kept trying to become a path. "No mirrors," she said. A fresh paper slipped from her fingers and took a ripple apart before it could believe itself.

Fuzanglong raised the water blade the height of his palm and thinned it to a fine edge. "Give me the surge," he told Sia. "I will turn it so the pool does not drink."

Sia for a moment peered through the dreaming to the Force the longed to call for, the aide she wished could be at their side at that very moment. Two swords in the darkness, shining and standing as a passionate wall of safety she had long come to trust. However, she saw what they themselves faced at that moment. Ella and Tobias in the Dark, in need of Light of their own. She would have to rely on her own strength and her friends here.

"Marcus," Sia said, feeling the umbrella's lattice hum against her wrists. "I may need one more pin on the last stitch."

"I can give one," he said. His voice was stretched thin but steady. "Place me at the end."

Sia looked at the seam and not at the crown. The coin-wide wound wanted to remember how to be a mouth. The earlier stitches held. The cross-weave she had laced with Winter's calm kept its left and right edges honest. The pressure was wrong, but it was simple. Pride had built a siphon and was trying to slam it through one point.

She opened the pattern a finger's width, just enough to take in new threads without tearing. The umbrella warmed along the steel pole, the red cloth runes answering her breath with a soft rise and fall. "I need the lines," she said, more to the work than to the people behind her. "If he is pulling on them, I can catch them."

"Catch is not enough," the Dreaming said from across the pool. "They are mouths as long as he names them to be."

"Then I change their names," Sia said. She thought of doors and halls and all the small rules that kept the Museum's peace. She thought of the way her sketchbook had learned to listen when she told it what a page was supposed to be. She thought of the first time she had closed a threshold by calling it what it really was. Her hands steadied.

The cords of bad light reached the coin. The Pride General braced. It would take everything it had pulled and send it through in a single crowned blow. Sia set the umbrella point an inch above the seam and lifted clean, as if she were taking hold of loose threads with a needle instead of a weapon. The pattern accepted her hand. The threads gathered.

"Now," she said to the weave. "Not open. Closed. Not mouths. Doors. Not in. Away."

The cords stuttered. For a breath they did not know what they were. Sia hooked the line of Winter calm through the Dream pattern and turned the threads back along themselves. The image in her head was simple on purpose. It was a siphon flipped. It was a road sign turned around. It was a drain learning to plug.

The Pride General pushed harder. The crown flared. Bastian met the low edge on the haft and drove it down and away from the arch. His dented bracer split another thread and held. He set his feet again and did not chase. Kaelan snapped a whispered prayer and cut a new ripple off the General's heel. The mirror collapsed before it could become an argument. Fuzanglong lifted his blade and carried a wide heat surge into mist beyond the pool's rim. Not a single drop touched the water. Mia adjusted the band at the Pride General's center with careful pressure. The bind allowed standing and nothing else.

Sia pulled. The hooked threads remembered the feel of motion and tried to run the wrong way. She showed them the right way with the only things that counted here. Law. Witness. Place. The Hunt's spear stood at the border with lightning still whispering along the iron. The crows watched like clerks with clean hands. The Garden kept its tone. The arch kept its hum. That was enough to name what should happen next.

"Marcus," she said, eyes on the seam. "There. Seal."

He laid the last line of heat exactly where she had pointed, a small weld that turned a curve into a lock. The stitch took. The pattern closed like a zipper pulled with two hands.

All at once the cords tightened outward. They did not feed the coin-seam. They collapsed along the route they had traveled to get there. Sia felt the motion pass back through the wrong light like a tide reversing. She did not need to see the far gates to know what was happening. The sense of open mouths became the sense of closing doors. One by one the lines went slack as if someone had cut them close to the wall and let the ends drop.

The backlash tried to whip into the Pride General. Mia's bind held him straight. Bastian set the blade away from the arch and gave the force a bad angle. Fuzanglong lifted and turned the last shiver of heat sideways into a harmless curtain of spray. Kaelan shook out her burned fingers and smiled the small, tired smile she saved for spells that finally let go.

The first collapse hit the Pride General's crown like a hook on a chain. The second turned the hook. The third pulled. The helm bowed. The plates along the ribs creaked the way ice does when it starts to break from the inside. Ash sifted out of a joint and vanished before it reached the ground.

The crows clicked three times in even rhythm. The herald did not move his hand from the spear.

The Pride General found a few words. "Unlawful," it said, and even in that single word there was an attempt to make the world agree because it had declared it so.

"Witnessed," the Earlking answered. He did not raise his voice. "Trespass marked. Breach attempted. Chains drawn from other gates. The door held. The pull returned to the hands that made it. Ledger is clean."

The Pride General's pauldron folded. The lightning mark flared and went out. The crown brightened once, like a last idea trying to stand up, then guttered. The armor sagged forward and shrank into itself. It did not fall like a body. It collapsed like a bad story finally told to stop. Ash and a rim of black glass remained on the exact line where the spear had pinned it.

Mia eased the bind and let it dissolve. She wiped her upper lip with the back of her wrist and breathed until the frost on her fingers lifted. "Held," she said, voice even again, "and done."

Sia did not look at the ashes for long. She looked at the seam. The coin in the world had shrunk to something smaller than a thumbnail. The stitches she had laced across it sat true. It would be tempting to keep pulling until the scar went flat just because it could. She did not. The Garden liked honest marks as much as honest doors.

"Last knot," she said. She pulled a final line through the cross and cinched it gently, then smoothed the weave with the flat of her palm. The pool's light dipped, then rose. The arch's hum fell back to the calm tone it had started the day with. The pressure in the ground eased by slow degrees, as if the land had unclenched a muscle.

The Dreaming lowered her hand from the pool. Something in her shoulders let go. It was not dramatic. It was relief. "That is what it needed," she said.

Sia kept her hands on the umbrella another breath, then lifted away. The red cloth runes faded to a soft glow. The steel pole cooled under her grip. The crook felt light for the first time since they had stepped to the line. She exhaled and felt the shake in her arms move out through her fingers and leave.

Bastian shifted his weight and checked his bracer. The strap had torn through one hole and made a new one. He threaded it back and tied it in a knot that would hold until there was time for real repair. "I am good," he said. "No breaks. Plenty of scuffs."

Kaelan flexed her hands and hissed a little as air touched the singed edges of her fingers. "I have a burn salve in my kit," she said. "After we are done speaking oaths."

Fuzanglong let the water blade ease down and fold into the pool. The ring's light sank to a bright seam just under the surface. "The Garden is clean," he said. "No heat went where it should not."

Marcus leaned his head against the umbrella's crook and breathed in and out like someone who had held a part of the sky long enough to feel it fight back. "That was my line," he said. "I have nothing safe left. I can hold as I am."

The Earlking took his hand from the spear and stepped to the exact edge it marked. He looked at the ashes, at the black glass, at the tiny scar in the air, and then at Sia. "Law is satisfied," he said. "No tooth took him. No killing word. He died by his own pull with witnesses. That matters."

"It matters here and in the Wilds," the herald added. He did not sound pleased. He sounded finished.

Thanatos watched the seam and nodded. "The wound will fade," he said. "Leave it honest. Do not polish over the scar."

The Dreaming faced Sia. "The Garden has work every day," she said. "You have other roads. It is time to say what is true and let things be what they are."

Sia lifted the umbrella so the crook rested again at her wrist. She spoke to the room that was not just a room. "I will carry Faerie passages inside the Dream road," she said. "I will close doors that feed Hell. I will leave honest doors alone. I will answer when the Wilds call for seam work, and I will keep the Garden in mind when the city tries to make everything square."

Mia stepped in beside her. "Winter will stand for that work when you ask," she said. "I will hold what you stitch if you need hands. I will not let anyone drag on a chain in your shadow."

Kaelan inclined her head. "Summer will heal where the crossing bruises," she said. "No toll when it is for keeping the world whole."

The Earlking touched the spear and gave a single nod. "The Hunt answers a formal call on lawful trespass," he said. "Witnesses will come when you name the line."

Thanatos did not add a speech. He put a hand to the birch and watched the way the light sat on the bark. The Garden stayed bright. The pool stayed clear. The arch kept its tone.

The Dreaming let out a breath she might have been holding for years. "Then I am done," she said, not with sadness. "There is a chair here that does not hurt to sit in. I intend to learn what a quiet day feels like."

Sia's anchor ring pulsed once. She felt the pattern in the umbrella answer. The world did not change shape. It felt like a house after someone fixes the door that has stuck for months. The first time it swings clean you notice. After that it is only a door that works.

Bastian re-tied his strap tighter and tested it with a tug. "The line is clean," he said to no one in particular. "That is my favorite way for a line to be."

Kaelan finally uncorked her salve and dabbed it on the red edges of her fingers. She made a face and smiled anyway. "We should make sure the Unseen hear that the pressure dropped," she said. "They will sleep better."

"First light," the Earlking said, glancing up at the crows. They lifted and wheeled toward the trees as if the time was already on their calendar. "Moot to seal what you have named. United Seelie if the words hold."

"They will hold," Mia said. She did not sound like she was guessing.

Sia looked at the tiny scar in the air and then at the pool. The work felt finished in the right way, the way that left you tired and also taller inside your chest. "All right," she said. "Let us write it down and go eat something that is not panic."

The Earlking's mouth turned at one corner. "We can do that," he said. He rapped the spear butt once. The line shimmered and settled. The Garden breathed. The road ahead pointed away from fire and toward oaths.

CHAPTER 21

Seelie United

SIA

Dawn laid a silver stripe across the pool and turned the birch trunks into quiet pillars. The Hunt's spear stood planted at the waterline, its crossbar level and sure. Two black crows perched there like punctuation, heads tilted, eyes bright. They were not showy about it. They were witnesses, and everyone seemed to feel that.

Sia stood with the umbrella grounded at her boot, palm resting on the crook. The red cloth hummed low, the runes calm instead of loud. Mia took her place on Sia's right with Winter sitting steady in her shoulders. Kaelan stood to the left, kimono sleeves tidy, fingers wrapped where paper had singed them last night. Bastian wore his axe across his back and a fresh wrap on his bracer. Fuzanglong drifted a hand's height above the grass, glow softened to match the hour. Marcus stayed small on Sia's collarbone, present and quiet.

The Garden made room for guests and then filled the space again. Titania came first, light catching on gold thread woven through a mantle that did not need it. She smiled like summer often does, warm and slightly dangerous if you forgot to respect it. Mab followed with no glitter at all, only the kind of gravity that stops a room from lying to itself. The Earlking stepped out of the trees in layered leather and fur, antlers shadowing the spear line. His one good eye looked like a chip of blue ice pulled from deep water. A Tuatha envoy arrived between heartbeats, Brigid by the look of the soft fire at her hands. An Unseen pathfinder joined last, face hooded, presence like a place your eyes slide past on purpose. The Dreaming stood by the pool, one hand skimming the surface. Thanatos leaned a shoulder to a birch and nodded to Sia once, as if to say, You are on time.

No bells. No speeches. The crows clicked, and that was enough to begin.

Mab set her palm to the spear's shaft just below the crossbar. "Venue holds," she said. "Witness stands."

Titania stepped to the rim of the pool and met Sia's eyes. "Name the order," she said.

Sia looked from Summer to Winter to the Hunt, then to Brigid and the hooded guide. She spoke clean and simple. "United Seelie Alliance," she said. "Summer. Winter. The Hunt. The Tuatha. The Unseen."

The crows clicked once together. The pool brightened like a breath taken in.

Mab lifted her chin a fraction. "Winter pledges guard on seam work," she said. "When the Dreamer holds a door or closes one that feeds Hell, Winter will keep teeth off her hands."

Titania's smile thinned into something serious. "Summer pledges healing at worked doors," she said. "We mend what closes clean and what was harmed on the way."

The Earlking tapped the spear butt with two fingers, almost lazy, not lazy at all. "The Hunt answers lawful calls," he said. "Name trespass at a line and we will make it matter."

Brigid's flame dimmed to a warm coal. "The Tuatha will bless tools and roads when called on fair terms," she said. "Edges that do not turn, bridges that do not lie."

The Unseen pathfinder spoke softly enough that the birches seemed to lean in. "We lend sighted paths when named correctly," they said. "Once for entry. Twice to hold it. Never a third time unless the debt is clean."

Sia set the umbrella's tip to the soil and felt the Garden's tone sit under her hand. "I take Faerie passages into my mandate," she said. "I will close the doors that feed Hell. I will leave honest doors alone. I will not turn the Garden into a wall. I will keep it a place that lives."

The Dreaming watched her for a long, quiet second and then nodded. "I lay down the burden that belongs to Faerie," she said. "I have kept these gates alone for longer than was smart. They are not mine anymore. Let the work go where it belongs."

Thanatos did not step forward. He did not need to. "I remain," he said. "I watch while she learns. I do not run the room."

The crows clicked again. The sound felt like ink drying.

Costs were spoken and closed without drama. Mia touched her upper lip and showed clean skin where blood had been, then dropped her hand. Kaelan flexed her fingers, Brigid cooling the last sting with a brush of heat that felt like spring instead of fire. Bastian tapped his rewrapped bracer and left it at that. Marcus admitted nothing but sat a little heavier against Sia's collar. Sia let her arms ache and did not make it into a story.

"Done," Titania said.

"Done," Mab echoed.

The Earlking's mouth turned at one corner. "Done," he said, as if the word tasted good.

The crows clicked a third time, sharp and final. The spear seemed to settle deeper without moving at all.

There was no more to say in that circle. Sia looked to the Dreaming. "May I open a door from here," she asked. "We need to check our home."

The Dreaming lifted her hand from the pool. Light rolled once and steadied. "This is your threshold now as much as mine," she said. "Do it."

Sia breathed in the Garden's tone and set the umbrella's crook to the air. The steel pole sang a quiet line she had learned on the road. Runes along the red cloth woke like embers under a bellows. She drew a rectangle where the air already wanted to be a door and wrote one clear address into it: Sanctuary. The frame formed with a soft chime, Museum bell answering from very far away and very near at the same time.

Bastian glanced at Mab and then at Titania, reading the room like a soldier who knew courts. He stepped to Sia's side without asking. "If you go," he said, "I go."

No one argued. It landed like a promise he had made earlier and was only now cashing in.

Sia looked around the circle one last time. Titania inclined her head, all sunlight and long memory. Mab's eyes warmed a degree, which for Mab was the same as a hug. The Earlking gave the smallest nod, antlers cutting a new shape in the morning light. Brigid smiled like a hearth that would be there when you needed it. The Unseen pathfinder was already fading at the edges, which Sia took as approval. The Dreaming let her shoulders lower, relief honest in her face. Thanatos arched a brow that meant be careful and I am proud of you, somehow both at once.

"Thank you," Sia said. The Rule of Three tugged at her tongue. She did not push it. Once was enough here.

She turned the handle and swung the door inward. Warm Museum light spilled across Garden grass. Charles's desk lamp glowed within, thresholds singing a clear welcome. Sia stepped through with Mia,

Kaelan, Bastian, Fuzanglong's gentle shimmer, and Marcus's small weight steady at her collar. The door closed after them, clean as a book shutting on the right page.

THE GARDEN DOOR OPENED into warm light and polished wood. The Museum bells answered Sia's threshold with a clean, even chime, one tone from the entry hall and another, softer one from somewhere deeper in the hotel. The air smelled like lemon oil and old paper. The floorboards under the rugs kept their steady creak, the kind that lets a building say I am here and I am fine.

Charles looked up from his ledger and lifted a small brass token to acknowledge the passage. The token flashed once, as if it approved of them. "Garden door," he said, mostly to the book. "Neutral entry, no toll."

"Thank you," Sia said. Her voice sounded normal again. The umbrella's hum eased down from ready to resting, the red cloth hood giving one last pulse before the runes settled.

Mia came through at her shoulder with Winter held quiet beneath her skin. Kaelan stepped wide to make room for Bastian's weight, then smiled at Charles in a way that counted as a greeting without opening any ledger. Fuzanglong's white glow slipped in last and folded itself to the size of a long scarf of light, respectful of the ceilings.

Marcus crouched on Sia's collarbone, tiny claws careful in the fabric. Even small, he looked wrung out. Sia touched the crook of the umbrella to her shoulder so he could lean on something that was not her. "Head home," she told him. Calm, not a command. "Rest. I'm about to come there anyway."

He nodded, too tired to argue, which said enough. "Okay." He took one slow breath, then unraveled into a ribbon of smoked glass and was gone, the way projections go when they choose peace over pride.

Brigid was already crossing the hall from the fireside parlor, sleeves rolled to the elbow, hands warm without heat mirage. "Hands," she said gently to Kaelan.

Kaelan blinked, remembered, and offered them over. The skin across her fingers was pink and tight where paper had singed her. Brigid rubbed a small circle at each knuckle. It felt like standing near a hearth after coming in from a snowstorm. The sting eased. The skin cooled. "Better," Kaelan said, surprised at how quickly relief arrived.

"Do not argue with craft fire," Brigid said, smiling. "Just treat it kindly."

Goibniu followed her at an unhurried pace, eyes taking in everything and filing it in places most people do not have. He stopped in front of Bastian, took the Green Knight's forearm, and checked the bracer wrap with a blacksmith's frown. "Your strap wants another hole," he said.

"It does," Bastian admitted.

Goibniu led him two steps toward a side table, pulled a punch from a pocket that should not have held a punch, and cut a clean new hole through the leather with one firm press. He fed the strap through, tested the pull on it, and nodded once. "It will hold," he said. "Try not to pick fights with stone next time."

"I will try," Bastian said. He sounded like he meant it and also like the world would tempt him to fail.

Mia tilted her head when Brigid looked her way. The new mantle sat steady in her eyes. You could see Winter there if you knew what to look for, but it did not look like someone else wearing her. It looked like Mia wearing more of herself. Brigid touched two fingers to the center of Mia's brow and then to each wrist. "You pulled without breaking," she said. "I am setting a soft ward to remind your binds to rest when you rest."

"Thank you," Mia said. Her shoulders loosened, just a little, as if a weight had learned to share itself politely.

Sia stood still long enough to feel her own arms complain and then stop complaining. The umbrella's weight had become a friendly thing, familiar as a backpack you forget you are wearing until you take it off. She set the crook to the floor and let the steel rest against her palm so the last of the Garden's hum could drain.

Charles left his desk and reached up to the master threshold board. It looked like a window full of tiny bells and marks, each line tied to a door or a rule. He hung something new on the west post, careful as if it had teeth. It was a small antler carving the color of old bone. "Gift from the Hunt, I believe," he said. "If I hang it here, it will only ring when trespass crosses. I prefer our guests ring the normal bell."

"It is a tally," Sia said. "For lawful calls. If I ask the Hunt to take a trespass on our line, that will make it true."

"Useful," Charles said. "Hopefully quiet."

Kaelan slid Sia's map from her sleeve pocket and laid it on the desk. The vellum had picked up a faint sheen since the last time Sia saw it, as if the Wild had decided to fold a little of itself into the paper. Sia touched the lower corner. A tiny spiral with a harp inside it bloomed near Marshall, no ink pot needed. "The Tuatha mark for friendly river crossings," she said. "That should stop the bridge from playing tricks when we are tired."

"Bless them for that," Charles said, and meant it.

Fuzanglong's glow dimmed further. "I will withdraw my projection," he told Sia, whiskers brushing the air in a small bow. "Too many thresholds bother it if I linger."

"Rest," Sia said. "We will call you when we need the patient voice."

"Please do," he said, and he went like a candle being pinched out, a neat close instead of a fade.

Truth padded in from the stairwell with the solemnity of a queen on patrol. She sniffed Sia's knee, then Mia's hand, then Bastian's boots as if this were the order of importance for the day. Her tail thumped the exact number of times it takes to say welcome back without getting overly emotional about it.

Bastian reached down, palm open. Truth allowed three seconds of knuckles on her crown and then moved on, dignity intact. "Good dog," he said. It sounded like praise and a vow at the same time.

"Rooms are ready," Charles said, back to Sia. "Brigid set tea on the long table for after you wash the road off. I logged the Garden accord in the private ledger, if anyone asks tomorrow why the bells have such good manners."

Sia nodded. She looked at Mia, who nodded back with that twin awareness that says I am here and I see you, not just the part of you that fixes things. Sia felt her chest loosen in return.

"Bastian," Kaelan said, gentle, because the question belonged to him. "Are you staying with us."

He glanced down the hall to the east wing as if a thought stood there waiting for him. "A while," he said. "The Garden sent you home. I prefer to guard what the Garden sent." He left it there. It was not a court answer. It was a person answer. Sia let it stand.

"Then you are a guest of the Museum," Charles said. "Neutral ground applies. If anyone, including the Hunt, wants to argue about you sleeping under this roof, they can do it over tea in my office while the hotel listens."

Bastian smiled in a way that made him look suddenly and unfairly handsome. "I look forward to the tea."

"Showers," Mia said, already turning toward the stairs. "And food that is not from a pack."

"Ten minutes," Sia said. "Then the long table."

Kaelan lifted her hands and rolled her newly cooled fingers like a pianist getting ready. "If the table tries to recite a poem at me, I am going back to bed."

"It will not," Charles said, deadpan. "Not on a weekday."

They took the stairs. The runner's pattern flashed under their feet like calm water. Sia paused on the landing and looked back once. Charles was hanging a small note under the antler tally that read CALLS BY SIA ONLY in tidy script. The bells on the board made a sound like someone clearing their throat and then being quiet on purpose.

In her room, Sia left the umbrella on the bed for a heartbeat and touched the steel pole with two fingers. It was cool and smooth and hers. The red cloth hood glowed just enough to answer. "Good work," she told it, because tools listen when you thank them. She washed until the road was a memory on the towel and put on a soft shirt that did not remember smoke or ash.

When she came back down, the long table was set with simple things that tasted like actual food. Bread with salt and butter. Soup that had decided to be chicken and stuck with it. Tea that did not try to solve problems, just sat with you while you thought about them. Brigid poured. Goibniu sat with his hands wrapped around a mug as if heat and he had a private conversation. Kaelan took a bowl and did not pretend she would eat daintily. Mia ate like someone who remembered she was human and hungry. Bastian broke bread like a ritual and then relaxed into the chair as if he had finally been allowed to be off duty for one hour.

Sia ate, drank, and let the room do the part of the work that rooms do when they are built for safety. The Garden would keep for the night. The accord was written in the air and in the bells and in the looks that had passed between old powers and new. There would be debriefs and plans and the next door to open. In a few minutes, she would step outside to check the wardline, just to make sure the town felt the same way the bells did. For now, she let the quiet do its job. She breathed. The Museum breathed with her. The day bent toward evening without worry.

AFTER THE BOWLS WERE empty and the tea was down to a comfortable warmth, Sia slipped her map into her pocket and stepped out through the Museum's front doors. The porch boards gave a friendly creak. Cool night air met her face and carried the usual small-town sounds, only softer. No sirens, no hard voices. Marshall felt like it had taken a deep breath and decided to keep it.

She set the umbrella tip on the top step and listened. The wards sang under the streetlights, a low harmony braided through power lines and gutters and old brick. Threshold craft should have ended at the property line. It had not. Over the months they were away, Sanctuary's rules had spread like ivy in slow motion, tracing seams, settling into places that wanted to be calm.

Across the street, two guys finished loading a van and almost bumped shoulders at the back doors. Sia could feel that moment where a dumb shove could have turned into something worse. Instead they both laughed and stepped sideways like the same idea had landed in each of their heads at the same time. A girl jogging past paused to let a cat cross the sidewalk and then waved at the cat like it could understand her, which it probably did.

Kaelan came to stand beside Sia with her arms folded under the sleeves of her kimono. "You feel it too," she said.

Sia nodded. "It reached past the lobby. Charles's bells learned new routes, and the town decided to believe them."

"This is not mind control," Kaelan said, eyes scanning the block. "It is weather. It makes storms less likely."

"Exactly," Sia said. "People still choose. They just have to push harder to choose bad."

Bootsteps sounded behind them. Bastian stopped at the porch rail and leaned an elbow on it, gaze moving the way a guard's does when he lets his guard down only a fraction. He watched the corner where the bar lights used to spit trouble on weekend nights. Tonight, the sign hummed the same as the streetlights and the door stayed shut.

"Your house is doing more than keeping a roof safe," he said.

"It's not a house," Sia said. "It's a place that remembers what it is for."

Mia pushed the door open with her shoulder and joined them, a mug in both hands. Winter sat quiet in her eyes, not sharp, not loud, just present. Truth followed, did a lap of the porch like she was checking the border, and then flopped into the spot that gave her the best view of the sidewalk.

Sia stepped down to the walk and stopped at the edge where the Museum's steps met the town's concrete. The line used to feel like a wall. Tonight it felt like a seam sewn tight. She reached out with the umbrella, barely a touch, and the runes on the red cloth answered with a small pulse. The steel pole gave back a soft hum, pleased, as if the day's work had left it in a good mood.

A flick of motion at the corner of her eye drew her attention to the brick beside the door. Someone had tucked a thin strip of bark under the house number. Sia slid it free. Dark lines ran across the pale wood in a pattern that did not mean anything until she let her eyes relax. The path showed itself then, a simple curve and a pair of notches, plus a faint cross mark near the base. Unseen script. The kind you only recognized if someone had taught you what to look for.

Kaelan leaned in. "Hidden route," she said, keeping her voice low. "One league only."

Sia nodded and slid the bark into her map. "I will copy it before we use it. One league is enough when it is the right league."

Inside the lobby, the antler tally from the Hunt hung at the threshold board where Charles had fixed it. It caught a bit of streetlight through the glass and threw a soft white reflection onto the ceiling. Sia imagined it ringing once, sharp and clear, when someone tried to take what was not theirs. She did not want to hear that ring often. It was good to know it would try to speak if it had to.

Marcus's absence tugged at her shoulder out of habit. She felt for him anyway, the way you reach for your phone after you set it down. The projection thread was quiet, which meant he had made it home and slept. Good. She would see him in person soon enough.

"Winter Front is still active," Mia said, eyes narrowed like she was watching weather systems. "You feel it."

Sia did. Most of the pulses she had learned to track were gone or fading. The Garden handoff and the alliance had shut a lot of doors. One place still hummed like a live wire. Far north, far cold. Winter's job. It would stay Winter's job, only now they would share the load when the Wilds were at risk.

"We chose this," Sia said. "Close doors that feed Hell. Leave real doors alone. That means we keep an eye on what feeds and what heals."

Kaelan looked up at the Museum's tallest windows, where warm lamp light traced the glass. "Sanctuary as a base changes the math," she said. "You can step to the Garden without walking through everything in between. We can answer a river, fix a seam, and be home in time to wash up."

"It gives us speed," Bastian said. "I prefer to move fast when I know the road."

Sia checked the sky. The stars looked lower than usual, like they were listening. The wardline blurred the edge where town ended and dark began, and it did it without stealing the night's personality. It just took the last five percent of sharp from it. That was enough to keep people from breaking.

She turned back toward the door. "Tomorrow we sleep in. After-noon, we copy the path the Unseen left us. Then we check the Garden line and make sure the accord is holding from both sides. After that, seam work when it calls. No hero moves."

"No hero moves," Mia said, and bumped her shoulder against Sia's like the words themselves were a kind of tether.

Kaelan smiled. "And I will handle Summer courtesies with no debt attached. We will not trip a ledger by saying thank you wrong."

"Please do," Sia said. "I am not in the mood to owe anyone for a fruit basket."

They went back inside. Charles was closing up the night book and setting the pen to rest on the spine. He glanced up, read their faces in one look, and nodded. "Town is quiet," he said.

"It is," Sia said. "Your wards stretched their legs while we were gone."

"They do that when the neighbors approve," he said. "We baked good habits into the thresholds. People learned them without being told."

Sia paused at the base of the stairs. "Thank you, Charles."

"You are welcome," he said, and he said it like a man who enjoyed the craft for its own sake.

They headed up. Truth trotted ahead as if their destination had always been the same bed at the same time. Sia touched the umbrella to the doorframe of her room before she went in, a small habit that felt like knocking on wood and also like writing her name on the day.

She set the umbrella by the nightstand. The steel lattice gave one last contented shimmer, the red cloth hood dimmed to its resting glow, and the soft green sheen along the pole caught a slice of lamplight like a wink. Sia stood at the window and looked out across Marshall. The street was quiet. The town was settled. The Garden door was closed and would open when she asked it. Tomorrow would be about maps and rest and maybe laughing at something small.

For now, she listened to the building breathe, and she let herself match it.

Epilogue

Ella

THE PLANE DOOR HISSED and let in cold that smelled like wet stone and sea. Ella followed the slow shuffle down the jet bridge with her shoulder pressed to a long canvas bag. The bag fit her side like it had been tailored. Inside, Veritas slept. The weight felt honest. The strap dug at the bruise above her right collarbone, a reminder that China had taught and taken in equal measure.

They stepped into the bright clatter of arrivals. Fluorescent light flattened everything. Signs pointed toward baggage, taxis, and a city that waited beyond the glass. Tobias held his phone to his ear and nodded through a line of clipped sentences. The set of his jaw said he was coordinating three people at once. It was the same look he wore before a breach, only softer here among families and suitcases.

Ella's phone buzzed with a message from Sia:

you two down safe?

She thumbed back a quick yes, then added:

> Yes. We're good. Scotland is gray and perfect. Tobias is wrangling Paladins. I will text again tonight.

Her brother ended the call with a small sigh that was not defeat, just the sound a plan makes when it fits. "Garren's splitting the team," he said, turning toward her. "Half to the western isles, half to the abbey. We meet the first group in Inverness and move north from there. They finally gave the name for the stack of work they have been hiding. Project Grail."

Ella tried the words in her mouth. They tasted like old stories and fresh trouble. "That sounds subtle," she said.

"It is not," Tobias said, mouth slanting. "But it is honest. We are following a trail that wants to be found."

They fell in with the crowd. The airport had the same universal rhythm as every airport, only the voices were softer and the announcements carried clearer. A boy with a dinosaur hoodie stared at the canvas bag and then grinned at her like he had noticed a secret and would keep it. Ella winked back.

Sia again: seriously, how are you?

Ella glanced at her right arm before she answered. The cut had closed days ago, a clean line just above the wrist that traced the place where a lesson had turned sharp. In Longwang's hall the air had tasted like rain even when it was not raining. The Dragon God had asked her to hold still while he named storms. She had learned to let a current pass through her without taking her with it. She had learned how to put the sword down before it put her away. The mark on her arm was thin and pale and would fade. She touched it with her thumb and felt only skin.

I am good, she typed. Tired, smarter, less scared of the bright parts. China helped. I will tell you everything when we get home. One month, give or take.

Sia sent a heart that looked like a red leaf. Ella smiled at the screen and let the small warmth settle where worry usually sat.

Baggage claim fed people in a slow loop. Tobias did a quick scan for their packs, then for exits, then for faces he knew. He was not hunting. He was counting. "Team Excelsior will be in place by tomorrow night," he said. "Lucretia and Martha are flying through Dublin. Greg and Andrea are already on the ferry list. Terrance has a line on a watchtower where we can sleep if we have to."

"Let me guess," Ella said. "The ferry smells like old coffee and the watchtower smells like old rain."

"Old iron," he said. "If we are lucky."

Her phone buzzed again with a text from 0Sia:

> tell Tobias I am proud of him even when he does not think he needs to hear it. And tell him Mia says hi.

Ella held the screen up. Tobias read and tried to hide how much he liked it. He did not succeed. "Tell them I am proud of them," he said. "And tell Sia the town feels different in her messages. Charles's bells must be doing something clever."

Ella typed the reply and slid the phone into her jacket. A cold draft touched the back of her neck as the sliding doors opened ahead. She adjusted the bag so Veritas rested more comfortably along her spine. The canvas hid the line of the hilt. You would have to know what you were looking for. People here did not.

Outside, taxi lanes moved in clean lines. The sky had chosen a solid gray and seemed proud of it. Distant hills held their shape like giants who had learned how to sit still. Ella drew a slow breath and tasted salt from a sea they would see tomorrow if the roads cooperated.

"Project Grail," she said again, mostly to herself.

Tobias heard it and nodded. "Pieces on a board we have not seen in a long time," he said. "The abbey kept quiet for a reason. Someone decided we were ready for the rest of the story."

"Or they ran out of time," Ella said.

"Then we do not waste ours," he answered.

They found their packs and shouldered them. Tobias kept his sword case plain and unbranded. The canvas bag pulled a little to the right and Ella shifted her balance to match. The movement felt practiced. It felt like the end of a long drill and the start of a real test.

At the taxi stand, a driver with a knit cap and tired eyes lifted a hand in a half wave. "You want city or country," he asked.

"City tonight," Tobias said. "Country in the morning."

"Fair," the driver said, and helped them stow their gear.

As the car pulled away, Ella looked back once through the rear window. The airport glass held the sky like a mirror. For a heartbeat she saw her own face and Sia's text reflected over it. She thought of a garden on the other side of the world where a door now opened because Sia asked it to. She thought of the Dragon God's voice naming the shape of a storm until she could feel the edges of it inside her bones.

Her arm did not ache. The cut was just a line. The fear that had ridden her shoulder since Veritas woke for the first time had shifted into something else. Respect, maybe. Not for the sword. For herself while holding it.

Tobias's phone buzzed again. He listened, then said, "Understood," and hung up. "One more change," he told her. "We are meeting a local contact before dawn. The abbey thinks this will move quickly."

"Good," Ella said. "I am tired of flights. I want roads."

"We will get both," he said.

Streetlights came on in a neat sequence. The city gathered itself for evening. Ella leaned back and let the motion carry her forward. She typed one last message to Sia.

We are fine. Home within a month. Keep the door warm.

She hit send and slid the phone into her pocket. The driver took an exit toward the river and the lights flicked across the window in bands. Ella rested her hand on the canvas and felt the steady truth of the blade at her back. The work ahead was hard. It was also clear.

To Be Continued in: Veritas, Book 5 of the Living Myth Saga